THE
HUNGER
OF CROWS

Also available by Richard Chiappone

Liar's Code
Opening Days
Water of an Undetermined Depth

THE HUNGER OF CROWS

A NOVEL

RICHARD CHIAPPONE

CROOKED
LANE

NEW YORK

Copyright © 2021 by Richard Chiappone

Published in the United States by Crooked Lane Books, an imprint of The Quick Brown Fox & Company LLC.

Crooked Lane Books and its logo are trademarks of The Quick Brown Fox & Company LLC.

Library of Congress Catalog-in-Publication data available upon request.

ISBN (hardcover): 978-1-64385-700-8
ISBN (ebook): 978-1-64385-701-5

Cover design by Meghan Deist

Printed in the United States.

www.crookedlanebooks.com

Crooked Lane Books
34 West 27th St., 10th Floor
New York, NY 10001

First Edition: November 2021

10 9 8 7 6 5 4 3 2 1

For absent friends, Sherry Simpson
and Geffrey Von Gerlach.

Beware that, when fighting monsters, you yourself do not become a monster . . .

—Friedrich Nietzsche

AUTHOR'S NOTE

Although the town of Homer, Alaska, is a very real place, numerous liberties have been taken for the sake of storytelling and in the interest of privacy. Some of the geographical details of the land and the sea, most of the business names and their relative locations on the Homer Spit or around the town, and all the characters in this work of fiction are entirely made-up. Any resemblance to real places or people—living or dead—is pure dumb luck.

—Richard Chiappone

PROLOGUE

Homer, Alaska

LIKE ALMOST EVERY other divorced—or nearly divorced—guy in Homer, Scott Crockett has been coming into the Orca Grill after work a lot lately. He seems to be leaving the jobsite earlier every day. It's only four in the afternoon now, and he's drinking his second IPA. The door to the bar is open, and in the sunlit doorway the owner, George Volker, is firing yet another waitress. The girl, a redhead who doesn't look old enough to work in a bar, is crying, pleading, hanging on Volker's arm with unmistakable intimacy.

Scott exchanges glances with the bartender, Shire Kiminsky. "Shire, what the hell? That kid's only been here a week, and Volker's already hooked up with her? How old is she?"

Shire rolls her eyes and sets some clean glasses on the bar. "She's twenty-one. I checked."

The girl whines, "George, don't do this to me!"

Volker hugs her and looks their way, shrugs like it's out of his control.

"The man is amazing," Scott says. "I gotta borrow his aftershave."

George Volker is short, ordinary looking, and must be close to sixty. The only physical exercise Scott has ever seen him attempt was bending over one time to pick up a nickel off the floor of the bar. Yet he somehow attracts a steady stream of young, incompetent waitresses who get romantically involved with him before he inevitably fires them. It must be the aging hippie look. The silver ponytail, the earrings. The guy goes through women like a king salmon in a school of candlefish. This latest one—Scott thinks her name is Tammy—may be one of the loveliest yet, if not the best waitress anyone's ever seen.

At the doorway, Tammy buries her face in Volker's chest and wails, "I said I was sorry about the deep fryer!"

"Take it easy." Volker pries her off, eases her out the door. "I'll give you a good reference."

"How can you fire me after five days and give me a good reference?"

"I'll say a fishermen's bar is not a suitable environment for a young woman of your refined temperament."

Shire scoffs. In a low voice she says to Scott, "Do you believe the bullshit this guy can sling?"

Scott sighs. "He does get the ladies."

"Oh, Scottie, so lonely, and not even completely divorced yet?" she says with playful mock sympathy. "Seriously, do you really want a wingnut like Tammy? She told me she thought the deep fryer needed more *water*. Volker has to drain the whole thing."

"Water." Scott laughs.

Volker finally sends the girl off. He walks back into the bar, groaning. "Shire, you're gonna have to work more hours. The first Princess cruise lands next week. We'll be swamped."

"No way." Shire shakes her very blond head. "I told you, George, my kids get off school on Memorial Day. I'm spending more time with them this summer. I leased my boat out to one of the Golovin brothers for the whole season."

"You're not going to fish?" Scott asks, astonished. He's known Shire Kiminsky since high school. Took her to their prom nearly thirty years ago. She's been a highliner—one of the best commercial fishermen on the bay—since she got her salmon permit and her own boat in her early twenties.

"I'm going to crew for a couple weeks on my brother's boat out west. Other than that, I'm spending the summer with my girls." She turns back to Volker. "Part-time, George. That was the deal. I'll help you out a couple times a week until you find a competent server with more than a room-temperature IQ."

"Shit." Volker collapses onto a barstool and reaches for his laptop. "I have to run a new ad. But all I get are ditzes!"

"No, George," Shire says, with authority, "all you *hire* are ditzes. If you based your decision on their experience instead of their tits, this wouldn't be a problem."

Volker looks at Scott. "Crockett, you ever consider a job in the exciting field of food services?"

"Thanks, George, but I'm too old for you."

"No more young ones, I swear," Volker says. He raises his right hand.

Shire snorts. "Right."

"I'm serious." Volker opens the laptop. "From now on, I'm looking for a smart, good-looking, unmarried, middle-aged woman who wants to live in the most beautiful place in Alaska. That's all I want."

"Yeah, me too," Scott says, and looks down into his empty glass.

"You had your chance." Shire reaches across the bar and pats his hand. She smiles fondly. "But no, the girl next door wasn't exotic enough for Scott Crockett. He had to marry the dark and mysterious Trina Malkovian." She winks at him. "Big mistake, my friend. Huge."

"Don't I know it." He stands, stretches. "See you later."

He walks out of the bar into the afternoon light. It's April, a month after the equinox, and the days are getting longer quickly now. The bay is calm, the tide rip at the end of the spit creating only the slightest chop. A sport boat cuts through the sparkling wave tips, trolling for salmon. Further out, a herring seiner heads for the fishing grounds. Blue-white glaciers cling to the old volcanoes on the other side of the bay. Crows and eagles and gulls pitch across the spotless sky.

Volker is wrong. This isn't the most beautiful place in Alaska.

It's the most beautiful place in the world.

PHOENIX, ARIZONA

CHAPTER

1

THE GUY SEEMS safe enough to Carla. Or maybe she just wants him to be. She's waitressed at the Sierra Vista for over a year, and she's met a few men here. More than a few. It's a cop hangout, and in her experience most cops are decent guys. Not that there aren't exceptions. She's been here long enough to know which regulars are likely to be trouble and which aren't. But there's something more to this stranger. He's harder to read.

It's late on a slow Tuesday night, and Carla's waiting for the kitchen to fill what'll be the last food order of the shift: chimichangas for the three twentysomething regulars huddled around a pitcher of Coors like they expect to hear it speak to them. Even out of uniform, the young guys have *rookie patrolmen* written all over them. They're polite, and that's nice. But she knows it's because she's got ten years on them. She could do without being reminded of that.

A very slow night. So she's free to watch a good-looking new guy when he walks in.

He's big, broad in the shoulders and very tall. Midforties maybe, but fit. None of the worn-out-cop paunch most of the regulars his age carry. Handsome and clean-shaven, with a short, expensive-looking haircut. The effect is ex–law enforcement meets pro football star with looks. She knows that type all too well: men who've been too attractive for their own good—or anyone else's—all their lives.

But there's more to this one. She's seen a thousand guys walk into every bar she's ever worked in intent on forgetting their jobs, their lives. Especially police. That's more or less why cop bars exist. With this new guy, it's not just the weary *I've been through all the shit cops have to deal with in this world and you haven't* attitude. It's more serious than that. He's trying hard to shed himself of something unpleasant. She can see that from across the room.

She sets a tray of glasses on the bar and watches him. He's wearing a cheery face, but she can tell he's forcing it. He glances at the TV, and the trouble coalesces around his eyes again.

Carla looks at the TV.

Manny, the owner of the Sierra, has turned off the relentless sports channel and is watching CNN. Like most news in the past few weeks, it's about Gordon McKint, military contractor and billionaire asshole of the highest order, now running for president—independently. Neither party will touch him. Congress has launched yet another investigation into McKint's company, Sidewinder Security. This one involves the murder of civilians somewhere in the Middle East. Carla can't keep track of it all. Doesn't want to.

McKint's on the screen. There's his signature eye patch. Manny's got the sound down too low for her to hear the megalomaniac, thank God. She can't stand his voice. Can't stand the news at all these days.

Apparently, the handsome stranger feels the same way. He shakes his head almost imperceptibly and turns away from the TV. As tall and straight-backed as he is, Carla pictures him leaning on his elbow at the bar for a drink, like a Clint Eastwood loner. Instead, he heads for the two-top in the corner. He can barely fit his legs under the table. He sits straight in the chair, takes off his long-billed black hat and sets it on his lap. That's nice. Not many guys bother to do that in here. Christ, you practically have to remind some to take theirs off when they're getting in your bed. Maybe this guy's meeting a woman? Kind of late in the evening for that.

That thought goes out the window when he makes eye contact with her across the room. Now he seems to genuinely brighten. It's not the carnivorous, pussy-crazed leer she's learned to steer clear of, but hungry in a pleasant, more appealing way. "Horndog optimism," her best girlfriend Sally calls it.

She motions that she'll be right over. He nods.

"Order up!" the cook calls to her from behind her. She delivers the plates of bulging chimichangas to the three young guys, then walks over to the stranger's table.

"Will there be others joining you?" she asks, handing him a menu.

"Just me," he says, and a shadow moves across his face. Sadness of some kind?

"Something to drink?"

The shadow vanishes again, and he smiles. The change happens so fast she's a little startled. But the smile is brilliant. "Ketel One, rocks, please. A splash of club soda, not tonic. Lemon wedge, not lime."

"Ooh, fussy," she says, and grins so he knows she's teasing.

"I've heard it said." He chuckles.

"Ketel. Rocks. Soda. Lemon." She leaves him reading the menu.

He's still absorbed in the thing when she returns with his drink. He doesn't even look up at her approach.

"Spoiler alert." She sets the vodka on the table. "The hero dies before the dessert list."

He looks up from his reading. That smile again. "You're right. The plot's a little obvious." He hands her the menu. "Just the drink, then."

Carla turns and walks away, resisting the urge to joke again. *Leave 'em wanting more*, her mother always says. *Drives men crazy.* She ought to know.

Carla goes about her job, feeling his eyes on her. She resists the urge to look his way.

Manny announces last call. The rookies ask for another pitcher. The complicated stranger orders a second vodka and makes it clear he's looking for company. When she delivers the new drink, he holds out his hand to her and says, "D'Angelo." He makes a show of reading her name tag, as though he hasn't already done that. "Uh, Carla."

They shake. The manicured nails finish her off.

When he asks what time she gets off work, she says, "Soon."

* * *

At closing time, Manny stops her as she punches out. He's a portly, avuncular second-generation Latino who treats her—and all the servers and cooks—like family. A former murder cop himself, his face is creased with concern. "Carla, you don't get in his car with him. You take your own truck. You hear? And call my phone if anything happens. You got my number on one-touch, right?"

Carla scoffs. "Come on, Manny."

"Hey, I'm serious," he says. "I don't know this guy, and I can't get a read on him. There's something hinky about him."

"Jesus, I'm thirty-eight years old. You can't make me stay in my room."

"The way you live." He shakes his head, puffs up his cheeks, and blows out a long breath. "You should talk to my pal Carmine from Sex Crimes. He'll tell you what happens when these things go bad."

"I *have* talked to Carmine from Sex Crimes. I'd rather stick my hand in the garbage grinder than do that again."

Manny sags, defeated.

"You're sweet, Manny. Someday I'm going to marry a man just like you."

"Good," he says. "Then *he* can worry about you."

She kisses him on the cheek and heads for the door.

*   *   *

Carla follows D'Angelo in her truck to his house, a perfectly refurbished Paradise Valley midcentury multilevel. It has staggered flat roofs and a terrazzo walkway. A water feature made from a stock tank is the centerpiece of the gated courtyard leading to the enormous heavy glass front door. This isn't the first time she's gone home with guys to expensive houses. She was a social worker at Maricopa County Hospital for years before burning out and going to work waiting tables, and she dated enough doctors to staff a clinic of her own. But this is classier in an understated way you just don't get with radiologists or, God forbid, surgeons.

She doesn't ask what he does for work, and he doesn't volunteer. But he clearly makes more money than any police job pays. An enormous window-wall in the living room looks out onto some kind of undeveloped land. No lights of any kind. An arroyo veers away in the desert darkness, his patio floodlights fading off into ghostly saguaros and brittlebush.

Against one wall in the front entryway is a long, narrow table. Propped on it is a framed picture of him with his arm around the shoulder of a teenage girl. She's clearly going to be tall and dark, like D'Angelo. Something about her handsome face resembles his.

"Your daughter?"

He nods, a forced smile tight across his lips.

On the other side of the girl in the photo, another man about D'Angelo's age has his arm around her waist. He's Latin looking and wearing a Mexican wedding shirt, a white linen guayabera.

Carla doesn't ask, but D'Angelo seems to want to explain. "My best friend from the Army. He was her godfather. That picture was taken at his family's place in Juárez. They gave her a quasi quinceañera. Simplified for Anglos." He looks at the picture with obvious fondness, and something else. "That was a very good day."

Carla knows enough not to ask any more questions. She looks away at a heap of mail on the tabletop. Something from the American Cancer Society, something else from Arizona Oncology Associates.

He sees her looking at that. He attempts to recover with alacrity. "Just got back from a trip." He takes her elbow. "Come on." He leads her into a huge kitchen that looks like acres of stainless steel. The stove and range hood, the dishwasher, the side-by-side freezer and fridge.

"Drink?"

She nods, taking in the jumble of copper pots and pans hanging from a rack of hooks over the big granite-topped island.

"Vodka okay?"

She nods again and watches this extremely tall and powerful-looking guy slice a lemon with surprising delicateness.

He hands her the drink. He holds up a small carry-on bag. "I'm going to throw this in my room. Why don't you sit out back?" He opens the sliders to a Saltillo tile patio. The night air is warm, but comfortable. "It's a nice time of year for it, before it gets so hot."

"Sure," she says, and sits on a love seat with thick red cushions. "They say the longer you live in Phoenix, the less the heat affects you. But I've been here all my life, and the summers are starting to get to me too."

He turns to walk back into the house. Over his shoulder he says, "The longer you live anywhere, the older you get. Maybe that makes it harder to take the heat."

"Yeah," she mutters to herself. She has a birthday coming in a couple months. "Maybe."

The patio is mobbed with pots of aloe and other desert succulents. A bougainvillea bush the size of a tree. Mexican sun and moon plaques, brightly painted plaster geckos on the posts supporting the patio cover. A big clay wood-burning chiminea. The place smells like Mexico. She feels like she's on vacation.

When he comes back out, they sit and talk about the weather, the lack of rain. A good waitress can make small talk about things she neither knows nor cares about. She gets a sense that he's doing it too, but she doesn't complain or even comment. In spite of the lingering feeling that he's holding something back, she's content to believe he's just trying to be sociable. It's a nice change from the pants-around-the-ankles opening gambit these kinds of hookups start with all too frequently.

She's been divorced ten years now. How many one-night stands have there been? She's not counting. But the real question is, how much longer can she live like this? Shit. She doesn't even want to think about that right now. This is too nice. It's such a great house, and a beautiful evening. The cloying smell of creosote bushes clings to everything. Somewhere nearby in the dark, a mockingbird is singing its ass off like somebody forgot to mention it's the middle of the night.

D'Angelo is in no hurry. Relaxed is refreshing. God knows she's seen urgent enough times. "Are you hungry?" he asks. "I guess I should've had something at the bar."

She shrugs. "Not sure. I could eat, maybe."

"I could fix something. Spaghetti carbonara?"

"Now I'm sure."

He leads her back inside. He seems to live alone. There is no sign of a woman, anyway. No houseplants. No art on the walls. There's an apron hanging from a hook. But it's a black bib apron, nothing feminine about it.

They switch to red wine that tastes far better—and far more expensive—than anything they serve at the Sierra Vista. Nothing she's ever been willing to pay for. At least he doesn't make a fuss over it. God, she hates when guys do that. The ear-nose-and-throat docs were the worst, for some reason. D'Angelo just pops the cork and pours. No rituals.

She likes that he's a bit of an enigma. He looks like a tough guy. She can see that his nose has been broken and fixed. His knuckles look like they're made of stone. And when he crouches to open a low drawer, she notices the white scar line that cuts across the top of his skull as straight as a bullet. But he's picked up some style somewhere along the line.

"You drink red wine with white pasta all the time?" she teases.

"Call me an iconoclast," he says.

He's picked up some education too.

"An iconoclast?" She has to smile. "Someone who tears down religious artifacts and beliefs?"

"Is that the real meaning? Well, I've seen people make this stuff into a religion." He swirls his glass and drinks again.

"But not you, right?" She gives him a dubious grin. "Come on, this isn't exactly box wine, D'Angelo."

He shrugs. "I did a favor for a guy at Total Wine. He sent me a case of the stuff." He points to a barstool at the granite-topped island in the middle of the kitchen. "Sit," he says. "Let's see what's in the fridge." He starts ferrying groceries to the island. A deli meat package. Another of cheese. Organic brown eggs. Organic romaine lettuce. Nothing cheap.

She decides to pry, just a little. "You know a guy at Trader Joe's too?"

"Normally I do my own shopping, but the guy who does my cleaning picked up some things and stocked the fridge for me. I was looking forward to some home cooking, but I thought I'd stop for a drink first. The Sierra Vista was the first place I saw on my way from the airport."

"Lucky me," she says, and salutes him with the wineglass.

He has the egg carton and several small bags and packages in his arms. There's a *New Yorker* on the counter top where he's trying to set them down. "Hey, would you move that, please?" He nods at the magazine.

Carla picks it up and glances at the cover as D'Angelo opens the carton of eggs. The name on the subscription reads *Cosmo D'Angelo*.

"D'Angelo is your last name? I thought it was a very exotic first name." She chuckles. "Not that Cosmo isn't. I like that."

He shrugs. "Everybody calls me D'Angelo. Ever since I was a kid. Except my grandmother. But you can call me Cosmo if you prefer."

"If I do, I won't remind you of your grandmother, will I?"

He laughs. "You look a lot like her, actually." He opens a thin package wrapped in white butcher's paper. "Aha. The pancetta is sliced the way I like it." He waves a thin, almost transparent disk of the pink meat marbled with white fat. "Good. More surface area than the crumbled stuff they sell prepackaged. Crisps quicker." He pulls a huge knife off a magnetic wall strip lined with others of all sizes and begins chopping the pancetta into tiny bits.

"I see," she says, enjoying this. For the first time all night, he seems genuinely engaged in the moment. Nothing hidden now. Whatever was bothering him is gone. Or on hold. Or very well disguised.

They slide into a comfortable silence. Carla has always liked being someplace where nobody knows where she is, what she's doing. She's been craving it more and more lately.

She watches D'Angelo crack eggs and grate Parmesan cheese with those big hands of his. The pancetta sizzles in a frying pan, the fatty, animal aroma making her hungry for more than food. Water boils, the pot lid rattling. He makes Caesar salad dressing in a glass bowl: more eggs, more cheese. He splashes mustard and Worcestershire sauce into the mixture without measuring. Red pepper flakes. He crushes garlic with a mortar and pestle, opens a tin of anchovies and mashes several of them too. He pinches one still-whole fillet from the tin and pops it in his mouth, sliding the open tin across the granite to her.

She can tell it's a test to see how adventurous her tastes are. She slips an anchovy into her mouth with relish—she loves the salty, bristly fish—and licks the oil from her thumb and forefinger. "These are really good."

He waggles his eyebrows at her and goes back to focusing on the salad dressing. He whisks light olive oil into the egg mixture until it's almost as thick as mayonnaise, tears some romaine into a salad bowl. "I have some croutons around here somewhere." When a timer goes off, he strains the pasta.

She eats so fast she embarrasses herself. "Damn, I didn't know I was that hungry."

He laughs.

This is too good. All of it. She knows it. This guy can't be this perfect. She can't help thinking that he's acting. A performance of some kind. When he smiles across the table at her, that glimmer of something serious looming behind his eyes has returned. Sadness, maybe? Grief? Hopefully it's not anger. She shoves the thought aside, finishes her pasta and her salad. Drinks her wine. It's all delicious.

She tells herself to watch out for this guy. And in the next second forgets it completely.

* * *

In bed he's a little rough, but not selfish. She can feel his tremendous strength, though. She'll have some finger bruises on her thighs, but it's not like she has anyone to hide them from. No complaints from her.

Afterward, he gets up and goes into the bathroom. She rolls up on her side and sees the time on his nightstand clock.

"I gotta go," she calls out. "It's really late. I'm beat."

"Are you sure?" he calls back from the bathroom. "Get some sleep. I'll fix you breakfast later."

Jesus, the guy is a food freak. *What else?* she wonders.

"No, really, I have stuff to do this morning," she lies, less comfortable now, suddenly intent on leaving. But there's something else she needs to do before she goes. Something she's done plenty of times. And not something she's sharing with this guy. Or any other.

She quietly slides open the top drawer of his nightstand.

At home she has a drawer of her own for the many small items she's taken from men before. Nothing valuable. Sunglasses, lighters, a lucky rabbit's foot. Wallet photos—although those are getting rare in the age of smartphones. Most items were purloined when a man fell asleep after sex. Or like now, when he left the bedroom for some reason. There's almost always a chance to grab something small. Her mementos.

Her girlfriend Sally scoffed at that. "Mementos are reminders of a fun time, Carla. You're counting coup, like the old Native American warriors."

"You only count coup from an enemy," Carla responded.

"Yeah? Well, maybe that should worry you."

It does worry her. Her mother, a spectacular aging beauty, has mementos from men too. Big ones. A house, cars, a swimming pool. They aren't from one-night stands, but they might as well be.

With D'Angelo still in the bathroom, Carla goes through the nightstand drawer. There's a pistol of some kind—not uncommon in the bedrooms of cops—condoms, pens, reading glasses. A passport. She opens it. His full name is Cosmo Anthony D'Angelo. Born in Buffalo, New York. He's forty-five. She flips through it. There are so many stamps from so many countries, hardly any blank pages remain. She closes the passport and notices a small black-and-white photograph, the margins yellowing, edges curled with age. In it, a much younger D'Angelo—wearing a camo uniform and holding some kind of machine gun—stands alongside a table where three men are seated. He looks to be in his early twenties.

She picks it up, sits upright, and swings her legs over the edge of the bed. She sets the passport back in the drawer and closes it. She'll keep the photo. It'll be a memento, no matter what Sally says.

Before Carla has a chance to look more closely, she hears the toilet flush. She hops off the bed, grabs her jeans off the floor, and stuffs the picture into a pocket. She's pulling them on when he comes back into the bedroom wearing a bathrobe.

"Sorry you have to go," he says. He rolls his eyes toward the bed. "We could have a rematch? Work up another appetite for breakfast." He grins with playful mock seductiveness.

"I need to sleep."

Again, he seems safe enough. But there's still something barely concealed that he isn't letting out. There's a heaviness weighing down the corners of his mouth when he smiles. The first word that came to mind when she saw him earlier walking into the Sierra Vista was sadness. Maybe regret is closer? Is he regretting something that happened? Something he's done?

Something he's *about to do*?

That makes her shudder involuntarily.

He notices. "You cold?"

"I'm fine, but I really have to go." She zips her jeans up, watching his eyes.

"That was nice," he says. "Can I call you? Cook you something a little more substantial for dinner some night?"

"More substantial than pasta? I'm stuffed."

He laughs. "Okay, something fancier, then. Let me show off. I'll fix something that goes with the snotty wine I forced on you."

Joking like that, he seems so normal again that she almost gets back in bed. She's been single and hooking up like this a long time, and she hasn't gotten hurt yet. But something is wrong here. "Come by the Sierra if you want to see me." She sees the surprise and a minor bruise to his ego blossoming in his eyes. Again, there's something inscrutable stirring behind it all. Manny's concerns about her flash through her brain. What if there's something seriously wrong with this guy? She feels a sudden need to get out of the house. She buttons her blouse and heads for the bedroom door.

Silent now, he follows her back through the kitchen. She grabs her handbag and keeps walking. At his front door, he suddenly reaches out and wraps his big hands around her upper arms and turns her toward him. A jolt of panic shoots all the way to her ankles. But he just gives her a peck on the lips and releases her.

"I'll stop by soon," he says. There's that warmth again that she was drawn to back at the restaurant. He seems his former charming self. Though, once again, the change is too abrupt.

She has to stifle the urge to run down the driveway. "Yeah, sure."

In the truck, flushed with relief, her instincts are still flaring. There's something off about this guy. Something underneath the charm. Something menacing. She's glad she didn't encourage him to contact her again very enthusiastically. *Hinky*, Manny said. He talks like an old cop. He is an old cop.

Carla backs down the drive, glancing at D'Angelo one more time.

He's standing in the doorway in his robe, watching her. He doesn't wave. He doesn't smile. He watches.

This guy is definitely hinky.

* * *

The scare she had at D'Angelo's house has mostly dissipated by the time she gets home. She should be comforted by her own familiar things. The clothes she left draped over every thrift shop chair and table in the apartment. Her houseplants. The small framed painting—one of her mother's original acrylics, a self-portrait—hanging over the kitchen sink. But she can't shake the feeling that she's just avoided something terrible. The guy didn't do one single untoward thing all night, and yet she feels lucky to be away from him for some reason. Still on edge, she pulls the photo out of her back pocket and looks at it more closely. The first thing she sees now is the eye patch on one of the men sitting at the table.

Gordon McKint.

It's not just the eye patch. Anyone can wear an eye patch. She recognizes the face, even twenty years or so younger.

An involuntary moan leaks out. *Fucking McKint?*

On top of the ongoing questions about the man's business practices—the bribery, the money laundering, every kind of complex, ethically suspect shit the man has been accused of—are persistent rumors of much more violent criminal activities, all of it so opaque she has only the vaguest notion what it means. And she just stole a photo of him doing God knows what. God knows when. Or where. And what exactly is her new friend Cosmo D'Angelo's role in all this? Good question. Her blood races.

She studies the photo. There are two men at the table with Gordon McKint. One is a dark-skinned, mustachioed man in a military uniform. An officer of some kind. The other is also dark, but wearing a suit and a thin tie. Given D'Angelo's youthful look, this must've been the nineties. And something about the room, the hacienda-style wrought-iron work over the window, makes her think of Latin America. Her mind turns to a drug deal of some kind, though there's nothing on the table in front of the men but papers. Is that ethnic profiling? Probably. But Carla's last name is Merino; her grandfather was from Monterrey, Mexico. It's Gordon McKint's baleful reputation and D'Angelo's intently vigilant expression—not to mention his automatic weapon—that evoke this suspicion, not the color of the other men in the picture.

She collapses onto a kitchen chair. The room is spinning. What the fuck has she done? She sits there for some time, holding the photo at arm's length as if McKint might leap up off the paper at her. Her heart thunders in her ears. What does she do with this thing? How can she possibly guess? Who would know? Who? Think! She feels like she's going to fall out of the chair, maybe just lie on the floor until McKint's goons come for the photo. For her.

Then it dawns on her. Lisa Yi, the one person she trusts to know what any of this might mean. They were in grad school together in Tucson. Now Lisa is at the *New York Times*, an investigative reporter covering mostly Gordon McKint's nascent presidential campaign in recent weeks. It's three hours later in New York. Seven in the morning there. Lisa Yi is a compulsive workaholic like no one else Carla has ever known. She'll be awake.

As she waits for Lisa to answer, Carla locks the door of her apartment. Like that could stop Gordon McKint or his shadowy, almost military organization.

She tells Lisa about the photo.

"McKint?" Lisa asks, her voice immediately rising. "Are you sure? Is he with guys who look like foreign military officers, by any chance?"

"Oh, it's McKint all right." Carla studies the photo. "One of the others looks like brass, and one is a well-dressed civilian. They could be foreign, I guess." She tells Lisa about the way the room looks. "But it could also be a Mexican restaurant right here in town. The military guy could be an American officer from Fort Huachuca, for Pete's sake. What do I know about uniforms?"

"Listen to what I'm going to tell you." Lisa's breathing ratchets up as she explains that a photo has reportedly surfaced. "It's from a time when McKint was in Colombia with the CIA. And it could ruin his political hopes, maybe even put the asshole behind bars." Lisa says the photo is thought to be in the hands of radical anti-McKint bloggers. "If that's what that is, Carla, I have to have it. The public needs to know."

"I don't know if that's what this is. I could scan it with my phone and text it to you," Carla offers.

Lisa freaks. "No! *No!* Do not send any image of that! This phone isn't safe. I don't want that picture out there in any digital form where it can get copied, captured, or altered until I have the original hard copy in my hands."

"Are you sure?"

"Absolutely. If digital copies get out before the original is vetted, McKint will declare it a fake. It'll be worthless as evidence against him. Where the hell did you get that thing?"

Carla tells her about her one-night stand with the handsome foodie. When she mentions the passport and recites his full name, Lisa groans. "Cosmo D'Angelo? Do you know who he is?"

"Please tell me he's just a nice-looking guy I slept with last night."

"D'Angelo's an operative in the Phoenix office of Sidewinder Security. McKint's company. I've tried to find out what he does, but it's never clear. I do know they want to take over all the security along the U.S.-Mexico border. McKint already owns the detention centers. He wants the enforcement branch too." Lisa says something more about the photo bringing McKint down, but Carla's ears are roaring now. She can't make it out.

"What's an operative?"

"He's a guy McKint sends to cut your horse's head off! Are you listening to me? I'm talking about Sidewinder having a private army on the border with Mexico paid for by American taxpayers. What do you think they're going to do if they find out you have something that could stop them?"

Carla looks at the photo again. "But there's nothing criminal going on in the picture. It could be a card game, for Christ's sake."

"Some former FARC rebel claims a high-ranking Colombian Army officer stole millions in American foreign aid money with the help of someone in the CIA. McKint testified in open congressional hearings that he never met that Colombian colonel in his life. If this is the picture people are talking about and it proves he lied to the feds, that's a felony. The same one that put Martha Stewart in jail."

"And then he can't run for president. And his company doesn't get control of the border either."

"You're getting the idea now. Carla, people get killed for less than that."

"What should I do?" Her heart starts to racing again.

"Get as far away from your apartment as you can. Right now. When D'Angelo discovers that picture's missing, he's going to track you there. Don't take anything but the clothes on your back. Don't call me on your cell again. Don't use it again, ever. Drive to someplace safe and call me from a pay phone. I'll send someone to pick up the picture from you. And we'll help you find a place to stay for a while."

Carla feels her stomach clench. Lisa Yi is not inclined toward hyperbole. She's a prizewinning journalist and dead serious most of the time. "Wait a minute. Why can't I just return the thing to D'Angelo? I could mail it to him or something."

"You can't do that. Do you want that maniac McKint for a president? We have to have it, Carla." Now there's a new tone to Lisa's voice, a hungry, almost greedy tinge to it. "This is going to be huge. And D'Angelo's more dangerous than you know. One of his employees in Phoenix recently died in a suspicious-looking suicide."

"What the hell is a suspicious-looking suicide?"

"Check out last Sunday's *Times*. I wrote about it. Later! You don't have time for this now. Just get out of there!"

Carla feels weak. It's four in the morning and she hasn't slept yet. "Maybe I should call the police?"

"The police?" Lisa Yi shrieks. "Are you insane? Cosmo D'Angelo won't be stopped by police. Run! Right now. I'm not fucking kidding, Carla. Take that picture with you and go!"

2

Aᴄᴛᴇʀ ᴛʜᴇ ᴡᴀɪᴛʀᴇss named Carla leaves, D'Angelo staggers to his room and falls facedown on the bed. He sleeps until dawn in his robe on top of the covers.

He wakes up feeling better than he has in two weeks—most of which he spent in a certain country he won't ever admit having visited. There is no stamp in his passport with its name.

It was not a pleasant trip. A job, not a vacation. *Nobody* vacations in that country. D'Angelo likes to think of himself as a negotiator, but he knows they don't send him into a situation until there is no chance of negotiating. This wasn't the first assignment of its kind for him—he's been doing unpleasant things for Gordon McKint in places like that for twenty-two years—but it was a bad one. Hastily thrown together. He hadn't been in on the minimal planning. His job was to persuade a local chieftain to embrace Sidewinder's interests. The guy needed a lot of persuading.

It didn't really require D'Angelo's skills. Just brute force. Which he could still do. But so could many of the newer goons the company was bringing on board, is spite of McKint's declared intent to become completely legitimate. D'Angelo had hoped to ease into late middle age working behind a desk, not the wheel of an armored vehicle. Everything about this last "negotiation" was off. He's glad he made it out alive. And frankly not sure how much longer he's going to be able to pull that off.

He's never been happier to be home again than he is this morning.

Maybe that has something to do with a certain waitress named Carla?

Yes, it was just a one-night stand, but then again, he finds himself liking the thought of it going in another direction. It doesn't have to be love and marriage like in some old song. It could be something, though. Maybe something like the arrangement he has with a Southwest Airlines flight attendant—he's been told he's not supposed to say stewardess now—named Annalisa. She overnights in Phoenix from time to time. He tried to call her last night when he got home from his trip, but she wasn't in town. Now he's kind of glad. Stopping in at the Sierra Vista turned out okay. It wasn't just the sex with Carla, which, God knows, he needed. He'd just spent two weeks in a place where you didn't want to take your flak vest off, let alone your pants. Carla seemed so comfortable being at his house with him. Everything about her was comfortable. He had to smile when she pulled up in his driveway and parked behind his Navigator in that old Toyota Tacoma pickup with the cab-over camper. Not a cowgirl rig, exactly, but a definite lifelong Phoenix vibe to it. Maybe it was the standard transmission. Which she handled effortlessly, setting the emergency brake and stepping out of the cab in one very sexy stride. You have to like a gal who's comfortable with a stick shift.

He liked talking with her, cooking for her, eating with her. That very grown-up feeling of comfort she gave off. She got a little jumpy at the end, but maybe he came on too strong. He'll stop by the Sierra soon. Turn the D'Angelo charm machine on high. See if he can get her to loosen up again.

* * *

The first person to see today is his daughter. Jennifer.

Yes, he'll eventually have to go into the office and debrief his immediate superior at Sidewinder, Phil Lundren, on the details of the trip overseas—details nobody wanted transmitted over the phones. But not until after he goes to the hospital. He rolls out of bed.

He takes a shower and dresses and does the pile of dishes and pans left from the spaghetti carbonara. He's got some time yet until visiting hours start at St. Joe's, where Jennifer is. Again. *Jesus.* She was doing so well this time. When he left to go out of the country, she was staying with her mother—his ex-wife, Rebecca—and looked like she was truly recovering.

But the cancer flared up again while he was away. Unable to reach D'Angelo, Rebecca called Phil Lundren. Lundren, controlling cocksucker that he is, didn't relay the news until D'Angelo was finished with the job and in Frankfort on his way home. He has to admit he couldn't have just picked up and left in the middle of that shitstorm anyway. And really, all his training and experience tells him he was better off not having a sick daughter on his mind. Still, it rankles him that Phil Lundren, of all people, has so much control over him.

He brews the first good coffee he's had in two weeks and savors it, but the thought of Jennifer sick again and the specter of talking to Lundren have conspired to demolish most of the upbeat mood he awakened with. He decides to make something good for breakfast before he heads to the hospital. That'll cheer him up.

He cracks three eggs into a bowl and starts scrambling them. The vapors off the olive oil shimmering in the hot pan, the aroma of the peppers sizzling, ignite memories of the Italia Imports store in the old neighborhood. His sister Rose called it "the stinky store." She wouldn't set foot in the place. But he loved those smells. The big cheese wheels sweating on the glass counters. The long salamis hanging from the ceiling like meaty stalactites. He loved the smell of food. All kinds of food. Always has. Still does.

When he was eight or nine years old, he'd go to the store with his grandmother. The nice dark-eyed ladies there in aprons and hairnets always came out from behind the counter with a slice of mortadella or a chunk of stringy scamorza cheese for him. Sometimes a bottle of orange soda to wash it down. They would pinch his chin and tell him how tall he was, how handsome.

He liked watching his grandmother pick through the huge woven basket of live Mediterranean land snails for the dish she called *babbalucci.* The snails were shipped to America while estivating, dormant inside their hard, striped shells, a dense mucous membrane stretched tight as a drum skin across the opening. His grandmother would shake each one up close to her ear, trying to determine whether the snail was alive inside. If it had died and dried up, it would rattle against its shell. She had to be sure before she dropped them into the tomato sauce. You didn't want a desiccated snail in your *babbalucci*. D'Angelo learned very young that life and death were serious matters—even in your kitchen.

He flips the peppers and pours the eggs over them, still worrying about his daughter but his mood improving.

Ah, to cook like his grandmother. Pig's knuckles in tomato sauce with lima beans. Golden chicken broth with carrot coins and pastina. Veal cutlets·dipped in egg and fresh parsley, browned in garlicky olive oil to a golden sheen he will never match. He loved staying at her house in the old Italian neighborhood when he was a child. He would sit on her front porch those summer afternoons, pushing the creaky old metal glider with one foot, reading Jack London and Arthur Conan Doyle, breathing the heady scent of the honeysuckle bush and the aromatic magic escaping from her kitchen.

He sighs, takes the frying pan off the heat, and slices a ciabatta roll, a little surprised at how hungry he is. He ate pasta with Carla at two in the morning. How can he be hungry again?

Who knows? Who cares?

He bites into the peppers-and-egg sandwich, thinks about his grandmother once more, his childhood, and for a rare moment, Cosmo D'Angelo lets himself forget about the world as he knows it to be.

Then he remembers the photograph in his nightstand drawer.

Fuck. Another unpleasant task ahead.

Jennifer gave the photo to him before he left to go on the job. For most of the two weeks he was over there, whenever the situation was stable enough, he stared at the damned thing, knowing how she wanted him to use it. And again during the four plane rides and the thirty-seven hours it took to get home. Then last night after getting Carla situated on the patio, he carried his travel bag into his room, took one more glance at the photo, and stuck it in the drawer with his passport. After all that scrutiny, he still hasn't decided what to do with it.

He knows that Jennifer is going to ask him. He could've happily gone all day today without thinking about that.

He finishes his breakfast and resists the urge to pull the thing out of the drawer and look at it again. What's the point now? It will only remind him once more that he's spent the last two decades doing Gordon McKint's dirty work. Twenty years ago, when McKint left the Agency to start Sidewinder, he asked D'Angelo to join him in the private sector. D'Angelo believed him when he said the ugly stuff would wind down. As the company grew and became putatively more legit, he kept hoping for that. He still is.

Now there's a whole new strata of management types—in Phoenix, and in Sidewinder headquarters in Virginia—but most of them have never fired a gun or used a sharp knife to cut anything other than a piece of avocado toast. So, his corner office in downtown Phoenix and the million-dollar house notwithstanding, it's D'Angelo they still call when something messy needs doing.

He used to have a soldier's pride in that.

Used to.

Now the question is: is that the only reason McKint has kept him around all these years?

3

CARLA HAS BEEN driving almost steadily since she hung up on Lisa Yi, threw some clothes together, grabbed her tip money stash, and left her apartment. Dirty dishes in the sink. Laundry on the floor. AC running. One last look around reminded her that any place she spends more than a few days ends up looking like a biker hideout. What difference does any of that make now?

If that photo is as important as Lisa says, and if Cosmo D'Angelo is who she says he is, he has access to computers with the capability to hack into just about anything. Assuming he has discovered the photo is missing, he might already have Carla's name and address from the Sierra Vista's payroll records. Or he could just lean on Manny—who's a tough, old ex-cop but no match for the huge, much younger D'Angelo. That's *if* he's discovered the photo is missing. That's a big if, and Carla simply has no safe way to find out whether it's true or not.

She left a voice mail for Manny to tell him she wouldn't be in that night. Nothing more.

Then texted her best friend, Sally: *I'm going away for a while. Don't worry. Seriously. Call you when I get back. Water the plants please? Love u.*

On her way out of town, she hit two different ATMs. Withdrew as much cash as each would allow. She didn't want to dally in Phoenix until the banks opened. The rest of her savings will have to wait until she feels safe enough to risk online banking. Online anything. If she ever risks that again. She tried a third machine, but it declined her debit card.

Now she's cut up that card, her Visa card, her J.Crew card, and all her others. She's smart enough not to use them, but she doesn't want to risk the temptation to do that if things get tight in the near future. At the moment, she has nothing in her wallet but cash and her driver's license—which worries her, but not as much as driving without one. The last thing she needs is to get stopped for some reason without a license. A police report would tip off Cosmo D'Angelo of her whereabouts faster than just about anything. Not counting the photo, there is nothing else in her purse except her makeup, some Altoids, a bottle of zolpidem, and her passport. She'll need that to get into Canada, because she's driving north and she's not stopping until she can no longer feel him out there behind her. She doesn't care if that means the North Pole.

Maybe Alaska? She's watched about six TV reality shows set there. The place seems to attract an unlimited supply of weirdos and freaks. Maybe they just thrive in a place so huge there's room for everyone. Plenty of privacy. The kind of place where a person with secrets could disappear pretty easily. She doesn't find the distances daunting. She likes to drive, always has. That's why she asked for the Toyota Tacoma with the camper in the divorce.

The hardest thing is letting go of the phone. It's amazing how attached a person can get to something that is never out of her hand, or her pocket, or her purse for more than a few minutes of every waking hour. She understands she needs to shed it but keeps telling herself that the possibility of being located by it is overblown. Fiction. Hollywood nonsense about GPS and spy satellites and shit. She's gotten three texts from Sally wanting to know what's going on, Carla jumping every time the phone vibrates. The last one is a plaintive *WTF? Please?* And what Carla really wants is to call her back and tell her the truth, so Sally will say everything is going to be all right, the way Sally always does. But that's not going to be possible now. Not if she's going to disappear.

The phone rings again, and she almost reaches for it. She needs to get rid of that thing before she answers it like one of Pavlov's mutts.

4

AT THE HOSPITAL, D'Angelo is pleased to find that Rebecca hasn't come in yet. Talking to her always leaves him feeling guilty, though he's not sure why. It was her idea to split, and a good one. But as glad as he is not to have to face her now, this means Jennifer is going to get right to the question of the photo. She's a straight shooter. Just like her father. Even as sick as she is, there'll be no tap-dancing around that thorny topic.

Walking into her room, he's surprised and delighted to find her sitting up, smiling and looking well, despite the patchy peach fuzz growing in over the baldness he's almost gotten used to in the past few months. She's even thinner than when he last saw her two weeks ago. Still, she looks much better than she sounded on the phone when he called her from the airports in Frankfort, New York, and then Dallas. Better than she sounded just last night when he called again as soon as the wheels touched down in Phoenix, too late to visit the hospital, desperate then for a distraction, and needing a drink.

"Hi, Pops."

"Do you feel as good as you sound?" he asks, ignoring how gaunt she's become.

"At the moment," she says, a spectacular grin on her face.

"That's good, right? Things seemed pretty bad when I called your mom from London two days ago. Even last night, you didn't sound like this."

"I don't know. I woke up this morning feeling okay. The doc was in early. My numbers are better than usual. This shit comes and goes, and I don't think they have a clue how or why."

She's right about that. The cancer has been maddeningly unpredictable and erratic.

"Eighty-eight percent," Dr. Singh, Jennifer's oncologist, told D'Angelo and Rebecca at the start of this whole nightmare last fall when the diagnosis came in. That was the probability that Jennifer would beat the cervical cancer they were just starting to treat. An intense woman with beautiful brown skin and eyes like an ocean squall, the doctor said she saw this kind of thing all the time and that with an otherwise healthy twenty-five-year-old woman like Jennifer, there was a "very high likelihood of complete recovery."

"Eighty-eight percent probability." Not eighty-five percent, which would have seemed like a broadly rounded number tossed off to sound encouraging. And not ninety percent, which would've reeked of pure hyperbole. Eighty-eight. Like the number of keys on a piano. The specificity of it was what lulled him into believing that Jennifer was going to be all right. "Complete recovery" were the exact words Dr. Singh had used, eyes flashing with expert certainty. D'Angelo liked the confidence she exuded, her apparent competence, the impression he got that she was basing her judgments on hard facts. That's the way he always tried to do his job.

But it hasn't gone as well as predicted.

D'Angelo resists the urge to say something stupidly hopeful. "I don't know what to say."

"Say you've decided," Jennifer says.

"Jen . . ." he stammers. "I . . . I just got home, late last night."

"And . . . ?"

"I'm working on it. It's complicated."

Jennifer is what she calls a social media nano-influencer. She runs an anti-McKint website, *gofactyourself.com*. Her blog has a small but rabid following. She hates McKint more than the cancer itself. She shakes her head and sighs. "Look, Dad, I could've sent it to the *Washington Post* or the *Times*. I could've posted the thing myself."

"And yet, you gave it to me," he says. "I asked you before and you never gave me a straight answer. Why *didn't* you post it?"

"Because coming from me, the assholes you work for will say the picture is a fake. That it's just an attack from an irrational McKint hater."

"And why will they say that about you? Whose fault is that?"

She grimaces. "I know. I have to admit, we've posted every single negative thing about him that has come over the virtual transom. We may have overplayed our hand." She leans forward and looks like she's about to climb out of the hospital bed to implore him. "But this is the real thing. You know that. And now I'm not sure anyone wants to hear from us anymore. Not even the legit media."

"I see. But if it came from me . . ."

"Yes. Coming from you, an insider, his old war buddy. Coming from you, the guy who does whatever it is you do for him, it will be huge news." She sags back into her pillow, her breathing strained.

"Jen, take it easy." He reaches to touch her shoulder.

She shakes him off. "Look, I know you're loyal to that one-eyed bastard. I know you believe all that semper-fi bullshit. But the asshole is running for president. The photo could stop his fucked-up campaign in its tracks. That's what I want!"

Yes, the "semper-fi bullshit" his daughter will never understand is part of it. "Like I said, it's not simple."

"I know, Pops." Jennifer hugs herself with those skinny arms. "I know it's because you're in that photo. I mean, I don't know what you guys were doing there in that room back then. And I don't really want to know. But McKint lied to Congress about meeting that Colombian colonel. The picture could finish him."

"I lied to them too, Jen."

"I know. And I don't want you in jail. It's just that . . ." She pauses to find a way to say it. "Yes, I feel good this morning, but I may not have a lot of time left. You know that. I need you to do this. Find some way to turn it over to the feds without hurting yourself. Trade the photo for immunity or something."

She's been this passionate about politics, about everything, since she was a teenager. And he wants to help her, but she hasn't thought it through the way he has. "Jennifer, if I give this to the media . . ."

"So, destroy it then!" Her passion turns to anger. He's seen that switch flip a hundred times since she was a teenager too. "Burn it! Go ahead. At least then I'll know where you and I stand."

She doesn't say *before I die*. But he hears it.

This is a conversation he's been having with himself since she gave him the photo. She's right. He's still a soldier to the bone. The thought of turning on his own former commander has had him tying himself in knots. Still, Gordon McKint hasn't become a billionaire and major player in the biggest of the big leagues by adhering to romantic notions like loyalty and camaraderie. D'Angelo knows that.

"Jen, give me just a little more time. Please?"

"Time," she mutters. "Sure." She closes her eyes.

"Jen . . ."

He stops when a short, older nurse bustles into the room carrying a piece of paper. She checks it against the chart on the bed frame, then reads Jennifer's monitor screen. "How you feeling, honey?"

Jennifer just shakes her head. "I was feeling pretty good for a while there."

"Yeah. I heard when I came on shift." The nurse smiles and points one thumb at D'Angelo. "Is this your boyfriend?"

Jennifer opens her eyes, rolls them his way. "This?" She chuckles. "This is my bodyguard."

The nurse looks D'Angelo over. "I believe it." She squeezes Jennifer's foot through the blankets. "Hang in there, young lady. Dr. Singh will be in soon."

When she's gone, Jennifer closes her eyes again. All the hopeful health he saw in her face when he arrived has drained back out again. Is he doing her any good being here? Is this visit for her? Or for him?

"Listen, Jennifer . . ." he says, not really sure what he's going to say next.

His ex-wife walks in. They've obviously had their problems. But right now, he's very glad she's there. "Rebecca." He kisses her cheek.

"Ah, it's the man of mystery. Welcome back, D'." She gives him a fond look. "I'd ask where you've been that no one could get ahold of you for a week, not even your office, but I know you'd have to have me killed or something if you told me." She scoffs. "Don't you ever get tired of that cloak-and-dagger stuff?"

"You have no idea."

She smiles. "You look good. You here to see your daughter? Or do you have some new bullet holes that need patching up?"

"I was just leaving. I have to get to the office." He turns to Jennifer. "I'll be back right after work. I'll bring you some Imperial Wok. You can't tell the food from the medicine in this fucking place."

That gets a laugh out of Jennifer. The first one he's seen in a while. "Dad, give me a hug before you go," she says.

D'Angelo leans over the bed. Jennifer wraps her arms around him, a tube dangling from one wrist, a monitor bracelet of some kind on the other.

She whispers, "Do the right thing, Dad. You know what it is."

5

IT'S JUST AFTER eight in the morning when Carla's eyes become so tired she decides to pull off the big highway and take the old switchback road to the rest area on top of the Hoover Dam. As scared and anxious as she is to put miles between herself and Phoenix, she still feels the magic of this place as soon as she steps out of the truck. She's glad she stopped.

Once again she gasps at the size of the dam, the immensity of the effort it took to build the thing. She can feel it vibrating in the six million tons of concrete beneath her feet. The whole structure hums like a gigantic electromagnet. How many times has she stopped here on her way to or from Vegas with her husband? Or, after the divorce, with some of the other social workers or nurses from the hospital where she used to work? It's been ten years since she left the hospital. It's been that long since she's been here.

She parks and puts the troublesome phone in her purse, walks to the Monument Plaza on the western end of the dam, and reads the plaque beneath the two massive bronze art deco sculptures. Towering over the plaza and mesmerizing her with their strange, stylized dignity, the winged gods sit imperiously on thrones backed against the cliff face. It's only fitting that they should overlook the celestial star map, a twenty-six-thousand-year clock built into the terrazzo deck. It's designed to pinpoint the configuration of the heavens on the day of the dam's completion in 1935. Even if violent lunatics like Gordon McKint finally obliterate life on earth, some alien visitor in the distant future can situate this massive human effort in time.

Carla loves the sound of the words *axial precession* on the monument's plaque, though she only vaguely understands how this astronomical clock is calibrated for eons. All of which brings her back to a critical question: with Cosmo D'Angelo and all his first-class computers looking for her, just how much more time does Carla Merino have on this planet?

She pushes the thought out of her mind for the tenth time today and studies the two giant statues a moment longer. She must've been eight or nine when she saw them for the first time with her mother—and some guy. There was always some guy. Carla's well aware that the same could be said of her.

She remembers her mother pondering the handsome bronze faces of the gods, their powerful winged arms straight up overhead, biceps like boulders. "I have to get one of those," she said.

"You want a statue?" the man with her asked. "For what, the yard?"

"Not a statue, silly. A man with wings." Her mother winked at her. "And muscles like those. A god. Is that so much to ask?"

Carla was still young enough to be entertained by her mother's repartee. That didn't last much longer.

It now occurs to her that earlier, when she fled the apartment, and Phoenix, maybe forever, she left messages for Sally and Manny but not a word for her mother.

Another thing she didn't do on her way out of Phoenix was stop at a pay phone—as Lisa Yi advised—to arrange handing over the photo to the *Times*. Somehow the thought of letting go of the thing, even to Lisa, is untenable. If she did, she'd still have to run, and then she'd have nothing to bargain with. *Bargain with?* Who is she going to bargain with? Cosmo D'Angelo? Just how would you go about that without getting yourself killed?

Her phone rings, and she almost yelps. It's only Sally again. Carla wants to answer, badly. Wants to talk to someone who isn't trying to kill her. But if she answers, will that put Sally's number on D'Angelo's radar? The phone rings again, the temptation to pick up almost too much. She runs to the stone parapets at the edge of the dam and hurls the thing out into the abyss. It plummets to the Colorado River more than seven hundred feet below.

She looks at the winged gods one last time, gets back in the truck, and drives.

CHAPTER

6

I T'S NEARLY NOON when D'Angelo pulls up to Sidewinder headquarters in south Phoenix.

Something's wrong. And it's not just the phalanx of MCKINT FOR
PRESIDENT signs incongruously staked out across the lawn. They look
like a small army of some kind guarding the otherwise nondescript,
single-story concrete-and-glass structure in the equally nondescript
business park. The signs are new. And they make him cringe. The
idea has always been to keep a low profile. Everything about Sidewinder Security is more or less secretive. The sign on the building is
so innocuous you have to know where to look for it. Apparently the
announcement by the company's founder has changed all that. He
should have seen this coming. Gordon McKint's face was on every
TV screen in every airport D'Angelo slogged through on his way
home from the other side of the planet. He grimaced at the sight of
the Sidewinder Security logo looming behind McKint as he told his
adoring followers just how he was going to solve, as he called it, the
"immigrant crisis." So much for secretive.

But there's something wrong *inside* the building too. Something is different. He can feel it in the taut faces on everyone. The
quiet is unusually severe, even for a place housing as many secrets
as this one. It puts him on alert.

Trudy, his office manager, looks positively bleak. She says,
"Welcome back, boss," and chews her lower lip. There's a tremulous

emotional catch in her voice. Trudy is not known for wobbly emotions.

He looks around. In the cubicles, the data analysts and tech mavens bow before their computer screens with what could be taken as their usual reverence for all things digital. But it's not. It's something else. Something more. He can almost taste it in the air.

It's fear.

He can see it in Trudy's face. He can see it in the posture of the whole team.

"What the hell is going on, Trudy?" he asks, pitching his voice low, privately.

She pulls her lips in, hisses, "It's about Kevin." Her eyes dart past him and back again.

"Our Kevin?" He knows only one Kevin. "With the yoga mat and the funny hair?"

Trudy looks like she's about to start weeping.

"Kevin Dykstra?" he asks, and she sniffles and nods.

In his stretchy pants and long-sleeved T-shirts, Kevin Dykstra is a New Agey anomaly among the other Dockers-clad techies and analysts. In his twenties, he may be the youngest person on the payroll here in Phoenix. D'Angelo marvels whenever he sees him ride up to the building on his bicycle—D'Angelo hasn't ridden a bike since he was about eleven—or sees him sitting on his ergonomic chair, clacking away at his keyboard. He can't help thinking about what he himself was doing at that age: who he was shooting at, or who was shooting back. Kevin will never know the thrill of either. D'Angelo isn't sure whether to envy or pity the kid.

He likes him, teases him about his man bun, calls him Buntaro after a Samurai character in Clavell's *Shōgun*. The kid doesn't get it but doesn't care. He just smiles and keeps on working. A data junkie, he's happy as long as he has a problem to solve and a computer to solve it with. He can fix anything. Hack anything. Find anything. Anything.

An alarm is starting to vibrate inside D'Angelo. If Trudy were the only one acting this way, he'd write it off as her typically dour mood. But *everybody* in the place?

"Kevin Dykstra?" He tries to lighten things. "What did he do, hack into the Pentagon?"

Trudy's face flashes sudden awareness. "Oh my God. You don't know."

"Obviously," he says, the alarms getting louder. "What happened?"

Trudy grabs a Kleenex and sniffles into it, teary eyes shooting around the room again. D'Angelo looks that way too. One of the techs is watching them from her cubicle; her head snaps back to her screen again. *What the fuck is going on?*

"Trudy?" he says. "Tell me."

"Not here." She nods toward D'Angelo's office. "Inside."

*   *   *

He gets Trudy settled in a chair near his desk, still sniffling. "Kevin's dead!" she blurts, sobbing now.

"Yeah, I was starting to get that. How? What happened?"

When she pulls herself together enough to talk, she says, "He hung himself! In his family's cabin, up north in the mountains." She stops. "Didn't Mr. Lundren tell you?"

Now the internal Klaxons are blaring.

"Mister" Lundren sent D'Angelo out of town, out of the country, to do a job that really didn't require his vast experience or talent. That alone was a little suspicious and had D'Angelo wondering. Then one of his own people commits suicide while he's gone? There are no coincidences at Sidewinder Security.

He reins in the anger. "No, I guess he forgot to tell me. When did this happen?"

"Almost two weeks ago, I think. Two or three days after you left on your trip, maybe. I could look it up."

He forces himself to speak calmly. "Sure, why don't you do that. Thank you."

Trudy stands to leave, but stops. "It was so terrible. I mean the way it happened. Poor Kevin. The police think he hung himself from the stovepipe on a woodstove and it broke or something. The cabin caught on fire, and that started a forest fire that burned for days. I think they have it under control now."

"A fire."

It's April and almost a hundred degrees already. Even up in Flagstaff where the daily temps are ten to twenty degrees cooler, there's little likelihood that anyone has been burning firewood lately.

"Uh-huh," D'Angelo says. He asks a question he already knows the answer to. He could write this script. "And so I guess there was no suicide note? No texts on his phone to anybody?"

Trudy shakes her head. "I don't think there was anything left after the fire. Not even much of a body. I'll get you the newspaper article. But Mr. Lundren can probably fill you in on the details. Do you want me to set up a meeting?"

"No, I need to check in with him anyway."

A suicide with no note. A body reduced to ash. Perfect.

It wouldn't have been Phil Lundren himself getting that dirty, of course. He doesn't have the skill set for that. Or the balls. But there are a couple others at Sidewinder who do. There's a reason Lundren has leapfrogged past him up the company food chain, though he doesn't go back anywhere near as far as D'Angelo and McKint do together. And it's not because of his field skills. He's never been in the field. Never fired a gun. The business is changing, and Lundren has climbed a very different ladder to the top level. D'Angelo worked his way up with live ammunition and boots on the ground in places like Cartagena and Kabul and Kinshasa, where his job was keeping McKint alive. The rungs on Lundren's ladder are made of spreadsheets and PowerPoint presentations. His job is keeping McKint alive too, but in the equally hazardous terrain of board meetings and fund raisers.

Yes, it's a two-tiered business now, the old-school practices rapidly being replace by newer, more publicly palatable behavior. And D'Angelo is smart enough to know that—the occasional need for his primitive services notwithstanding—it's never going back. He needs to find out what really happened to Kevin Dykstra. And most importantly, why? What the hell did the kid do? The trick is finding out without anyone knowing he's looking.

They took out one of their own people?

So much for the "semper-fi bullshit."

* * *

When Trudy goes back out to her work area, D'Angelo walks to Phil Lundren's office. He doesn't call first. He wants to surprise

Lundren, keep him off-balance if he can, see if anything about Kevin Dykstra slips out.

He walks past Kevin's now-empty workstation. The computer screen is dark. His special chair is gone, but his New Age crystal is sitting on his desktop. D'Angelo steps in and picks it up. Puts it in his pocket.

Lundren puts on a show of being pleased to see him, but D'Angelo can see in his face that he isn't happy he showed up unannounced. "D'Angelo, welcome back." His face goes a degree or two brighter. "Coffee?"

Phil Lundren is a couple years younger than D'Angelo, almost as tall, with a plain face and a plain midwestern voice. He keeps something like a smile on at all times, as if he's not sure when one is actually appropriate. He's a born manager of people. A natural salesman. Which is a requirement for those jobs anyway. It's not charm exactly. Cosmo D'Angelo has indisputable charm. The kind that gets him what he wants or needs. What Phil Lundren possesses is the ability to get *other people* things *they* want. Mainly, Gordon McKint. If Lundren has ever had an original thought or idea of his own, D'Angelo hasn't seen any evidence of it.

"No coffee, thanks." The Kevin Dykstra thing has already put him on edge. Snapping at Lundren won't get him what he wants. He won't say anything about Kevin until he sees if the subject comes up.

It doesn't. Lundren wants to share some good news. "You're getting a bump, my friend. Moving up a notch."

D'Angelo has been wondering if this would happen. Gordon McKint's decision to throw his hat into the presidential race means that Sidewinder Security will have to adopt a kinder, gentler public face for a while. Starting with fewer unflattering news items about their handling of detained immigrants along the border. McKint's plan to privatize the Border Patrol is the centerpiece of Sidewinder's shift from profitable but messy rebellions and civil wars to nice, stable domestic situations right here in the U.S. He has pledged to remove himself from Sidewinder's management if elected. But once he's in office? With the power that brings? It'll be business as usual on a scale never seen before. And no need to wade through bloody foreign mud.

All of which requires some shifting in personnel. In other words, less Cosmo D'Angelo and more Phil Lundren.

"You are going to be—and this is straight from Gordon himself—head of special services, here in Phoenix."

"Special services. Great. I assume you're moving up too," D'Angelo says.

"You're looking at Gordon's new campaign manager."

"You're moving to Virginia?" Now that is good news.

"DC, actually. The campaign headquarters is in the District, just a few miles from our offices in Arlington."

Lundren's smile looks as close to genuine as D'Angelo has ever seen it. Obviously, it's for his own ascendency to the national stage, not D'Angelo's own mostly lateral move. He's been making "special services" decisions since they opened the Phoenix office.

"Good for you, Phil," he says. "Congratulations."

"Good for both of us. You're going to be in the office now. Always. Period! No more jungles. No more deserts—except our own beautiful Mojave, of course. No more sticky stuff. Let the young guys handle that." He gets thoughtful for a second. "Actually, we're going to need to keep the rough stuff minimal during the campaign." The smile returns. "You deserve a break, Cosmo. This is it. And a nice pay raise too."

"Wonderful," D'Angelo says. Still no mention of Kevin Dykstra.

"So," Lundren says, "fill me in on that job. It's my last piece of business here before I head to the East Coast."

They talk about the details they couldn't put in emails. An hour later, D'Angelo stands to leave Lundren's office. He puts his hands in his pocket and feels the crystal.

Lundren still hasn't said a word about Kevin Dykstra. D'Angelo debates whether to bring it up or keep mum and launch his own surreptitious search into the matter. He's almost to the door when Lundren pretends to remember something.

"Hey, you heard about the young guy from data who we lost? Dykstra?"

"Trudy just filled me in. First I heard of it." He pitches it so that Lundren will get the message.

"Yeah, I didn't want you distracted while you were over there."

"Sure," he says. "Any ideas why he did it? I mean, there's no note, right?"

"Nothing survived the fire." Lundren looks away. The sure tell of a bad liar.

"Is that right?" D'Angelo says, neutrally. "I'll see if Trudy wants to organize a memorial for him or something."

"Yeah, sure. Thanks."

D'Angelo reaches for the doorknob.

"Hey," Lundren says, as if it just came to mind, "were you in on the vetting of the kid when he was hired?"

D'Angelo shakes his head, curious to see where this goes. "Why? Something sketchy come up in his background? Something they missed?"

"Nah," Lundren says. "I just mean you and the kid knew each other for a while, right?"

The alarms again.

"Yes. I knew Kevin Dykstra and I liked him. He was a straight arrow. Funny hair and all."

"Sure. Let me know if there's a memorial. I'll be in DC, but I'd like to contribute something."

"Thanks, Phil. I'll let you know."

You lying motherfucker. We don't kill our own people.

*   *   *

D'Angelo knows better than to make any inquiries into Kevin Dykstra's so-called suicide here in the Sidewinder offices. If he's going to get any enlightening information about this, it will have to be from outside sources. It's not the first private inquiry he's had to make. Sidewinder Security is populated with covert operatives, former spies, and ex-agency spooks and ghouls trained in elicitation and duplicity. Asking questions is like juggling live grenades. It's one of the things he used to love about the job.

He spends the afternoon pushing Jennifer's condition out of his mind and catching up on messages and business matters that have accumulated while he was away. When he sees a grinning Phil Lundren leave the building, glad-handing his way through the analysts and cryptologists—obviously on his way to DC to help with

McKint's campaign—he can only bite his lip. He'd like to take Kevin Dykstra's crystal and shove it down Lundren's throat.

What the hell was Kevin Dykstra up to that brought that down on him?

The whole thing makes D'Angelo alternately furious and tired. He almost mutters a cliché that seems apropos: "I'm getting too old for this." But he stops himself. Because if can you say it, you might start believing it. And if you believe it—if only for a minute— you're right.

CHAPTER

7

B Y NOON, CARLA has driven straight through Las Vegas, all the
frivolous wasted weekends she's spent there no longer having
any nostalgic currency for some reason. She can barely remember
one. Maybe once your future seems like it's about to be erased, the
past goes with it too somehow?

She drives until she needs gas and pulls into Cedar City, Utah,
a pretty little town on the edge of Zion National Park. Sagebrush
and stunted trees climb the desert hills into higher, snowcapped
mountains to the east. Ski country. The tourist town looks so peaceful. A nice place to live, maybe. Someplace easy for a good-looking
woman to get a waitress job—for cash under the table. Maybe she
could find a campground and live in the camper for a while until
the summer temps get too hot. Who would look for someone in
Cedar City, Utah? Who's ever even heard of it?

She entertains the ridiculous idea for another half minute before
snapping out of it. She buys gas, pays cash, and drives on.

Exhausted now, she makes it another hour before dozing off at
the wheel. Jolted awake by the howling horn of a swerving oncom-
ing driver, she pulls into the next rest area on her side of the highway. She's not sure where she is. It doesn't matter. The emptiness
of the landscape is comforting. High desert sprawls away in all
directions. Sagebrush and scrub oaks and sparse, brown grasses.
Except for the rest stop bathrooms in a low stone structure with

a red tile roof, there are no buildings anywhere. She parks in the shade of a big paloverde tree, then staggers out of the truck and climbs into her camper. She crashes on top of the sleeping bag on the foam rubber mattress, her cheek pressed against the cool nylon fabric. With her eyes shut, the steady woosh of cars and semis passing on the highway synchronizes with her heartbeats. She's asleep.

When she wakes up, it's midafternoon and her truck is no longer in the shade. The camper is sweltering. She climbs out and goes into the women's room. She splashes water on her face, looks in the mirror, and cringes. God, her birthday is in July, just three months away. Thirty-nine. She looks a hundred. She's known for some time that she is just not going to age with the rather frightening grace her mother has. That woman has a mirror she talks to, like a certain queen from a fairy tale.

Carla presses her fingertips to the puffy skin under her eyes as if she can push it back into her face. It's not the late night out, the lack of sleep, or the stuffy hangover sinuses from D'Angelo's expensive Pinot Noir that she's seeing. This is what fear does to you.

She takes out her makeup and does her face. It's not simple vanity, although she's well aware of her capacity for that. She does it so she can look in the mirror and recognize the Carla Merino she is going to spend all her time striving to keep alive. She's not going to knock herself out for some wrecked-out hag. And really, who else does she have to look good for now?

Back in the truck, she drinks half a bottle of water and looks at the photo again.

Alert now, clearheaded, the fear reasonably under control, she considers her options.

She has two choices. She could give it back to D'Angelo, or she could give it to Lisa Yi to use against McKint.

She has a feeling that even if she sends it back to D'Angelo, or to Sidewinder Security, right now, McKint isn't going to just forgive and forget.

And if she turns it over to Lisa and the media, she'll make an enemy of him for life. His attack dog, D'Angelo, will hunt her down sooner or later. She'll have to have a sure way of completely disappearing before she attempts that.

But there is a third way. What if she destroys it? Burns it and throws the ashes into the desert? They might not believe she did it. And if they are as vicious as their reputation for violence hints, she really doesn't want to think about what they might do to her to find out if she's lying.

The first two options terrify her; the third pisses her off.

At the county hospital, three-quarters of her clients were Mexican or Central American immigrants—legal or otherwise—who needed all the things social workers provide for people and who have little money, less power, and no legal protections at all. The last thing those people need is for Sidewinder Security to control their lives. McKint has to be stopped.

But for now, she needs to keep moving.

She almost puts the photo back in her purse but thinks better of it. She opens the glove box and thinks better of that too. She looks around inside the cab of the truck. There's a barely detectable slit in the headliner fabric directly overhead. She spreads it open with her thumb and one finger and slips the photo up inside. The fabric closes back over it. It's nearly invisible again.

Putting the truck in gear, she pulls out of the rest area and follows the frontage road to the next highway entrance ramp heading north. A sign says SALT LAKE 235 MILES. Boise is another three hundred or so. She'll think about the whole matter again when she hits Canada. It's probably not far enough, but it's a start.

8

D'ANGELO MAKES IT through the afternoon without smashing anything, anyone.

He's in the Imperial Wok, waiting for the takeout he's ordered. Jennifer's favorite—the Shanghai Dinner Special. One shrimp foo yong, one fried rice, one house lo mein, two egg rolls.

He's a fair hand in the kitchen himself, but he has purposely never learned to cook Thai, Japanese, or Chinese. If he did, he'd never leave the house.

He's been coming to the Imperial Wok for as long as he's lived in Phoenix. When Jennifer was a girl, it was a regular destination for them on his shared-custody weekends. The owner, Mrs. Chen, has become somewhat of a confidant—God knows, he doesn't have many others—and she's told him that she gets offers from land developers almost daily. He happens to know she owns the whole strip mall the restaurant is located in. "So much money!" she says. "But then what am I going to do? Not work?"

It's a good question. Across Seventh Street he can see yet another new restaurant under construction. The street is lined with them. When did Phoenix become a foodie mecca?

It seems like it's happened overnight. You can still get a traditional veal chop or a recognizable plate of linguini and clams at Christo's, of course, but now the whole town is overrun with joints for people intent on paying too much money for too-clever food.

Trattorias serve grilled pizzas with pine nuts, kale, and chorizo. Overpriced finger food emporiums seem to believe they invented the idea of putting meat between two slices of bread. And Mexican food? People used to be happy with the ubiquitous Filibertos. Now the hipster crowd demands carne asada with pomegranate, hibiscus flower, and tamarind-spiced wine reductions. Apparently there's a competition to concoct the entrée with the most ingredients.

Hoping to be happily surprised, D'Angelo has tried enough of those places—well, not the idiotic fusion joints—and most times he's been left neither happy nor surprised. All he wants at the moment is to eat some takeout with his daughter at the hospital, go home, and drink a very tall glass of vodka. Several, actually.

Mrs. Chen comes out with his order. Behind her, he can see into the kitchen. All the cooks are tiny, older Mexican women with strong Mayan features. Mrs. Chen shouts orders in a Chinese-English amalgam to the women. They don't appear to speak either language, yet somehow the food turns out great. That's one of the things D'Angelo likes about the unassuming place. Crammed in a strip mall between a NAPA Auto Parts and Nita's Nails, there's a counter up front and an uncomfortable wooden bench if you want to wait inside for your food instead of in your car. There are even a few small booths for those determined to have the full sit-down Imperial Wok dining experience. The banquettes are covered with hot-orange vinyl, the tabletops in matching Formica. He once asked Mrs. Chen if the blazing orange color has some significance in Chinese culture. She told him studies show that you can turn over tables faster with hot colors. So much for cultural significance.

"D'Angelo!" She puts the bag on the counter, grinning. "You look terrible."

"Thank you, Mrs. Chen."

She lowers her voice, goes serious. "How's your daughter?"

"It's hard to know," he says. He hands her the money for the food. "Thank you for asking."

"So young still," shaking her head. She rings up the sale, gives him his change. "I made the foo yong a little spicy the way she likes it."

D'Angelo thanks her again and turns to leave.

He's almost out the door when a tall, heavy goon with a lizard tattoo crawling up his neck pushes in. Shaved head, badass scowl.

He tries to shove D'Angelo out of the way. D'Angelo instinctively sets his feet, blocking him. They stand, face-to-face. The guy glares at him. Mean eyes. Mean mouth. Mean everything.

D'Angelo feels the stifled anger about Kevin Dykstra he's had simmering on a back burner all day boiling into something more immediate, more violent, and far more therapeutic. Anger, channeled in a useful way, is just what he needs. But he doesn't want to tear up Mrs. Chen's restaurant satisfying his own suddenly murderous mood.

"My fault," he says, and steps aside.

The creep gives him a victorious sneer and pushes on into the restaurant.

D'Angelo walks to his car. Two parking spaces away is a jacked-up Jeep with a Confederate flag sticker and a rifle rack in the rear window. A rolling cliché. Not hard to guess whose ride that is. He's about to get in his car when his phone rings. He sets the food bag on the hood.

It's Rebecca. Her voice is quaking. "Are you on your way? Don't stop for food. Jen's not going to be able to eat. She's having a bad time again, Cosmo."

She called him Cosmo. Not good.

"I'm on my way."

Heart revving, he grabs the bag of food and opens the driver's side door, but something in the restaurant window catches his eye. The tattooed creep is at the counter, waving his hands in Mrs. Chen's face. He must be saying something unpleasant. D'Angelo can make out Mrs. Chen's disapproving look from across the parking lot. He has the feeling that when Mrs. Chen disapproves of something, you can see it from outer space. He hesitates, half in the car. The hospital is at least twenty minutes away.

Mrs. Chen crosses her arms over her chest and says something back to the big goon. Two of the tiny kitchen ladies come out carrying huge knives, clearly very loyal to her. D'Angelo sighs. This will only take a minute. He starts back across the parking lot toward the restaurant. He can smell violence coming. It's like fresh coffee calling.

The creep leans over the counter and, with one thick finger, pokes Mrs. Chen in the middle of her chest above her folded arms. She rocks back on her heels, almost stumbling. The guy spins away from the counter and stalks out the glass door, shoving it open so hard it slams against a tall concrete ashtray and cracks. Reveling in that small victory, he takes two more steps before he sees D'Angelo coming his way. Too late.

D'Angelo punches him in exactly the same spot he poked Mrs. Chen. A full-shouldered right, driven into his breastbone with all of D'Angelo's 238 pounds and as much anger and frustration as he dares reveal in public. Anger at Lundren and McKint. Frustration at his inability to stop the disease that is killing Jennifer.

The creep buckles, gasping. D'Angelo draws back to finish him off with another to the jaw. Then he sees Mrs. Chen and the cooks gathered in the doorway, watching. No need to make this any messier.

He crouches over the guy, yanks his wallet out, and pulls out all the bills. "You just bought a door, fuckhead."

He takes the money to Mrs. Chen.

He returns and grabs the creep by his shirt and hauls him upright. He shoves him across the parking lot to the Jeep. The guy is starting to get his breath back. D'Angelo plants another fist in his belly, crumpling him again. The guy hangs on his side-view mirror.

"Look," D'Angelo says, "if you get out of here before my friend Mrs. Chen calls the police, neither one of us will have to talk to any cops. Do I need to tell you you're never eating Chinese food again? It doesn't agree with your stomach."

The guy nods that he understands.

"Good." D'Angelo gets in his car and drives. With Rebecca's phone call echoing in his head, he can't even enjoy the post-violence buzz he's come to be so fond of. The smell of Mrs. Chen's food almost sickens him. And then there's the Phoenix afternoon traffic. It takes him over half an hour to get to St. Joseph's.

Things are worse than Rebecca let on when she phoned him. She meets him coming into the lobby.

"What're you doing down here?" he asks.

"She's in ICU. It's bad, D'. Real bad."

There are good days, and there are bad days. And then there are days like this.

*   *   *

It's almost midnight when D'Angelo gets home from the hospital. Jennifer is still in ICU. He and Rebecca waited for hours but never got in to see her again. Her condition is listed as *stable*. That's both better and worse than the possible alternatives.

He pours himself a drink. He feels like just slugging it from the bottle but forces himself to take the time to put three ice cubes in a short old-fashioned rocks glass. He sets a slice of lemon on top of them and pours the vodka through it. He leaves just enough room for a splash of club soda, drinks it in two long swallows, and makes another.

His mind races from one thing to another, pointlessly. Jennifer. Kevin Dykstra. McKint. Lundren. Jennifer again, and again.

Her last hug, her last words to him . . . He's trying not to use the term *last words*. Her *most recent* words to him keep coming back. "Do the right thing. You know what it is."

If only.

He walks into the bedroom and sits on the edge of the bed, holding his drink between his knees.

That goddamned photo.

Jennifer gave him the cursed thing the day he left to go on the overseas job. One of her sources in the anti-McKint internet world had come by it somehow. D'Angelo took it with him out of the country on the job, studied it each time he found a peaceful, secure minute in the two weeks of madness there. He looked at it again and again on the several long plane trips going over and coming home. And what did it tell him?

The thing was two decades old. It had been snapped in Colombia, without D'Angelo's or Gordon McKint's knowledge. Each time he studied it again, he found himself looking at his then twenty-seven-year-old self, standing behind McKint in his camo fatigues and armored vest, cradling his M16.

He couldn't stop studying his much-younger face. Looking for what? He wasn't sure. Isn't sure now. Maybe the kind of certainty he once felt about his role in everything McKint stood for.

Where did such assured devotion come from? And more importantly, where is it now? What exactly is he certain of anymore? Until these past few weeks, he would have bet that his smart, hotheaded, twenty-five-year-old daughter Jennifer would outlive him. *That* was something he could be certain of. He isn't putting money on that now.

He's always believed that the often-shady, sometimes-violent things he and Gordon McKint have done over the years in the name of drug interdiction, regime change, or counterinsurgency were needed to fight constantly evolving threats to the United States. Now, as the company shifts to domestic security contracts, the focus seems more and more on threats to the bottom line. How much pride is there in border security? Does he really want to devote his life to protecting America from the little old ladies who cook for Mrs. Chen?

Yet he owes Gordon McKint almost everything he has in this world. That much he knows for sure.

The day the photo was taken, he'd driven McKint to a small town in the mountains a few hours from Cartagena. As they approached the village, McKint told him the meeting was off book. "You mention this to no one." It wasn't the first time they were going dark. McKint was CIA. Who could tell if *anything* he did was sanctioned? That was half the pleasure in the job.

They met the Colombian colonel and the civilian in a hotel room in the village. No introductions were made. D'Angelo checked the room to make sure it wasn't a surprise-party kidnapping or assassination. When he declared the place secure, McKint sent him out into the hall to guard the door.

Some time later, just as McKint came back out of the room, a concussion grenade crashed in through a window. McKint wasn't seriously injured, but D'Angelo was deafened and dazed. Small-arms fire poured into the building. The Colombian colonel staggered into the hallway, screaming, "Get out of here!" obviously not wanting to explain to the regular Colombian army what he was doing there with the CIA officer. Gordon McKint hauled the barely conscious D'Angelo out the back of the building.

On the drive back to Cartagena, they got their stories straight: they'd been ambushed going to meet an unknown informant, someone they never did see. McKint didn't want *his* superiors knowing about the meeting any more than the Colombian officer did. D'Angelo understood that this incident was way the fuck off book.

D'Angelo drinks the last of his vodka and sets his glass on the nightstand.

Jennifer doesn't have much time, and he wants her to know the truth about what he decides to do—one way or the other. He owes her that.

One more look at the photo, and then he has to decide.

He pulls the nightstand drawer open, but his phone rings, and he turns and picks it up off the bed next to him. It's Rebecca. "The hospital just called, Cosmo."

"So soon?" he asks, his whole body feeling the weight of this.

"Fucking cancer," Rebecca says, chokes, and hangs up.

He sets the phone down, turns back to the drawer, and pulls it the rest of the way open.

*   *   *

It's been three days. Three days of sobbing family members, Jennifer's friends. Condolences from everyone at Sidewinder. Three days of planning and paperwork at the funeral home. Three days since Carla Merino stole the photo, and with it any chance of D'Angelo honoring his daughter's dying wish.

D'Angelo stops back in at the office on his way home from Jennifer's wake. He spent the day there with Rebecca and her family—he has none of his own left. Maybe if he plows through the work that has certainly piled up during the day, he can get his mind off Jennifer's death for a few minutes. But he can't concentrate on the job, his thoughts constantly gravitating back to Carla Merino, the photo she stole three days ago, the fact that he's still looking for her.

How would she even have known what the photo meant or that it was a threat? That's a nagging question. But now that he has her phone records and has seen the call to Lisa Yi at the *Times*, it looks like she's given the thing to them and has gone into hiding with their help. Was she working for the *Times* all along? He can't see any connection to them—other than that phone call. How would she even know he had the photo? And where is it now? Why haven't they splashed it? Gordon McKint has been all over the news for days, whipping his supporters into a frenzy over what he calls the "immigrant menace" threatening America. Trying out sound bites.

Seeing what incites the most hysterics. That photo will stop him in his tracks. It will put him—and D'Angelo—behind bars.

If the *Times* had the photo, they would never sit on it. Never.

If they don't have it, what the fuck has Carla done with it?

He pulls into the parking lot, still wondering about that.

He recognizes the one car in the lot besides the guard's. Andy Krall, the oldest guy in the Phoenix office, is at his desk when D'Angelo lets himself in. Andy has been with Sidewinder since the beginning. Before that he worked with Gordon McKint and D'Angelo in parts of the world D'Angelo never wants to see again. He's been a mentor at times. And one of the very few in the company D'Angelo trusts.

Andy stands and leans out the doorway of his office, his jowly face dark with sadness. "I'm sorry I couldn't make it to the wake today, Cosmo. We're all sorry about your loss. I can't even imagine."

D'Angelo can't remember Andy ever calling him Cosmo before.

"Thanks, Andy." Andy has adult children of his own, grand-children. D'Angelo steers the painful conversation to the subject of work. "You're at it late. What's up?"

"Nothing serious. A little trouble at the facility in Nogales. Something else shaking over by Sierra Vista." He shrugs. "It's all border, all the time now."

Andy is a language expert, fluent in several Central Asian and Caucasus dialects. He ran Sidewinder's group in Uzbekistan, where their subcontractors are building an irrigation project at the Sea of Aral. His real job was providing surreptitious support for some quiet CIA programs designed to keep the region America friendly. But Andy's been reassigned to the southwest border project now. Many of their best people have been. D'Angelo knows Andy isn't a lot hap-pier than he is about McKint's new emphasis on domestic contracts.

"Yeah, I saw Gordon on the news again today," D'Angelo says. As always, he avoids saying anything that could sound like criticism of McKint or Sidewinder policies. Andy is also adroit at staying neutral. While this is their home office and the building is empty except for the two of them, it's quite conceivable that the company is listening in on its own employees. If they've learned anything over the years, it's that people trained to spy, spy on each other. "Modern life, I guess," D'Angelo says, and walks to his office.

What a day. In a lifetime of direly unpleasant situations, Jennifer's wake felt like the worst punishment he's ever endured. Rebecca—still clinging to Catholic rituals D'Angelo has long jettisoned—insisted on the open-coffin visitation, a gruesome, medieval ritual he abhors. In spite of the embalmer's arcane arts, and contrary to what a well-meaning mourner assured him, Jennifer didn't look at all like she was sleeping.

He sits at the desktop and cleans up some administrative stuff.

This isn't going to take his mind off Jennifer's death. Or Kevin Dykstra's—which he has been quietly investigating outside the building. And it certainly isn't going to clear his head of Carla and the missing photo—also being pursued in secret.

He picks up Kevin's crystal and holds it up to the overhead lights. It doesn't refract the light the way a diamond or even glass might. It seems to absorb it. How did this kid go from the left-brained, analytical thinking of the Air Force Academy to a belief that this piece of rock contains life-enhancing healing properties forged in the fires of the earth's creation? Or something. D'Angelo tried to read about it, hoping Kevin's alleged mysticism would reveal something about why he died.

He asked a friend at the FBI—an old Special Forces brother—about Kevin Dykstra's death. On hearing the name, the guy slipped up and said something that made D'Angelo believe the feds had talked to the kid. Now why would the FBI be talking to a Sidewinder Security employee, secretly? D'Angelo couldn't get any more out of the agent, but he could fill enough blanks to see that Kevin Dykstra, computer maven extraordinaire, had stumbled onto something in his rambles through the labyrinths of Sidewinder's incoming data stream. Something that cost him his life.

Now, looking into the crystal, it occurs to him that Kevin and Jennifer were almost exactly the same age when they died. The cancer had come roaring back the same day he visited her for the last time. She was in a coma by the next morning. He never got to talk to her again about what he's finally decided to do with the photo. If he ever gets it back. He never got to talk to her again about anything.

Tomorrow is the funeral, and then he'll take some time off work. Gordon McKint himself called again to insist on it. And to say how sorry he was about Jennifer's death, of course. It almost made D'Angelo laugh. Almost.

"She posted some unpleasant things about you, Gordon."

"Story of my life. I never take it personally." McKint sighed. Even over the phone it sounded fake. "It was her job, and she worked hard at it. Like her father. We all have a job to do. Right now, yours is to take some time off."

Gordon made it sound like compassion. Maybe he's capable of that. It's hard to tell with him. But D'Angelo knows that this is partly because a man in his distracted state is going to make mistakes. And this is a business where mistakes can cost lives. Or is McKint just trying to get him out of the office again so he and Lundren can pull their next stunt? Are they gradually easing him out altogether?

"Gordon, I just got back. Literally," he said. "Four days ago."

"That was no vacation." McKint was insistent. "Go. Andy Krall will manage while you're away. He can call Phil if he needs help, but we're not launching anything new for a few months during the campaign. Things will be quiet. Take as much time as you like. A month at least."

In truth, he could use some time alone to think about all the things his daughter said to him in the last few months of her far-too-short life. And some time to track down Carla Merino and that photo. He doesn't have to be in the office to do that. With access to Sidewinder's codes, he can search for Carla on his own equipment. And there are plenty of independent contractors out there willing to do legwork on the ground, for a price. The trick is to find the photo without Phil Lundren or McKint knowing he's looking for it. Let alone that he once had it and lost it.

He'll tell them he's going to take a few weeks off and go for a long drive across the Great American Desert. Get his head straight about Jennifer's death. A "spirit quest" or "walkabout" or whatever the Kevin Dykstra types call such things. He doesn't know too much about spirits. As far as he can tell, this hard life on earth is all there is. Existentially speaking, if he can't cook it in a frying pan or shoot it with a gun, it doesn't exist.

Two things that *do* exist are Carla Merino and that fucking photo. But where?

PART II

HOMER, ALASKA

Two Months Later

CHAPTER

9

WHEN THE FEROCIOUS pounding explodes against the door of her camper, Carla shoots upright on her sleeping pad, pulse surging, hands thrown out in front of her as if blocking a blow. For a second she thinks D'Angelo has somehow tracked her all the way from Phoenix. But she has a feeling that if and when he comes for her, she won't hear anything. Until it's too late.

She slumps back on the sweat-damp sheet, nerves jangling. More likely it's just Volker. Jesus, he's been possessive lately. Making plans. Talking about marriage, for Christ's sake. The two of them running the Orca Grill together. Happily-ever-after shit. Not that the idea sounds so horrible. It's not. The bar's a moneymaker and Volker's not a bad guy, if a little clingy. And she's really beginning to like this town on the bay. But his plans involve paperwork. Public records. There are serious reasons why she can't do any of that.

Volker started in on it again last night. When she demurred once more, he brought up Billy Griest, one of the young regulars in the bar. It got ugly. She hadn't wanted Volker to find out about that little slip in judgment. She thought she'd been discreet. She'd certainly never meant to hurt him. But she has a birthday coming, and she let the flirtation with Billy go too far because she wanted to be reassured—she despises the archaic expression that sounds like something her mother would say—that she still has what it takes.

There's more banging on her camper door, accompanied now by girlish giggling that tells her it isn't Volker. It's Shire and her five-year-old twins, there to take Carla dipnetting for salmon.

"All right, all right," she groans. "I'm up."

She's wearing just her underwear and her watch—which says it's seven thirty AM, though the sun is already high enough to beam through the skylight overhead. The camper is stuffy and too warm. She kicks the top sheet off and remains on her back. The sweat on her skin cools quickly. She closes her eyes. Just a few more minutes of sleep. Please.

She's been living with George Volker for six weeks. But, last night, after the fight with him in the bar in front of all the regulars, she slept in the camper in the parking lot instead of going home. Volker can worry a bone like a Chihuahua, and she didn't want to spend the whole night rehashing the Billy Griest thing. He'll get over it.

She almost dozes off again when some kind of big SUV rolls in and parks alongside her truck, gravel crunching under the tires. A door slams. Men are talking—no, shouting—to each other in the parking lot. About fish. Of course.

She pulls the curtains back and squints at the uncommonly clear sunlight. First time after weeks of rain. Outside her window, a few feet away, a skinny young fisherman with rock-star hair and an orange trucker's cap leans into the rear of the SUV, extracting fishing rods. Her window is directly at his eye level. All he has to do is turn his head. He straightens, oblivious to her presence, slams the door shut, and walks off toward the marina, tackle in hand. He presses his key fob, and the vehicle lock clicks shut.

Well, shit.

Fish and fishing. Fishing and fish. It's all anyone in Alaska seems to think about. Nothing can distract these guys from the pursuit of scaly, cold-blooded sea creatures. Not even a half-naked cocktail waitress in a camper in the parking lot of a bar. Okay, a sweaty, middle-aged cocktail waitress. Still, there was a time she would've had every man on that coast climbing through her window. Now there are twin five-year-old girls and their mother pounding on her door.

The girls bash the sheet-metal door again. It sounds like they're using hammers. "Carla!" they scream. "Dipnetting!"

The whole town is fish crazy. The regulars at the bar make a living at it. The tourists fish for sport. The locals—even the children—apparently live to kill as many fish as they can, by any means possible. Well, she wanted to get as far from Phoenix as she could.

The banging continues.

"All right! I'm coming!"

She swings her feet to the floor. The carpet is gritty with gravel and sand, her clothes scattered across it. There are two Alaskan Amber cans and a box of chocolate-covered graham crackers on the floor, an empty sardine can on the little counter top. Last night's dinner. She stands and pulls the sheet off the pad and wraps it around her shoulders. "It's a good thing I love you girls!" she says through the door. She slides back the dead bolt.

The door flies open. Shire Kiminsky leans into the camper, white-blond hair glowing under the morning sun. "You have to get a phone, Carla." Shire's twin midlife surprises, the equally blond Irene and Alice, push into the doorframe at each hip. Shire's wearing a pale-blue tracksuit, white stripes down the arms and legs. The twins wear tiny knee-high rubber boots and flower-print dresses with bright-orange life jackets buckled over them.

"Hello, girls," Carla says. She sits back onto the sleeping platform. "Did your ship go down?"

The twin on Shire's right hefts a miniature baseball bat. She holds it out to Carla and points at the words burned into the wood: CAPTAIN SHIRE'S FISH WHACKER. The other one brandishes a long-bladed filleting knife, safely encased in a plastic sheath. "We're going dipnetting," she says, shyly. As an afterthought, she adds, "For salmon."

"That's right, Carla. And so are you," Shire says. "When was the last time you did something fun outdoors?"

Shire Kiminsky has to be the healthiest cocktail waitress in North America. All freckles and regularly flossed teeth, sun-pinked cheeks, and more energy than the big bang. She's forty-five and could pass for the twins' older sister. Alaska born and raised, she holds a charter captain's license but has leased out her halibut boat so she can spend summer days with her girls. Evenings she waits tables with Carla at the Orca. And tough? If somebody needs to be eighty-sixed from the bar, Volker has Shire do it. God knows she can be a lot scarier than he ever will.

Shire. Good to her kids, hardworking as a sailor, discreet with men. It's sickening. Carla loves her.

"Fun? Outdoors?" she moans. "What am I, a fucking chipmunk?"

The girls giggle. One of them tugs on her mother's jacket, stage-whispers, "Carla's swearing again, Mom."

"And she's almost bare-naked," the other girl adds. "Again."

Shire took Carla in when she first got to town. She lived with them for nearly a month before moving in with Volker. The twins know her all too well.

Now she gives the girls a mean look and hisses, "Squealers!"

They laugh.

Shire says, "Carla's going to wash her mouth out and put some clothes on now. Aren't you, Carla?"

"Yeah, yeah. They're around here someplace."

Shire picks Carla's jeans off the floor. "You know, they have these things called hangers now." She throws them at Carla. Carla shrugs off the sheet and climbs into the jeans.

With the door open, cool air from the small-boat harbor wafts in and makes her shiver. Beyond Shire and the girls, she can see more fishermen trooping across the parking lot. Cars and trucks towing skiffs rumble down the road to the boat launch. At the top of the ramp leading down to the marina, two young fish plant work-ers in blood-smudged rubber bibs lean against a dumpster, smoking under a cloud of hovering gulls. A big commercial fishing boat of some kind motors out of the harbor, rigging heavy with electronic equipment flashing in the uncommonly bright sunshine.

What a place. Not yet eight in the morning, and the sun's already high in the sky. It will dally there for another eighteen hours. After two months, the almost constant daylight is weirding Carla out, making her feel exposed all the time. At least it's rained most of the time since she got here. Today the unclouded brilliance of the sun feels like a searchlight trained on her.

Shire says, "What you need is a boat ride, and a nice stack of sockeye fillets to get you through next winter."

Next winter? The idea makes Carla squirm. Where will she be by then? Will she even be alive? Not if Cosmo D'Angelo finds her.

She gropes for something else to think about, trying not to turn her agitation on Shire and the kids. "Why are my two favorite little girls playing with knives and clubs? Whatever happened to Barbie dolls and sock monkeys?"

The twins dart from their mother and prance across the gravel, hacking at each other's life vests, squealing, "Sock monkeys!"

"And why do we have to go fishing, Shire? Your brother's a commercial fisherman. You can't need the fish."

"Because the girls love it, and so do I. And everybody needs to get out and kill their own food once in a while. You are aware that salmon don't actually live on Styrofoam trays at Safeway, right?"

"I guess."

"Hey!" Shire picks one of Carla's sneakers off the floor and throws it at her. "Look up there in the sky." She points with one thumb over her shoulder. "You see that ball of light? That's the sun."

"I'm from Arizona. Big deal. The sun." She pretends she has no opinion on its prominence today.

"In this part of the world, we don't see it like this all that often. But it's shining right now and the salmon are running. Around here, that makes people smile. Try it." Shire throws the other sneaker at her. "Smile."

Carla catches the shoe and pulls her lips back to show her canines.

Shire frowns. "We'll work on that later." She leans farther into the camper, picks up the sardine can, and curls her nose. "Jesus. It smells like a crab fisherman crawled in here and died."

Carla flashes on the anchovies she shared with D'Angelo at his house in Phoenix. She turns away and paws through the sheets for her shirt.

Shire is on a mother-rant. "You can't live like this. You've been in town two months and still haven't got a phone or PO box. And now you're breaking up with Volker? What are you going to do, live in this piece-of-crap camper?"

"I'll move back in with you!" Carla grins at her and waggles her eyebrows. "I can help raise the girls!"

Shire has to laugh. "Please. I put something to eat in front of them the other day, and Irene said, 'Fuck this shit!' I wonder where she learned that. And I'd rather they aren't sexually active until first grade, okay?"

"Trying to be helpful." Carla finds her T-shirt, pulls it on.

Shire sighs, her girl-next-door face going serious. "Come on, Carla, Billy Griest is more than fifteen years younger than you. I know. I've carded him. What were you thinking?"

"It was an accident!" Carla grabs her sneakers, pushes Shire out of the way. She sits on the steps of the camper to put them on, wincing at the bright sunlight. "Look at me. I'm almost forty. Four-zero. My boobs are racing my ass to my ankles. It's nice to know that I still have what men want. Okay?"

Shire scoffs. "Get in line, sister. Try having twins at your age."

"Don't you want to feel . . . you know . . . wanted?" Carla says. "I mean, desired?"

"Wanted? In *this* town?" Shire snorts. "You work in a bar full of mostly divorced guys who spend weeks at sea. All a woman has to do to feel 'wanted' here is fall on her back." She pauses to check on her girls. They're trying to creep up on a flock of crows that hop into the air and fly as the pair approaches. Shire turns back to Carla and lowers her voice. "You know, this may come as a surprise to you, but there are other ways besides sex to get the attention of men."

"Oh, listen to Miss Good Judgment, who got knocked up with twins at forty. Something tells me there was a penis involved in that life-changing event." Carla ties her sneakers and stands, locks the camper door. The morning sunlight licks every bumper and windshield in the parking lot. Standing out there in the open now, she's twitchy again. "All right. Let's go netting. But I have to run by Volker's first. He's gone to Anchorage on a Costco run, won't be back until happy hour."

Shire looks at her watch. "Make it fast. We can't get into the cove on the low tide."

Carla nods and fishes her keys out of her jeans. She inhales deeply, trying to offset the jumpiness the cloudless morning is causing. Along with the natural ocean scent of brine and fish, the breeze off the harbor reeks of diesel and dumpsters. Disquieting around-the-clock daylight aside, the very strangeness of this place is also reassuring. Two mature bald eagles sit atop a tall construction crane, scanning the beach for an easy meal. She's so far from Phoenix now. It's another world here. *A safer one*, she tells herself. She wishes she believed it.

She slides into the driver's seat, rolls down the window.

Shire leans in. "Why don't you want to smooth this over with Volker? What's so wrong with him suddenly? I mean, yeah, he's a bit of a dork sometimes. But he's not mean. I'll take dorky over mean any day."

"He seemed very cool. You know? When I first met him. Now he's getting all domestic. I can't do that again. I just can't."

Shire keeps her eyes on her daughters. "Seeming cool to new waitresses is more or less George Volker's life's work." She pats Carla on the shoulder. "Only this time, I think the goof is really gone for you."

"He cooked me poached eggs. For *breakfast*."

Shire nods, blond ponytail radiant in the sunlight. "That's when most people eat poached eggs, hon."

"He's talking about getting married, making me partner in the bar."

"What the hell is wrong with that? The Orca is a freaking gold mine."

"I guess." Carla wishes she could tell Shire why her name can never appear on a marriage license. Or why it already feels she's been in one place too long. "It pisses me off, having him making plans for me like that," she says instead.

"You're out of your mind. But I guess it's your life." Shire straightens and calls out to the twins. "You girls don't go down that ramp until I get there!"

"I don't know how you do it, Shire," Carla says. "I really don't." She's come to love the twins, but she thanks God once again that the only child she ever attempted to raise was the one she married. She starts the truck. "I'll go to Volker's house, get my things, meet you down at the boat."

"Okay. I'll gas up. Be at the dock in an hour. I've got sandwiches, bug dope, and a pair of hip boots you can borrow. We'll go kill some fish. It always cheers me up."

Alaskans. Fish crazy. Every single one of them. She starts to back the truck away from the Orca, shaking her head. Shire waves for her to stop and walks back to Carla's truck.

Carla leans out the window. "Now what?"

"Listen, you're going to need a place to stay until you get back with George. Why don't you use my family's cabin on Loon Island for a while? Just until you find your own place, or come to your senses and apologize to him. I don't want you living in this thing like a hobo. When we're done netting, I'll show you the cabin, give you a key. And the key to the skiff. I won't need it for a while."

"The skiff?" Carla is a little surprised. "You think I'm ready for that?"

Shire has been training her to handle the small boat for weeks. When the commercial salmon season opens, they're going to crew on her brother Elrond's seiner. Carla has surprised both Shire and herself with her natural ability at seamanship—even in fairly rough water.

"The weather is good, and it's a short hop across the bay to Loon. And you're a born sailor, girl," Shire says. "You should join the fleet."

"Couldn't I just date them?"

Shire laughs. "Just promise to apologize to George tonight, okay? Even if you don't go back with him, maybe he'll let you keep the job at the Orca. The tips are the best in town."

"Thanks, Shire." Shire's been good to her. Everyone here has. Even George Volker. The reality shows make it seem like Alaska is a haven for every nutjob and socially incompetent troll on the continent. A catch basin for the detritus of society. And maybe it is. But there are human beings here too. Good ones. It could be a great place to live. A safe place. Hopefully.

She puts the truck in gear and turns out of the Orca parking lot onto the spit road. It's a three-mile drive to town from the bar and marina, but there's very little traffic heading toward the land mass. Coming the other direction, however, a steady line of cars and pick-ups and RVs—the early-morning fishing crowd—streams out onto the spit toward the small-boat harbor.

She flips the visor down to block the sun and feels marginally less exposed. She tries to convince herself yet again that this place, so far from anywhere, is in fact safe.

On the right-hand side of the spit road, the interior of the bay is dead flat. A woman in a yellow top throws a Frisbee into the water for a frantic black dog. On the seaward side, soft rollers curl onto the sandy beach. Small shorebirds and much larger gulls patrol the surf line, picking out morsels. They give a wide berth to an enormous bald eagle, worrying some kind of fish carcass.

A cluster of small businesses sit on a wooden plank platform up on posts. White-sneakered tourists crowd into the doorways of halibut charter offices and coffee shops. There's a Native Alaskan art gallery with exquisite whalebone and walrus tusk carvings. Her mother, an artist of some repute in Phoenix, would love the craftsmanship in those.

My mother. Christ. It's a lovely day. Let's think about something pleasant.

She passes a family wearing matching black Orca Grill hoodies posing for a photo in front of a bronze sculpture. The statue depicts a bearded mariner, monument to the men who've drowned fishing Alaskan waters. Behind them the bay glitters like a bowl of blue sequins. Across the bay, the Kenai Mountains tower over the heavily forested shore.

Carla does the reassuring math. She drove nearly four thousand miles to get to the town of Homer. The spit juts another four miles into the bay. Loon Island is farther yet.

It's about as distant from Phoenix, Arizona, as you can get. But is it far enough?

She glances overhead at the small slit in the headliner. She's had the photo for two months and still hasn't figured out how to do anything with it that won't get her killed. And now she's going fishing with five-year-old girls.

Well, she has to keep up the appearance of normalcy if she's going to survive. And around here, murdering fish is what passes for normal. She turns the radio on and drives to Volker's house.

10

Scott Crockett ties off the bow line of the *"C" Lady* to the fuel dock cleat and steals a furtive glance at the office window, praying that his almost-ex-wife Trina isn't peering out from her desk in accounts receivable. If there were any other place on Kachemak Bay he could fill the boat's tank—any other place at all—he'd happily pay an extra five bucks a gallon to avoid her. Ten. Thankfully, she doesn't seem to be around.

He turns to the sound of footsteps on the dock behind him.

"Trina's gone to lunch," Kyle, the chubby teenage dockhand, says warily. The kid has certainly been privy to whatever version of Scott's divorce opera Trina has shared with the staff. Never mind all the screaming matches she and Scott have indulged in right here in the marina over the past few months as the marriage fermented into the bitter paste it has become. The poor kid may be thinking Scott has come looking for another smackdown.

Scott holds his hands up. "Take it easy. I just need fuel."

Kyle reaches for the diesel hose, obviously relieved. "Going dipnetting? Everybody's going dipnetting. I never seen nothing like it where I come from. Women, children, old grannies. Where's your net?" Kyle glances around the boat.

"I thought I'd try catching them on a rod and reel."

Kyle looks at the rod lying on the canvas hatch cover over the aft hold, the bright tinseled streamer knotted onto the end of the line. "That a fly pole?"

Scott kneels on the deck and unscrews the brass cover on the fuel tank.

"Flies? In the middle of the ocean?" Kyle looks at him like he's just suggested hunting moose with a sharpened stick. "Shit."

Scott feels his face warming, everything about fly-fishing suddenly seeming affected. What kind of a poser has he become? He's a working guy, a journeyman carpenter, an independent contractor. He straps on a tool belt and hammers nails every day of his life. Fly-fishing? He knows a sheetrocker who took up fly-fishing, and now the guy is teaching creative writing classes at the community college up in Eagle River.

He should be fishing like a man: trolling for king salmon, or dragging herring chunks across the bottom a hundred feet down for halibut. He shouldn't be fishing at all. He should be back on shore meeting women.

Kyle hands him the hose. He inserts the nozzle in the opening in the deck, starts the diesel flowing. Turning the conversation away from his suddenly ridiculous-sounding plans, he says, "How about you? Got your fish put away already?"

"Nah, I only been here less than a year. Not a resident yet. If I could dipnet, I sure would. How many salmon you allowed?"

"Twenty-five fish for the head of household and ten more for each additional member of the family."

"Like a wife?" Kyle asks, a sudden slyness in his voice. "You get ten for that?"

"Yes, Kyle. I believe the Alaska Department of Fish and Game recognizes a wife as a member of a family."

Kyle goes silent, apparently thinking about that. A moment passes. Scott closes his eyes and inhales the dizzying diesel fumes rising from the tank belowdeck. He feels the sun on his face and thinks about the next four days, in the boat, alone. No Trina. No lawyers. Peace. Quiet. Fish. The boat is big, the cabin comfortable. The galley is stocked, the fuel tanks filling now. He would stay out there the rest of his life if he could. It's one way to avoid trying to start over again.

Kyle is asking him something. "Makes you kind of wish you stayed married to Trina, don't it?" He glances at the office window like he isn't sure whether Trina is there or not either. Like she might come flying out of it at them, claws out, teeth bared. "I mean, ten extra fish is a lot."

Scott looks at him. "You work with her every day, Kyle. Would *you* marry Trina for ten extra salmon a year?"

Kyle thinks about it a second. "Kings?"

Scott shakes his head ruefully. "Sockeye." He stops pumping and pulls the nozzle out and hands it over the rail to Kyle.

"Oh." Kyle hangs the gas nozzle in its cradle, notes the number of gallons, the total price. He pulls his hat off and peers inside as if the answer to the Trina question is stitched into it. He tugs it back on his head and takes Scott's credit card into the office.

Nearby, two large gray-and-white gulls sit on the rail of a Boston Whaler. For no apparent reason, one of the birds turns to the other, opens its fierce yellow beak, and screams into its partner's ear. *Gulls must mate for life.*

Kyle comes back out onto the dock. "Ten sockeye, huh?" He hands Scott the credit card and clipboard, but he still hasn't answered the Trina question.

"That's what I thought," Scott says. He signs for the fuel and pushes off.

The *"C" Lady* is fifty feet away from the dock, motoring toward the cut in the rock jetty enclosing the boat harbor, when Kyle yells over the clamoring gulls, "I'd marry her for ten extra lingcod! Maybe."

Scott just nods and steers for the opening in the break wall.

"They'd have to be big ones, though!" Kyle yells.

Scott smiles. They'd have to be fucking monsters.

*   *   *

As he approaches the jetty, he's cut off by a massive steel vessel chugging toward the opening, rails gleaming in the sunlight. The name *MADMEN* shouts from the dark-blue transom in white letters. It's a hundred-footer, a long-liner, one of the biggest in the harbor. The sight of it dredges up a wave of memories. Years ago, in those dead winter months short on construction jobs, he crewed on commercial boats like this one. And crabbers. And pot fishers. Anything big enough, wide enough, heavy enough to ply Alaska's most dangerous, storm-torn winter waters. The Bering Sea, the Gulf of Alaska, the open North Pacific. From the November red king crab seasons to the March halibut openers, Scott froze his ass and risked his life alongside so many other young lunatics looking for adventure and unmatchable crew-share paychecks.

He hasn't been out to sea for years now, except for sport fishing, of course, something that suddenly, in the shadow of the passing *Madmen*, feels more pathetic than ever. On the huge boat's aft deck, he can see two young crewmen laughing, spirits soaring in the warm midmorning air as they head out for the sablefish or cod season openers.

Trina made him promise to quit commercial fishing after the *Polar Huntress* went down in the Shelikof Strait one February night. Heavy crab pots stacked too high on the deck. Everything coated with frozen sea spray. Forty-knot winds and twenty-foot seas conspiring to roll the ship over in the troughs. Three men gone forever, and Scott a hero who had never wanted to be one, and never would be again. He shakes off the thoughts. He doesn't need to relive that icy nightmare on a day like this.

The *"C" Lady* drifts forward. Scott shifts the two Volvo inboard engines into reverse for a second, then back into neutral again to let the big commercial vessel pass. Behind him there's a line of sport boats and charter six-packs waiting for the *Madmen* to exit the harbor.

He watches the ship glide out of the cut, gulls panic-flapping off their nests among the shit-splattered jetty rocks. It disappears behind the break wall, only the tall radio antennae and the hydraulic line puller visible now above the boulders, beckoning. *Come with us*, it says. *Be a real fisherman again. Be a man. There are worse things than death. Things like boredom.*

Finally exiting the cut himself, Scott keeps his speed low in the wake of the *Madmen*, the long-liner slowly building power. Scott is happy, waiting for the big vessel to round the point at the end of the spit. He's still admiring the bulky, serious-looking form of the ship, still vaguely entertaining the idea of commercial fishing again—now that he's a single man once more.

Not everyone in the line of smaller boats behind him is as patient. A big Lund aluminum skiff roars by, just thirty feet off his starboard beam, a dipnet handle jutting over its transom. The skiff cuts between Scott and the beach, its big Yamaha outboard open-throttle despite the LOW WAKE signs on the dock posts. Shore anglers jump back from the heavy wake, fists waving, middle fingers brandished. Inside the cabin of the *"C" Lady*, Scott can't hear their shouting, or the laughter that he sees on the faces of the two women and two children in the skiff. Standing at the wheel of the center console is Shire Kiminsky.

She has her twins in the boat with her now. Every time Scott sees them around town, he can't help thinking about Shire's parents, 1970s homesteaders, come to Homer to grow their own organic everything. They're still a quirky blend of *Mother Earth News* and Tolkien. She has a brother Elrond, a sister Gal. Over the years Scott's known them, there has been a progression of horses, goats, dogs, and cats named Gandalf and Frodo and Bilbo and such. Someday young Alice and Irene will realize they got off easy.

Shire grins at him and waves as she gooses the throttle again, the bow of the skiff dancing up out of the water. The little girls hug each other and buckle over with laughter. Scott was frankly surprised when Shire had the twins, at her age—like everyone else in town, he still doesn't know who the father is—but she seems to enjoy them immensely. She's raised them to be real Alaskan kids. They were practically born in that boat.

That makes him sigh. He should have married Shire, or someone like her—someone wild and fun loving, someone who it might've been fun to raise kids with. Unlike Trina, who surely would've made it an even worse slog than their marriage already was. Scott has already added Shire to the expanding list of local women who've begun to appeal to him in a testicle-tingling way lately. But—even if she'd have him—does he want to take on kids at his age now? He honks the boat horn and shakes his head at her, laughing now himself.

In the forward seat of Shire's skiff, another waitress from the Orca sits face-into the bow spray, hanging onto the painter, leaning back, boots jammed against the deck to keep herself in her seat. Her brown hair lashes out behind her from under a blue bandanna like a bundle of horsewhips. He's studied her over the rim of a beer glass more than once. She has a long straight nose and murky gold-green eyes exuding a wise-to-men toughness that positively harpoons him. He figures she's about five years younger than he is—just another divorced middle-aged woman working in a fishermen's dive bar—but way too good-looking, as unreachable as the stars and planets to an ordinary guy like him.

Scott can't think of her name. Now *that* is exactly why women like her will always be banging guys like Volker. Guys who own bars and wear ponytails and earrings. Guys who never forget the name of a good-looking woman. Ever.

Scott has a crazy desire to warn the waitress that, despite his dorkiness and his age—the guy has to be pushing sixty—George Volker doesn't stay with one woman very long. And then he reminds himself he isn't in charge of the waitress's love life. He isn't in charge of her anything. Or any other woman's anything now, for that matter. He really *does* have to stop trying to save them. Trina came with the word *trouble* scrawled across her forehead like the price on the windshield of a used car. He neither kicked the tires nor looked under the hood before signing, because that was back when he still believed he could make anything work.

He watches the skiff overtake the lumbering *Madmen*. When she's just ahead of the huge steel prow, Shire swerves hard to port, cuts right across the front of the bow, and heads out onto the bay. Shire was right. He really should've married her.

Women. What is he supposed to do now? Spend the rest of his life trying to look cool? Like Volker? Grow his hair long and start hanging around bluegrass concerts, chatting up anything with tits and a peasant blouse? It's a horrifying thought.

With the *Madmen* finally clearing the end of the spit and most of the other boats in line now gunning up on step and racing around him, Scott checks the console. The engine temps are good, rpms where they should be. He pushes both throttles forward and feels the satisfying power building, vibrating through his hands, his feet. If the marine weather forecast were better, he'd run out around the distant tip of the peninsula to the open water of the Gulf of Alaska and spend the night anchored up in one of the remote coves on the other side. It's a five-hour trip through some potentially rough water to the outer islands where he likes to fish for lingcod and rockfish. The forecast is just not clear enough to attempt that yet. Instead he sets the autopilot for Goat Cove directly across the bay from the spit. He'll spend the morning there with the army of dipnetters from town. If he's lucky, he can put a couple sockeye in the boat.

If he's *very* lucky and the weather clears, he'll take off for Chugach Pass and a few days in the remote unpopulated Gulf.

*   *   *

Scott anchors the *"C" Lady* in eighty feet of water on the east side of Goat Cove. When the stern swings outward toward the bay on the receding tide and the anchor feels set, he shuts down the engines. He pulls on his hip boots and puts his rod in the Zodiac inflatable, lowers it off the stern. Hooking the swim ladder over the transom, he climbs down into the Zodiac and yanks the little outboard to life.

The tide is almost at the low water mark, lots of mud flats on both sides of the creek channel flowing out into the cove. But the inflatable skiff can negotiate very skinny water. He wends his way up the channel until he comes to the line of skiffs and inflatables pulled ashore to wait out the tide change. He cuts back on the outboard just downstream from the waterfall that blocks the returning salmon from going any further upstream. In the wide pool at the base of the falls, a dozen locals lean into their dipnets, hauling the trapped sockeye out onto the mudbanks.

He noses the Zodiac to shore on the bank opposite Shire Kiminsky's big Lund. Scott's boat is the only one on that shore. It's shallow and not a good spot for dipnetting—the fish are in the channel hugging the other bank where all the locals are—but he's not going to use a net. He takes the fly rod and climbs out.

Shire and her twins and about nineteen other dipnetters are lined up shoulder to shoulder along the bank of the creek channel. Shire is netting, and the waitress—he still can't recall her name—is picking the salmon out of the webbing and tossing them to the twins. One girl clubs them unconscious with her wooden bat; the other slits their gills and bleeds them. Together, slathered with mud, the girls stack them in an enormous plastic ice chest like a couple of tiny blond deckhands. They are having such a good time. An Alaskan day at the beach.

He walks upstream along the muddy bank and finds a place closer to the falls where he can make a long cast across the channel into the milling salmon. He's careful not to throw too far and hook one of the three-foot-wide nets. He's feeling incongruous enough among the others with their food-gathering efficiency, his hobby seeming more ridiculous than ever. No one pays any attention to him, least of all the waitress.

Here at the head of the cove, surrounded by heavily forested mountain flanks, there is no breeze at all, no sign of the bad weather predicted for the outer reaches of the bay. It's a beautiful day full of sunlight and fish and laughter. A day of luck for almost everyone, it seems. He even manages to land a couple fish on the fly rod. And still, for some reason, he doesn't feel lucky. Maybe seeing the waitress across the channel, just out of reach, reminds him that this is as close as he is ever going to get to a woman that exciting at this late point in his life.

The waitress takes a turn leaning into the river with Shire's long-handled net, the little twins cheering her on. Scott keeps casting and retrieving, pretending he's not watching her. Her expression is intent, her hair pulled back in the blue bandanna, the sun flashing on her earrings. She's right there, a dozen yards away. And what does he do? He casts, over and over and over again, as though he really is more interested in the fishing than in her. When he hooks a salmon that breaks the surface in front of her, she looks up and smiles quizzically at him across the water. He stupidly fails to smile back at her or say any of the many clever things he's fantasized saying to strange women for the last few years of his married life. He just plays the hooked fish to his feet and lands it. When he looks up again, the waitress is busy struggling to lift the awkward net and a fish of her own.

*   *   *

It's evening now, and it's been such a beautiful day. Sunshine, blue skies, and sockeye salmon. But the forecast is iffy for the waters east of the Barren Islands. So Scott has been anchored all afternoon. Long after he saw Shire, her twins, and the great-looking waitress set out for home on the rising tide, he dallied, hoping the weather report would improve. He hauled the Zodiac back on board and stowed it. He worked on a wiring problem in his GPS unit. He went down into the engine room and checked the fuel filters. The weather was so nice most of the afternoon that—in spite of the building clouds in the southwestern sky—he has been lulled into thinking it will hold. It's six PM when he pulls anchor and decides to attempt a run around Point Pogibshi to the other side of the peninsula. The wind is already starting to pick up.

Kachemak Bay has three-foot seas, but the *"C" Lady*—which is forty-five feet long and wide beamed—handles those well. He makes good time, until he's two miles short of the point. There he hits the storm as it comes howling out of the Gulf of Alaska. Facing mounting waves that are going to be a lot worse around the corner, he turns back. He considers his autopilot. He could set a course directly for the spit and the boat harbor, cutting straight across the open bay—it will shave off a couple miles—but with the wind suddenly shifting even farther to the west, the waves have a lot of fetch and will batter his port beam. He'll be wallowing in the troughs all the way. It'll be safer to hug the near shore, tuck in behind the islands, and hole up for the night. Still, it's a rough trip, even for the *"C" Lady*. A smaller boat wouldn't have a chance.

11

D'ANGELO HAS KNOWN for weeks—her license plates popped on the Customs and Border Protection grid—that Carla entered Alaska at the Alcan–Beaver Creek Border Crossing from Canada. He assumes she'll be working for cash, probably waitressing. People usually go to what's familiar, and that's what her records show she's been doing for ten years. But Alaska is a huge place with a high rate of alcohol consumption and a lot of places to eat and drink, spread out over an area almost the size of the Lower 48 states. There are dozens of towns and villages hundreds of miles remote from the road system, accessible only by boat or plane. She could be anyplace from Ketchikan to Nome to Dutch Harbor. He couldn't very well go from town to town knocking on doors looking for her. He caught a lucky break: a FedEx delivery to Carla Merino's mother Sara, a prominent artist in Scottsdale. Shipped from Homer, Alaska.

D'Angelo arrives at the Ted Stevens International Airport in Anchorage at six PM, spirits soaring until he finds that the last flight of the day to Homer has been canceled. The plane is stuck in Kodiak. Some kind of storm.

Weary from the five-hour flight from Phoenix, he collects his baggage. Off to one side of the busy baggage claim area, he unlocks the handgun case and makes certain his pistol is still there. It's a Colt Combat M1911 worth nearly two thousand dollars. Might an underpaid baggage handler with a yen for fine firearms find it irresistible? It's possible.

The pistol is still there. So is the stun weapon he's brought for quieter situations. It would be nice if he didn't have to use either one, but he's determined to get that photo from Carla Merino. Whatever it takes. Wading through a sea of tourists, he makes his way to the car rental desks.

A Camry is the biggest sedan they have left. It's billed as "ergonomically advanced" but isn't really designed for drivers six feet four inches tall. By the time he turns south onto the Seward Highway and leaves Anchorage, his legs and back are already cramping up. He has 215 miles to go. Still, it feels good to be actively in pursuit now, after all these weeks.

It's not nearly as easy to track someone down as Hollywood and thriller authors make it look. Especially when you're trying to keep the search a secret from almost everyone in your office. It's been a frustrating two months. And Jennifer's death has derailed him, shattering his focus, but at the same time, it gives him more purpose than ever. He never got to tell her what he'd decided to do with the photo. And then he lost the thing. Unforgivable.

And unprofessional. A civilian could make excuses for himself about being distracted by the death of his daughter. But even without the uniform, Cosmo D'Angelo is a soldier, always will be. He has a duty to find the photo.

Thank God Gordon McKint insisted he take a few weeks off. He was able to do most of the searching online at home, away from prying eyes at the office. And thank God for Andy Krall, the one person in the company he can trust. Andy doesn't know anything about the photo. He thinks D'Angelo is tracking Carla for personal reasons—which he is, in a manner of speaking. He cooked for her, and she stole from him. There's no way not to take that personally. Luckily, Andy despises Phil Lundren as much as D'Angelo does, and he's not happy about the death of Kevin Dykstra either. Andy has kept D'Angelo connected to Sidewinder Security's giant search engines through a ghost link that nobody is going to see unless they know to look for it. And he's making sure D'Angelo's search results never get kicked up the pipeline to Lundren. Luckily, Lundren has been busy in Washington trying to control the media fires raging around each new accusation leveled at Sidewinder. Now, with just a little more luck, he can find Carla and get that photo back without Lundren or McKint knowing he once had it and lost it.

It will take nearly five hours to drive to Homer. He's hoping there are some decent restaurants along the way.

12

I$^{\text{T'S A FEW}}$ minutes before eleven o'clock and an unusually slow night at the Orca Grill. This afternoon the cruise ship departed for Anchorage and then the weather got snotty, driving the remaining tourists into their hotels or Winnebagos earlier than usual. Now only the usual cluster of regulars hover at the bar: four almost identical "marina rats" with stubbly gray-white beards, seaworn eyes behind wire-rimmed trifocals, oil-stained fingers. All of them tilting on their barstools like the staples pinning their asses there have pulled out.

They've been busting Volker's balls all night about Carla's indiscretion with Billy Griest—there are no secrets in a town this small—and they're still at it. Jimmy Thompson, the loudest mouth in the North Pacific, passes his hat down the bar. "Old George here obviously can't give that girl what she wants. Everybody, chip in, and we'll buy him some of those blue pills. What do they call them? Starts with a *V*, I think. Three syllables. *Vagina?*" And his sea lion laugh. "Harnk, harnk, harnk!"

That isn't why Carla slept with Billy, and Volker knows it. But he refuses to debate the matter with these guys. Maybe he's getting wiser with age. He grins at them and opens a new bottle of Jameson's. "Sure, Thompson, pick up a Costco-size bottle of those for me, would you? I'll hire a couple new waitresses." He turns away and sets the whiskey bottle on the glass shelf behind the bar.

In the mirror, he sees Carla walk in the door, backlit by the moody gray evening light.

After a rare day of brilliant sunshine, the weather turned vicious about an hour ago, the wind clocking around from the west and gusting to gale strength. The forecast was off by twenty knots and ninety degrees. Just another unpredictable-weather day on the coast of Alaska. Now the sun is low in the northwest and blotted out by the storm clouds piling into the bay. Behind Carla, Volker sees two tourists stagger past, pinning their hats to their heads as they lean into the wind.

Carla shuts the door and pauses to fix the blue bandanna she's wearing around her wind-tossed hair. One of the regulars spots her in the mirror and says, "Uh-oh."

The others turn on their stools.

Carla comes around the end of the bar. She glances at them. "Hi, boys."

They nod, sip their beers, look elsewhere. Even Jimmy Thompson knows enough to say nothing.

Carla looks at Volker. "Can we talk?"

"Sure." Volker points to the kitchen. Carla pushes through the swinging half doors. He follows.

She has a small travel bag over one shoulder. She's going somewhere. The thought stabs him, but he isn't going to ask where and have her tell him it's none of his business. Nor is he going to be the first one to bring up Billy Griest and have that whole subject discussed in front of the guys at the bar. He's learned a thing or two about fighting with a woman. Start with something she can't deny. "You moved your stuff out."

"Yeah, I need some space. You know . . . for a while."

Volker feels a thickening sensation in his chest. What the hell? He's broken up with too many women to even remember. It usually doesn't feel like this. Maybe it's because this time he's not the one who fucked up? That's a first.

In spite of his intention to avoid the Billy Griest issue, he can't seem to help himself. "You need space?" he says. "Or a space-*man*?"

"Meaning?"

"Meaning Billy Griest isn't exactly the sharpest hook in the tackle box!" That comes out way too loud. He thinks he hears the regulars tittering out front.

Carla sighs and sits back against the kitchen counter, arms crossed. The blue bandanna low on her forehead makes her look like a gypsy or something.

"Look, I'm sorry, George. Really, I am. That's what I came to say. I shouldn't have done that. I'm sorry I hurt you. It was a dumb mistake."

"And now you think you can just waltz back into my life?" The stupidity of that hits him as soon as it's out of his mouth. It sounds like dialogue from a sitcom. She's already moved her clothes out of his house. Does she look like she's trying to "waltz back into his life"?

Carla stands straighter and smiles sadly. She puts one hand on his arm. "Let's give it a couple days, okay? Take a little break. I'm going to stay in the Kiminskys' cabin on Loon Island."

"Tonight?" he asks. "It might get rough out there."

"We came across after dipnetting and it wasn't bad. Shire let me run the skiff. We checked the forecast after dinner. Shire said the wind is out of the south, and the mountains are mostly blocking it on the water between here and the island."

"What time was that?" Volker says. "You know how fast it can change?"

Carla scoffs. "George, it's late. I'm tired. I just wanted to say how sorry I am." She turns and walks out of the kitchen with him following again.

The regulars all fidget, refuse to make eye contact. Like he doesn't know they've been listening to every word. Jimmy Thompson hunches over his beer and whistles some familiar tune Volker can't place.

"One favor?" Carla says. "Can you give me some vodka to take over? Shire says they don't leave booze in the cabin when they're not there. Too many break-ins. I forgot to stop at the liquor store."

"Sure," he says, not certain why. He's spent the whole day imagining the guilt he would heap on her the next time he saw her. The vituperation. Now he's not even sure how they're leaving things. Is he still the injured party? Of course. But this sure doesn't feel as satisfying as he thought it was going to.

He pulls a bottle of Stoli out of the cupboard under the bar. Holds it up to her. A peace offering? Why is *he* making peace? He usually has the upper hand in these things. He fiddles with the band on his ponytail as he watches her stuff the bottle in her bag.

"Thanks, George." Carla shoulders the bag. She pulls a bag of tortilla chips off the display rack and waves them at him. "This okay?"

Volker nods. He isn't going to try to put his foot down about a bag of corn chips.

Carla leans in and gives him a peck on the cheek. "Thanks again."

George realizes he's fussing with his ponytail again and drops his hand to his side as he watches her heading for the door. The guys at the bar turn that way too. When the door closes behind her, Jimmy Thompson says, "Wow, George, I guess you told her!"

Volker ignores their laughter. The whole thing has left him exhausted.

"Drink up, boys," he says. "I'm closing early."

13

CARLA WALKS OUT of the Orca into the damp night air and circles around to the back of the building on her way to the docks. Contrary to what she just told Volker about the wind not being too bad, it's blowing straight into her face. But once she's behind the building, it drops off. It doesn't feel too strong. She can do this. She doesn't want to spend another night in the camper in the parking lot. It reminds her too much of the long drive and the many roadside nights on the way to Alaska. Maybe she should've just smoothed things over with Volker? Maybe. But she likes the sound of being away on an island.

With her bag over her shoulder, she heads for the ramp to the docks. She gets as far as her truck, parked near the back door of the bar, and stops. The photo is still hidden up in the headliner of the cab.

Shire was right about the fresh air and sunshine. Carla hasn't thought about the photo all day—not while dipnetting or even during dinner at Shire's house. Hardly thought about D'Angelo all day either.

She walks over to the truck. Should she leave the picture in it? It's parked under the huge parking lot lights, looking as old and road beaten as it is, with crow shit splatters on the windshield and rust ulcers on the fenders. There are two security cameras on the eaves of the Orca. Two more on the other corner of the building.

Volker seems convinced that there are all kinds of thieves out there dying to rob the few hundred dollars that ever accumulate in the register in this age of credit cards. Nobody is going to risk his security system to steal her eighteen-year-old beater.

Still, on Loon Island she'll be farther away from the damned photo than she's been at any time since taking it. As much as it has upended her life—not to mention its continuing potential for getting her killed—there's something disquieting about being that distant from it. What's up with that?

She stands at the door of the truck a moment longer, fingering the keys in her pocket.

Fuck it. Maybe she can forget about it for a couple days.

She strides down the big aluminum ramp to the docks.

All she has with her is her travel bag, the bottle of Stoli, and some lime-flavored tortilla chips. She's left men before with less than that.

* * *

Though it's almost midnight when she steers the skiff out of the cut from the marina, the bay is lit by the sickly yellow glow from the ever-present solstice sunlight, now seeping under the clouds from behind the snow-topped volcanoes to the northwest. The water is wind-riffled but not too choppy, and Carla feels a surge of confidence about crossing to the island.

There are no other boats in sight. That's unusual, even for this late hour. People come and go across the bay all day and most of the night, it seems. But not tonight. When she throttles up and powers past the End of the Road Hotel & Resort and rounds the tip of the spit, she finds out why.

The wind has shifted and is coming out of the west, not from the south as forecast. The mountains aren't blocking it, and the water that was so calm earlier this afternoon is now churning. She throttles up the engine and the skiff lifts up on step, the hull planing across the wave tips without plowing. She can do this. She grips the wheel hard, crouches slightly to absorb the shock of each wave, and jams her knees against the steering console. She's going to Loon Island.

Halfway there, she hits serious trouble where the water emptying into the Gulf of Alaska collides with incoming wind-driven whitecaps. The skiff plows into a maelstrom that pummels the aluminum hull and nearly knocks her off her feet. She yanks the wheel hard starboard to tack into and through the wind the way Shire has shown her, but she can't get the skiff back up on step. It's wallowing and nosing through the waves instead of over them. A wall of frigid, glacier-fed seawater sloshes over the bow, filling the boat to the tops of her sneakers.

She glances back over her shoulder. The lights on the hotel at the end of the spit look just as far behind her now as the island is ahead. Like Shire said, Carla's surprisingly good with the skiff for a woman who's spent her whole life in the desert. But the boat is bogging down as the icy water fills it.

Still a mile from Loon Island, a huge wave slams the skiff and jostles it sideways in a trough, and a second, even bigger wave hammers the stern so hard it pops the cowling open on the outboard. When another wave smashes over the transom again, the motor coughs and shudders to a stop. She cranks the starter. Nothing. Powerless now, the skiff begins to founder. All around her, sea-green waves rise and fall like pistons.

The radio crackles with static and unintelligible chatter that sounds like Shire's voice, then goes dead.

14

B Y THE TIME Volker ejects all the regulars from the bar and closes down the kitchen, it's almost midnight. He's pulling the chain link security fence down over the whiskey shelves when his phone rings. "Orca," he says. "We're closed. Unless you're female, young, and lonely."

"George, wait!" It's Shire, her voice agitated, none of her usual confidence in it. "Is Carla there?"

"She left a half hour ago. Maybe longer now."

"Can you catch her? There's a small-craft warning. The advisory just caught up with the weather. A local squall is coming. It could turn into something bigger. You know how it is."

Volker feels a sudden weight on him. "Well, shit, Shire. You're the one who told her it was safe." He walks through the kitchen to the back door with the phone to his ear. "Hold on a sec. Maybe she didn't go out. Maybe she's in her camper for the night again." Carla's truck is parked behind the building in one of the employee spots.

Overhead, murderous-looking clouds boil up the bay. Against the storm's gloom, the mercury lights atop the lamp poles smolder like white coals. The parking lot is devoid of life, the wooden boardwalk fronting the shops and charter offices deserted. On the beach, multicolored tents shimmy insanely with each gust.

Volker walks out into the wind and pounds on Carla's camper door. Tries the handle. It's locked. "Nah. She's gone, Shire."

Shire groans. "Son of a bitch, I wish she'd get a fucking phone. Check and see if my skiff is in the slip?"

"I'll call you right back."

He locks up the bar and hurries against the wind to the wooden sidewalk overlooking the small-boat harbor. From the railing he can see that Shire's skiff is not in her slip on the long floating dock below. He calls her back and gives her the bad news. "She's out there. Can you call her on the radio?"

"I just tried. She's not answering."

They agree there's nothing to do until the wind drops off again.

Despite Carla's assurances, Volker wonders how capable she is with a small boat in big weather. If Shire's worried, he's worried.

He walks back to Carla's truck and hunkers in the lee of her camper. He lights a joint. It's powerful Matanuska Thunder; the shit will make your eyeballs do the backstroke. He sucks the smoke in deep. Ignoring the wind, he folds his arms across the cab of the truck and rests his chin on his sleeve. Have they broken up? How is it possible that he's not sure?

A car he recognizes goes by on the spit road and honks. It's Landry heading home from the restaurant at the End of the Road Hotel & Resort. His window rolls down and he yells, "Trolling for men, Volker? Try the public toilet!" Volker waves absently. Maybe that's what he should do, go gay. He's getting too old to be hosing young waitresses, and God knows none of the women in town his age will have him. He really does seem to get along better with men.

He takes another hit and tries once more to figure out where he and Carla stand now. She takes her clothes but says she'll see him again? And now she's out there on the near-dark bay in a twenty-foot skiff in a storm like this? Women! Jesus, what a confusing pain in the ass they are.

He realizes he's biting at a hangnail on one thumb. That pot was supposed to be calming. He throws the exhausted roach on the gravel, steps on it, and pulls another joint out of his pocket. Maybe this one will help.

15

It's nearing midnight, and Scott is now anchored in the lee of Loon Island, which blocks the wind still roaring over the bay. The cove nestled in the concave curve of a tall spruce-topped bluff is calm and quiet, the water showing little sign of the gale except the slow swells curling into the boulders at the foot of the bluff. He can hear but can't see harbor seals woofing to each other in the shadow of the cliff face. A few yards off the *"C" Lady*'s stern, a huge male sea otter floats on his back, tearing a crab apart, uninterested in the boat or Scott. Baitfish dimple the surface. He kneels on the forward deck and checks the deadfall on the anchor line. He's still a little quaky after the ill-conceived and nerve-fraying attempt to round Point Pogibshi just as the storm hit. In the near-dark of the late hour, he can see the tops of the spruce trees, high above, quivering in the still-powerful west wind.

Thankful that he decided to turn back at Point Pogibshi and follow the shoreline eastward to Eldridge Passage and the protection of the islands, he stands and stretches his back. His hands are tight from gripping the wheel. He could use a drink, dinner, and some sleep. Maybe tomorrow the storm will blow through and he can try to head out to the rockfish grounds again. He tests the deadfall on the anchor line with his foot once more, his cautiousness reinforced by the memory of his brush with drowning on the *Polar Huntress* years ago. Satisfied, he goes into the cabin of the boat and fixes dinner.

He sips a glass of Black Box merlot as he cooks one of the salmon fillets on the galley stove. He has another glass with dinner. He's drinking more of the cheap box wines these days. He's drinking more, period. He does the dishes and pans and puts them away. When the cabin is shipshape the way he likes it—a fussy habit that Trina called a "pathology"—he goes to the cupboard over the galley and pulls out the Maker's Mark.

As late as it is, and as nerve weary as he is, he's unable to sleep. The insomnia has been getting worse these past few years. He misses the deep slumber he knew on those crabbers and long-liners. He misses the absolute exhaustion from the frenetic madness of the time-limited openers, quotas to fill. Taking his breaks collapsed against a bulkhead in his dripping rubber bibs, instantly unconscious. No trouble sleeping those days. But it's not just the dreamy oblivion he misses. It's also the joy of doing something so undeniably, so preposterously risky. Building houses isn't even close.

If he's going to be awake, he might as well get something done. Another long-standing habit. He opens one of his tackle boxes and takes out a spool of heavy monofilament line, a pack of stout treble hooks. Using his crimping tool, he spends an hour tying up some yard-long leaders to use for trolling with herring bait; there are some fish you just can't catch on a fly rod. He tests each leader, clamping the treble hook in his needle-nosed pliers and yanking on the line until the monofilament almost cuts into his hand. Then he carefully coils and sets each one aside on the table.

Still not sleepy, he's thinking about that long-liner, the *Madmen*, again. It really got to him this morning. Though maybe not as much as that waitress from the Orca did.

He gets up and puts the coiled trolling leaders into the tackle box, thinking about her now. Why would an exciting, sexy woman like her take up with an ancient, ponytailed dipshit like George Volker?

Add it to the list of things he will never understand about women.

He finishes his bourbon and goes out onto the aft deck to take a depressed leak. The night air off the water is cool. The bay is about forty-five degrees this time of year. He can see yellow daylight gilding the mountaintops to the north. It's hard to tell whether that's just remnants of the lingering sunset or the jaundiced start of the coming dawn. The stern has swung toward the cliff face. Without looking at the tide tables, he can tell the water is lying slack and low. He looks at his watch. Twelve thirty AM. Another day. Another tide. Same old Scott.

Carla! Out of the darkness, the name flashes into his brain. *Carla.*

"Carla," he says, zipping up, happy to have recovered the lost name. "Carla, Carla, Carla."

As he turns back toward the cabin, something catches his eye at the periphery of the deck lights' glow. Something skating into the cove on the breeze. It drifts closer and he grabs the boat net, scoops it up, and swings it under the nearest light. It's an unopened bag of tortilla chips. The label reads: NEW, HINT OF LIME FLAVOR!

It's like finding an artifact from another culture. Trina monitored their health and nutritious diet for so long, he can't remember the last time he's eaten a corn chip—or any other kind of junk food. Well, brothers and sisters, this man is free now. And what does a single man about town pair with tortilla chips? Bourbon, of course.

He takes the chips inside the cabin, refills his glass, and sits reading the ingredients on the foil bag. What the hell is maltodextrin? It sounds like one of Trina's worst nightmares. He pulls open the bag, pinches one of the tortilla chips between his thumb and forefinger, and sets it on his tongue. He's half expecting to hear his arteries slam shut, to feel his blood pressure surge to his brain case and strike him dead with a massive hemorrhage. Instead, a sensation of joy begins to emanate from his mouth, spreading through his whole body, a dizzying feeling. He realizes he's smiling. He chews and swallows the chip.

Whatever else the great philosophers and statesmen have said about freedom, however many ways they have defined it or described it, he, Scott Crockett, newly divorced carpenter and up-and-coming wild man, is perhaps the only person in the history of the world who knows for a fact what freedom actually *tastes* like.

It's something like roasted corn, but wonderfully salty. With just a hint of lime.

He's reaching for his second chip when he hears the frantic pounding on the hull.

CHAPTER

16

D'ANGELO PULLS INTO the scenic overlook parking area high above the choppy waters of Kachemak Bay. The wind is raging. A mass of angry black storm clouds roil and loom overhead. He parks the Camry near a sign declaring that the town nestled at the foot of the hill is the "Halibut Capital of the World." He gets out and stretches. Five hours in the plane and nearly five more in the car have his lower back aching, legs stiff. He leans on the steel guardrail at the edge of the cliff, gripping the brim of his long-billed cap against the rising wind. Although it is nearly midnight, remnant Alaskan summer daylight lingers. Even from that height, he can see the white horses stampeding across the surface of the sea.

Jutting out from the base of the hill, a long, narrow spit of land reaches halfway across the mouth of the bay. Against the lucent gray water it looks like a black finger, crooked as though beckoning the incoming gale. Lights of small businesses dot the spit. A cluster of them marks something larger perching on the very tip of it—the End of the Road Hotel & Resort, where he has made a room reservation. The panorama is like a miniature version of Cape Cod but ringed with ragged, glacier-draped mountains right out of an Alaska visitors bureau brochure.

The wind hammers a copse of tall dark conifers on the edge of the cliff, and they bend in unison like rows of yoga junkies in a city park. When a smattering of rain sprays him, he pushes off the railing and crams himself back into the car. He flips the wipers on, checks his phone for the list of bars and restaurants in the town. The Homer Holiday Inn Express is the first drinking establishment on the only road in or out of this place.

Exhausted, he sighs, "The Holiday Inn it is," and drives down the long, curving hill into the town.

*   *   *

The bar on the ground floor of the hotel has two small windows and is dimly lit. Maybe to mimic true nighttime darkness, a rarity in the Alaskan summer months. He sits at the bar and orders a Ketel. The aroma of frying food seeps from a doorway behind the bar. The kitchen apparently. That's hopeful. To keep a low profile, he flew coach from Phoenix, and the dismal, foil-wrapped sandwich the airline offered is now just a memory of disappointment. On the long drive from Anchorage down the mostly unpopulated peninsula, there were few promising-looking restaurants. By the time his hunger really kicked in, nothing was open. Hopes up, he asks the bartender for a menu.

The bartender, a beefy guy with wavy red hair and a huge, also-red moustache hovering over his upper lip like a parade float, says, "Sorry, pal, kitchen just closed."

"No problem." D'Angelo flashes his friendliest smile. He'll ask about Carla, in time. "Just the drink then."

He takes the vodka and swivels on his stool, looking as best he can like another happy tourist in a bar full of people just like him. He keeps the ersatz smile glued on his face and scans the room.

Nothing surprising for a self-proclaimed fishing mecca. A couple graybeards in finger-smudged ballcaps hunch like gargoyles over the bar, nursing beers. D'Angelo pegs them as either commercial fishermen, boat mechanics, or carpenters. Maybe all three. It's hard to tell in coastal towns. There are several sets of sunburned, late-middle-aged tourists wearing mall-walker sneakers, Costco jeans, sweat shirts announcing they've been to Denali National Park or Seward or Glacier Bay.

More interesting is a gang of athletic-looking women in their late twenties or early thirties wearing T-shirts with boat names— *Nauti Mermaid Charters, Two Gals Fishing*—dancing to some nondescript alt rock, appletinis waiting for them at their table. From their windburned cheeks, firm biceps, and several bandaged fingers, D'Angelo guesses deckhands. One of the older-looking girls gives him a game eyeballing. He resists the urge to reciprocate. He's working. He offers his hopelessly-married look instead.

He checks out the waitress working the room. She's all wrong. Older. Heavier. Androgynous. Nobody would use that last word regarding Carla Merino.

A burst of sudden laughter turns his attention back to the dancing deckhands. They're hanging on each other, bent double with hilarity. He feels himself sag. Jennifer didn't make it to their age. It hasn't even been two whole months, he tells himself. Most days now he can go without thinking about her for hours at a time. Progress. Still, the sight of young people having a good time always impales him. Conventional wisdom is that, in time, he'll get over it. Someday he'll be able to picture her in every group of dancing young people he sees. Healthy. Strong. Swaying to the music. Laughing. Alive.

The bartender drifts his way, asks him if he needs another.

D'Angelo declines. He doesn't know how many more places he'll have to cross off the list before he finds her. He needs to keep the booze down to one per venue.

He puts on his cheery traveler face. "Hey, did you have a waitress named Carla working here a couple weeks ago? I thought maybe this is where I met her. Now I'm not sure." He laughs as if embarrassed. "It was my first trip to Homer, and I'll admit I hit more than one watering hole that night. Honestly, I don't even remember the names of half the places."

The bartender shakes his head, definite. "No one but Jeanie there. Been with us for years. A room this small? It's a one-woman job."

"Sure," D'Angelo says. He pushes back from the bar. "Thanks."

"Good-looking gal?" the bartender asks. "This Carla?" His moustache darts side to side obscenely. He looks like he might twirl the ends with his fingertips.

D'Angelo leers back at him. "A keeper."

"You might try the Orca Grill. The owner's got some kind of radar that picks up the cuties when they cross into the town limits or something."

"Ha! That right? Lucky guy." D'Angelo is still doing the hail-fellow-well-met routine. "The Orca, huh? Sure, I might've been there. Where's that again?"

The bartender tells him how to get to the road leading out onto the spit. D'Angelo gives the dancing deckhands one last appreciative glance and turns to leave. He turns back and calls out to the bartender, "Any chance the kitchen will still be open out there?"

CHAPTER

17

THE THUDDING ON the hull of the *"C" Lady* continues. For a second, Scott thinks the tortilla chip has already destroyed his brain. Then, out of the darkness surrounding the boat, a voice shrieks, "Help!"

He grabs a flashlight off the console and darts out onto the aft deck. The wind through the trees on the bluff seems to have tapered off, but swells are still rolling into the sheltered cove. Off the port corner of the transom, a body encased in a bright-orange survival suit bobs spread-eagle, belly-up. The one-piece heavy neoprene suit, with its hood and sewn-in gloves and feet, has a zipper up the front like a rubber onesie for a giant baby.

Scott falters, his mind turning to that night on the *Polar Huntress*, the big boat listing sharply starboard, about to roll over as he frantically zipped Donny Chesterson, the youngest crew member, into the last suit they had on board.

The voice from the water jolts him back. "Help me, for Christ's sake!"

He trains his flashlight on a pale face peering up at him. A woman's face, framed by the tight neoprene hood, like a nun in a hot-orange wimple. Only she doesn't talk like a nun.

"Hey, asshole! Can you get that fucking light out of my eyes?" She paws the smooth fiberglass hull at the waterline with the awkward neoprene gloves. "Help, goddammit!"

"Wait!" He pushes the fly rod off the hatch cover, rips the hatch open, and yanks out the swim ladder. He hooks it over the transom. "Can you climb it?"

She manages to grab the ladder but can't pull herself up with the weight of the survival suit dragging her down. "Son of a bitch!"

Scott leans over the rail. With the weight of the suit, she's a lot heavier than he thought she'd be. He grabs with his other hand too and, with both arms straining, hauls her over the transom. They fall together on the deck, water sloshing. His shirt and pants wet.

Scott stands, slapping water from his pant leg.

She sits back against the gunwale, gasping. "I thought I was going to fucking die."

The deck lights shine on her face. It's the waitress. And he knows her name. There really is a benevolent God in the universe. "You're Carla, right? From the Orca? Are you okay?"

"I'm freezing. There's water inside this thing."

The suit is zipped up only halfway to her chin. Her coat is soaked.

"Well, you don't have it zipped up all the way."

"It stuck!" she says, gasping, yanking at the zipper tongue without success.

"Take it easy." Scott reaches to help her. "How'd you get out here?"

"Shire's boat." She keeps yanking on the zipper. "Goddamn this thing!"

"Shire?" Involuntarily, he looks out across the water. "Is she out there?"

"No. She loaned me the skiff."

"Where the hell were you going in that storm?"

"To her cabin!" she snaps at him, and frees her head from the hood. "Get me out of this fucking thing!"

"All right, all right." He pulls her to her feet, yanks the zipper down. Her jeans and jacket are drenched. "What happened to the boat?"

"Filled with water; motor's drowned or something. Goddamn waves."

He holds one sleeve as she pulls her arm out, then the other. The suit slumps around her ankles. She extricates her feet and stands, water oozing from her sodden sneakers. A blue bandanna sags across her forehead. She shivers violently and falls back against the transom, almost pitches overboard.

He holds her by one arm. "Hang on. Let's get you inside." He hustles her into the cabin, past the galley and down the three stairs to the sleeping bunks under the foredeck. "You may be hypothermic. How long were you in the water?"

She's trembling, her jaw clenched. "I don't know," she says through her teeth. "It felt like a year."

"Okay, get those wet clothes off. Climb into that sleeping bag." He points to the bedroll on his bunk. "I'll get you some dry things."

She nods and unzips her jacket.

Scott goes into the head to find a towel. When he comes back out, her jacket, sweater, and blouse are on the floor. She's wearing a lacy, deep-red bra. He throws her the towel. "Dry your hair; get in the bag." He busies himself picking up her clothes. It's the closest he's been to a nearly naked woman in months. The closest he's been to a woman, period. He stands with the pile of wet clothes. He's about to put them in the head when she says, "Help."

She's sitting on the edge of the bunk. Her bra is off now, but she hasn't taken her sneakers off, and her jeans are tangled around her ankles. She looks dazed. Her eyes seem unfocused.

"Hang on." He drops the wet clothes and kneels to pull her sneakers off. That close to her, the smell of her wet body makes him inhale raggedly. Jesus. He yanks her jeans the rest of the way off.

She's wearing read underpants that match the bra. Unselfconsciously, she hooks her thumbs into the elastic and slides them down.

Scott almost leaps to his feet, turning away again as she kicks them off and scrambles into the sleeping bag. She pulls the bag up to her chin, wraps the towel around her hair. "Thanks."

Crazy feelings barely in check, he looks at her now lying there in his bunk, wet hair clinging to her cheeks and neck. "My clothes are going to be way big on you. Just stay in the bag for now. Maybe we should get you over by the stove, get some direct heat on your hair. I'll cook up some soup or coffee. You okay?"

"I'm half drowned, half frozen. Do I look okay?"

It's all he can do not to blurt, *You look great*. He says, "Let's get you by the fire." He throws her soaked things on the deck in the head, then comes back and slides his arms under the sleeping bag and lifts her off the bunk, blood rushing to every corner of his body. He has to keep talking. "How the hell did you get into the immersion suit in an open skiff?"

"Shire made me practice doing it. We're supposed to go commercial fishing with her brother in a few weeks somewhere."

"Sure. Elrond. I think he's got a permit for the Chignik district."

"Those waves," she says, mostly to herself, and shudders. "God."

Scott carries her, still wrapped in the bag, to the dining nook. He tucks her in at the table on the banquette seat nearest the stove. She still looks a little dazed, though her eyes are brighter now. "Give me a wrist." He feels her pulse, then lays his palm across her forehead. Her skin feels cool but not dangerously cold. Touching her makes his heart race, and he has to swallow before talking. "Your pulse is strong, you're fairly warm. You don't seem too hypothermic. Still, you should maybe get some warm food inside you."

He crouches at the little refrigerator under the counter in the galley and pulls out a Tupperware container of leftover rockfish chowder he brought from home—easy to heat up and gobble while trolling. He empties the container into a pan, sets it on the stovetop. He has to resist the urge to wash out the Tupperware. He sets it in the sink and runs water into it.

"I'd take a shot of that Maker's." She points at the bourbon bottle, still on the table next to the tortilla chips. "Hey, is that my bag of chips?"

He laughs, relieved to have the pressure in his chest, in his groin, off his mind for a moment. "I didn't find any guacamole." He sets a clean glass on the table in front of Carla. "I'm going to radio the Coast Guard, tell them Shire's Lund is out there somewhere, swamped. I'll tell them your condition and see if they think you sound hypothermic. They can send a fast boat with a medic, or even a helicopter if they think it's that bad. Or I could pull anchor and motor back to town. But you seem okay."

"Sure," she says. But she doesn't look sure. She's quiet, her face troubled. What is she thinking? He's survived a sinking boat. Maybe he knows a little about how she feels.

He hands her his cell phone. "You should call Shire and tell her about the skiff. Maybe let Volker know you're okay?" He picks up the radio handset. "I'll radio the Coasties."

"Wait. Don't do that," she says, softly. She hasn't touched the phone, the glass, or the bourbon bottle.

Scott stops. "Wait?" The heat from the galley stove is suddenly stifling.

She bites her lip and nods.

"You don't want me to call the Coast Guard?"

"No. I mean, yes, that's what I'm saying. No Coast Guard." The sleeping bag slides down and one small breast comes uncovered, the nipple as rigid and pointy as a roofing nail. It should whip him into a frenzy of longing again. It doesn't. Casually, she pulls the sleeping bag up to cover herself. "Sit down, er . . ."

"Scott," he says.

"Scott. Yeah. I know you from the bar. You're a carpenter. Glacier IPA, right?"

He's more than a little pleased. "Yes, a contractor," he says. He feels himself blush with embarrassment. She doesn't seem to notice. She's not all there. Drifting. Her mind on something else. "Carla?"

"Sit down a minute, Scott."

"That look on your face tells me we're both going to need a drink." He sits across from her, pours bourbon into her glass, refills his own.

Carla throws the whiskey at the back of her throat, swallows. "I need to tell you something."

Scott would say he has a sinking feeling. But that's not a term he ever uses.

"Yeah?" Scott says. "You want to start with telling me how come I'm not talking to the Coast Guard? Because Shire's skiff is not going to sink with all its floatation compartments. It's just going to wallow under the surface. And if I don't report this and some boater runs into it, people could get hurt." He looks at his watch. "It's one o'clock now. The first fishermen of the day will be on the water by five. Even if nobody crashes into the skiff, someone's going to find it and report it. Shire's your friend. You want her to think you're at the bottom of the bay?"

"Just for a while." She picks his phone up off the tabletop but sets it down again. "Just until we get somewhere safe. Then I can get word to her. Shire can keep a secret."

"Whoa. 'Until we get somewhere safe'? Who says we're going anywhere? And safe from what?"

"I don't want anyone to come looking for me. So if they think I'm drowned . . ."

Incredulous, Scott scoffs, "Are you telling me you scuttled Shire's skiff to get away from George Volker?"

"No, that was an accident. We were breaking up, and I just didn't want to spend the night with him hassling me about it. I didn't have anywhere to go. Thought I'd spend a couple days at Shire's cabin on the island. Then maybe move my camper to the RV park up on the river for the summer until I found a new place to live." She swallows the last of her bourbon and pushes her glass across the table toward him. "I didn't know about a storm coming up, those monster waves and all . . ."

"Yeah," he says, "the forecast was all wrong. I planned on going out around the point and spending the night on the outer coast. I had to turn back and hole up here. And this boat is twice as big as Shire's skiff."

"Well, I was sitting here thinking how glad I am that I didn't drown. But now that it looks like I'm probably dead"—she hesitates—"what if that might be the best way to leave it?"

"You want to be 'probably dead'?"

She shrugs. "Maybe. For a while."

Scott frowns, thinking about that. The boat shifts on a swell. Something thumps on the deck. He looks out the doorway to the stern. "I think my flashlight's rolling around out there." He wants to stand and go deal with it. He doesn't. "All right, this is not about Volker. I'll bite: why do you want to be 'probably dead'?"

She pauses a second. "The truth?"

"I live in a fishing town. I haven't heard a true story in years. Humor me."

"Fine," she says. "There's someone after me."

18

VOLKER IS STILL out in the parking lot of the Orca, leaning against Carla's camper, watching the tortured clouds twisting in the stormy night sky and worrying about Carla, when a dark-green sedan pulls in and stops directly behind her truck. He sees the rental sticker on the car, but the guy driving is no tourist. A big man with a cop's shaved sideburns wearing a leather jacket and a long-billed cap like one of those SWAT team gunslingers in the movies. The stranger doesn't get out. He just sits there and scans the Arizona plates on Carla's Toyota. Then he takes a quick glance at the security cameras on the back of the Orca and types something into his phone, which is propped against the steering wheel before him.

Volker walks over.

The guy turns off his engine but remains sitting in the car. He rolls down his window. "Man, this really is the end of the road, isn't it? End of the *world* is more like it." His voice is friendly, but something about his eyes sends a chill through Volker.

"I'm closing up," Volker says.

"I thought you could serve until five?"

"Legally, yes, but my diehard, regular degenerates are getting too old to stay up that late anymore. It's all tourist families and early-bird fishermen nowadays. It's a shame, really, people controlling their drinking like that. Kind of sad, actually."

The guy opens his mouth to say something just as a gust slams the rental car so hard it rocks on its springs. Volker's ponytail whips the side of his head. A ball of dried sea grass and kelp barrels across the parking lot like a beachfront tumbleweed, passes between Volker and the car, and crashes against the building. When the wind eases, the driver says, "Carla Merino?"

"I used to go by that name," Volker says. "I had it legally changed to Susan." One corner of the man's mouth curls up a touch. Volker would call it a smile if not for the dead-meat eyes above it. He decides not to get too cute with this guy. "Isn't this when you flash a badge, Officer?"

"Private," the guy says. "Where is she?"

Volker can't help himself. "Gone fishin'."

The driver sighs like he regrets what he has to do next. He scans the uninhabited parking lot, cracks open the car door, and sets one foot on the gravel.

"All right, all right, take it easy," Volker says. Does he want to put this guy onto Carla? Well, it can't hurt to tell him she's gone out. It's a big bay. "Seriously. She went out in a friend's boat." He just won't tell him where.

"Is that right?" He still has one foot on the ground, holding the door against the wind. What looks like a very expensive cowboy boot sits in the damp gravel, the pointy toe laced with curlicue stitching. Artistic merit notwithstanding, it isn't a boot Volker wants to get kicked with. Over the wind, a persistent dinging clamors from the dashboard, the key still in the ignition. "She's out in a boat with a friend?"

"Not with the friend," Volker says. "She took the boat. She's alone."

"Alone?" The guy looks past Volker at the bay, now almost indistinguishable from the clouds crowding it. "In this weather? Why would she do that?"

Volker decides to go with the truth. The guy's some kind of pro. He's going to find out everything anyway. "She works for me and we had an argument in the bar, and she left and took her friend's boat out. That's all." The wind nearly knocks him off his feet. The sound of heavy surf throbs in the night air. "Seriously."

"Better be a big boat."

"She in trouble with the law?"

"I told you, I'm private."

"So, somebody's looking for her."

"*I* am." The guy lets the dashboard dinging go on as he studies Volker's face. When he's apparently satisfied Volker's not withholding more, he pulls his leg back into the car and closes the door. He stares at Volker, daring him to say the next dumb thing. "Where is she going in the boat?"

"To her friend's cabin on Loon Island."

"The same friend who loaned her the boat."

Volker nods. Talking to this ghoul is starting to make him twitch. He reaches behind his head and fingers his ponytail as if to reassure himself it's still there.

"What's her friend's name?"

Volker tells him, and the guy writes it down in a small notebook. "Kiminsky? That end in an *i* or a *y*?" He writes what Volker tells him. "And you are?"

Volker answers that without smartassing, nerves jumping. He wishes he had another joint rolled and ready to burn. A fat one.

The guy starts the car and pulls something up on his phone. "So, George, tell me about this End of the Road Hotel and Resort." He holds up the phone with the photo of the hotel for Volker to see. "Food any good there?"

"Not bad. Lots of seafood, of course," Volker says, happy to see him leaving and sure he's just missed a beating to remember. Or hopefully forget. "About a mile on up the road. You can tell if you've gone too far: you'll be underwater. It's too late for anything right now. They have good breakfasts, though. Try the crab omelet."

The guy's smile is incredibly warm. The metamorphosis from sheer menace to comforting charm is astounding. This is someone you never want to play poker with. Or lie to. Still smiling like an old friend, the man says, "Thanks. I'll sleep well knowing that." He puts the car in gear, holds his foot on the brake. His face goes icy again as suddenly as it warmed. It makes the Gulf of Alaska wind seem positively tropical. "You're sure she's not home in your bed right now, right?"

"I wish," Volker says. It's the truest thing he's ever uttered.

"But you have cohabitated. Is that correct?"

This guy is some kind of cop for sure. Or wants Volker to think he is. Well, the truth isn't going to hurt Carla now. "She moved out yesterday. Took all her things. I don't know where she plans to live. Maybe with Shire or one of my other waitresses. Maybe in her camper."

The guy in the car studies the camper for a few seconds. Then the car starts rolling. A business card flies out the window and flutters to Volker's feet. Volker steps on it to keep the wind from blowing it away. When he bends to pick it up, the guy guns the engine and spins out, the tires peppering Volker with gravel.

"Asshole!"

The card reads *Cosmo D'Angelo*. No other information except a phone number.

The guy gives a couple merry toots on the horn and speeds up the spit road toward the hotel.

Carla. What in the hell has she done to put this thug on her trail?

Man, he wishes he had that other joint.

19

S COTT STANDS AND goes to the galley stove, his back to Carla. *A woman on the run. Great.* The pan of chowder is steaming. He ladles some into two bowls. "Someone is after you."

Carla doesn't respond.

He turns back to the table. "Seriously?"

She nods. Under the yellow, low-voltage cabin lights, her eyes look golden. He carries the bowls to the table. "Have some of this. It'll warm you up." He sits down opposite her, facing astern.

"Thank you," she says.

"So, tell me about this someone who's supposed to be after you. A man?"

"Yes, a man." She takes a spoonful of chowder, lifts it to her mouth, but hesitates. "Not a nice man," she says. Her hand trembles as she tastes the soup. "Scary, actually."

"I see." He looks past her and out the open door to the aft deck. The wind has settled further and the water shimmers, a silky bronze in the predawn half-light. Over the transom he can just make out the dark mass of the island. A loons calls, its mournful wail echoing off the cliff face. The next few days were supposed to be carefree and easy. This sounds like neither. He should pull anchor and take this woman back to town and save himself whatever headaches he's sure she's going to precipitate. Right now. But God, she looks good sitting there, hair all messed up, wrapped in his sleeping bag, slurping rockfish chowder. Christ, he isn't even fully divorced yet and he's become as hormone addled as every other untethered male in town.

"Fine," he sighs. "A guy is after you. Why is that not really a surprise?" He's still not hungry, but he sips his soup. "Husband?"

"No, not my husband. I don't have a husband at the moment. A guy I let pick me up at the place where I was working in Phoenix." She swallows some soup. "He's . . . um . . . sort of dangerous."

"Look, after just getting out of a long, unhappy marriage, I don't need some whole new variety of grief that obviously comes with you. And I really don't feel like solving mysteries. Just tell me who the guy is, please?"

"All right." She sets her hands flat on the table on either side of the bowl. "His name is Cosmo D'Angelo. Nice looking, very tall, well built, well groomed, forty-five years old."

Scott eats his chowder and nods to keep her talking.

"He was quiet, polite. Looked like a cop. I went home with him. He seemed harmless."

"The words you used a minute ago were *dangerous* and *scary*."

Carla cringes. "I had no idea when I met him."

"Okay. So, what happened?"

"I have a kind of embarrassing habit."

For an instant, Scott thinks she's going to go into details about her sex with the guy. He feels himself blanch. "A habit?"

"Sometimes I keep a memento from a guy I've been with."

"A memento?" he asks, relieved.

"In case I never see him again. So when D'Angelo was in the bathroom, I found something in his nightstand and I took it."

"Wait . . ." He's not sure if he heard that right. "You stole something from the scary guy who's now chasing you?" He sets his spoon down and rubs his eyelids with his fingertips. "This is starting to give me a headache. What the hell did you take?"

"An old black-and-white photo. I grabbed it and closed the drawer before he saw me. He didn't suspect anything. I went home."

"That's it? You went home? And then you drove four thousand miles to Homer, Alaska? To take up halibut fishing? And now he's hot on your tail? That photo must be very valuable. Or very dangerous."

"It's both."

"An old snapshot?"

She nods. "When I got home, I looked at it more closely. It's an old Army picture of Cosmo D'Angelo—twenty years ago, maybe—with three other guys. D'Angelo is holding one of those assault rifle things. It looks like the guy he's guarding is . . ." She hesitates, clearly not sure she wants to continue.

"Is what?"

"It's Gordon McKint."

"McKint?" A cold feeling of dread starts tugging at him. "Are you sure?"

"Of course. He looks like the same vicious asshole he is today. Eye patch, smirky mouth. Only twenty years younger. Like I said, D'Angelo's just a kid in the picture."

"Oh, man . . ." Scott's stomach curls in on itself. "Listen to me, the picture, you still have it?"

"Not on me. But yes. I have it."

One knee starts vibrating under the table. "Christ, Carla. Have you read the papers in the past week? Seen a TV? McKint's out there telling his followers that if he's elected, he's going to deputize every one of them to make citizen's arrests of any 'suspicious' immigrants they see. The guy is insane."

"What?" Carla frowns, brow knit. "That doesn't make any sense. How can a president deputize people?"

"It doesn't have to make sense. It only has to make his followers feel powerful."

"Yeah, well, he's good at that," Carla says.

Scott tries to find a way to dismiss the dread growing in his gut. "Look, your friend D'Angelo knew McKint years ago in the Army. Maybe it's no big deal. Now that McKint's famous, maybe D'Angelo dug up an old picture of him to show it around to the guys he works with or something. Maybe it's nothing."

Carla silently shakes her head.

"What?" Scott asks. "This gets worse?"

"Cosmo D'Angelo works for McKint at Sidewinder Security, the military contractors."

"Assassins is more like it." Scott pours himself another bourbon. Drinks it in two gulps. The bourbon feels like it's scorching the lining of his stomach. "Actually, nobody knows what those guys do. And you stole a photo of McKint from them? Great."

"My friend at the *New York Times* thinks the picture could stop his run for president. Maybe put him in jail. It's got something to do with South America. Colombia. McKint lying to congress about it."

"Jesus, Carla, if that photo is evidence . . . Gordon McKint is not a guy you want for an enemy."

"I didn't see him in the picture until I got home and looked closer!"

Scott runs his fingers through his hair. "And this is why you want to be presumed drowned now?" He wants to scream at her, *Because you're running from Gordon fucking McKint?*

So much for carefree and easy.

She eats her soup, head down.

"All right," he says, keeping his voice level, "let me think."

There are a dozen questions he'd like answered, starting with why—if this photo is so dangerous to McKint—this D'Angelo character had it at his house. But none of that matters right now. There's really only one thing he needs to know.

"Carla, what the hell are you planning to do with that photo?"

She sips her bourbon and swallows. "When I got out of grad school, I got a job as a social worker at the county hospital in Phoenix. Idealism up the wazoo. All I saw there, day after day, were indigents. Homeless people. Sick people. Poor people who needed help. And a lot of them were Mexicans, Guatemalans, Hondurans."

She pauses. Scott waits.

"What I'm trying to say is, I could only do so much for them, could barely put a dent in their problems. It was endless. Like fighting a forest fire with a squirt gun."

"Does this have something to do with McKint's detention centers on the border?"

"Did you ever read that bloody western novel about the American mercenaries who go down into Mexico to wipe out the Indians that are attacking Mexican farmers? The Mexican government pays them for the scalp of every Indian they kill. Well, it doesn't take the mercenaries long to figure out that the Mexican farmers' scalps look exactly like the Indians'. Nobody can tell them apart. And there's money to be made."

"Jesus. They start killing everybody?"

Carla nods. "Sidewinder owns the detention centers along the border. And if McKint gets his way, they'll take over the Border Patrol. What do you think will happen when they get paid to detain people, and also get to decide who to detain? I'll tell you what: they'll pick up every brown person they can find." She stops and looks straight at him. "If I can do something with that picture to stop those assholes, I will."

"Like turn it in to the FBI? They could put you in witness protection, give you a new name."

"I could've done that months ago. Only I'm not a witness to anything. And the anti-McKint bloggers say he's got people *inside* the FBI."

"Is that possible?"

"A couple months ago, a Sidewinder whistleblower was supposed to testify against McKint to the FBI. He died under suspicious circumstances. It was supposed to look like a suicide. He worked in Phoenix. Do you want to guess who his boss was?"

"Your boyfriend, D'Angelo."

Carla just nods again and goes back to eating her soup, carefully spooning each mouthful to her lips as though it's still hot.

He wants another drink but decides he might need to stay sharp. He watches her eat for another minute, the hum of the generator and the cries of night birds the only sounds. "Well, you're right about one thing. They'll definitely be coming for you if they find out where you are." An involuntary chuckle escapes him. "Jesus, Carla, there're some sharp fillet knives in that drawer by the sink. Why don't you just take one and cut my liver out?"

She looks up, pushes her bowl aside, and pours herself another drink.

"You ever hear the feminist saying *Cinderella didn't ask for a prince; she just wanted a night off and a dress?*"

"What the hell does that mean?"

"It means, thank you for pulling me out of the water, but I haven't asked you to keep rescuing me. Just take me back to town. I'll figure something out."

"You *do* understand that your name is going to show up on a Coast Guard missing-persons report when somebody finds Shire's skiff swamped out there in a few hours. Sidewinder must have more computers than God's tech department. D'Angelo, or somebody like him, could be here by this time tomorrow."

"Like I said, you don't have to get involved. I got this far, didn't I?"

"Yeah, you're doing great."

Unable to sit still with everything she's told him ricocheting around in his brain, Scott stands and walks to the door of the cabin. He instinctively checks the distance between the boat and the cliff face, the wind direction, the way the tide is running. The swim ladder is still hanging over the transom. He half expects to see a scuba-clad assassin coming over the rail, Uzi blazing. Too many movies, he tells himself. Does he want to get involved with Carla?

Yes, he'd like to do the right thing now. But is this some sick attraction to danger, a little excitement in his life? Or just simple horniness running amok? He's not sure which explanation is more stupid.

The orange survival suit is lying on the deck in a heap. Again, the *Polar Huntress* disaster sparks to life in his mind. Donny Chesterson paralyzed with fear as the vessel listed and began to take on water. Scott grabbing the kid and practically stuffing him into the survival suit, shoving him over the rail as the boat rolled. The icy sea lunging at them. Scott wearing just his old float coat. Luckily the Coast Guard helicopter was already on the way. There have been times since that night when—high and dry and safe and warm—it has all felt like an adventure to remember with a kind of perverse fondness.

This is not one of those times.

CHAPTER

20

FITFUL RAINDROPS SMEAR the windshield as D'Angelo pulls into the End of the Road Hotel and Resort, an unremarkable two-story building with drab gray wood siding and a mossy shingled roof. It could be a midlevel hotel anywhere in the country. If not for the location. And what a location. Squatting at the tip of the spit, it's flanked by the churning sea on three sides, surf pounding the beach pebbles. A panorama of mountains and glaciers across the bay glow blue-white beneath the nearly black sky. The one-of-a-kind setting is obviously a magnet for visitors. License plates from a half dozen states are on display in the parking lot. But with the late hour, the rain, and the raging windstorm discouraging beach walks, there's no one around. The tourists are apparently tucked in for the night. D'Angelo presses his cap to his head and hurries through the sea-damp air.

The lobby is empty, silent. Behind the front desk, a tiny, dark-eyed, middle-aged woman looks up from a magazine. She glances at the clock on the wall and frowns like she's not getting paid enough to have to check in guests at such an hour. She has a perfect helmet of inky black hair and laser-straight bangs above a serious, nearly paper-white face. She looks like she should be inspecting nuclear test sites in countries that aren't supposed to have nuclear test sites.

The woman sighs theatrically and stands, glowering at him, lips welded. She's much too stiff for him, but after the enervating drive from Anchorage to the end of the road and the less-than-fruitful conversation with George Volker, he could use a smile from any person of the opposite gender. This one looks like a tough sell. Still, it's a rare day when Cosmo D'Angelo can't get a woman to show her teeth—one way or another. He gives her a smile designed to defrost Siberia. It has no effect.

"Name?" she says. The room temperature plummets further.

"Cosmo D'Angelo. I called yesterday."

"Yesterday?" Her brow furrows even more. "Yesterday. For a room, tonight?" She looks at the computer and scowls. "You're lucky you got anything in town on such short notice." She clearly resents even speaking to someone so cavalier about making reservations. There's a trace of an accent. Eastern European. Russian, maybe. She glares at him. "It *is* summer, you know."

"It was spur-of-the-moment. I suddenly realized I've never been to Homer, Alaska. Had to see it. Call it an emergency." He turns the heat up on the smile. But the weather report for this gal is calling for record low temps. No pleasantries in the forecast. Zero percent chance of humor.

"Credit card and driver's license." She slides the room rental agreement across the counter.

D'Angelo reads the bottom line, stunned by the rack rate. He's gotten better deals in London and Paris. She isn't kidding about Alaskan summer exigencies. It's going to take some creative accounting to expense this trip without anyone at Sidewinder asking what he was doing on the far edge of North America. He can deal with that once he's eliminated the Carla Merino problem.

"Room two-oh-three. Left at the top of the stairs." She holds out a card key, eyes gray as gravel. She says, "Welcome to the End of the Road" without a hint of welcome.

He shuts down his smile, stores it for another day, another less-challenging encounter. He takes the card key without further cleverness. There's no point in trying to melt this particular glacier. He hopes he's just tired from the long trip, not losing his touch completely. "I don't suppose the restaurant is still serving food."

She looks at the clock on the wall, rolls her eyes his way, arches one eyebrow. "Breakfast is at seven AM."

"Well, thanks, then." Pride more than a little wounded, he heads for the stairs. He hopes to hell the rest of the women in this town are a little warmer than this one. He's seen friendlier border guards.

21

SCOTT'S STILL AT the cabin door, enjoying the cool air and resisting the urge to pick up everything off the deck. The fly rod, the survival suit. Tidying up.

She didn't ask for a prince. Listen to her. Drop her off at the marina and go fishing.

If the wind dies off, he might be able to get out around the corner of the peninsula later today. There are miles of ragged, glacier-carved coastline along the Gulf of Alaska. Deep bays and long, fjord-like coves. Dozens of uninhabited islands. Literally thousands of square miles of ocean to fish.

To the east he sees fast-moving sea ducks speed past, black specks against the silvery-pinkish light. That's the idea. Keep moving, as fast as you can.

All he has to do is pick up the radio and make the call. He can keep Carla's name out of it—except how's he going to explain to the Coast Guard how he knows about Shire's foundered skiff? And the urge to help her is no small matter.

Trina used to tease him by putting a jigsaw puzzle together on the dining room table and purposely leaving the last couple pieces lying on the tabletop where he could see them. A crossword puzzle with all but a few words filled in, the pencil tantalizingly lying on top of it. She found his inability to resist helping her finish them entertaining—until she found it unbearable.

She would shake her head and say, "Scottie, you've never met a damsel you haven't tried to help, have you?"

Scott knows his inability to leave a puzzle unfinished has more to do with his OCD compulsions. But his rescuer tendencies are no small matter either.

"Scott, are you all right?" Carla says.

He turns. "Sure." He's not sure how long he's been standing there.

"I meant what I said."

He brushes that aside. "Your name is going to pop up on Sidewinder's search system when somebody finds that skiff and Shire tells the Coast Guard about you. That's sure as hell going to bring D'Angelo or one of those guys to town. But it'll take some time for them to get here. We can talk about it some more in the morning."

"It is morning," she says.

He looks at his watch: three fifteen AM.

"*Later* this morning." He walks to the table. "Come on. I'll carry you back down to the bunk. Let's think about getting a little sleep."

She holds the sleeping bag against her collarbone as he lifts her in his arms. Her face inches from his. Her hair smelling like the sea.

"Why are you doing this, Scott? Why not just call the Coast Guard and be done with me?"

"I'm still trying to figure that out."

He carries her down to the sleeping area and sets her on the bunk. "You want one of my T-shirts to sleep in?"

"Thanks."

He hands her a huge, green T. As she pulls it on, he turns away and rolls out another sleeping bag on the opposite bunk.

"You sound like you know a lot about this spy stuff."

"Not really." He fusses with the bedroll. "I watch a lot of movies. But I agree that the key is for you to appear to be dead."

"Sorry I can't give them a body."

"I'm not," Scott blurts. Feels himself blush. He opens a cupboard over the bunk and yanks a pillow out. "You're probably safe for a day or two. As long as you've been careful and they don't already have any idea where you are."

She doesn't answer.

He turns back. She's sitting up in the sleeping bag, holding her head in her hands.

He sits on the bunk opposite. "Carla? There's no other way for D'Angelo to connect you to Homer, right?"

She looks stricken, face pale. "I thought it was safe. It's been two months."

"What? What did you do?"

"Shire's brother Elrond gave me some sablefish, and I shipped some frozen to my mother in Scottsdale two days ago. FedEx." She hurries to add, "But I paid cash and used a phony name!"

"Not good, Carla. They were surely expecting you to contact your mother. If they saw that FedEx delivery, they could hack into their tracking system and get the package's point of origin. Does your mother know anybody else in Alaska?"

"I doubt it."

Scott looks at his watch again. "FedEx overnights frozen seafood shipments. Say the package got to Phoenix yesterday afternoon, maybe twelve hours ago . . ." He raises his eyes to hers. "Hypothetically, if D'Angelo caught a flight to Anchorage last night, he could already be in Homer."

Carla looks at him, teeth clenched. "Sorry."

He shrugs, hoping it doesn't reveal how bad this really is.

They sit, looking at each other for a second.

Her eyelids are drooping, but the deep-green shirt brightens the gold in her irises. They pull him in. He gets a grip and says, "You really want to use that photo against McKint? You're sure?"

Carla nods. "I've waited and waited for two months while he's on TV every day, whipping people into a frenzy of hatred. If I can convince D'Angelo and Sidewinder that I'm dead, this is my chance to use the photo against them."

"How's it supposed to suddenly show up if you're dead?"

Carla chews her lower lip, thinking. "How long before the Coast Guard calls off the search for me?"

"I'm not sure. A few days, I guess. Why?"

"Okay, when everyone thinks I'm dead, I'll go see Shire, give her my keys, and ask her to get the picture out of my truck. I'll give her the number for my friend at the *Times*, Lisa Yi. Shire can say she found the picture in my things *after* I drowned. So they'll think I'm dead."

"The picture is in your truck?"

"Yeah, in the cloth on the ceiling of the cab."

"The headliner?"

Carla shrugs. "I guess. If that's what it's called."

"And where's the truck?"

"Parked behind the Orca."

"Shire?" Scott feels his heart tightening. "Carla, think about what you're saying. What if D'Angelo is already on his way? You want to get Shire and her kids involved with that guy? You said yourself, he's not a nice person."

Carla looks sick. She swallows hard. "I don't know. I mean, no, of course not. Fuck! Shit! Fuck!"

Scott shakes his head, almost laughing. "Nice language. Well, it's solstice, nearly twenty-four hours of light in the sky, and the spit will be a tourist anthill for the next three months. D'Angelo can't very well break into the truck in broad daylight and start taking it apart. And at night the marina is lit up like a ballpark. Plus, there're security cameras all over the place. Still, we're going to have to get to it before he figures out a way. I just don't know how."

Carla looks at him. "You're talking like you've decided to help me."

He tries to change the subject. "You were so gung ho about saving the world, you quit social work and became a waitress?"

She groans. "Yeah, how's that for idealism?"

"I don't know. These days, serving people alcohol sounds like a humanitarian act. And how does stopping McKint change the world? I mean, really, for how long?"

"You're right. It won't change the poverty. Maybe nothing will. But it could keep things from getting a lot worse."

"Yeah." Scott stands and looks down at her. "Maybe."

"Scott. If I can stop McKint, I'll help a lot of people down there, all at once."

"I have to think about it." He walks back up the stairs and through the cabin and out onto the aft deck. The wind above the cliff has gone silent. The swells are getting smaller. The cool air feels good. Somewhere in the gloom, a gull keens. Farther out on the bay, a ship's horn moans. He wishes he were on it. Maybe not.

He could call the Coast Guard now and go back to being

another divorced guy in a small town brimming with them, working the same job he's been doing for years, and indulging himself in
what passes for luxury in his world: fishing for salmon and halibut
in the same bay he's been fishing all his life. Or he can help Carla
do something good, something important.

And put himself in Gordon McKint's sights?

Fuck. Shit. Fuck. She summed that up about right.

He stows the fly rod and the landing net, stashes the swim ladder in the aft hold. The survival suit is a problem. It has Shire's name
and numbers on it. Is it better for the suit to show up empty, sug-
gesting Carla wasn't able to get into it? Or is it better if the thing is
never found at all? He handled the suit when she came aboard and
doesn't know if anyone can identify him from DNA or some other
modern science gimmick like the cops on TV always use. That's
almost certainly Hollywood nonsense. But if the thing disappears,
forensics will be moot. Disappearing is easy enough on the ocean.

The fathometer says there's ninety feet of water under the boat
where he's anchored. It's not a good fishing spot, the bottom muddy
and featureless. No reason for divers of any kind to visit. Boaters
rarely use the area for anything other than hiding out from storms.

He stands for a moment, looking at the survival suit lying on
the deck, pushing back the memories it evokes. Then he kneels
and stuffs an eight-pound torpedo-shaped downrigger weight into
each foot of the suit, zips the thing up, and drops it over the side.
It plummets into the black depths like a cartoon Mafia victim in
cement shoes, the orange neoprene arms flailing madly overhead.
His own hands grip the rail so hard they ache. When he pulls them
off, his fingers are trembling. How did he find the courage to save
Donny Chesterson's life that night? It's amazing what you might do
when you just don't have time to be frightened.

He returns to the cabin and puts his bourbon glass in the galley
sink with the soup bowls. He runs hot water and washes everything, sets the dishes in the drying rack. He tells himself he's just
keyed up about the whole Carla thing, but understands that he'll
never get to sleep with dirty dishes in the sink. Know thyself. Even
the embarrassing parts. Especially the embarrassing parts.

He turns off the generator, and the boat plunges into absolute
silence. Even the birds have called it a night.

Carla is already asleep when he gets back to the bunks. He stares at her face a moment. She looks older now than she seems when she's awake, swearing and mouthing off. Older and somehow even more attractive.

He's heard men complain about women coming into their lives dragging a load of personal baggage with them. Carla should have her own container barge.

Is she trouble? Oh, absolutely.

Does he care? Not much.

He climbs into the port bunk and lies there, not the least bit sleepy now. Waves softly slap against the hull. The anchor chain groans and clinks as the boat shifts on the tide. He does love sleeping on the boat. Alone. Having a lovely woman in the next bunk doesn't take away from that at all.

One of his subcontractors, Frank Bass, an electrician, lifelong bachelor, and reliable smartass, recently said to him, "You're getting divorced? *Mazel tov*, man. All the pussy in the world now!"

"Nice, Frank," Scott said. "Very classy, my friend. Sophisticated."

"Aw, come on, Scottie. Lighten up. 'Happily married' is an oxymoron. What's not to love about divorce?"

Right. What's not to love about defying the Coast Guard and having some combat-trained goon hunting him? All because of this woman whose problems Scott simply cannot let pass.

Having been raised Catholic, he honestly should've expected nothing less. Somewhere in heaven or hell, Sister Mary Claire is laughing her ass off.

22

CARLA AWAKENS IN the bunk, disoriented. Sunlight streams through the porthole in the bulkhead above her. Sunshine? For the second morning in a row? Has to be some kind of record for this place, given the two months of almost-constant clouds and rain she's endured since arriving. Once again, the clear bright light makes her feel exposed—even down here in the bow of Scott's boat. She has to remind herself that only one person on earth has any idea where she is now, and he's a friendly, harmless carpenter. Decent, smart, and nice looking too.

But there's something else going on. In spite of the menacing sunshine, she's feeling awfully upbeat for some reason. She lies there in Scott's sleeping bag another moment, mystified, until she realizes it's bacon. Bacon is going on. Scott is cooking bacon, and the thick, greasy aroma always evokes the same memory.

* * *

She was eleven, staggering not yet fully awake down the hallway into the kitchen of the big house in Scottsdale, coaxed along by a scent she'd never awakened to before—not in that house. Her mother would've eaten bacon right after she volunteered to donate a kidney to a complete stranger. Yet there was a skinny man wearing a T-shirt and baggy board shorts at the big five-burner stove, his legs like overtanned sticks extending to the unlaced Hush Puppies on his feet. He turned at the sound of Carla pulling out a chair at the kitchen table.

"Hey, little lady. Ready for a bite of heaven?" He had shaggy blond hair with lighter highlights. A sparse moustache the same colors. Talked with a cowboy drawl. *Little lady.*

She gestured toward the frying pan. "Where'd you get that stuff?"

"The bacon? Just ran to the Quicky Mart. The inside of your fridge looks like a feed-and-grain store. God save me from vegetarian food Nazis." He turned back to the stove. "I mean, your big sister's fun, but Jesus!"

My big sister. Did any of those guys really believe that?

"We better eat that before my sister wakes up," she said.

This poor dummy didn't have a chance. He hadn't been notified that this was a one-night stand.

There were always men, from as far back as Carla could remember. Mostly one-nighters like this one. But some others moved in long-term—meaning for as long as her mother needed them—and were like pets. Like dogs, or not-very-clean cats hanging around the place. They were generally balding, paunchy, older guys named Ronnie or Bert and Bud. Carla got used to them being there: slouched hungover on the sofa watching sports or sleeping on a chaise longue by the pool in their old-man boxers. Carla always understood that those guys were from outside the local art world, where her mother had a name and a certain artistic appearance to keep up. It took her a little longer to figure out that their money was how her mother could afford to navigate that world in the first place.

They paid to have the patio tiled. A sun-room added onto the house. New pool decking. In return, her mother made sure they got everything any man could want from a woman—until she got everything she wanted from them. The transaction took exactly as long as each job lasted. Carla liked them. And felt bad for them. Some brought her little gifts and acted like they were her father.

My father.

Of course this memory veers down that path. Carla doesn't remember her father—she was too young. But how many times did she hear her mother's version of his overdose? "Halcion," she would say. "He always had trouble sleeping." A pause. One arched eyebrow. Her best half smile. "But not anymore, of course."

* * *

Memories evaporating, Carla sits up in the bunk and inhales the bacon fumes filling the boat. She cranes around to see Scott in the galley, his back to her. Her wet clothes are draped on the bench seat, on cabinet doors, dangling from the handle of the little refrigerator. "God, that smells good," she calls out.

He turns at the hip. "Good morning. I put out some things of mine. I think they might be pretty big on you, but yours are still wet."

She slides out of the sleeping bag. "What time is it?"

He's spread some of his own dry clothes across his neatly made bunk. Declining the big white jockey shorts and the heavy canvas work pants that would fall right off her small hips, she pulls a red flannel shirt on over the T-shirt and rolls up the sleeves. It hangs just short of her knees, covering all the things you are expected to keep covered at breakfast. No need for pants.

"About eight o'clock," he says.

"I didn't think you'd let me sleep that long." She glances out the sun-filled windows, half expecting to see a boat approaching, D'Angelo at the helm. She finger combs her hair as best she can— it's gummy with seawater salt—and climbs the steps to the warm, food-scented galley. Scott is leaning over a heavy iron frying pan, bacon grease snapping like fireworks.

"You were sleeping pretty hard. I've been up a while."

"I can see that." She nods toward the stove. "The last man who cooked for me wants to marry me. The *second* to last man who cooked for me wants to kill me. Maybe I should fix my own meals from now on."

"Volker cooked for you? I wouldn't have guessed. He looks more like a pickled-eggs-and-extra-smoky-jerky kind of guy. Maybe because I only see him in the bar. He asked you to marry him?"

"He tried to woo me with poached eggs."

"That's how he gets all the young ones? I'll have to write that down."

Carla is more pleased about being lumped into that age category than she cares to think about.

Scott plucks the bacon strips out of the frying pan and sets them on a paper towel. "I don't dislike George. I'm just jealous. I'm happy to hear you only moved in with him to hide out. I mean, if he's what women want . . . That's too depressing to think about." He hands her a coffee. "Sit."

Carla sits over her coffee mug, looking out the boat window at the wispy fog patches lingering over the cove. A handful of black-and-white birds of some kind paddle in erratic circles, their reflections cruising upside down beneath them. A sea otter lounges on the slick surface, belly to the sky, toes in the air, wearing his own fur survival suit. Hard to believe that water tried to kill her last night.

Scott sets two plates of fried eggs and bacon strips on the tabletop, slides into the seat across from her. "Eat up, and we'll get out of here."

Ravenous, Carla stuffs bacon in her mouth and mumbles, "Where will we go?"

"When Shire's skiff is found, your name will be on the radio today and in the papers tomorrow: the *Homer News*, the *Peninsula Clarion*, and the *Anchorage Daily News*. We can't just sit here a week until the search for you is called off. We need to get you someplace where nobody knows you. Someplace you can lay low until we figure out how to get the picture out of the truck. I was going to say we could pull anchor, head out around the point, and shoot for Seward. It's just a long day's boat ride from here."

"Why? What's in Seward?"

Scott laughs. "A lot of drunk fishermen. Just like here. But nobody knows you there."

"God, I've been here two months, and I'm so sick of drunk fishermen."

"You're starting to sound like a real Alaskan woman."

"What do you mean you were 'going to' suggest Seward?"

"It's a moot point now. It's calm here, but there's a small-craft advisory for the other side of the peninsula. Storm warnings. Winds from the east. Seas to eight feet. We might make it alive, but a head wind like that would beat our brains out all the way. And if anything went wrong with the boat . . ." He lets that fade out. "Sorry."

"So, what do we do?"

"In my divorce deal, my ex is keeping the house I built in town. I get this boat. Fine with me. But I can't run my business out of it. So I'm fixing up an old house I own on the river fifteen miles north of town at Anchor Point. Nothing fancy. Couple acres with a gravel pit on it. I keep my construction equipment there. If we can get you up there unseen, you can hide for a few days while I find a way to get to your truck before D'Angelo does."

"That'll be the first thing he does when he hears I'm dead, won't it? I mean, he's got to figure I either had the photo on me when I drowned or it's in the truck."

Scott shrugs. "Like I said before, right now the truck is too exposed. He can't get to it where it's parked any easier then we can."

"That's good, right?"

"Yeah, I guess. It'll give us time to figure out how to grab the photo."

"And then what?" Carla asks.

"I'm fucked if I know." He shakes his head. "I'd say I'll drive you up to Anchorage. You give the thing to the FBI. But if you're right about McKint having people inside the feds . . .."

He finishes his food and stands. "Well, we can't stay here. Half the captains on the bay know this boat. Somebody will come investigating why we're sitting here before the day's out."

He starts the engines. The boat vibrates with their power. He lets them run while he carries their empty plates and cups to the galley and runs water on them. "Will you wash these while I pull the anchor?"

"Sure." She goes to the sink.

Scott sits at the wheel and flips a switch. Carla feels the boat shift as the anchor line tightens. It feels good to be doing something. To be moving. But then a thought hits her.

"Scott, how do we get through the docks and up to your hideaway without me being seen?"

He turns and smiles. "I have an idea."

"You have an idea?" She scoffs. "One that includes keeping me alive?"

"Half the guys in the marina know you from the bar. And even if they didn't, they'd never let a woman like you pass without eyeballing her. You're going to turn heads, and we don't want that kind of attention."

"What do you want me to do, put on a disguise?" she jokes.

Scott doesn't laugh.

"Oh, come on. What, a fake beard and moustache?"

"It doesn't have to be that dramatic." Scott keeps his eyes on the anchor chain clanging into its hold in the bow of the boat. "Every day, some new young guy shows up on the docks looking to crew on the commercial boats. They've been watching *Deadliest Catch* and want in on the glamour and excitement of the most dangerous job in America."

"I know a few crab fishermen. *Glamour* is not the word that comes to mind."

"A lot of them learn that real quick and take off for warmer, safer jobs on dry land. That's why the Salvation Army store is loaded with almost pristine work clothes."

"So . . . ?"

"So there's going to be one more scrawny young deckhand in the small-boat harbor. Very soon."

23

Araucous cawing rousts D'Angelo out of an earthquake dream he knew was a dream but couldn't climb out of. He'd been in an earthquake in Turkey once. Single scariest day of his life.

He sits up, squinting at the morning light pouring through the sliding glass doors to the room's balcony. An enormous, glossy black raven is perched on the railing, squawking at a group of equally black crows strafing it and shrieking their opinions of its species. The raven sounds like it's gargling with rocks, the much-smaller crows like children imitating an older sibling. What are they saying? It's clearly not friendly.

D'Angelo climbs out of bed and raps on the glass. The raven's head swivels. It mutters something toward him with obvious irritation and launches off the railing straight into the squadron of angry crows. The aerial bird battle flaps out of sight. He flips on the coffeemaker and finds his way to the shower, muttering in his own language that he should have brought some good coffee packets with him.

Hunkering to fit his tall frame under the showerhead, he lets the hot water drum on his skull, thankful that he's finally dreaming of something other than his daughter. Even earthquake dreams are better than that.

The coffee steams in the pot when he comes out of the bathroom. He throws a robe on and takes a cup out onto the balcony in spite of the cool early-morning air. The midnight storm had been brief, and now the bay is calm under clearing skies. Soft, residual swells roll past the end of the spit. He sips the coffee and grimaces. Funny, after all the years spent drinking camp coffee unfit for human consumption, only four years into management and city life he's already a caffeine snob of the first order. Surely the hotel must have an espresso bar. He leans over the railing and tries the coffee again. He dumps the cup onto the rocky beach below.

On the other hand, the scenery is spectacular.

He takes in the view, instinctively determining the compass rose—an old habit from years in the field when directions made a difference between life and death. The balcony faces due south across the Kachemak Bay. To the west, the open waters of Cook Inlet stretch to a horizon jagged with dormant volcanoes and the mountains of the Aleutian range. Eastward, the bay is shouldered by low hills dotted with the houses of the town on the north shore. On the south, snow-topped summits sit shrouded with leaden clouds. Two blue glaciers, lucent against the gloom, wind between conical peaks like the frozen rivers they are. At their base, a thin layer of cottony fog carpets the water as far as he can see toward the head of the bay.

A dozen yards away from the hotel, a motion catches his eye. The low morning sun flashes white on the bellies of small shorebirds soaring along the surf line. On an apparent whim, the flock abruptly folds over on itself like a sleight-of-hand trick and lands on the pebbled shore, suddenly invisible. There's mystery everywhere.

It all makes him wish he were just a tourist gawking at this beautiful place. He isn't looking forward to the work he has ahead of him today. But Carla Merino must be dealt with.

That damned photo. If he'd acted decisively the moment he put his hands on it, none of this would be necessary. If only he'd gone straight home the night he got back from that tough job overseas instead of to the Sierra Vista for a drink. After two weeks among potential enemies, he thought Carla Merino was exactly what he needed. Now look where he is. He wishes he'd never met her. Right now he wishes he'd never met Gordon McKint. But then, where would he be? Hell, *who* would he be?

From the balcony he can hear the clink of silverware and plates. Someone is having breakfast out on the restaurant deck.

Jesus, he's hungry.

He dresses, hangs his Nikon around his neck, and heads down to the hotel restaurant to find out how good those crab omelets really are.

Over the bar in the restaurant, a TV screen shows the face of Gordon McKint, glaring belligerently with his one good eye. Luckily, the sound is muted. D'Angelo has eaten enough meals listening to Gordon McKint over the years. More than enough.

*　　*　　*

After the breakfast—omelet very good, coffee not so great—D'Angelo drives to the marina. He parks and walks down a steep aluminum ramp to the docks. Somebody there might verify—or dispute—that Carla Merino went out into last night's gale in a small boat. He's stepping off the ramp onto the dock when he sees a hard-hulled Alaska Department of Fish and Game inflatable towing an aluminum Lund skiff. He walks along the dock and stands near the slip where they tie it off. It's not hard to see that the skiff has spent some time more or less submerged. A foot of muddy water sloshes in the hull. The cowling on the big outboard motor is missing, the center console festooned with sea grass and long kelp tubes. D'Angelo loiters close enough to hear the fish cops telling someone that early-morning dipnetters found the swamped boat on the other side of the bay. Two names are mentioned. Shire Kiminsky. And Carla Merino. He hears the words "presumed drowned."

Apparently, that much of Volker's story is true.

Word gets out quickly. In minutes the harbor master, State Troopers, local police, and the Coast Guard swarm the dock. A reporter from the town's weekly newspaper shows up, a nice-looking middle-aged woman with a tremendous pile of crinkly black hair streaked with silver. She's wearing a blue raincoat, black-and-yellow-striped tights, and the brown rubber knee boots half the people on the docks have on their feet. Somehow she makes it all work.

D'Angelo ambles past the cluster of law enforcement types, slouching as he walks, trying to look as much like a simple curious tourist as he can manage. That's a stretch, him being much taller and a lot fitter than most of the paunchy sightseers wandering the docks.

He stalls there as long as he can, mingling with a group of aging, Patagonia-clad ecotourists—all high-end optics and stainless-steel water bottles—waiting to board a big catamaran for a birding charter. Listening in on the police conversations, he holds the camera to his face and aims it at a crow perched on the wide gunwale of a commercial seiner. The bird has a blue-black mussel clamped in its beak. It bashes the shell against the aluminum rail with a musical, bonking sound.

If Carla is dead, where is the photo?

An older, overgroomed woman with perfectly coiffed auburn hair mistakes D'Angelo for one of the birding group. The only person without binoculars or a gigantic camera, she looks out of place in that crowd. Her clothes more tailored, less outdoorsy than the others. The lightweight loafers all wrong for a boat deck or a stony beach. "Is that some kind of sea crow?" she asks him.

D'Angelo shrugs, puts on an embarrassed grin. "Beats me. I'm new to this."

"Me too," she says. "I got talked into it."

One of the men in the group turns their way and scoffs. "There is no such thing as a sea crow. It's a common American crow. Or maybe a *Corvus caurinus*, the northwest crow. But we're probably a little out of their range."

The woman turns away from the pedant and leans closer to D'Angelo. "I like 'sea crow.' It's a nice name."

"It really is," he whispers back, then notices the police talking to a short, middle-aged woman with a blinding white-blond ponytail. Beside her are two small girls wearing diminutive life jackets. The boat's owner? If so, she's the friend of Carla that George Volker mentioned, Shire Kiminsky. Another looker—this town seems loaded with them—but way too wholesome for his taste. The appeal of the girl-next-door types has always been a mystery to him. He likes women a little less pristine looking. Carla Merino, for example.

Shire Kiminsky looks distraught, close to tears. But she's no china doll. Ignoring the muck in the recovered boat—she also wears the brown rubber knee boots that seem de rigueur among the locals—she hops down into it. With obvious experience, she scrutinizes the damage to the outboard. The little girls stand on the dock in matching boots of their own, looking up at the uniformed giants towering over them.

"She was heading for your cabin on Loon?" a Trooper about D'Angelo's size asks Shire Kiminsky. "Any chance she made it to the island? I mean, maybe she just didn't tie the skiff off well enough? Boat drifted off during the night, swamped? You said she doesn't have a phone. Maybe she's over there asleep in a warm bed?"

"I don't think so. When Fish and Game called to say somebody found the skiff, I phoned Heidi Skirlin. She lives down the beach. Nobody's been there."

"Anything missing from the boat?" someone asks her.

She stands in the skiff, looking alternately sad and perplexed. "I keep most stuff lashed down or stowed. But everything that was in this locker is gone." She flips the locker open. "Fire extinguisher, hip boots, survival suit, first-aid kit. The key is on the ring I gave to Carla. She must have gotten the locker open before she went into the water. Maybe trying to get some floatation. Looks like one of the life vests is gone too."

"Survival suit?" a Trooper asks. "You carry an immersion suit in your skiff?"

"I was using it to train Carla." Her voice catches. "She was going to crew on my brother's boat next month." She looks at her little girls.

The Trooper presses on. "Is your friend capable of suiting up in a swamping boat?"

"She got pretty good at it—for a girl from a big city in the middle of a desert. But that would be a tough stunt in a storm." Her voice cracks. "God, I should've never let her—"

"If she's in the suit, still floating out there," the female reporter asks, "would she still be alive? The water being as cold as it is?"

"If she's in a good immersion suit, maybe." The Trooper looks at his watch. "Figure she went into the water around midnight during the storm. That's nine hours, ten maybe. That's a long time, but we've got the chopper out, our boats searching the downwind beaches and coves. We can hope." He pauses, grimaces. "But if she's just in a life vest . . ."

"Aw, jeez," Shire Kiminsky says, sobbing openly now. "*Carla*." She climbs up out of the skiff and takes her daughters' hands. They cling to her, looking equally distraught.

The authorities talk some more, asking her for information about the missing Carla Merino. D'Angelo already knows as much or more about her than they do, except where she is, and if she's alive or not. Only Carla Merino knows those two things. Unless, of course, she isn't alone. That idea starts pecking at his brain like a hungry crow.

The actual birders board the catamaran, so D'Angelo walks back to the ramp and starts up toward the parking lot above. He runs straight into George Volker coming down it.

Volker stops abruptly fifteen feet uphill from D'Angelo as if he just stepped on an invisible rake, a stunned look on his face. His eyes shoot side to side, like he's thinking of bolting, maybe even diving into the harbor. D'Angelo walks up close, smile in place. "Pretend I'm an old friend," he says softly. "Right now, dipshit. Do it. Say hello and look happy to see me." He takes Volker's right hand in his. Now Volker looks like he really *is* going to jump. D'Angelo grips that wrist with his other hand. He smiles even wider, like he is delighted to find his old ponytailed friend there. "The police can't protect you from me." Still smiling like the birth of a star, he adds, "Smile, or I'll feed you to the crabs. Understand?"

Volker manages a pained grin, a nod. "I got a call. I have to talk to the Troopers."

"Good. Go on down to the docks and talk to them. Just never mention our chat last night about Carla. Never mention me at all. Right?"

Volker nods again.

D'Angelo releases Volker's hand. Loudly, he adds, "Hey, thanks for the tip on the End of the Road omelets. First class!" He turns away, takes two steps up the ramp, and looks back down over his shoulder. Volker, still planted in place, is staring up at him, a sick look on his face. "That crab is so delicious," D'Angelo calls out. "What on earth do those creatures eat?"

When Volker turns and continues down the ramp, D'Angelo climbs the rest of the way to the top. He walks along the plank boardwalk and into the aroma cloud of frying food. The omelet he ate earlier was first class indeed, but much too small. He looks at his watch. It's just after nine AM. If he eats a second breakfast now, he can fit another meal in before dinner. He's going to be in this town until Carla Merino shows up, and his instincts are crackling. Her missing body. The missing survival suit. Is this his training at work? Or is it his persistent hunger that's making him feel she's still alive somehow? If she is, it's somewhere close by. After all, this is the end of the road and the beginning of nothing but water. How far can a person get from here without a boat?

He'll stick around a couple days, try the restaurants, look at the birds, check out the local women in their rubber knee boots. If Carla *does* wash up dead and proves him wrong, he'll admit his error and find some way to take apart her truck. Though not right there in the parking lot of Volker's bar. It will take a lot of work to disable the security cameras, hot-wire the truck, and drive it somewhere more private. All without being noticed. He hopes she's alive; it would be so much easier to just ask her for that photo. Especially as persuasive as he can be.

Elicitation—the art of drawing information out of people—is essential in his trade.

24

VOLKER STANDS BESIDE Shire, listening to the cops question her. One of the young coastguardsmen gawks, unaware how obviously he's ogling her. She's a mom, and forty-five, but still a knockout—although, in Volker's opinion, his own ponytail looks better than hers. Usually high energy and lively, she's quiet now. He's never seen her look so glum. Carla and Shire became close almost as soon as Carla arrived in town. It looks like Shire misses her as much as he does.

He realizes the cops are done with her and talking to him now.

"So, you said Ms. Merino stopped in the bar late last night?" an extremely serious Trooper asks. The cop is a stranger to Volker. Volker would remember this guy trying to fit in under the Orca's low doorway. He's rail thin and very tall—even for the Staties, who like them large. And no sense of humor—again, even by Trooper standards of mandatory humorlessness. He wears his hat with the chin strap cinched so tight it looks like he's trying to hang himself. Volker resists the urge to ask if that hurts. His name tag says *Sgt. Demmet*.

"Yes, we talked around midnight, I guess."

"Did you argue?"

"Not really," Volker says. "It was friendly. She said Shire loaned her the skiff. I told her to be careful."

The Trooper turns to Shire. "Did you witness that conversation, ma'am?"

Shire shakes her head, wipes her eyes. "I was off last night, home with my kids." She glances toward Irene and Alice, lying on the dock on their bellies, heads hanging over the edge, watching the writhing white sea anemones clinging to the pilings in the water below. "The girls and I canned salmon and watched *The Little Mermaid*. Again." She snorts a half laugh and dissolves into tears.

Sergeant Demmet's nostrils quiver at her display of emotion.

Volker reaches an arm around her and squeezes in what he hopes is a comforting way. Dispensing comfort isn't usually the reason he puts his hands on women. "The bar was pretty empty," he tells the dour Trooper. "But I'll give you the names of the three regulars who heard me and Carla talking. Believe me, there is nothing on this earth those guys would like more than sharing the details with you."

Sergeant Demmet nods, unsmiling and clearly waiting for Volker to volunteer something more, something incriminating, maybe. Volker has served uncountable thousands of drinks to cops of every kind over the years, and he knows they suspect everyone of something. It's hard to blame them. If you have a job where people lie to you every chance they get, you can't help thinking everybody's lying to you. The skipper of the halibut boat in the next slip has told the cops he saw Carla take Shire's skiff out *alone* a few minutes before midnight. Still, Trooper Stone Face here looks very hungry for a collar.

"Is there anything else, Officer?" Volker keeps it as sweet as he can. A lifetime of cultivated sarcasm makes that difficult. Still, he's willing to try. That's just the kind of great guy he is.

"You see any strangers around the bar last night?"

"Nobody special." Volker involuntarily glances back and sees Cosmo D'Angelo up on the boardwalk overlooking the marina, pretending to be reading the menu pinned to the door of High Tide Fish & Chips. If the lanky Trooper's face is made of rock, D'Angelo's is pure ice. Mostly it's the way the bastard can shift from deep-space cold to long-lost-pal mode without blinking. Now *that* is scary.

He hears Sergeant Demmet's voice coming in from the edge of his consciousness. Even in full Sherlock Holmes mode, he must see this was an accident. He's losing interest. "Okay," he says with a sigh, as if he's obliged to ask one more thing. "Is Ms. Merino's vehicle still parked in your lot?"

"It was there a few minutes ago. Toyota Tacoma. Two thousand one, I think."

"Do you have a key?"

"There's an extra stashed in one of those magnetic boxes, up in the left rear wheel well."

Sergeant Demmet writes again.

Volker glances back up at the boardwalk. D'Angelo is still dicking around, running one finger down the menu signboard like it's the most fascinating thing he's ever read.

Demmet is saying something. "Mr. Volker, call if you think of anything else." He hands him an Alaska State Trooper card.

Volker guesses it's his week to collect cards from various jerks. "Sure, right."

"I'd like to take a look at Miss Merino's truck now," Demmet says. His radio goes off. He steps away and answers the call. When he's done, he turns back to Volker. "I have to go. I'll meet you at your bar later this morning." He tips his hat to Shire and walks away down the dock.

Volker glances up at the boardwalk in time to see Cosmo D'Angelo disappear into High Tide Fish & Chips.

Shire is very quiet. Even the twins are subdued. One of them—Volker can't tell them apart—says, "Mom, is Carla in heaven now?"

Shire looks like she's going to start crying again. She crouches to their level. "I think it would make Carla laugh to hear you say that." She pats the girl on the head. "No, I don't think she's going to heaven anytime soon. Not Carla. I think she's out there waiting for us to find her." She looks out across the harbor at the cut in the jetty. "If I can get the motor fixed, we'll go out today and look for her, okay?"

The girls lean into Shire in an impromptu three-way hug. One of them throws a tiny arm around Volker's leg and tries to pull him into it. He finds something like a smile to stick across his mouth and silently renews his personal oath to never date women with children, strong religious beliefs, or food allergies. It is impossible to compete with stuff like that.

Shire looks up at him and says, "Poor Carla."

"Yeah," Volker says, staring up at High Tide Fish & Chips. "You got that right. Poor Carla."

25

So, Carla Merino has apparently drowned. D'Angelo has to wonder why he doubts that. A hunch? Is it too convenient, or too farfetched? Not really. People who live on the water like this drown all the time. The problem is that Carla's name is going to pop on Sidewinder's name-recognition-alert list when the Coast Guard declares her missing. He needs to call Andy Krall and get him to make sure nobody at the office sees that and wants to know why she's on that list.

He tries Andy's number. It goes straight to voice mail. D'Angelo leaves him a vague message that doesn't mention Carla's name. As he hangs up, a young and almost frighteningly friendly waitress ushers him to a booth in the High Tide restaurant overlooking the bay. Outside the big window, boats cut sun-sparkled wakes across the water and gulls careen into the light surf.

"Best table in the house," the girl says.

It's too early for the lunch rush, and she has no one but him to fuss over. She leans across the table for the unneeded silverware on the far side. She smells of something earthy. Incense? Pot? Patchouli, maybe.

"Coffee?"

She has long brown hair that glows with the chemical sheen of self-inflicted, bargain-priced dyes. Her face is the color of pork & beans, a hue no doubt requiring plenty of sun bed assistance in the brief and mostly cloudy Alaskan summers. A pale gold stud glitters on the side of one nostril. She flashes him a smile like a piano keyboard. He has a weak spot the size of Australia for waitresses. But not this goofy, or this young.

"How old are you?" he asks.

"Old enough to know better but young enough not to care." More teeth. She hovers, grinning conspiratorially.

"Well, then, uh"—he reads her name tag—"Tara Ann, I'll keep that in mind. If it's okay for now, I think I'll just have an espresso and a look at a lunch menu. I *can* get lunch this early, right?"

"You can get anything you want."

"Good to know," he says neutrally. He decides to halt the word play before Tara Ann implodes. "Give me a minute."

"Suit yourself." She emits a tiny sigh and strolls off.

D'Angelo scans the menu. He expects nothing more than the usual fish and chips but is pleased to see the place has a few enticing local items. He's trying to decide between the razor-clam fritters and the salmon-and-cod cakes when Tara Ann returns and places the cup of steaming espresso on the table next to his phone. She stands there beaming like she's single-handedly cultivated, picked, and roasted the beans herself.

As D'Angelo opens his mouth to order the clams, his phone starts vibrating on the tabletop. The salt and pepper shakers tremble. Concentric rings emanate across the surface of the espresso.

Tara Ann says, "I have that effect on men."

D'Angelo reads the incoming number on the vibrating phone and feels his mood tank. It's not Andy Krall.

Tara Ann hovers over him with her order pad. He gives her a dismissive look. "I need more time to decide."

She pouts and wanders off.

D'Angelo stares at the incoming number. A chill runs down his arms. Phil Lundren instead of Andy. He tastes his espresso and picks up the phone. No sense pretending he doesn't know why Lundren is calling. "That was fast, Phil. The woman just drowned last night. You're taking time out from Gordon's campaign to deal with this?"

"I can't say I'm happy about it." Lundren has perfected his menacing tone as he's climbed higher in the company. The guy can't wish you a happy birthday without it sounding like a threat. "Your phone tells us you're already there. Homer, Alaska? That means you'd already located the Merino woman yesterday, *before* she went into the drink."

This isn't good at all.

"Her name popped already?" He asks what he already knows to buy a little time.

"Yes indeed. Carla Teresa Merino. One of our earnest young techies discovered she's someone we've been searching for. Only, here's the good part"—Lundren pauses for effect—"*we* haven't been looking for her. But someone near and dear to us has." The irritation in his voice amps up a notch. "You've been busy in your spare time the past couple months, my friend."

"One of the children traced it to me already? Wow, that was fast."

"Yeah, wow," Lundren says. "And I'm just now hearing about this woman you've been tracking so covertly that no one in your own office even knows about it? Except your pal Andy Krall, I assume. Two months? This does *not* make me comfortable."

"I was doing a background check. Protecting myself from ruthless women. A sweet guy like me could get taken advantage of."

Lundren knows how to play that game. "You know what your problem is, Cosmo?"

"Which one?"

"Your problem is you actually *like* women."

D'Angelo resists the temptation to retort.

Lundren sighs dramatically. "Okay, you don't want to talk about Carla Merino? Fine. Let's talk about your daughter, then. Let's talk about Jennifer. Any new thoughts on her quest to destroy us while she was still alive?"

While she was still alive. Lundren definitely knows how to play. D'Angelo is thrown off a beat, which leaves him staring out the window, considering hanging up.

A mature bald eagle soars past and lands on the beach in the middle of a cluster of gulls, scattering them like billiard balls in a hard break. The eagle hops a few feet to the fish carcass the gulls were sharing, pins it under one huge foot, and rips into it with its hooked yellow beak. You don't have to be the earliest bird to get the fish, just the fiercest. It looks a lot like the world D'Angelo works in. Talking about Jennifer is still difficult. Talking about her to Lundren is torture.

"Phil, you know that Jennifer and I barely spoke for the past couple years because of her feelings about Gordon. What the hell does any of that have to do with Carla Merino?"

"A couple months ago, a source we have at the *Times* told us that pain-in-the-ass so-called journalist Lisa Yi was wetting herself about a photo that supposedly puts Gordon alongside a certain Colombian colonel back in the nineties. A photo someone was giving to her."

"And?"

"And this morning a flag went up on Carla Merino's name, so the analysts pulled everything you've been accumulating, Cosmo. Including her phone records showing that Merino called Lisa Yi the same day she vanished from Phoenix, Arizona, of all places—where you happen to live. Today she turns up apparently dead in Homer, Alaska. And what do you know? Our old friend Cosmo D'Angelo is there too."

"So what? Carla Merino and Lisa Yi went to college together. Carla was probably telling her about this tall, handsome guy she met in Phoenix. How charming he is."

Not knowing how much information Lundren has on where that photo came from, he can only stall. Maybe Lundren will get struck by lightning in the next minute or two. Maybe one of his ex-wives will walk in and shoot him. One can hope. "I still don't see this connecting to Jennifer."

"Let's say, just as a wild guess, your daughter the anti-McKint fanatic acquired the photo somehow and couldn't publish it herself because *gofactyourself.com* has no credibility anymore. Say she knew your girlfriend, Carla Merino in Phoenix. And say she gave Merino the thing to give to Yi at the *Times* because Yi and Merino are old sorority sisters."

This isn't the worst-case scenario for D'Angelo. Lundren thinks Jennifer gave the photo to Carla. He's out of the equation in that theory. So far. Unless Lundren is just throwing him a curve here. "Then why hasn't the *Times* printed it yet?" he asks.

"Because Carla Merino didn't give it to them. She stole it and disappeared."

"What? You're looking at my search materials, Phil. Carla Merino's not remotely political or connected to anybody spooky. Why would she steal the thing?"

"To blackmail Gordon, of course. If such a picture exists, he'd pay plenty to have it disappear once and for all time. Who wouldn't?"

"And has Carla Merino tried to blackmail Gordon? I haven't heard about that."

"No." Lundren coughs, clears his throat. "Maybe she's trying to get up the nerve. Like you said, she's a civilian. How's she going to know how to hand the photo off to Gordon McKint for ransom money without us coming down on her like the wrath of God—which we most certainly would?"

"How do I fit into this delusion?"

"Maybe your daughter asked *you* to get the thing back from Merino. Maybe that's why you got friendly with her at the restaurant. But then Merino split."

"Phil, I met Carla Merino in a bar the night I got back in the country from a job I was doing for you. She and I had a little fun. She left town suddenly the next day. Her family is worried about her. I'm trying to find her to help them out. It's a simple story you're trying to make complicated. I don't know anything about any legendary photo. And Carla Merino is a dead end now. Literally. An hour ago, I saw that boat she sank being towed into the docks."

"If she's as dead as you say she is, what are you still doing on the coast of Alaska?"

"Waiting to see if the body turns up," he lies smoothly. "For the sake of her family. If you like, I'll check and see if she left behind a photo labeled *Secret Picture of Gordon McKint*."

"Tell you what," Lundren says, "why don't I send someone to help you find her. You know . . . dead or alive, as they say."

D'Angelo feels his heart rush a beat. This is definitely not the way he wants this conversation to go. Tara Ann is heading back toward his table. "No need to send anyone, Phil. But thanks for the offer. Great talking with you. Gotta go."

"Wait!" Phil Lundren breathes, obviously choosing his words with care. "Cosmo, you're a valuable asset. Don't make me fix this."

D'Angelo hangs up. His phone immediately rings again. Lundren. He shuts it down.

Tara Ann waves her order pad at him. "Decided?"

He shakes his head. "Change of plans. I have to go."

He leaves money and walks out into the morning light and the racket of the always-screaming gulls.

He tries Andy Krall again. Andy might be able to tip him off if Lundren is sending someone to find him. Plus, he should apologize for getting Andy in trouble.

Andy's phone goes straight to voice mail once again.

Lundren's words *dead or alive* were clearly not limited to Carla Merino.

"Damn."

26

Dısguısıng Carla as a deckhand is their plan, and that seems to have put Scott in good spirits. He's bright-eyed and calm as he steers the *"C" Lady* back across the bay to the town. At his insistence, Carla stays inside the cabin, but the huge windows offer a 360-degree view. The morning is clear and calm at the moment, the minimal wave tips dancing with sunlight. Birds everywhere, taking off from or landing on the sparkling blue surface. A spectacular Alaskan summer day unfolding. Scott points as they pass a mother otter floating on her back, her young pup perched on her belly. Carla smiles. It should make her feel good to be moving, but the closer they get to town, the more her nerves twitch.

Scott doesn't seem to notice. He's busy keeping an eye on all the other vessels crisscrossing the bay. Carla can't help wondering if one of them is carrying Cosmo D'Angelo, armed, angry, and determined to prevent her from using that photo.

She forces herself to find something else to think about, to talk about. "This is a nice boat, Scott," she says. "It's kind of big for one guy, isn't it?"

Scott laughs. "It's way too big for one guy. My folks left it to me when they died. They had a charter business in summers. I crewed on it with them when I was in high school, before I started working on the big commercial crabbers and such. I'd never buy one this big—even if I could afford it, which I can't. I sort of keep it for the memories, I guess."

When they get close to the spit, he says, "Here's the plan. You go down into the bunk area and stay low now while we're docked. I'll swab the deck and wash the salt off the windows and get the boat shipshape. All the things I usually do, so the guys in the next slips don't think anything is out of the ordinary. Okay?"

Carla nods.

"Then I'll lock you in and go pick up some work clothes for you. Stay belowdeck and away from the windows while I'm gone."

She starts down the stairs to the bunk area and stops. "You're sure this is going to work?"

"Yeah, really. The harbor's going to be super busy on a day like today. People coming and going all over the place. Nobody is going to notice one more young deckhand. You'll be fine. Now, get down."

Carla climbs down the stairs and sits on the edge of the bunk, telling herself she'll be as fine as Scott seems to think she will. When she feels the boat suddenly slow to enter the small boat harbor, her heart skips. Again she tells herself not to worry. In a few minutes, the boat bumps against the dock and she hears Scott go out. His footsteps are heavy on the deck above her as he does something to tie them to the dock. Then he comes back in and shuts the engines down. A thick silence prevails in the claustrophobic sleeping area.

She looks up the stairs and watches him stow his fishing rod in the cabin, put some kind of weights in buckets on the back deck. He looks down at her. "I'm going to hook up the freshwater hose and the shore power." He goes outside and washes down the decks with a garden hose, scrubbing them with a long-handled brush. Several people he apparently knows walk by on the docks, and he chats briefly. About fishing. About boats. When he's done, he leans into the cabin door and quietly says, "I'm taking off. You okay?"

"I'm fine," she says, but suddenly feels sick, her stomach knotting. She looks up the stairs at the windows in the cabin above, D'Angelo on her mind again. "I'll be all right," she says. She can hear her own voice quavering.

Scott walks back into the cabin and comes down the stairs.

"What's the matter? This is going to work."

She chuckles ruefully. "My mother would love to see me now. She always said I was going to get into serious trouble one day. If she knew about D'Angelo, she'd hork up a lung screaming *I told you so.*"

Scott says, "That's at least the second time you've mentioned your mother. Last time you made some crack about wanting to hurt her. What's up with you and her?"

Carla exhales. "I don't know. Maybe it was just normal teenage girl stuff. But it got pretty ugly." She relaxes a bit, talking. "Adults—parents—have all the power. Bad behavior is the only weapon a kid has. I figured that out in junior high and started running wild."

"Running wild?" Scott waggles his eyebrows comically. "Love to hear the juicy details."

"Let's just say I was a very naughty girl, and my mother and I still have sort of a hate/hate relationship."

"Yikes."

She has to laugh. "Yeah, yikes."

"Okay, look." He sits next to her on the bunk. "I'd love all the details, but right now I'm going to go get those work clothes for you, and we're going to get away from here and up to Anchor Point. You'll feel a lot better there."

"You don't have to do this, Scott," she says. "I told you I didn't ask for a prince."

"Maybe I always wanted to be royalty." He's trying to cheer her up. She has to like him for that. "I mean, what am I supposed to do, feed you to this shark? Or turn you over to the police, which would be the same thing? Even if they lock you up, there are ways for people to get to you inside any jail."

"God," she says, "I don't want to die wearing orange. Not with my coloring."

Scott smiles, clearly happy to have her joking. "Just stay hidden for now." He puts an arm around her shoulders and gives her a squeeze. Carla feels something more than simple safety in it. She's happy to have it but not sure this is what they need right now.

Scott may have had the same thought. He pulls his arm away a little too quickly.

"All right then," he says. "I'll be back in an hour. We'll hustle you out of here and tuck you in at my house on the river until we find a way to get that picture out of your truck."

"This is a first, a man clothes-shopping for me."

"It's a first for me too."

He climbs the stairs.

She leans out from the bunk and watches him slide the cabin door closed. She hears the lock snap shut and goes cold. The thought that D'Angelo might already be in Homer looms in her mind, dread rising in her veins. Now she can't run if she wanted to.

She calms herself. Scott's a good man. And she's already missing his company in a way that's surprising. Is she feeling something genuine for him? Or is she just using him the way her mother uses men to get what she wants?

*   *   *

There were always men in the house, from early childhood to the day Carla moved out when she was fifteen. Most were harmless enough. Tragic, really. Fools.

Then Ashton Bolt moved in.

It was the first time her mother broke her own rule of keeping only men who could pay their way. And hers. Ashton was an adjunct English professor at the college. He could barely pay his phone bill. He made little money on his books, despite the "huge fuss" (her mother's words) that critics were making about his latest collection of poems.

It was a whole new situation. Ashton didn't take her mother out to dinner. Didn't add to her already overstuffed jewelry cache. He took no interest in the house or the pool. And he certainly wasn't financing remodeling projects. In fact, it seemed that her mother was taking care of *him*. He drove a Kia, for Christ's sake. But Ashton was a "nationally recognized" poet, her mother was quick to point out. The prestige he brought her among the art crowd was heady. For the first time in Carla's life, her mother seemed almost happy. Which might have been nice for Carla too. If not for Ashton.

He was the first of her mother's men to notice Carla in a creepy way. He kept it subtle enough in front of her mother. Who could be more subtle than a poet? But he also made sure Carla was aware. Lechy looks. Pervy comments. It went on for weeks. At first she almost liked the attention, considered using it to provoke her mother. But she was too smart to get into a sexualized competition with a grown woman of her mother's vast experience. Her mother was either oblivious to the whole thing or pretending to be.

When Ashton finally went too far, Carla told her mother. The reaction was predictably disappointing. Her mother didn't blame Ashton. Didn't even consider throwing his child-molesting ass out of the house. Sure, Carla had been sleeping around with boys since ninth grade. But she was only fifteen. Ashton was thirty-five. And her mother completely came down on *his* side? Carla was a whore. A cock tease. She had to hear about the slutty way she dressed. As usual.

It was their last big fight. And Carla's last night under that roof.

*   *   *

Why is she thinking about Ashton Bolt now, more than twenty years later? A better question might be, how the hell has she ended up locked in the cabin of a boat in a harbor on the coast of Alaska?

The glimmer of optimism Scott's escape plan momentarily inspired is fading fast. She can't help thinking that if things really go sideways and D'Angelo somehow finds her, she might die right here in this bunk. On this boat. In this marina. In a town that's barely a speck on the lonely edge of the continent. Her mother always said men would be the death of them both. *Even your mother is right sometimes.*

Unable to relax, she gets up and goes into the bathroom.

Throw some water on your face. Snap out of this!

The light from the single porthole in the tiny room is meager. The mirror is spotlessly clean—no surprise there—but old and marbled with silver streaks. She squints into the clouded glass and shudders at the sight. Her hair is clumped and snarled, sticky from the seawater. She looks like one of the homeless women in the parks in Phoenix. Walking wreckage, from their bedroom slippers to their floppy hats. This isn't just the sinking skiff and the dunking in the bay. This is what two months of relentless fear looks like.

She leans closer to the mirror again and sees not only her face but her whole life.

This is Carla Merino. Almost forty years old and still waiting tables. She might be doing that at fifty. Sixty. Still hauling heavy trays, back aching, shoulders frozen, veins going blue.

That future—or one like it—is already starting to show in her tired face. Yes, she's still a good-looking woman. Always will be. Good features. Strong chin. Great nose.

But being young again?

That ship has sailed. And what's left behind on the dock is looking pretty rough right now.

She bites her lip and shakes her head.

She has an idea.

It's not going to make her any younger, but it might keep her alive long enough to start taking care of herself. That thought stops her. Jesus, she's in a truly life-and-death situation and she's fucking around with her appearance? Well, vanity is as good a reason to keep living as any.

Plus, Scott is looking for a disguise for her. Maybe she can help with that.

He said there were sharp knives in the drawer. She crouches as she climbs the stairs and crawls on her hands and knees to the galley, pulls on a drawer. It clatters open. There are four or five knives of different sizes and types. Also a pair of heavy kitchen scissors. Even better.

Carla takes them and crawls back down the stairs to the bathroom. The sink bowl is about the size of a bucket, and she can't get her head under the faucet. So she splashes handfuls of water on her hair and combs it out with her fingers as best she can. Then she pulls a thick lock of it straight down against her collar bone and snips it even with her chin. For the first time ever, she wishes she had been a hairdresser, not a social worker.

She gets it mostly even all the way around and cleans up the hair clippings. Rinses out the sink. She checks the new haircut in the mirror, running her fingers through it again, the ends jagged in spite of her best efforts. It's a different look for her, and that's at least part of the purpose.

She yanks her blue bandanna off the bathroom door handle and wraps her hair down. Only the saw-toothed ends protrude. It gives her something of a pirate look. She hopes.

Her shirt is wet now, and the galley stove has gone cold. Shivering, she climbs back into the sleeping bag just as the porthole above her bunk goes dark like a shutter has dropped. She jumps, nerves charged, until she realizes it's only the weather changing again. The first slanting splatters of rain streak the glass. Carla pulls the sleeping bag up tighter under her chin, thinking how she's been spending her life lately. All the one-night stands. All the harmless mementos she managed to accumulate.

Yes, it's been admittedly empty, but without serious trouble.

Until Cosmo D'Angelo came along.

The rain falls harder.

CHAPTER

27

ON THE DRIVE between the marina and the Salvation Army store, a moss-green sky spits rain across Scott's windshield. Continents of cloud shadows collide on the bay. The rain builds in hesitant fits. He flips the wipers on as the droplets accumulate.

All along Pioneer Avenue, tourists stroll the sidewalks wrapped head to ankles in Gore-Tex and nylon and rubber. Patches of blue sky lean against the heavy gray shoulders of an incoming cloud bank as if trying to push it back out into the Gulf of Alaska. Then a squall unloads, sheeting the windshield, pummeling the truck roof.

The weather just can't make up its mind. Brother, does he know that feeling. On the way to the thrift shop, he felt so relieved to be off the boat and away from Carla, he actually slowed in front of the police station. Almost flipped the turn signal on. All he had to do was walk in and start talking. Only he didn't.

Now he sits in the parking lot, waiting for the squall to back off to make a dash for it. Is he really going to do this? Buy Carla a disguise, smuggle her out of town and up the road to his house on the river? And then . . . ?

What in the hell is he doing? Deceiving the Coast Guard—after all, he owes them for saving his life. Defying some professional killer. Potentially antagonizing Gordon McKint, one of the most infamously dangerous men in America. Risking his own life for a woman he found floating alongside his boat. The question is a fair one. Well, he's wanted something exciting to happen for a long time. Carla is certainly that. The last ten hours have already been more interesting than the last ten years.

Sure, he could call the Troopers, meet them at the boat, turn her over. And then what? Explain how she happened to be tucked away in the *"C" Lady*, safe and dry, miles from where Shire's skiff was found?

He's reaching for the door handle when a big black Lincoln Navigator pulls up next to him in the parking lot. It's exactly the kind of rig goons from shady organizations like Sidewinder Security drive in TV shows. His nerves quiver. The driver of this one, however, is a large square-headed woman with short pink hair. Scott has seen her around town. Trina knows her from the library guild or something. She's finishing an ice cream cone. He relaxes, chiding himself for the paranoia.

"Car food," Trina called it one time as she and Scott were walking across the Safeway lot and noticed a similarly large woman slouched behind her steering wheel, eating a deep-red cupcake. "What dieters eat in the car before they go home with the family groceries," Trina explained. "Bet you a hundred dollars the back seat's full of nutritious low-fat everything."

Trina always told him he should be more observant about the world around him—about people, especially. It's another thing he's going to work on, now that he's free to reinvent himself. *Reinvent.* He saw that word in a magazine at the place where Trina insisted he get his hair cut—where she gets her hair cut. It was an article about some snotty celebrity who had recently refurbished a tarnished public image. *Reinvent.* Scott likes the sound of it. Maybe that's what he's doing right now, here at the Salvation Army store. An ordinary carpenter and home builder, about to buy a disguise for the good-looking, presumed-dead cocktail waitress he has stashed on his boat. A woman being hunted by a trained assassin.

He gets out of the truck. The rain slows to a sprinkle as suddenly as it started. The woman in the car next to him pops the remnant tip of the ice cream cone into her mouth and climbs out. He follows her into the store.

Reinventing himself?

Sure, why not? At this rate, he might be the Thomas Edison of self-reinvention.

28

T HE RAIN SLOWS to a sprinkle again as D'Angelo drives by the Orca and once more looks at Carla's truck, still parked behind the building. It's possible that the photo is at the bottom of the bay in her pocket. But, if Volker was telling the truth—he's pretty sure Volker is too scared to lie to him—Carla took all her clothes and things from his house. It's unlikely she would take them out in the skiff. So the truck and camper now hold everything she owned. Unless something else turns up soon, D'Angelo is going to have to take it apart, no matter how inconveniently visible the damned thing is.

He needs to get to it before Lundren sends so-called *help*.

Given the security cameras—and in spite of the bright mercury lights—he'll have to break into it in the few hours of near-dark around midnight. Preferably with a very loud diversion, and a face mask. He hopes he has time to wait until tonight.

All of this is assuming that Carla is actually dead. It wouldn't be due diligence to ignore the alternative possibility that both she and the photo are together and perfectly safe. Some kind of scam, organized to make him think she's gone, isn't out of the question. Given unlimited time, D'Angelo could hang around until either her body shows up or she makes a mistake and reveals herself. But thanks to fucking Lundren and the threat of his muscle arriving in town, it has to be a rush job now. Never ideal.

In the meantime, there's someone he needs to talk to.

He parks outside the harbor master's office overlooking the small-boat harbor, waits for it to empty. Through the windshield he watches the mostly unsuspicious people of this place. In spite of the suddenly rainy weather, scores of sightseers—as ubiquitous up and down the spit as the bald eagles, gulls, and ever-present crows—loiter about. They seem oblivious to the drizzle and are no doubt innocent of nefarious intent. Down in the marina, a half dozen kayakers—slender, fitter-than-thou types—load brightly colored fiberglass sea kayaks onto the deck of a water taxi. Fishermen of all sizes and shapes come and go from boats of all sizes and shapes, carrying tackle and ice chests and the long-handled nets everyone seems to own. The entire town appears to be clad in all-weather gear. Raincoats. Rubber pants. And those brown rubber knee boots, of course. Mere shitty weather is not going to keep these people indoors.

Whether or not Carla Merino actually died in that bay, a whole lot of fish are destined to.

A big, white-bearded fisherman wearing what looks like a nineteenth-century Russian shirt, modern jeans, and knee boots exits the office. The harbor master appears to be alone. D'Angelo heads for the door, considering how best to get the information he needs. He knows better than to lean on a guy in a position of authority like the harbor master. This will take guile—which is a lot more interesting than muscle anyway.

29

TRYING TO KEEP the cool, sea-damp air out of the sleeping bag, Carla pulls the thing snug around her again. Another cold draft finds its way in anyway.

"Shit!" She slides down into the bag until her feet hit the bottom.

How long has Scott been gone? It feels like hours.

There in the bunk area, the walls veer together to form the bow of the boat. With the porthole gone dark, they feel like they're closing in. She tries to relax but feels like she's lying in a huge vise, a giant hand cranking the walls of the boat tight around her.

If she could just go up into the main cabin with its big windows, maybe she could see the horizon, the mountains across the bay, the old inactive volcanoes, the glaciers. It's funny how she's become used to those snowy rock piles. No, it's more than that, more than just being comfortable there among them. She's actually begun to feel at home here, the relentless daylight notwithstanding. And now she'll have to leave. Find a new place to live. How the hell do you get a new identity?

The walls move closer. What would it hurt to just go up into the cabin and take a look around if she stays low?

She crawls up the stairs on her hands and knees. Slides on her belly onto the bench seat on one side of the galley table. Staying very low, she raises her head just enough to see over the bottom sill of the window facing the ramp and harbor master's and the shops and parking lots.

Outside the rain-splattered glass, the world looks normal enough. Rubber-clad fishermen, boat owners, tourists coming and going. Just another wet summer day at the end of the road, Alaska. Was she expecting to find Cosmo D'Angelo in full combat gear looming on the other side of the window? Why does he have to be some kind of commando assassin or something? It seems that in a better, more just universe, she could have met a lot more men without this happening.

In the midst of her thoughts, she realizes someone is coming down the dock directly toward the *"C" Lady*. A woman in a red raincoat. Carla crawls back down the stairs and into the bunk. She hears footsteps on the deck, then the metallic rattle of someone fiddling with the padlock. She cranes her neck around the corner of the bunk and peers up the stairs. Through the small window on the cabin door, she sees a woman's head, thick black hair fluttering over her shoulders in the rising wind. The door slides open on its runner.

Carla ducks back into the bunk, presses herself against the wall under the porthole.

The woman steps into the cabin. She has a key. It can only be Scott's ex-wife. Trina, Carla thinks he called her. She hears the woman moving something. Opening cupboards, opening drawers. Lifting something, dropping it again—the lid on one of the storage compartments. She's searching for something. Carla cringes in the bunk and crushes herself against the wall.

The woman apparently finds whatever she's looking for and goes quiet. Carla can hear her muttering. She has to peek. Can't help herself. She reaches back to pull her hair tight and hold it behind her head, then remembers that she's cut most of it off. She makes sure the bandanna is secure and presses half her face out far enough to see the woman.

She's sitting at the galley table, head down over a notepad, writing something. She has olive skin, black eyebrows, thick black hair with a silvering part down the middle. When she finishes writing, she stands suddenly, yanks her hood up, and pulls the zipper up to her chin like the gesture is punctuating her last sentence. Carla ducks back into the bunk.

"Fuck yourself, Scott," the woman says, resignedly. "Just fuck yourself."

Then Carla hears the pen hit the tabletop. Footsteps. The door slides shut, the padlock clicks again.

When she's certain the woman is gone, she crawls up the stairs and under the galley table. She reaches up and feels around until she touches the notepad, pulls it down. On it the woman has written,

I signed today. It's officially over. I hope you're happy. Actually, I don't give a shit if you're happy or not. You can have your precious boat. But I took my lucky flasher and hoochie. I hope you never catch another fish again as long as you live.

It's signed, *Jesus Fucking Christ.*

Carla slides the notepad back up on the table. She remains underneath, feeling embarrassed and ashamed to have eavesdropped on Scott's private life. His wife's too, now that she thinks about it. Like she doesn't have sufficient drama of her own?

Who was the famous Russian guy who said all happy families are the same, but all unhappy families are unhappy in their own way? Whoever it was, the smart bastard nailed it. Maybe he could explain what the hell a hoochie is too.

Well, Scott has been more than decent to Carla, and she owes him at least the appearance of privacy. When he gets back, maybe she'll tell him she saw his wife come aboard but didn't come out of the bunk. Plus, Carla has to admit, she's kind of liking the big goof a little more than her rescue from the briny deep merits. Thank God she's been too preoccupied to do anything stupid about that.

Yes, she needed him to rescue her when she was in the water. His boat was still on the surface; hers was not. And yes, at the moment, she needs him to help her get out of the harbor unnoticed. And hopefully to get that fucking photo out of her truck. But, goddammit, she does *not* need him in her bed.

She's almost sure of that.

She sits squatting under the table a while longer, considering her relationship with Scott. Listening to the footsteps of people coming and going on the dock, she enjoys the less-claustrophobic openness of the cabin. Then she realizes that someone has stopped walking next to the boat. A shadow looms across the banquette next to her, and her nerves flash. Someone is looming outside the window. She shoots out from under the table and scrambles down the stairs on all fours, hops back into the bunk, trembling.

Christ. She's going to die of a heart attack long before Cosmo D'Angelo ever gets to her.

CHAPTER

30

THE HARBOR MASTER is a thickset guy in his fifties or early six-ties, with short, fine white hair and the tired expression of a man who has spent his life looking people straight in the eye. No doubt the kind of guy who takes his job seriously. This is going to call for more than waitress-melting charm.

D'Angelo leans on the counter top and says, "What's with all the law enforcement in the harbor, chief? Pirates?"

The harbor master chuckles. "Not yet, thank God. A local gal's gone missing, presumed drowned in last night's blow." He straight-ens the papers before him until the counter top is as orderly as every other surface in the room. "What can I do for you?"

With a mix of camaraderie, authority, and neediness in his voice, D'Angelo asks a few questions about the harbor and hints that he's looking for someone who might be on a boat berthed in the marina.

"Is this official?" The harbor master clearly wants to see some ID.

Sometimes looking like a cop helps, sometimes not so much.

"Let's just say I could show you a badge, but not one that fits this particular jurisdiction. Besides, this is outside the purview of my job. It's personal."

The harbor master frowns. "Hmm. Personal." He makes it sound like an embarrassing word he doesn't appreciate hearing spoken.

D'Angelo spies the family photo sitting upright on the man's desk. In it the harbor master sits on a plaid couch between a middle-aged woman and a teenage girl. There is no such photo of D'Angelo with his wife and Jennifer as a teenager. She was four months old when he left.

"You have children?" D'Angelo asks. He doesn't let the harbor master answer. "Even if you don't, you can imagine how far wrong a girl can go in this world today. All the temptations . . ." He sighs like he just lost his last dollar in the world's last slot machine, which is exactly how he feels now talking about fathers and daughters.

"I see," the harbor master says, his frown softening into something less guarded, more concerned.

D'Angelo takes a deep, theatrical breath the way characters in novels are always doing and discovers he's only partly acting. He lets it out like a locomotive braking. "Just hypothetically, say you were looking for a runaway girl who got mixed up in some very ugly, not at all legal stuff . . ." He pauses, letting the harbor master's imagination fill in the blanks. "What I'm saying is, sometimes legit police tools are just not enough. Sometimes a guy's gotta have more in his toolbox than a badge. I'm sure you've seen enough to know what I mean."

"You think she's here in Homer? On one of our boats?" The harbor master is hooked, already considering the possibilities. Then he apparently remembers his position. "We *do* have privacy policies," he says, almost begging D'Angelo to be a real cop on a real case. "Unless it's official, of course."

D'Angelo sags into the counter top like he's been carrying all that weight too long. He feels bad using the actual grief over Jennifer for this performance. Man, this business really is going to turn him into a soulless monster, as Jennifer pointed out to him more than once. Still, you use what you have at your disposal.

He gives the harbor master his weary-fellow-man-of-the-world smile. "Let's just say, what if you followed a girl this far and had an idea that she's gone out on a boat with someone to hide away?"

"Why can't she just get on a plane and fly out?"

"There's an FBI BOLO on her nationwide. She'll pop if her ID gets scanned by TSA."

"Hmm." The harbor master smiles, clearly liking the law-and-order camaraderie, being let in on all this inside information. All those acronyms. "Hypothetically?"

Another pained *We're all in this together* grimace from D'Angelo. "Of course. Say, hypothetically, she needs to stay off the grid for a bit. Where could she get to from here by boat?"

The harbor master turns to a big wall map showing a large chunk of south coastal Alaska and an equal amount of water. He points to the four-mile-long spit of land they're standing on, jutting due south out into the blue of the map. "We're here," he says. "There are small communities and artist colonies and oyster farms right across the bay here, but she'd get noticed in any one of those pretty quick. However . . ."

D'Angelo remains quiet, knowing the man is intent on solving the puzzle, determined now to offer ideas, enjoying being part of this. Whatever it is.

"If she *really* wants to throw somebody off her trail," the harbor master says, "and she has a good enough boat, she might could shoot across the Gulf to Southeast, or even all the way to British Columbia. Even Seattle, I suppose." He stares at the map and scratches the side of his head. "That would take a big boat, given the weather forecast for the next ten days."

"You know every vessel in this harbor, chief. What boats would be right for something like that? One that's fit and seaworthy. Hypothetically, again."

The harbor master thinks about it a second. "It would have to be a pleasure boat. The salmon season is just starting. The sablefish, cod, and rockfish seasons are under way too. And the halibut charters are super busy now. So the commercial guys aren't going to go on a joyride across the Gulf right now when there's money to be made here." He looks out the big windows facing the marina. "There are only so many privately owned boats the size and type you're talking about." He lists some names: *Wavey Days, Dream Weaver, Cape Cook.* "Those all have plenty of freeboard, working galleys, sleeping bunks, good electronics. There are probably a dozen others too."

"That many?" D'Angelo does nothing to hide his disappointment. "How big of a boat are you talking about."

The harbor master pulls his chin. "Well, let's see . . ." He looks past D'Angelo and grins. "Something about that size right there could do it."

D'Angelo turns to the window. A white fiberglass pleasure boat is docked in a slip right below the office. It's maybe forty feet long, wide beamed, with a flying bridge and nice lines. Older, but still a good-looking craft.

"That's the '*C*' *Lady*. It belongs to Scott Crockett. Local guy, a contractor. But trust me, he's not likely to get involved in anything squirrelly. Very straight shooter. Known him for thirty years. My daughter went to school with him. Good guy. Middle of a divorce right now, I'm sorry to say—maybe the first one in town that didn't involve another woman."

"Wow. That *is* a straight shooter."

The harbor master chuckles. "He'd never get mixed up with a runaway girl and drugs and such. Never."

D'Angelo smiles inwardly. He never mentioned drugs and takes a second to thank the gods that Jennifer's many rebellious under-takings didn't include much hard-core substance abuse. Like her father, she was way too serious to let go of control like that. "You're probably right," he says. "I'm grasping at straws here. I should hit the road."

"You know," the harbor master says, offhandedly, "Scott is a certified hero."

"Oh yeah? Iraq or Afghanistan?"

"Neither. Local. Saved a kid on a crabber that went down in the Bering Sea maybe twenty years ago. Risked his own life to get the kid into an immersion suit. Didn't have time to put his own on when the boat sank."

"Hmm. Good for him," D'Angelo says, and means it. "Kind of guy you'd want with you in a tough spot."

"Yes, he is," the harbor master says distractedly. "Kind of odd to see his boat back in here just now, though." He frowns, still looking out the window.

"What do you mean?" D'Angelo's radar kicks on. He keeps his tone innocently curious.

"Well, I talked to him yesterday just before he set out. He said he'd caught a break in his construction work and was going out for three or four days. That man loves his boat and the sea that floats it. Sounded like he was really looking forward to it. Guess he had a change of plans."

"Is that right?" D'Angelo says, again keeping it light. It doesn't sound like much, but he stores it anyhow. "Well, I should get going. Thanks again for your time." They shake hands and D'Angelo turns away. He stops at the doorway. "Hey, you got any good sushi in this town?"

"Sushi? I suppose. I don't go for it myself." The harbor master looks at D'Angelo like he's asked him to recommend a proctologist. He seems about to say more when he stops and peers out the window again. "Oh, that's strange."

"What?" D'Angelo looks that way and sees a woman in a red raincoat locking the padlock on the cabin of the *"C" Lady*. She steps over the gunwale onto the dock and walks up the dock toward one of the other marina ramps.

"Hmm," the harbor master says, "that's Scott's wife. I guess the divorce isn't final yet. I suppose I should let him know I saw her poking around. None of my business, really. But between you and me, I've always liked Scottie a lot more than her." He grimaces with mock terror.

D'Angelo chuckles. "Okay, chief. I promise I won't tell a soul you said that about her. Ever."

He heads for the door.

"Good luck with your daughter," the harbor master says. "I hope you find her okay."

"My daughter." He gives the harbor master a sly smile calculated to convince him he's seen through all of D'Angelo's hypotheticals. "Chief, you should've been police."

*   *   *

It's noon and raining softly again as D'Angelo leaves the harbor master's office. He crosses the boardwalk and heads down the ramp and onto the docks, deciding to take another glance at the skiff Carla supposedly sank. That was just about the last place she was seen alive. Maybe there's something there he can use.

As he passes the *"C" Lady*, he hears something move inside. It would be natural enough for somebody to be inside any boat in the harbor, of course. But he just saw the woman in the red raincoat—the guy's soon-to-be-ex-wife—lock the cabin. Who locks somebody *inside* a boat?

He stops and leans over the port gunwale to peer in the big window. A movement catches his eye, directly below the window. A shadow of something four-legged scurrying downstairs to an area under the foredeck. An animal?

Maybe this Crockett guy got custody of the family dog? Or— if he's not as clean-living as the harbor master implied—maybe the scary wife left a rabid fox in there as a little surprise for him. D'Angelo has certainly seen some divorces get that ugly.

In any case, it's got no conceivable connection to his problem. He walks on.

A couple hundred feet away, he finds Shire Kiminsky's skiff. Nobody around now. Also nothing of interest to him. Just a muddy aluminum boat with a very expensive looking trashed outboard. He's still standing there when his phone rings. Lundren again. D'Angelo doesn't answer. Again.

A few seconds later a text shows up: *Twenty-four hours. We don't hear from you, I send someone.*

If Lundren says "twenty-four hours," he really means as soon as he can launch one of their people. There are several big military bases and enough active-duty personnel in Alaska to start a couple medium-sized wars. No doubt plenty of ex-military guys have stuck around the Great Land upon their discharge. Maybe liking the huge empty spaces with few prying eyes keeping track of a man. Or his hobbies. Or his weapons.

Who knows how many there are lurking out there, armed to the teeth and itching to do something spooky? If Lundren is in a hurry to send muscle, chances are it won't be a professional coming from Sidewinder headquarters in Virginia. Or even one of D'Angelo's own men in Phoenix. It will be some gun-toting survivalist head case from Fairbanks or Wasilla. Even so, D'Angelo figures it'll take at least a day to get them to Homer. Hopefully enough time to find that photo before they show up.

Well, if Carla *is* dead, the only way he's going to find out standing around here is if somebody fishes her body out of the sea and dumps it on the dock. He just doesn't have time to wait for that to happen. He's got to do something. Anything.

He silences his cell phone and walks back to the ramp, passing the *"C" Lady* again. He glances in the windows. No sign of a dog. Nothing moving in there now.

Halfway up the ramp, a big, middle-aged guy comes walking down, his arms loaded with work clothes. He has a pair of those rubber boots pinched between the thumb and forefinger of one hand.

"Running away from home?" D'Angelo jokes.

The guy laughs. "Right now, that sounds pretty good."

At the top, D'Angelo walks over to a dumpster that reeks of fish. He drops his cell phone into a corner, hears it slide through the pile of bulging plastic garbage bags and hit the metal bottom with a clang. Lundren's people can still track it, and certainly will. But then D'Angelo will seem to be in the vicinity of the marina. Which will make sense to them a while longer. Now he can move around freely.

But move where? With the truck impossible to approach, he has nothing left do but watch the marina. That's where Carla was last seen, and that's where she's most likely to resurface—so to speak. Dead or alive.

He walks back to his car, scanning the docks below. Even with many of the halibut charter boats out on the water for the day, a steady stream of commercial fishing vessels and private sport-fishing boats and sundry other small craft come and go. None of them look one bit suspicious. Neither do any of the numerous people on the docks. They're either folks on vacation or working people doing their jobs.

Maybe, if he lives through this, he should retire and spend summers in this beautiful place for the six or seven broiling months when Phoenix is too hot for anything with a four-chambered heart. Working for McKint has made him more money than he needs. He could do some consulting work over the winters, just to stay busy. And summers in the Halibut Capital of the World? That's starting to sound good. He has to love a place dedicated to a big, ugly, bottom-feeding fish. And most importantly, one that's delicious.

He could lease one of those little shops there on the spit. Start a restaurant. All takeout. Italian, sure, but seafood only. No meatballs. Yes, there are already numerous fish-and-chips places lining the spit road. Halibut and salmon and cod on every menu. But how about an all-calamari place? A giant squid painted on the sign. He could call it *Tentacolis: Authentic Sicilian Seafood*. The slogan would be "Don't ask for the recipe, and nobody gets hurt."

Sure. One day soon. If he lives long enough.

He slides into the car. And waits.

CHAPTER

31

STILL SHOOK UP from when somebody looked in the window,
Carla stiffens when she hears footsteps on the deck again. She
risks a peek around the corner of the bunk. Scott unlocks the door
and slides it back, carrying a bundle of mostly black or brown
clothes and a pair of Xtratufs. He stops when he sees the note on
the table. "Carla? You all right?" he calls down to her, still staring
at the note.

"I'm fine." She climbs out of the bunk. "We had a visitor."

"She didn't see you, did she? You didn't talk to her?"

"Take it easy. No. She didn't know I was down here."

"Okay." Scott nods and walks the rest of the way to the top of
the stairs and hands Carla the clothes. "Good," he says. He walks
back to the table.

Carla holds out the Carhartt overalls in one hand, the bulky
gray hoodie in the other. "Do they sell anything except gray, black,
or brown?"

"You'll want to blend in," he says, distracted by the note. He
leans over the table, his palms on the Formica on either side of the
paper like he's afraid to touch it.

Carla strips off the flannel shirt and the T-shirt she slept in,
both still a little damp from her hair-cutting job. She climbs into her
equally damp underpants. Her bra is still too wet, so she sets it aside
and pulls on the thin fleece top he's brought her. It's long-sleeved

and fits snugly, the pile fabric seeming to radiate warmth across her torso. "Oh God, that feels good."

"Sure," he says, without looking up.

She steps into the heavy canvas overalls and yanks the shoulder straps tight, watching Scott pondering the note. "So how long were you married before you started cheating?"

Scott turns and looks at her quizzically. "What do you mean?"

"I sort of had to read that note to figure out who she was, coming and going from the boat like she owns it."

"Well, she *did* own half. But it sounds like it's all mine now." He stops and looks her way. "What makes you think I cheated on her?"

"Well, her heartfelt 'Fuck yourself' was my first clue."

Scott sits at the table, picks up the note, and holds it close to his face as though smelling it. "I never cheated on her."

Carla scoffs. "Right." She pulls on the overlarge hoodie and slips her feet into the boots. They're a little large on her, but manageable.

"No, really, that wasn't it," Scott says.

"Look, it's none of my business. I'm sorry. I—"

"She wanted a baby," he says. "We've been . . . I mean, we *were* married eleven years. I think I gave her the impression I wanted kids too. She's thirty-nine, and she feels like it's getting late, you know?"

Carla knows, all right. Wanting children isn't a problem she's had. But she can certainly feel for another woman pushing forty and second-guessing everything she's done up to that point in her life. "Scott, look, I was being a smartass. It's my default mode." She tugs the hem of the hoodie down on her hips. "How do I look?"

Scott studies her from the table. "Good. You look like the usual deckhand or young fisherman." He tosses her a black nylon watch cap. "Put this on over your bandanna and then pull the hood up." He stops abruptly. "Hey, you cut your hair."

"You noticed."

Scott nods. "Good idea. Once we get you settled in at my house, maybe we can do something to change the color."

"You keep hair coloring around the house?"

Scott frowns, thinking about something. "Listen, I'm thinking maybe we should get ahold of Shire and tell her what's going on. When you're safe. Maybe get her to pick up some dye or whatever."

She doesn't want to reveal how much the idea buoys her spirits. Shire's confidence. Shire's competence. Shire's sheer Alaskan gutsiness. But they've already decided not to get her and the girls involved. "You could go get dye. Why bring Shire into this?"

Scott scratches his head, thinking. In spite of the moment, she finds it charming. He's like a big kid sometimes. "I think she may be who we need to get to your truck. Volker will let her into the truck—if we could think up some excuse. Maybe to find something of hers in there?"

It makes sense, and she really would feel better with Shire helping. But . . .

Scott snaps out of his thoughts. "Hey, we'll talk about it on the way to the house. We gotta get out of here."

"Sure." She's acting like this is all in a day's work, but the thought of walking out into the marina in broad daylight is almost too much. "I don't know if I can do this, Scott. What if D'Angelo's out there?"

Scott picks up a yellow rubber raincoat and walks to the top of the stairs. "Let's keep moving. Put this on. It's bulky enough to hide your chest." He hands her the raincoat. "If he's here in Homer, he's seen the commotion over Shire's skiff. He's going to think you're dead. Really." He looks out the window and scans the docks as if he doesn't at all believe what he just said. "Come on. We'll walk up the ramp and straight to my truck. It's parked by the ice cream place. Just keep your head down and don't talk. Act like a sullen teenage deckhand, and nobody will suspect a thing. Wear these."

He hands Carla a pair of inexpensive plastic mirrored sunglasses.

"It's cloudy and sort of raining out there," she says, holding them up.

"Don't worry about it. You'll look like another cool young twerp. Those guys would wear their shades at midnight in a monsoon. Now, let's get out of here."

He waves her up the stairs and helps her into the heavy raincoat. "Yellow. Great. Well, at least I won't die wearing orange." She's joking to keep the creeping tension at bay a little. Her jaw has gone tight; the skin behind one knee twitches.

"You look right for this place. You're going to be fine."

He looks at her more closely. Differently, too. He's starting to go for her. She knows the look. This isn't the time for that, but still, it helps somehow. "Sure," she says. "I'm going to be fine." She wishes she believed it. She puts the sunglasses on.

He slides back the cabin door, scanning the marina again, his brow taut with concern. "You ready?"

She glances at the note on the table, trying to get her mind off what's out there ahead. "Scott, what's a hoochie?"

"What? What are you talking about?" He keeps looking across the docks, up the ramp.

She tells herself to keep talking, keep joking. "Your wife says she isn't letting you keep her favorite hoochie. Is it a sex thing? A boat sex toy or something?"

"*Boat sex*?" He looks like the question pains him. "It's a fishing lure! A rubber squid imitation, for Christ's sake." He leads her out onto the aft deck and slides the door closed on its runners. "Boat sex. Jesus."

Scott helps Carla climb over the gunwale of the *"C" Lady* and onto the dock. Buried under the big yellow raincoat, the hoodie, and the canvas bibs, she really does look like any other young deckhand or fisherman. At first glance. She tells herself this is going to work.

Scott hands her a duffel bag containing her damp clothes. "Just walk beside me now, like we're talking about the boat and fishing. Real calm like. We go up the ramp and straight across the parking lot. No stopping till we're in my truck."

Carla throws the duffel strap over one shoulder. Scott carries a white kitchen bag bulging with fillets from the sockeye he caught yesterday.

The tide is very low, and the ramp slants down to the floating docks at a precipitous angle. Luckily, no one is using it at the moment. Scott turns to Carla. "Remember, you're a moody teenage mope. Keep your head down like you'd rather be anywhere else on earth than here."

"I *would* rather be anywhere else."

"Shush."

They are halfway up the ramp when he stops suddenly. Carla peeks around him and sees Shire at the top, stepping onto the ramp from the parking lot. "Oh no."

She's alone, thank God. No sign of the twins. If they recognized her, they'd start clamoring for sure. On the narrow ramp, there's no chance of avoiding Shire. Scott goes up just ahead of Carla. Over his shoulder he says, "Shire's coming down, straight at us. Get close behind me and do like I do."

"I know, I see her," Carla whispers.

Scott waves to Shire. Again, over his shoulder, he says, "Don't say a word until I tell you." They meet Shire halfway.

Shire says, "Scott, did you hear about Carla and my skiff?"

"Yeah. I heard." He sounds calm. "I have to show you something," he says, "but you *cannot* react right now, here in public. Promise?" He sets his free hand on Shire's arm. "I mean it. Don't do anything excited. Understand?"

Carla feels her heart slamming on every beat.

"What?" Shire says. "I mean, sure. I don't know. What's going on?"

"There's a kid standing behind me. A new deckhand. Just look at his face," Scott says. "You hear me? Don't do a thing, Shire. Don't say anything more than hello. I don't want to attract any attention. Okay?"

"What the fuck, Scott?"

"I'm serious as shit, Shire. Do I look like I'm joking?"

Shire's voice levels. "Okay. Calm down. I'm cool."

Scott turns and pulls Carla alongside him. "Everybody stay calm."

Carla pushes the sunglasses down an inch and looks over the top of them at Shire.

Shire's face freezes. "Carla? Oh my God! What the hell?"

Carla opens her mouth to say something, but Scott squeezes her shoulder, hard. He says, "Carla's in trouble, Shire. I'm taking her to my place on the river. Go down to your skiff or whatever you were doing just now, and then meet us up at the house later. We'll explain everything."

He starts to turn away, still gripping Carla's shoulder.

Shire grabs his wrist. "Scott, I'll call you."

"No! No phones. Just come in person. Alone. No kids."

"Should I call the police?" Shire whispers.

"No, no, no. No police. Just come. And before you make the turn onto my road, you look in the rearview. If there's anyone behind you at all, you keep driving all the way to Anchor Point. Go into the inn or the gas station or something."

"Carla," Shire hisses, "what have you done?"

A couple fishermen are coming down the ramp from the top. "We gotta go." Scott steps aside and pulls Carla with him. "Go on down to the skiff, Shire. We have to get out of sight. Now."

He plods on up the ramp. Carla stays very close behind. They pass the two fishermen coming down and make it up to the board-walk. They walk through the milling tourists perusing the galleries and gift shops to the parking lot. Carla gets in the passenger seat of Scott's truck, head still down, as instructed. To anyone watching, she will hopefully look like a young guy with his attention glued to a mobile device. What could be more normal than that?

As Scott starts his truck, Carla glances across the parking lot at her Toyota, still parked behind the Orca. It's right there. Scott looks that way too.

"Can we get the picture?" She holds up her truck keys.

Scott looks at her truck again. He looks around the parking lot. He seems to be considering pulling up next to Carla's truck, jump-ing out, and reaching in to grab the photo out of her headliner. There's nobody in sight there behind the Orca at the moment. It would take only a few seconds. They won't have to involve Shire. "Can you do it?" she asks.

The words are barely out of her mouth when an Alaska State Troopers Ford Interceptor pulls up behind Carla's truck and stops. The Trooper gets out and looks at her license plate. Scott puts his truck in gear and drives.

32

IN SPITE OF Lundren's threat to send one of his goons, D'Angelo will have to wait until dark to make a move on Carla's truck. Without any immediate alternatives to pursue, he sits in the rental car in front of the harbor master's office for another half hour, watching the marina. There's nothing of great interest happening there, so he takes a moment and pulls his pistol out of its holster, keeps it low between his knees, and checks the chamber and magazine. Of course it's loaded. What kind of idiot would walk around with an unloaded weapon? But old habits prevail. It's best to be sure before he has to pull the trigger. Not that he really thinks Carla Merino is going to put up that much of fight. And if she did, he'd use the stun gun. If at all possible. Even so, like he said, it's best to be sure. He's going to get that photo, one way or another.

He's slipping the pistol back into the holster when he sees the guy he passed coming down the ramp carrying a bundle of clothes, now stepping off the *"C" Lady* onto the dock. It must be local hero Scott Crockett. With him is a young deckhand. Still no sign of a dog or any other four-legged animal. Was the kid crawling around in there? Curious.

With nothing else as interesting in sight, D'Angelo watches Crockett and the boy through his binoculars as they head up the ramp. They're halfway up to the parking lot when white-blond hair flashes into view. He pulls the binoculars away from his eyes and sees Crockett and the deckhand stopping to chat with someone descending the ramp.

Blond ponytail. Tracksuit. Shire Kiminsky. His alarms start vibrating. She just happens to know Crockett? That's possible, maybe even probable, in a town this small. But if Carla has faked her own drowning in a boating mishap, who might know something about that? The person who owns the boat, that's who.

He pulls the binoculars back up and watches her talking to Crockett and his young deckhand. The deckhand is mostly hidden behind Crockett's broad shoulders. All D'Angelo can see is a face full of sunglasses. Then the kid reaches up with one thin hand and pulls the glasses down a couple inches.

And there she is.

Two months' worth of work culminating before his eyes. "Son of a bitch," he mutters. "Hello, Carla."

Crockett hustles her up the ramp, sunglasses up, head down.

So there is no doubt that Carla and Mr. Legit are in the scam together. And now so is Shire Kiminsky. Funny how a boring day can turn into something else entirely. Crockett is a bigger rascal than people think. He left his wife for a dead woman.

D'Angelo loses them for a second in a crowd of tourists at the top of the ramp. And then he sees them getting into the Crockett Construction pickup truck.

"Shit." He drops the binoculars and starts the car. The spit road is clogged with barely moving cars and motor homes. Crockett's truck is five or six vehicles ahead of him, heading for town. Perfect. He can tail them as far as he needs to.

As he approaches the Orca, he glances over at Carla's pickup, still parked in the same spot near the back door. A lanky Alaska State Trooper is stepping out of a Ford Interceptor. George Volker walks out the back door wearing a flowered shirt over bulky cargo shorts, sandals. With the bay beyond him and the gulls overhead, all he needs is a boogie board. He crouches and reaches up under the wheel well of Carla's truck and hands the Trooper what must certainly be a key.

"Shit," D'Angelo says again. He hits the brakes, veering into the parking lot of Harbor Bait and Tackle, across from the Orca. He glances up the road at Crockett's pickup heading away toward town. With Carla Merino in it. Well, he can't be in two places at the same time. And he needs to know if that Trooper finds anything. "Shit!"

From Harbor Bait and Tackle, he has a good line of sight on Carla's truck. Volker is standing there, watching the Trooper glance inside the cab and then into the camper without putting any real effort into it. Understandable. They believe she drowned in the bay. Why wouldn't they? A woman goes out in a boat and disappears in rough weather. In Alaska. Good chance she's dead. Maybe they'll move the truck now. Hopefully someplace less public.

The Trooper's not there long. Exchanging a few words with Volker, he hands the key back to him. He climbs into the Interceptor and joins the conga line of motor homes, campers, and every kind of sport utility vehicle inching up the spit road.

D'Angelo relaxes. Carla's Toyota will sit there a while longer, no doubt. And it's still too exposed to search. He's about to drive off and try to catch up with Crockett's pickup again when he sees Volker climb into Carla's Toyota. *What in hell?* When gray exhaust rolls out of the truck's tailpipe, D'Angelo puts his car in gear and cuts across the road between the two lanes of slow-moving traffic.

He pulls in behind Carla's truck, blocking it. He gets out. Volker sits cowering behind the steering wheel. D'Angelo puts on a friendly face and knocks on the window. "George! What's happenin'?"

"I'm just moving the—"

Volker gets halfway out the door and D'Angelo hits him once in the ribs, a very controlled medium jab to get his attention. He picks him up by the front of his hibiscus-patterned Hawaiian shirt, pushes him against the side of the camper, and lifts him onto his toes.

"Jesus!" Volker gasps for breath. "What the hell, man? You punched me. I thought we were copacetic!"

"A love tap, George." He holds Volker an inch off the ground. "Good to see you too."

Volker's face registers exactly as much fear as D'Angelo wants it to. He lets him slide down the side of the camper until his heels are back on the gravel. He carefully straightens the front of the shirt. "Where're you going with Carla's truck, George? A luau?"

Volker massages his ribs. "That hurt."

D'Angelo leans in, curls his right hand into a fist, keeps that elbow tight against his side. "Don't make me ask again."

"Okay, okay. Chill, man. I was taking it to my crib! Just until Carla's relatives or somebody claims it."

D'Angelo fires up his fiercest, end-of-the-world eyes and cocks his elbow back another couple inches.

"For God's sake!" Volker yelps. "I need this parking spot. Really, man. I'm just moving the truck to make room before I open."

D'Angelo knows "too scared to lie" when he sees it. He backs off and gives Volker his atomic smile. "Sure," he says. "Here's what we're going to do." He leads Volker by one elbow back to the open door of Carla's truck. "You're going to drive it to your 'crib,' just like you started to do . . ." A thought occurs to him. "How were you planning on getting back out here to open the bar?"

"I was going to call my kitchen helper, Joey. Have him pick me up at my place. He's just a kid. A teenager. Leave him out of this. Please?"

Again. Too scared to lie.

"Of course," D'Angelo says. "Give me your phone."

Volker hands it over.

"Now, you drive nice and carefully to your house. No need to call young Joey. I'll follow you and drive you back here." He nudges Volker into the driver's seat. "I'll be right behind you." He pauses, puts a touch of menace into his voice. "There's nobody waiting at your house, right?"

Volker shakes his head. "I live alone. You know . . . now that Carla moved out, and now that she's . . . you know." He glances out at the water in the bay, a genuinely pained look on his face. Which tells D'Angelo that Volker's almost certainly not in on Carla's scam.

"Okay, George, drive the speed limit. Trust me when I say that you do not want to talk to any more cops on our way."

D'Angelo moves the Camry out of the way, and Volker drives Carla's truck out onto the road to town. D'Angelo slips into the tourist traffic, two cars behind him.

This is progress. Carla is alive. Crockett and Shire Kiminsky are in on it. And he'll soon have unfettered access to the truck. If the photo isn't there, he'll have nothing more to do but talk to Carla.

CHAPTER

33

CARLA IS LOATH to leave the photo behind in the truck on the spit but happy to be out of the harbor and on the highway out of town. As the road climbs higher and higher above the bay, it feels like they are physically rising above the threat she's been living under for the past twelve hours. The past two months. Halfway up the hill, she yanks her hood down and peels the knit hat and the sunglasses off. Scott glances her way but doesn't make her crouch down or put the shades back on. He must be feeling better—safer—too. "How're you doing?" he asks.

"I wish we had the picture."

"We'll figure some way to get it. Like I said, maybe Shire is the key."

She just nods, at the moment wanting only to feel the miles piling up between her and Homer and hopefully Cosmo D'Angelo as well. Scott apparently understands. He says no more.

At the top of the hill, the big paved overlook catches her eye. The sea-viewing area is half filled with cars and campers of all sizes, their occupants draped over the guard railing at the edge of the cliff, cameras and phones gobbling up the scenery. Kachemak Bay glitters in its deceptively alluring way hundreds of feet below. *Nothing but lovely blue water here*, it seems to say. *Get in your skiff and come on out!* A metallic taste fills her mouth, and her cheek twitches. She's seen just how unfriendly that water can get. Up close.

She peers across the bay at the ghostly forms of the mountains on the other side, the old volcanoes, Iliamna, Mount Redoubt. Then a wall of big trees looms between the road and the water, obliterating the view. The forest continues on that side of the highway for the next few miles, a world of shaggy evergreen woods interspersed with fields of tall grasses and broad-leafed plants.

Scott drives on, repeatedly checking the mirror like an escaped convict in an old movie. All he needs is the striped outfit. It makes her anxious again. She looks in the side mirror. Nothing behind them but Alaskan scenery. Trees. Bushes. More trees. In the distance, mountains and glaciers. And up close, clusters of purple-blue flowers hugging the shoulders of the road. Not even a car in sight behind them. However tense Scott is, she's ready to believe that no one is chasing them. Chasing her. She can believe that. Sure. Maybe.

She undoes the seat belt and wriggles out of the bulky rubber raincoat, twists to toss it into the back seat of the truck. There are toolboxes and power saws and big drills of some kind on the floor back there, the words CROCKETT CONST stenciled on them. There are other tools she doesn't recognize. There's a pair of muddy brown Xtratuf boots just like the ones she's wearing. Her sneakers are in the bag with her damp clothes.

She wishes she could do this without Scott. And she told him she wasn't asking for a prince. God, she wishes she had the photo in her hands again and didn't need him. Didn't need to get Shire involved. But she really has no other choice right now.

She turns back and buckles her seat belt, slides lower in the seat. Scott sits stiffly upright behind the wheel, clutching it with both hands, obviously tense. She says, "Scott, I'm sorry for all the trouble I'm causing you. Really. I am."

He glances at her. "Well, I could use some excitement in my life. I mean, if you hadn't floated into it, I'd be out there right now fishing. Alone." He pauses and laughs quietly, shaking his head. "God. Is that pitiful enough for you?"

Carla feels herself smile, the tension lifting like the fog over the bay. Scott's one of those rare, unguarded men who makes her happy to be talking with him. "Have you been a carpenter all your life?"

"I fished commercially when I was in high school. Paid my way through college." He glances over at her like he's not sure he believes she wants to hear his life story.

Carla nods. "Yeah, I've been here long enough to know that's what some Alaskan kids do. Joey the kitchen helper at the Orca wants to fish, but his mother won't let him. Too dangerous."

"It is dangerous," Scott says. "I almost got killed when I was twenty-five."

"You kept fishing after college?" she says, joking now. "Did you major in crabbing or seining?"

Scott laughs. "Look at you, knowing all the terms."

"I work at the Orca. The conversation is all fishing, all day."

He shakes his head. "I kept fishing because I was an English major. Which means I needed a real job. And I loved commercial fishing. I gave it up and started the contracting business after the crabber I was on sank and almost took me with it."

In spite of the warm sun beaming through the windshield, that chills her. "Yeah, well, I know something about nearly drowning."

"You sure do," he says.

They drive for a while in silence. "I'm glad you made it out alive," she says. And she means it.

"Same here," Scott says. His face reddens and his Adam's apple bobs as he swallows, hard. She can practically see his brain churning, trying to find something else to say. "How about you? You said you were a social worker?" he finally blurts.

She nods. "For about six years."

"What made you quit? Ship sink?"

"Something like that," she says. "The poverty. The misery. It was just one sad story after another. It wore me down after a while. It's hard to explain."

"Sure," Scott says.

He drives on in silence until a narrow two-lane appears on the left. He turns onto it and checks the mirrors again to see if anyone turns behind them. Carla finds herself checking too. Nothing and nobody. She'll be checking for the rest of her life. She doesn't even want to think about how long—or brief—that's going to be.

The smaller road is shouldered by short, bushy trees. She knows they're called alders. She watched Shire cut some to use in her smoker for salmon. Alders. Carla's learned that much about the outdoors since being here. Nature girl. That's her. Two months and she can name one tree and two fish. By the time she's seventy or eighty, she'll be identifying small brown birds.

A battered and rust-blotched flatbed approaches Scott's truck coming from the other direction. The approaching driver raises his forefinger off his steering wheel. Scott does the same.

Carla says, "What's that, some kind of back-road salute?"

"I guess. You tend to see the same eight or ten people every day on a road like this. No need to get too excited about it."

This secondary road is even curvier than the highway, winding around marshy ponds dotted with lily pads. In one lush green puddle, a moose stands ankle-deep in the shallows as if posing for a calendar, sloppy water weeds dripping from its jaws.

"Yearling bull," Scott says. "See the little nubby antlers poking out by its ears?"

Carla says, "Do you hunt?"

"Used to, all the time. Moose, caribou. Only small game for the past few years. Grouse mostly." He stops and thinks. "Last year, I don't think I got out at all."

"But you own a gun?"

"Guns. Plural. Rifles, shotguns." He chuckles. "In Alaska, if you don't have at least five guns, you're not allowed to own property or vote."

Carla nods, thinking.

"That's a joke, Carla."

"I know that," she says. "I'm just glad you have a gun." Still, it doesn't comfort her as much as she thought it would. "You're sure that even if D'Angelo is in Homer, there's no way for him to guess we'd be up here in these woods. That's true, right?"

"I can't imagine why he would," Scott says. "Nobody knows . . ." He pauses. "Except Shire."

"Well, I'm glad she doesn't think I'm dead now. Shire is smart and tough, and I want her by my side. But I'm still scared to get her sucked into this. Those girls . . ."

"I know. I shouldn't have told her to come up here. That was stupid. I should've just arranged to meet her someplace in town to explain things, after you were tucked in at my place. Ask her to go get Volker to let her into your truck."

"Why can't you call her? How come you told her not to call you?"

"I don't know." Scott's fingers fidget on the steering wheel. "In the movies, somebody's always listening in on other people's cell phones. The papers talk about satellites a hundred miles out in space with cameras so powerful they can see you taking a leak off your back porch. They say your own TV set can be used to eavesdrop on you. Really, I don't know what to believe. Except that Sidewinder has the latest of everything."

"They wouldn't be listening to your phone," Carla says. "D'Angelo doesn't know you exist."

"But he'll know it was Shire's boat you sank. He might be listening to hers." He sighs. "Like I said, I just don't know."

This isn't helping her nerves. She squirms in her seat.

Scott sees that. "Take it easy. We're safe now. Like you said, Shire is smart. And as long as she's careful, there's no way in hell this D'Angelo guy could associate you with me or know you're here in Anchor Point." He reaches over and touches her elbow. "Look, there's nothing up here except moose and squirrels. Really. Rocky and Bullwinkle live up ahead. I'll point out their house."

She snorts a laugh and hopes to hell he's right.

He drives another mile or so. She looks out her window at the passing forest, thinking about moose and squirrels. "Are there bears around here too?" she asks.

"Mostly black bears. Some brown bears down on the river once in a while when the salmon are in. Are you afraid of bears?"

"I don't know. I've never seen a wild one. But once when I was hiking with my husband in the mountains in Arizona, we saw bear tracks and I got scared about sleeping in a tent because I was having my period."

"Why? Are bears attracted to crabby women?"

"Ha." She punches him on the arm. They drive another minute in silence, and she says, "I like you, Scott. You make me laugh. My husband made me laugh. At least at first. Or that's the way I remember it." She sighs. "Shit, it was almost twenty years ago when we got married."

"God, you don't seem old enough to have been married that long ago. What are you, forty?"

"Forty?" She glares at him. "Do I look forty?"

"Oh, man. I'm sorry. How old *are* you?" He looks like he's going to be sick.

"Thirty-eight. And a few months." She pauses. "Eleven, actually."

He scoffs. "Only, thirty-eight and eleven months. I see. Nowhere near forty. Sorry."

"Look, you're single now. You'll be meeting women. If you're going to be dumb enough to try to guess a woman's age, just deduct five years from your lowest estimate. Ten, even."

"Actually, I meant to say, thirty. Honest."

That makes her smile. "Okay, now I feel better." She chuckles and looks out the window. "Liar."

"Boy, I won't make that mistake again," he says with mock seriousness.

He obviously likes making her laugh. Likes talking to her. And she likes that about him. Not wanting him to see how much, she laughs to herself.

She keeps her head turned and takes in this place called Anchor Point. They pass tired-looking houses wrapped in wind-tattered plastic fabric with the word *Tyvek* printed on it. Corroded sheet-metal trailers draped in blue vinyl tarps. Rotting wooden boats, rusting trucks and cars, dead snowmobiles and outboard motors strewn about the properties. Ugly dogs lounging proprietorially in rutted dirt drives. Every other road sign shotgun dimpled.

They pass a dented mailbox near the mouth of a dirt track branching off into an elderberry thicket. She peers up the leaf-lined drive at a shack that would appear to be abandoned if not for the child sitting in the weeds out in front of it.

She sees Scott look her way. He probably thinks she's surprised to find that people live like this. She's not.

"Pretty grim, huh?" he says.

"I know something about poor people, Scott. I met enough at the county hospital in Phoenix. Families of the sick. They were almost always uneducated and broke, and tired of being both. My job was to help them organize lives beyond organizing." She stops for a minute, thinking. "After I quit, I decided I'd rather serve drinks to people during the few hours of their day when they've convinced themselves they're having a good time."

The memory makes her weary. And angry.

Scott is quiet. He drives on through the woods.

They pass another house mummified in Tyvek fabric. She says, "How come some of those houses have that stuff all over them? Does some kind of aluminum siding or something go over the top of that?"

He chuckles. "No, they won't be putting anything over that, I promise you. Here at Anchor Point, Tyvek is considered a finish product. The real diehards won't even go that far." He points. "Look there."

Set back from the road a hundred feet on an alder-choked dirt track, an unpainted plywood shack the size of a backyard storage shed slouches into the surrounding brush. The plywood is weathered a silver gray, every nailhead bleeding rust stains. A wisp of dark smoke oozes from a pipe jutting through its corrugated metal roof.

"Old Ingerhausen will tell you he don't need no stinking paint. Let alone tar paper or, God forbid, that swanky Tyvek. That guy is the real deal."

A whiff of sulfurous fumes drifts into the truck.

"What the hell is he burning in there?" she asks.

"Coal. People pick it up off the beach. It's always wet, and it's high sulfur—God only knows what else is in the fumes—but it's free."

"Jesus, this place is like Appalachia."

"Sort of. We've got tweakers, rednecks, Holy Rollers. Maybe even some snake handlers too, for all I know. So, yes, in some ways it's like Appalachia. Except there are no folklorists telling us how colorful our 'traditional' lifestyle is."

"You say 'us.' You're talking like a local."

"I was raised in the house we're heading for right now. My folks left it to me. I've been fixing it up. Last winter when Trina and I were fighting all the time, I'd come up here and work on the place to get away. Spend a whole weekend alone sometimes, hammering and sawing, slinging taping mud. Happily."

Another truck passes in the other direction. More steering-wheel-finger waves.

"I didn't mean to pry," she says. "Okay, I *do* mean to pry now. After being in your boat and in your truck—this is the cleanest work truck I've ever seen, by the way—I'm guessing your house has that fancy Tyvek stuff all over it. Am I right?"

"Much worse," Scott says. "You'll see."

He drives another mile on through the forest. Carla peers at the few houses they pass, all in various states of disrepair and neglect. It seems a different universe from the gift shops and art galleries, the espresso bars and three-hundred-dollar-a-day fishing charters of Homer, fifteen miles and a couple thousand light years away. Is it far enough to keep her safe?

He slows to turn onto an even smaller, unpaved road cutting into the thick spruce forest. Small birds flit from one side of the narrow lane to the other. A scrawny squirrel darts out, looks aghast at the approaching machine, and flees back in the direction it came from. Shafts of sunlight beaming through the trees make the whole place look like the inside of an old church. Quiet and safe, Carla hopes.

Why is Scott bringing her and the trouble she obviously attracts to his home? She has to wonder: would he be doing this is if she were old, fat, and ugly? No chance.

CHAPTER

34

D'ANGELO FOLLOWS CARLA'S truck, Volker at the wheel, as it rolls the three miles of spit road and on across a causeway over a big estuary slough to the mainland and town. They pass the post office, a Safeway store, a gas station, and enough dining establishments to make his stomach cry out. Skinny Tony's Pizza, the Reluctant Clam, Bo's BBQ, a Thai place.

Regretfully leaving the potential lunch spots behind, he follows Volker up the big hill leading out of town. The sun is out at full summer intensity again, the sky pristine but for thin cloud fingers reaching across the bay. Gulls coast over the water. Above them, a half dozen eagles circle on updrafts over the bluff like synchronized swimmers of the sky.

Two women in running tights and T-shirts jog downhill, trailing a big black Lab wearing a red bandanna. D'Angelo wonders what the dog's name will be here. In his experience, most places west of the Mississippi, a male lab with a bandanna is going to be Cody. In Brooklyn, his name will be Max, or maybe Miles. Who knows what the local pet clichés are in Homer, Alaska? He hasn't spent much time this far north, though he's beginning to want to.

Everything about Homer makes him feel stupidly optimistic. What a place. Fabulous scenery, good-looking women, interesting food. He's practically ready to retire here, take up sport fishing. Right now he wishes he'd eaten something more. He hopes Volker has groceries. He could slam a sandwich while he's going through the truck. If the photo's not there, then he'll go find Carla and her friend Crockett. They are going to need to lie low for a while until Carla's drowning is yesterday's news. Crockett's house is almost certainly where they're headed. Occam's razor: the simplest solution is probably the answer.

Near the top of the long hill, the Toyota's right turn signal blinks on. Volker turns off the highway onto a secondary road that follows the ridgeline of the bench overlooking the bay. The terrain below is treeless meadows blanketed with small willows, grasses, and wildflowers. Alder thickets hug the gullies. D'Angelo is pleased to note the scarcity of homes and the distances between them. He'll have plenty of privacy if he has to tear the truck apart.

Volker drives another mile along the ridge over the bay, the densely green hills shimmering in the post-rain sunlight. Far below, the spit juts out into the blue water, the shops and restaurants just a blur from that distance. A quarter mile offshore, a boxy white cruise ship lies at anchor carrying an army of tourists ready to storm the town.

Tourism seems like a nice way to make a living. Relatively little damage to the world, at least at the art gallery and souvenir shop end of the business. God only knows what conditions the unfortunate bastards who make the T-shirts endure. Anyway, it sounds pretty harmless after what he's seen in his line of work. The thought of his own little food shack on the spit comes to mind again. Cook calamari, date some of the local fisherwomen.

He's lingering on the fisherwomen idea when Volker turns down a dirt-track driveway through a dense thicket. D'Angelo follows. The alders on each side reach across and mingle twenty feet above the gravel. At the far end of the leafy tunnel, Carla's truck rolls into a grassy clearing and stops in front of an A-frame house that all but screams 1972. Volker's crib. *Of course.* One look at George and he should have guessed it would be either an A-frame, a yurt, or a geodesic dome. D'Angelo has to wonder if George Volker even knows how entertaining he can be. He parks behind Carla's truck.

There are no other vehicles near the house, no signs of life inside. Front door tight, windows shut all around. No smoke from the chimney. He half hoped Volker's breakup story was a fake and that Carla and Crockett had driven up here to meet their pony-tailed coconspirator. But it's a pretty safe bet that the bartender isn't in on whatever they're up to.

He gets out and immediately takes in the nostril-twitching aroma of pot overtaking the damp forest smells, sees the smoke curling out the driver's side window of Carla's truck. Well, if you're going to be a cool guy and live in an A-frame with porch railings draped in fishing nets bejeweled with glass floats, you pretty much have to smoke weed too. That may be written into law somewhere. And the shit is legal here in the Great Land. So why not?

D'Angelo walks up to the truck and taps on the window. "Did you bring enough for everybody?"

Volker peers up at him through a cloud of blue-gray smoke and whimpers, "I don't know anything." He looks like he thinks D'Angelo might cook and eat him.

D'Angelo puts on his harmless face. "I just need to go through the truck, dude." He shows Volker his open hands. "Come on, open up."

Volker cringes and opens the door.

"Are you my friend?" D'Angelo asks him.

"What?"

"Just say yes and save yourself a beating."

Volker's eyes get bigger. "Well, I *want* to be your friend," he says.

"Excellent!" D'Angelo marches Volker over to the front of the rental car and presses one finger against his chest. "Then stay right here. Now that we're friends, I never want to lose sight of you. I don't think I can bear it."

Volker sits back against the hood of the Camry and pulls a fresh joint out of his shirt pocket. "Mind if I smoke?"

D'Angelo laughs. "Not at all. Just sit tight while I see what our lady friend keeps in her rolling boudoir."

He's reaching for the door to the camper when the sound of gravel crunching in the driveway turns him around. Volker lets out a long stream of grassy smoke and looks that way too. A black-and-white Crown Vic comes out of the alder tunnel and parks behind D'Angelo's Camry, the words HOMER POLICE painted on its sides.

D'Angelo shoots Volker a deadly stare. Quietly, he says, "Stay cool now, George. You understand that the police can't protect you from me or the people I work for, right?"

"The people you work for?" Volker goes ashen. "What the hell does that mean?"

"Use your imagination," D'Angelo says, and turns his most charming smile on the skinny cop, now getting out of the Crown Vic. "Officer."

The cop, a guy in his thirties maybe, walks up and announces himself as "Officer Kramer, Homer PD."

"Cosmo D'Angelo," he says with manly cheer. "Friend of George here."

The cop is another tall one. D'Angelo thinks if he were twenty years younger, he'd sign up. What a place to work. What kind of hardened criminals could they have in Homer? Diabolical anglers keeping a few salmon over the limit? T-shirt shoplifters?

Volker palms the joint and stands up from the hood of D'Angelo's car. "Hi, Tim. What's up?"

Officer Kramer launches into him. "Have you lost your mind, George? What the hell are you doing moving the vehicle of a missing person currently the subject of Coast Guard and police investigations?"

"Geez," Volker whimpers, "that sourpuss Statie Sergeant Demmet told me they were done with the truck."

"Well, the goddamn Troopers have no goddamn business telling you that you can goddamn move it. It's still an open city investigation. And did he also tell you it's legal to smoke dope outside in public?" He knocks the joint out of Volker's hand. "Because it's not."

Demonstrating surprising wisdom, Volker plays dumb and submissive. "I moved it because I needed the parking space. I thought—"

Kramer looks like he might shoot Volker if the fool keeps running his mouth. "Unless you've got a marriage license that says Mr. and Mrs. George Volker, with Carla Merino's signature on it, you drive this Japanese piece of crap back down the hill and straight to the cop shop. You got me? It's going into impound until either Carla Merino's family claims it or she Jesus-walks back into town across the surface of that bay."

Volker fiddles with the rubber band on his ponytail. "What do you need her truck for, Tim?"

The cop almost snaps back at him but deflates. "Honest to God, George, if your old man hadn't handed you a gin mill sitting on the most valuable piece of real estate in town, you'd still be mowing lawns and burning the money on skunk weed." It looks like talking to Volker is sapping the life out of him. D'Angelo sympathizes.

"But—" Volker says.

The cop cuts him off. "Think about it. Ever heard the term *foul play*? What if Carla Merino's body shows up with, I don't know, say, an Orca Grill ice pick in the back of her head or your name carved into her chest in satanic letters or something? You think maybe we'll want to look around at her last known address—which, according to the regular Orca degenerates, is either your house or her camper shell? You think maybe?"

Volker grimaces. "Oh. I never thought of that."

"Well, George, you just keep practicing that innocent-by-reason-of-stupidity routine. I've known you my whole life, and I will testify in any court in this great land that you are—at the very least—twice as dumb as you appear to be."

"Thanks, Tim," Volker says. "That's very supportive of you."

Kramer hitches up his belt, laden as it is with his Glock 19, pepper spray, Taser, and the other tools of his trade. He really does look like he wants to unholster something and use it on Volker. "The station," he says. "Right now. Let's go. I'll follow you to town."

Kramer turns toward the police car, then stops and looks back over his shoulder, scrutinizing D'Angelo in depth for the first time. His eyes narrow.

D'Angelo knows he's made.

"Law enforcement?" Kramer asks, eyes tight with interest.

D'Angelo shifts to *Aw, shucks, you got me* mode. Everything but grinding his toe in the driveway gravel. "Military police. Retired. That's how I know ol' George here. His nephew and I went through training together at Fort Huachuca. Thought I'd stop in and see him while I'm touristing the hell out of Alaska."

Something approximating a smile flashes across Kramer's face. With exaggerated incredulity, he says, "You're telling me"—he has to stop and laugh—"you're telling me that you're taking a day out of your vacation to spend time with George Volker?"

"Hell, you can only fish so much," D'Angelo says, as if he's missed the sarcasm entirely. "You know, I went out on one of those halibut charters, and dang! Did we catch fish. Those ugly buggers are something else, let me tell you . . ."

Kramer turns away, already as bored with the conversation as D'Angelo hoped he'd be. "Let's go, George. You drive this truck to the station and turn the keys over. I'll follow you there."

"Sure, Tim." Volker looks over at D'Angelo to make sure that's the correct response.

D'Angelo nods. "I'll follow you guys to the police station," he says helpfully. "Then I'll drive you out to the bar, George." Big toothy smile. Lots of goodwill. "No problem."

But having Carla's truck in police impound is a problem for sure.

35

CARLA SITS UP straight when Scott stops in front of a two-story house nestled in a clearing among the giant spruce trees. Freshly stained wood siding. Glossy, dark-green trim around the windows and the front door. Everything about the house appears fresh and new, even though he said it was the house he grew up in. It's much nicer than anything they've passed since turning off the highway at Anchor Point. "Pretty swanky for this neighborhood," she says.

"I wasn't shooting for the retired-yuppie look. That's just sort of how it turned out."

"Shire told me that the new money and the summer people are going to make it impossible for working folks to afford to live in town pretty soon. She says they'll have to move up here to Anchor Point and live with all you 'toothless firewood cutters.' "

"Toothless woodcutters." Scott smiles, shakes his head. "For a homesteader kid, Shire's a real snob. Do you know she has a master's degree in marine biology from some snotty East Coast school? Brown? Bard?" He shrugs. "She's right about the cost of real estate in town. Even up here now. And it's not just summer people driving prices up. I'm guilty of gentrifying Anchor Point myself."

Scott's house does indeed look posh compared to the sketchy places along the road. Glossy with the recent rainwater, the green metal roofing looks like it's been scrubbed by Mother Nature herself.

The windows sparkle in the midday sun. And it's impossibly tidy. No rusting appliances or old boat trailers in the front yard, no dead vehicles in the drive. The front deck has several big flowerpots sporting some kind of small blue-and-orange flowers. It has neither the aging-hipster feel of Volker's house nor the ragged, who-gives-a-shit look she expected from the home of an unmarried Alaskan male.

She glances at Scott, still sitting behind the wheel, watching her reaction to the house. She can tell he's proud, pleased that she's impressed by it.

"It's beautiful," she says, admiring the house a while longer. "Isn't there some shack owners association or something that's going to fine you for putting on siding and window frames?"

He smiles. "People around here think that any man who would voluntarily paint his own house is insane. I get a pass because, even though I got fancy and went away to college in glamorous Anchorage, I came back here and fished. And I still work with tools for a living. My neighbors treat me like a favorite not-too-bright cousin."

Carla peers up at the house. "Is it safe to leave the place empty when you go to work or go fishing? You said there are druggies around."

"There are some rough types up the North Fork of the river, but most of the people here are decent enough," he says. "My mother was a teacher at Anchor Point Elementary for about a hundred years. And my dad drove a heating oil truck. Everybody knew them both. Nobody messes with my house much. If I were an Anchorage lawyer or doctor stuffing my weekend fishing mansion with fine things, the punks would strip it to the framing."

D'Angelo and the photograph momentarily forgotten, Carla sits and studies the house through the windshield, considering Scott's account of the class structure here at Anchor Point. But mostly she's thinking that she's liking him way too much.

She steps out of the truck and parks the sunglasses on her nose. They walk to the foot of the porch stairs, the air thick with sunshine and the scent of the forest drying out after the rain. She can feel herself relaxing. Not even the bright sunshine bothers her now. Then a loud blast erupts nearby, and she yelps involuntarily, adrenaline coursing through her. It's followed by two more nerve-rattling explosions. "What the hell was that?"

Scott takes her elbow. "Take it easy. Somebody up the road is sighting in a rifle. Or shooting his neighbor's dog. Hopefully not his neighbor. You sort of get used to gunfire up here." He smiles. "Welcome to Anchor Point. Home sweet well-armed home."

Carla lets out a long breath. "Great to be here. Your house is lovely," she says honestly. "Truly lovely." They go up on the deck. Carla looks over at his garage, and beyond it the several huge yellow machines sitting around a small gravel pit. "What's with all the heavy equipment?"

"The excavator and stuff?" He looks that way. "I use them for foundations and septic systems, water lines. Stuff like that."

"Water lines. Ah, that's encouraging." She yanks off the blue bandanna. "I hope it means this yuppie hunting shack has a shower." Suddenly self-conscious about her looks, she tries to pat her hair down. The short, matted tendrils are too springy. "I'd like to get the seawater out of what's left of my hair sometime before I die for real."

Scott pulls out his house keys. "Come on. I'll show you the bathroom. While you're in the shower, I'll put something together for lunch."

"Lunch? Screw lunch," she says. "What time is cocktail hour around here?"

* * *

Scott's house is nearly as woody inside as out. Wide plank floors, stained wood doors and frames, stained windowsills, even a wood ceiling throughout with a translucent, pale-white finish. Carla smells paint thinner and sawdust. No question a carpenter lives there. A tidy one. The house is as clean and orderly as his boat. She should've guessed.

In the entryway, a neat stack of firewood sits next to an even neater pile of newspapers. Muddy work shoes stand side by side on a shallow rubber tray next to a pair of clean lightweight loafers. He's not even married anymore, and he takes off his shoes when he comes in? She resists commenting. He's doing her a gigantic favor here. And everything about the house gives her a time-out-of-time feeling, like some safe, magical place from a fantasy. The feeling of security is almost too silly to think about. "This is nice, Scott."

He kicks off his work shoes and puts the loafers on, looking at her sideways, maybe expecting a wisecrack to come on the heels of the compliment.

"No, really." She holds his elbow for balance and climbs out of her Xtratufs and sets them in the mud tray next to his shoes. They walk into the stark, minimalistic living room. There's an obviously new couch and a chair, both a safe tan-beige. A simple floor lamp with a creamy white shade. A wood coffee table, starkly barren.

"I had to take the old furniture out to redo the floors, and I ended up hauling it all to the Salvation Army store. My folks were the kind of people who bought furniture once every century or so."

Carla smiles. Her mother buys furniture the way people shop for groceries. Weekly.

Amid all the wood is a black iron woodstove that looks like it's never felt fire. And a gray metal cabinet almost as tall as Carla, two feet wide and nearly as deep. The word ORVIS is written above a big chrome dial. She gives Scott a quizzical look.

"A gun safe."

"How decorative." But she's happy to be reminded that he does indeed own guns. However magical the place seems.

There are no rugs, no paintings or photos on the clean, off-white walls. She says, "It's a nice place. Kind of sparse, though."

"What do you mean?"

She hears the injured undertone. "I think I was expecting animal heads or fishing poles on the walls. You're a single Alaskan guy, and you don't even have pictures of yourself holding up dead fish?"

He looks at the walls, a frown tugging at the corners of his mouth.

"Teasing," she says. "Jesus, Mr. Sensitive, I'm just saying I thought you'd have some faux-rustic Teddy Roosevelt crap."

"There's a dead porcupine on the road coming in. Been there a week. It's very flat. Maybe I can nail it up somewhere."

"That would be a stylish touch."

She wanders into the kitchen. The white tile counter top is pristine. No dirty dishes. No dishes at all. Not even a water spot on the stainless-steel sink. There is a pot rack suspended from the ceiling over the counter, serious-looking copper pans dangling from it. A small round table with a clean black-and-white plaid tablecloth and four chairs. The room looks like it's been staged by a real estate agent. She thinks of the magazine-strewn, used-coffee-cup-heaped chaos of Volker's house. Never mind the nightmare of worn clothes she left draped over every piece of furniture in her now-abandoned apartment in Phoenix.

Maybe she should hire Scott to follow her around straightening up after her for the rest of her life. By the look he's giving her right now, she has a feeling he'd sign up for that. Happily. She knows that look. He has a monster crush on her. She isn't happy with how pleased that makes her feel. What the hell is wrong with her? Shire Kiminsky doesn't need men to fawn over *her*.

She shakes off the thought. "How about I get that shower while you mix us a drink of some kind? Bloody Mary?"

"Come on." He leads her up a set of dark-stained stairs and into a bedroom with a wood cathedral ceiling bleached like the rest of the house. A similarly whitewashed beam supports the ceiling, a white ceiling fan hanging from the center of it. The guy likes white.

Scott crosses the bedroom and heads for the adjacent bath. Carla gravitates instead to a window looking out on a valley behind the house, a small river winding through it. On the slope downhill, the tall evergreen trees that surround the house give way to smaller bushes and grasses. Across the bottomlands, she can see thickets of alders running all the way to the scraggly-topped trees that line both banks of the river. She recognizes their tall, uninterrupted trunks and the sudden baskets of jumbled limbs crowning their tops. *Cottonwoods.* They grow along the rivers in Arizona too and are favored by the Hopi Indians for carving ceremonial dolls and spiritual figures. Her mother once did a series of metal-and-glass sculptures loosely based on kachina dolls, flagrantly appropriating the Native culture. They were a big hit in Scottsdale.

Peering down the river valley, Carla can see the sleeping volcanoes across the bay partly veiled by clouds, looking old and spooky and terribly sad for some reason. People say it's pure wilderness over there for hundreds of miles in any direction. No towns, no people. Maybe that's where she should go. Where she would be safe, living in a cave with the bears. She dials her vision back to the valley below. There isn't another house or building of any kind in sight, and she tries to let that lighten her crashing mood. Suddenly the seclusion of Scott's house is losing its magic. Something is making her blue.

"You like the view?"

Carla turns to find Scott standing in the doorway to the bathroom. "Scott, you ever think about living someplace else, other than Alaska, I mean?"

"Nah, look at all I have." He stops and grimaces. "Well, if I'd stayed married, I'd have a big beautiful house in town instead of this little one on a gravel pit. But I have a beautiful boat on a bay full of fish. I've got no debt, money in the bank. How many carpenters anywhere live that well? Alaska is blue-collar Nirvana."

Carla thinks about it, thinks about the apartment in Phoenix and the fact that she's still renting, driving an eighteen-year-old pickup truck. She's happy for him, a little envious too. "You're a lucky guy."

She hears the water running in the shower. "That sounds like Nirvana calling to me." She pulls the hoodie off over her head, unsnaps the straps on her Carhartt bibs, and walks into the bathroom.

"Towels." Scott points to a stack of big green ones. "Use whatever you need."

She brushes past him to the fogging glass shower enclosure. "Ah, wonderful." She's in the land of the wood elves now. And they have indoor plumbing.

CHAPTER

36

WHILE VOLKER PARKS Carla's truck at the impound yard under the watchful eyes of Officer Kramer, D'Angelo scrutinizes the security measures around the cop shop. Volker turns the key over to Kramer and climbs into D'Angelo's Camry. D'Angelo makes a show of waving a friendly good-bye to Kramer. He drives off with Volker cowering in the passenger seat.

"I couldn't help it," Volker whines. "I didn't know the police would show up!"

D'Angelo shuts him up with a murderous stare. He could throw Volker out at the next corner, but investing a few minutes to drive him out the spit road to the Orca could ensure that Volker keeps all this under wraps. "Just shut up, George."

Volker goes silent.

When they pull in behind the bar and stop, Volker points to the parking place that Carla's truck occupied. It's now filled with a big Winnebago, the rear of it wallpapered with what appear to be stickers from every national park in America. Volker gets his courage up enough to speak. "See? I told you I needed that parking spot."

"I thought that was employee parking," D'Angelo says to him.

"Are you kidding? When the tourists are spending money, nobody cares where anybody parks."

"Okay," D'Angelo says, "just so we're clear on this: if you say a word about me, about any of this, to anyone at all . . ."

"I know, man! Mellow out, would you? How stupid do I look?"

D'Angelo has to smile. "Some advice? Don't press people on that question." He glares at Volker until he opens the passenger door and gets out.

Volker closes the door and leans into the open window. "Could I have my phone back?"

D'Angelo cuts him a fierce stare. "I need to borrow it for a while. What's the password?"

"Six-nine-six-nine." Volker pouts. "Can I ask you one question?"

"What?"

"What do you want from Carla's truck?"

"Oh, that question," D'Angelo says, and pulls away. He sees Volker giving him the finger in the rearview mirror. That makes him smile. Good. Let him vent his anger. Better than getting heroic and telling one of his cop friends that a scary stranger is asking questions about the missing Carla Merino.

He pulls onto the road and drives back to the base of the spit and on across the estuary slough. On the other side a sign indicates the way to the airport.

The little airport is at the end of the narrow road surrounded by muskeg and swampland. Small birds wheel and dip over the wind-bent grasses at the end of the runway. The parking lot is almost empty, and inside the terminal it's quiet. No one there but one sleepy-eyed, middle-aged redhead poking at a computer keyboard behind the Bay Air Service ticket counter. The DEPARTURES AND ARRIVALS signboard above her shows that there will be no flights in or out of Homer for another three hours. D'Angelo pockets a parking envelope from the dispenser in the lobby and walks back outside.

In the long-term parking area, he wanders among the dozen or so vehicles, checking the dates on the paper slips on their dashboards. He finds a dark-brown Subaru hatchback of indeterminate age whose owners won't be back in town for several days. That's as much time as he needs. By then, either he finds that photo or Lundren's muscle shows up and this whole thing goes another way. He's hoping to avoid that.

As he fills in his blank parking slip with the license number and color of the rented Camry, a car approaches the airport. He stands still. It rolls on by to the UPS building a quarter mile farther down the road. Other than that, the area remains empty. A bird with long yellow legs launches off a stunted black spruce nearby, shrieking something that sounds like, *I'm running, I'm running, I'm running.* A crow waddles by between two parked cars, picking tidbits out of the pavement cracks, grumbling to itself. D'Angelo jimmies the door of the Subaru, breaks the ignition lock, and does what he needs to in order to start it.

He transfers his belongings into the Subaru, backs it out, and parks the Camry in its place with the new parking slip on the dashboard. Will it match the other half of the original deposited by its owners? No. But really, like Volker says, nobody's checking those things during tourist season.

Folding his legs into the little hatchback is a crunch, but the car is perfect for blending into the town traffic. In his short time in Homer, he's come to the conclusion that all locals drive either pickup trucks with wet dogs in the back or Subarus. Pity the Subaru owners with wet dogs.

He drives away in the Subaru. Whoever Phil Lundren sends to find him will be looking for the Camry. Whatever he's driving, there's no getting to Carla's Toyota now. The impound yard is fenced, barbed wire on top. Lots of lights. Security cameras, of course. Getting to the truck is going to be a major undertaking. And he doesn't even know if the photo is in it. So the next order of business is a visit to the one person who can tell him where it is— now that he knows she's alive.

He kicks himself for letting her ride off in Crockett's truck when he had the chance to follow them. Well, sometimes this job requires snap decisions. They aren't always going to be good ones. Hours have been wasted, but he has a pretty good idea where Carla is. As he drives out of the airport, he pulls out Volker's smartphone and Googles *Crockett Construction, Homer, Alaska.*

Driving through the business district of the town, he passes a restaurant called the Ethereal Eatery, and his thoughts turn to lunch. A sign says *Enchilada Lunch Plate!* He watches a teenage waitress with a long blond braid set food before tourists at a patio table. It makes him wonder who eats Mexican food cooked by Anglos two thousand miles north of the Mexican border.

Although right now, he'd eat Chilean empanadas prepared by Laplanders.

The air vents in the Subaru funnel in food aromas. "Damn," he mutters, and inhales deeply, taking as much sustenance as he can from the fumes.

He's so hungry he wants to punch somebody.

PART III

ANCHOR POINT, ALASKA

37

S COTT IS TUCKING celery sticks into the Bloody Marys when Carla comes down the stairs wrapped in a big green bath towel, her hair bound in a smaller one. He looks up and stammers, "I . . . I . . . you look, er . . . better." He runs his fingers through his hair.

She can see that he's a goner. She should mind that, but she just doesn't.

"I feel better," she says. She takes a seat at the kitchen table. He sets her Bloody Mary in front of her. "Thanks." She tastes the drink. "Perfect. You're a good cook, a good carpenter, and a good bartender. Do you do everything well?" It's shameless, but she can't help doing it.

His face goes bright pink. "There's more vodka in the freezer if you need it. I'm going to take a shower. You can throw your clothes in the washing machine."

"Then what?" She yanks the small towel off and fluffs her now-short hair.

Scott stares for a few seconds before replying. A goner.

"When Shire gets here, we'll talk to her about getting the picture out of your truck. And then we should wait here—maybe a few days, maybe a week or more before we try driving north—until you're, you know, officially . . ." He makes a throat-slitting gesture with one hand.

"A week? I'm going to need something to get my mind off D'Angelo," she says, and sips her drink. "Suggestions?"

Does he even know she's flirting? He was married for ten years, never cheated on his wife. She's being obvious, but he looks more confused than aroused. She decides to have mercy on him. "What do you do in your free time?"

"Free time?" He looks like he's never heard of the concept. He laughs. "I'm either building, fixing, or painting something. My Wi-Fi is spotty, but I got custody of the DVDs in the divorce. I hope you like Mafia movies. There's a Scrabble board around here somewhere." He sighs. "Look, all I know is carpentry and fishing. That's my life. One fascinating thing after another." He turns to go upstairs.

"Hey, Scott."

He stops and looks back at her.

She smiles. "I appreciate what you're doing. Thanks."

She means it, but she can see it only makes him want her that much more.

He staggers the rest of the way up the stairs.

*   *   *

Sitting in Scott's immaculate kitchen, Carla wonders if she could ever get used to this level of cleanliness and order.

She can't help thinking about an apartment she shared with a girl named Maryellen in grad school in Tucson. It was on the second floor of a U-shaped building wrapped around a swimming pool so fetid even she—with her minimum standards of hygiene—refused to stick a toe in it. Maryellen was the first person Carla ever met more comfortable with household chaos than she was. She would come through the door and start dropping things: books, papers, groceries, items of clothes. Wherever they hit, they stayed—for days, for weeks. Carla can't remember ever seeing Maryellen bend over and pick something up off a floor. Dishes in the sink, counter top slathered with food. Smudged glasses and coffee cups on every horizontal surface. Dirty laundry moldered in corners, on chairs, under beds. Farm animals would've walked out of there appalled. After visiting once and fleeing in disgust, Maryellen's mother donated a brand-new vacuum cleaner. Maryellen never took it out of the box. Carla didn't either.

She sips her Bloody Mary and smiles at the memory. Maybe Scott's orderly habits would rub off on her. If she stayed here a while. Well, even if that's not likely to happen—and she can't see how it might—she's here right now.

She can hear water running in the pipes. He's in the shower. She finishes her drink and stands. The vodka races to her brain. She heads for the stairs.

Is this a good idea? Almost certainly not—she should be focusing on staying alive, not fooling around—but she doesn't much care. Like she said to Shire, it's nice to feel desired.

*   *   *

The glass shower enclosure is completely steamed over. Scott's form is a shadowy six-foot-tall shape bent forward, head down, under the water spray. She drops her towel and opens the door, steps in. It closes behind her with a metallic click. Scott stands straight. He starts to turn, but she puts one hand on his hip. "I don't really like Scrabble," she says. "It makes people too competitive. And gangster flicks are so predictable."

With her other hand, she lifts the bar of soap off its shelf and runs it in circles between his shoulder blades, then down the small of his back, lower still.

"Shire claims there are ways—other than sex—for a woman to get attention from men."

He turns and faces her, the water splashing off his shoulders now. "She did?"

"You think she's right?" Carla asks, sliding the soap across his chest.

"Absolutely," he says, like it's a well-known truth. "Lots of other ways."

"Oh really?" She pretends to be fascinated. "Any that you want to suggest just now?"

"At the moment," he says, "I can't think of a single one."

In bed, he's enthusiastic, his mouth and fingers awkward but gentle. Carla enjoys his efforts, however unsophisticated. She stiffens into a shuddering internal explosion, holds it as long as it will last, and then drifts back down. The therapist who told her she pursued casual sex because it gave her a sense of control was wrong.

It was the complete oblivion of an orgasm she was pursuing. You can't think about anything else, anything at all. Sometimes that's the goal.

She rolls up onto her knees and elbows and says, "Let's get serious."

After the noisy part, they fall into the pillows.

CHAPTER

38

Lying next to Carla, Scott is floating in a fog of elation that nothing but actual two-party sex ever gives him and no amount of masturbation ever matches. It's a feeling he hasn't known for months.

He may have drifted off. At some point, he hears Carla let out a long, dramatic sigh. She looks worried about something. Time to talk. Not his greatest talent. It's important, though. He knows that much. For some reason, there was an old *GQ* magazine at the Anchor Point gas station, of all places. Waiting for his snow tires to be mounted, he read a how-to article about postcoital "pillow talk."

"Carla, relax. I told you, he won't have any way of knowing that we're up here."

"That's not what I was thinking about. For the first time in a while."

"Then what?"

"You know, if I want sex—like any healthy, oxygen-breathing human being should—I do what it takes to get laid."

"So, what's the problem? You're an adult."

"The problem, goofy, is that chasing pussy is an act of valor for men. When a woman initiates sex, she gets called a whore."

"It's not like you're doing it for money or something. I mean I hope you're not scheming to get your hands on my fishing tackle."

"No." She comes close to smiling. "Your wife already grabbed that valuable hoochie thing."

Scott is embarrassingly pleased to be lying in bed with this good-looking woman, talking. "That's what's bothering you?"

"I keep saying I'm going to stop hooking up like this with men I hardly know. I'm getting too old for it."

Just another man she hardly knows. Scott feels the sting that brings on. "Old?"

"Yeah. Lately, I've been worrying about the way I live. And my future. Even before the D'Angelo thing."

She has one hand resting between her legs, fingers absently twirling the hairs there, staring up at the ceiling as she thinks about what she's saying. He tries to concentrate on the conversation.

"Carla, everybody worries about the future—unless they're sickeningly rich or incredibly dumb." He hopes that sounds as wise as it seems to him.

"If I keep living like this," she says, "presuming I can stay alive a little longer, I'm going to end up like my mother: bitter and alone and depending on strange men for everything. And I'm not nearly as good at manipulating guys as she is. I worry I'll be so desperate when I'm her age I'll start posting ads on dating sites: 'Wanted: Straight male. Age twenty-one to ninety. Must have teeth.' "

The talking is good. Only now his body is interested in something else.

She looks down and sees that and shakes her head, smiling to herself.

"Oh well," she says, "since we're already here . . ." She pushes him on his back and straddles him. "Starting tomorrow, I'm going to straighten out my life."

They're still in that position a few minutes later when he hears his front door close with a thud. Carla stops riding but remains on top of him, fear freezing her face. "You hear that?"

Scott puts his hands on her hips, keeping her pinned there. "Quiet!" he hisses.

"Do you have a gun up here?" she whispers.

He shakes his head. "In the safe. Downstairs."

"You don't keep one next to your bed?" Louder now.

"I never wanted to shoot anyone in my bedroom. Until now. Shut up!"

She cups a hand over her mouth.

He feels her tense, about to climb off him, jump out of the bed. "Wait. Don't move," he says, trying to think this through. Would a professional soldier slam the door like that and alert everyone in the building? He strains to listen to what sounds like footsteps downstairs. He feels Carla tensing again. Those are *definitely* footsteps on the wood floors. No way he can get to his gun safe.

Then a familiar voice echoes through the house. "Scott? Carla? Where are you?"

Carla goes light. "Shire!" She wriggles off him. "Come on up."

Footsteps pound up the stairs.

Scott scrambles into the bathroom and cinches a towel around his waist. He walks back into the bedroom.

Shire Kiminsky stands in the doorway, arms crossed over her chest, face pink with anger. "Goddammit, Carla. I was practically planning your funeral and crying my eyes out! I'm going to kill you."

Wrapped in her towel, Carla runs to Shire, gives her a hug. "Good to see you too."

"Why am I always the only person wearing clothes when we talk?" Shire says. Then her indignation collapses. She hugs Carla back. "God, I thought you were dead. I was so happy to see you on the dock ramp. Even if you did totally wreck my skiff, asshole!"

"Sorry." Carla gives Shire a kiss on the cheek. "It was an accident."

"An accident that just happened to land you in Scott's bed?" She cuts Scott a cold look. "You think the two of you can put on some clothes and tell me what the hell this is about?"

"Yeah," Scott says. "I'll fix us some lunch and explain."

Shire turns back to Carla. "What the fuck did you do to your hair?"

* * *

Down in the kitchen, Scott assembles three salmon sandwiches and ferries the plates to the table along with a jar of pickles and Carla's corn chips. He brings three IPAs and sits next to Carla.

Carla's explaining to the still-angry Shire about her rescue from the bay, about the old photo of Gordon McKint, and about Cosmo D'Angelo.

Scott eats his food listening to her but worrying about his performance between the sheets. Thinking that years of marriage to one woman have given him a very limited toolbox of techniques. How would he know what various females might like? He'd only slept with five in his whole life before marrying Trina. Six, if he counts the bathroom remodel client, a much-older divorcée who lured him to her bedroom, ostensibly to see about a recessed-lighting problem. He isn't sure if that one counts because he was so freaked about the ethics of screwing a customer—not to mention wondering if he'd ever get paid for the job—that he wasn't able to come.

They eat and talk, mostly Carla, who tells Shire about fleeing Phoenix.

Shire fumes. "You think you're being stalked by a professional killer, yet you find time to get our heroic carpenter here to show you his lumber?"

"I needed to get my mind off the whole thing."

Scott stifles a sigh. That's all he is. A distraction.

"You mean the whole thing you never bothered to tell your best friend about for two months?" Shire asks.

"I'm sorry that I had to keep D'Angelo a secret. Really. I didn't want you and the girls involved." Carla turns to Scott. "And I'm sorry if I used you to make myself feel better."

"Um . . ." He needs to do or say something. He stands and goes to the counter and picks up the frying pan. There's one piece of salmon left in it. "Who's still hungry?" he says.

He turns back to the table and sees Carla and Shire stiffen, eyes wide.

From behind him, a man's voice says, "I am."

Scott spins around.

An enormous man fills the kitchen doorway. "I'm starving."

CHAPTER

39

"JESUS FUCK!" AT the sight of D'Angelo, Carla hurls herself against the chair back, gulping air. "Oh my God!"

D'Angelo's standing with one hand in his jacket pocket. He's wearing the same long-billed black cap he had on the night they met in Phoenix. It almost touches the top of the doorframe.

"Hello, Carla," he says flatly. "It's been a while. You changed your hair."

A nervous jolt shoots down the inside of her thighs. Her gut clenches. She wants to fly out of her chair. D'Angelo's dead eyes pin her to it.

She glances at Scott. He has the frying pan in one hand. He looks like he's going to make a move with it. D'Angelo holds up one palm and stops him with a shake of his head. "Everybody stay put." He keeps the other hand deep in his pocket. "No sudden moves, okay?"

"He's got a gun," Scott says.

"Listen to Crockett, ladies." D'Angelo turns that ice-water stare on Carla again. "You and I need to talk."

Carla's legs feel like they've already started running without her. She puts her hands on the tabletop and leans forward, not sure whether she's going to launch out of the chair or bend over and vomit. A trickle of sweat slides down her ribs. She hears herself emit a tiny groan and falls back into her chair. He's been terrorizing her for two months—from thousands of miles away. Now the source of all that fear is standing right in front of her. She moans, "Oh, fuck."

Shire says, "Take it easy, Carla."

That's not going to be possible as long as D'Angelo keeps those eyes on her.

He says, "The picture. You have it with you?"

She manages to shake her head. "Not here."

"Not here." His face darkens further. "The truck?"

"If I tell you the truth, will you let us go?" Her voice sounds funny to her, distant and vaguely electronic, like it's coming from speakers outside her head somewhere. "Will you?"

Shire and Scott are frozen, listening to the pair's every word.

"Well, if you *don't* tell me the truth. . . ." He lets that hang there. Watches her.

Carla's mind spins. Once he knows where the picture is, he won't need her. He won't need any of them. He could pull the gun out and use it. Kill them all. Scott said no one is going to think twice about hearing gunshots up here at Anchor Point. The thought makes her breathe faster. But if she doesn't tell him, will he start hurting people?

Before she loses her nerve, she blurts, "I stuck it up in the head-liner of the cab."

"So it *is* in your truck," D'Angelo says, his face blank. "Okay, who told you I had it at my house in Phoenix? Who do you work for?"

"What? *Work* for? What do you mean?" she sputters. "I just stumbled onto it in your nightstand."

D'Angelo nods. Carla can see he already knew that. Of course he did. If she'd been working for anyone, he would've found out by now. He's seeing if she's going to lie.

He says, "Why haven't you turned it over to your friend Lisa Yi? Or *any* of the media? What are you waiting for?"

He knows that she talked to Lisa Yi too. There's no way to guess how much he's found out. What he's heard. What he knows. She can't risk lying to him. "Before I let anyone print it, I wanted to make sure you couldn't find me."

"And you figured if you're supposedly drowned, you can do whatever you want with it?"

Carla nods.

"Did you and Captain Crockett here scuttle the skiff on purpose to throw me off?"

"No!" Carla looks over at Shire. "I wouldn't do that!"

Shire reaches out and lays one hand on Carla's arm. "I know, honey."

Carla turns back to D'Angelo. "I didn't know Scott was even out there. There was a storm! I almost got killed!"

He just stares, eyes as empty as deep space. Carla grits her teeth. What is he thinking?

He snaps back to life. "One last question. And this is the big one." He pauses a beat. "How much were you planning to charge Gordon McKint to give the photo back to him?"

"What?" Carla almost comes out of her chair again. "Charge? Money?"

"Blackmail?" Scott says. He sets the frying pan down on the counter and slumps into his chair. "Carla?"

Before she can answer, D'Angelo says, "At first I figured Crockett was in on the plan, but now my guess is you're playing him. Using him—like you used George Volker—to hide you until you can find someone to help you blackmail McKint and split the money. Is that how this is supposed to work?"

"That's not what I was going to do!" Carla turns to Scott. "Scott! Honest. You have to believe me. You know what I want to do with the picture. I told you the truth!"

"I know," he says, but he looks doubtful.

"Carla?" Shire says. She looks like she's also wondering if D'Angelo is right.

Carla feels like she's going insane. "Blackmail McKint? Jesus! I don't know how to do that!"

D'Angelo's face goes inert again. Impossible to read. She's not sure if he's even listening. Is he about to pull his gun out?

"Listen to me!" she says, "Yes, Scott was going to hide me until you gave up. But then we were going to take the photo to the FBI in Anchorage. That's it. That's all there is. Cosmo! What the hell do you want me to say?" Something is tightening in the back of her neck. "Scott, please. Tell him!"

"It's true," Scott says. "She wants to stop Sidewinder from taking over the Mexican border. Personal reasons." He looks at Carla fondly, then back at D'Angelo. "I believe her."

"Personal reasons," D'Angelo mutters. He seems to think about that for moment. He sighs, shoulders loosening. "Yeah, that's the conclusion I've been coming to about Carla lately too. I just had to be sure." He pulls his hand out of his pocket and pats both sides of his jacket with his palms. There's nothing in the pockets.

"What the fuck?" Shire says. "No gun? You scared the shit out of us!" She stands.

"It just means I don't keep one in my pocket." D'Angelo gives her an icy stare. "Don't push your luck."

Shire sits back down. "Asshole," she mutters.

"That's better," D'Angelo says. "Here's what's going to happen now. You three are going to help me get that photo out of Carla's truck."

"What?" Carla squeaks. "Help you?"

"Well, I can't stroll into the police station and ask for it. One of you is going to have to go and get it while I stay here with the other two until you get back."

"Hostages?" Scott says.

"Think of it as making a new friend."

Shire starts to object.

"You want me to get it myself? Okay. Fine. I'll just blow up a boat or two in the marina to draw most of the cops out of the shop and then force my way into the impound yard." His eyes flare up. "Because after coming this far, I am not leaving here without that fucking photo!"

Shire and Scott look as terrified as Carla feels.

"Well, now that we all understand each other," D'Angelo says, relaxing incrementally, "how about you make me a sandwich with that last piece of salmon, Crockett? And we'll figure out who's going to town."

Scott looks at Carla and then Shire, questioningly. They both shrug.

"Okay," Scott says warily. He stands again and goes to the stove. "But if we get you that picture, you have to go."

D'Angelo holds one hand up. "I swear: You help me get that thing, I'm out of here."

Carla's touched by Scott's attempt to protect her and still wondering what the hookup with him was about. She's feeling way too

warm about him for it to have been mere sport. *Shit.* Does she want
to get involved with a new guy right now in the middle of all this?
D'Angelo could revert to his death-threat mode any second. Like
he said: he doesn't have a gun in his pocket. That doesn't make him
harmless exactly.

At the moment he seems mostly interested in food. "Damn,
that smells good, Crockett. What did you put on the salmon, dill?"

Shire looks at Carla from across the table and rolls her eyes. She
mouths, *Asshole.*

"Yeah, dill. Come on, D'Angelo," Scott says. He reaches into
a cupboard and pulls out another plate. "You have to tell us why
you're so hot to get that photo. We know you and McKint lied
to Congress about meeting the Colombian colonel in the picture.
But even if you're convicted, that's a few months in a white-collar
prison. You guys could do that time standing on your heads." He
makes a sandwich like the others, pulls a napkin from a drawer.

Carla feels her nerve coming back. "Scott's right, Cosmo.
You've been making my life miserable for two months. Now you
want to sit and have lunch? And terrorize us into helping you? Are
you really that intent on helping McKint run for president? That
loyal to McKint?"

D'Angelo looks like he's deciding how to answer her.

She says, "This isn't about McKint's so-called immigration
emergency. You're not a racist like him. I've been to your house,
seen the picture of your Army friend from Mexico. And I've seen
your face when you watch McKint running his mouth on TV." She
pauses, catches her breath. "So what's this about? The money you'll
make if Sidewinder takes over the border? Is that all?" Carla hears
the pleading in her voice. She really doesn't want it to be about that.

D'Angelo is still. His face unreadable.

Nobody says anything for a moment. Somewhere nearby, a
crow squawks. A dog barks.

Then D'Angelo sighs. He takes a seat at the table between Carla
and Shire. Scott sets the plate of food in front of him. D'Angelo
silently picks up the fish sandwich and takes a huge bite.

Carla feels the terror dissipating. Maybe it was getting that
tirade out of her system. Or maybe it's being this close to him,
inches away now. She flashes to sitting on his patio chatting, eating

the spaghetti he cooked for her, climbing into his bed. She's heard it said that all humans are capable of becoming monsters. Well, maybe some monsters can be human.

"Oh man," he says, his mouth stuffed, "the tartar sauce is perfect."

Carla arches an eyebrow at him. "Cosmo? That photo?"

He takes a swig of beer, swallows. He nods.

"It's personal for me too, Carla."

40

THE ORCA IS half-full. It's too early in the day for the regular bar zombies, but a dozen tourists—all from the day's cruise ship—are sitting at two adjoining tables, nursing pitchers of local Red Knot ale and marveling at the Alaskan bric-a-brac hanging on the walls. Gold pans, gill nets, a long piece of feathery whale baleen. Volker makes sure everyone is set for the moment, then heads for the liquor storeroom off the kitchen for some Tito's to replace the freshly empty bottle behind the bar.

He's still wondering what a dead-eyed ghoul like D'Angelo wants so badly from Carla's truck. What he has to do with Carla at all. It's clear the withholding bastard isn't going to share that information. Or anything else. Not with all that secret-agent, need-to-know-basis bullshit he seems to wallow in. What a dick.

Cutting through the kitchen, Volker stops to say hi to his young helper, Joey, just arriving. Joey is hanging up his HOMER HIGH SCHOOL MARINERS letter jacket and putting on an apron. He's old enough to work at the Orca—washing dishes, busing tables—but not to mix or serve drinks. "Go, *Mariners!*" Volker shouts.

Joey smiles and knots his apron. "Hi, Mr. Volker."

Joey is the quietest, most polite teenager Volker has ever heard of. He loves embarrassing the kid with gross comments and crude, unsolicited advice.

"Dude, you're early," he says as Joey picks up a broom. "Don't you have some pointy-titted cheerleader you should be poking this afternoon?"

Joey shakes his head and starts sweeping.

Volker doesn't really need the extra help. He keeps Joey around because he promised the kid's mother he'd give him a summer job. Angela, a nurse at the hospital, is a worried, nervous single mom but a lot of fun in bed. She's also a helicopter parent of the first order. She doesn't want Joey out working on the boats, where he would make a lot more money than the Orca pays—but where he could also get hurt or even killed.

Volker was dating Angela when Carla showed up. Throwing Angela over for her, he considered reneging on the promise to hire Joey. But keeping the boy on the payroll is relatively cheap insurance in case he ever needs to get back into Angela's good graces. And the truth is, he enjoys the kid's company. Now that Carla is gone, he's suddenly remembering more of Angela's good traits than her bad ones.

"So, Joey," he says, as he unlocks the door to the liquor store-room, "how's your mom?"

*　*　*

Volker has the bottle of Tito's in hand and is just switching off the storeroom light when he hears a thud out in the kitchen. "You break it, Joey, you pay for it!"

He walks out to find Joey facedown on the concrete floor, a short, bald man standing over him. The guy has a ginger, chest-length beard that's braided and cinched with a leather thong an inch above the tip. He's hunched forward, hands balled in fists tight to his hips, bright-green eyes bulging with anticipation. "George Volker?"

"Hey, what the hell—"

Volker barely registers the blurred movement in front of his eyes but feels the sudden numbness spreading across his face, hears the Tito's bottle crash on the concrete. He's just figuring out that his nose is smashed and that he's on his back on the floor himself when the man crouches, grabs him by his shirt front, and says, "Carla Merino's truck. Two thousand one Toyota. Where is it?"

Carla again. Of all the problematic women Volker has known, she's taking first prize.

The little guy looms over him. He's wearing a white T-shirt with some thrash metal band logo on it, tucked into camo pants, tucked into combat boots. The floor-mat beard, the neck tattoos. Definitely an Anchor Point off-the-roader.

Those guys don't frequent the Orca much. What would they have to talk about with either the commercial fishermen or the tourists? None of them work or fish. None of them do anything, as far as Volker can tell. He knows the type, mostly from Atkins's gas station up there, where he fuels up because it's four cents a gallon cheaper than in Homer. There are always a few of the goons hanging around, gassing up their cobbled-together pickups with mismatched quarter panels and absent tailgates. Whenever one of them looks his way, Volker nods and says, "Hey, man," and hopes they recognize him as the defiant, antiestablishment type he's pretty sure his ponytail says he is.

"Are you listening to me?" This particular troglodyte now kicks him in the thigh so hard the pain rockets from his ankle to his armpit. The guy draws his boot back to deliver another one. "Her truck?"

"Stop!" Volker crab-scuttles upright against the stainless-steel sink stand. "The truck is at the cop shop. It's in impound! I swear! Go look!" He raises one hand to his bleeding nose, squeezes his cramping thigh with the other. His pants are wet with vodka. He has a shard of glass in the palm of one hand. Out of the corner of his eye, he sees that Joey seems to be unconscious but breathing. Angela's going to blame this on him somehow. "Jesus, why is everybody so interested in Carla's truck?"

The guy crouches so close to his face now that the beard tickles Volker's neck. Although everything about the man screams *tweaker*, his teeth are straight and brilliantly white. His breath smells fresh, though vaguely chemical, like some kind of household cleaning product. "Who's 'everybody'?"

"A big guy from out of town. Looks like a cop."

"Eye-talian name?

Volker nods.

"Yep." The creep is apparently unsurprised. "Impound, huh?" he says, eyes slit.

Volker nods as quickly as he can. A spear of pain shoots through his skull. "I turned it in this afternoon."

The thug straightens and peers down at him, twisting the end of his beard, no doubt deciding whether to believe Volker or beat on him some more. "If I drive all the way into town and it's not there, I'm going to come back out here and stick your head in that deep fryer until your ponytail is crispy as a corn dog. You do know that, right?"

Volker nods harder, his sinuses exploding.

"Okay then. Have a nice day." He turns and walks out.

Volker scrambles across the floor to Joey and rolls him onto his back. The left side of the kid's face is bloody, that eye swelling shut. Volker shouts his name, shakes his shoulders. Joey's right eye flutters open and stalls half-lidded.

"Joey! Can you hear me?"

"Mr. Volker?" Joey's eye finally seems to locate him.

"Say something," Volker says.

"I fucking quit, man."

41

D'ANGELO EATS RAVENOUSLY, biting off big chunks of his fish sandwich, gulping it down with the bitter IPA everyone seems to be drinking these days. The food is glorious, the garlic-flavored oil smoky but not burned. God, he hates overbrowned garlic. "Delicious. I think I might live to my next meal now." He sips his beer.

"The picture," Carla says.

"Okay. In 1997, I was with Joint Special Ops, providing ground branch protection for the CIA during the War on Drugs down in Colombia. It was chaos. Escobar was dead, and the other drug lords were slaughtering each other over his turf. Meanwhile, the Colombian Army and right-wing paramilitary groups were fighting the communist FARC guerillas. Everyone was financed by the coke we were supposed to be destroying." He stops to take another bite and a swallow of beer. "Chaos."

Carla says, "You were guarding McKint in the photo."

D'Angelo nods. "Gordon was a CIA adviser to the Colombian Army. I was his driver-bodyguard. One day we met two men at a little hotel in the mountains. One was a colonel in the Colombian Army. The other was some Panamanian lawyer. Long story short? McKint and the colonel were stealing DEA money by the truck-load. The Panamanian was laundering it for them."

"Who took the picture?" Carla asks.

"Not sure. My bet is the colonel had it done. He wanted something to bargain with if he got sideways with the CIA," D'Angelo says. "We'll never know. Torres was killed in two thousand one."

"So, how is this 'personal' for you?" Shire's skepticism is thick.

D'Angelo takes a breath and starts again. "This meeting was almost over when a concussion grenade came through a window. Small-arms fire poured in. A real shitstorm. I was dazed pretty bad. Gordon grabbed me and basically shot his way out of the building. I was in the hospital for a month. I still can't hear much out of this ear." He points to the left side of his head.

"Now you owe the prick your life." It's Shire again. "Fucking great."

D'Angelo continues. "Then a couple months later, Gordon left the Agency and asked me to join him in the new company he was starting."

"Sidewinder," Carla says.

"Yeah. Gordon predicted that the next twenty years were going to be one clandestine military engagement after another. America didn't have the stomach for all-out wars anymore. There were fortunes to be made working as contractors." He shrugs. "I took the job."

"And it's been a real moneymaker for you too, hasn't it?" Shire says, dripping contempt.

"Can someone control this woman, please?" He's almost laughing.

"Control?" Scott says. "I've known her for more than thirty years. I haven't seen it done yet."

"Okay. To answer her question then, yes, Sidewinder has made money all over the world. But today, we don't have to go so far to do that. That's why you see Gordon on TV ranting about the border."

Shire hisses something under her breath.

Carla says, "That's all it is? McKint saved your life, and you are forever indebted to him? So you're going to take that photo from us and give it to him?" She shakes her head. "That's some pretty disappointing B-movie shit, Cosmo."

"Do you know where I got that photo?"

Carla shrugs. "Lisa Yi thinks your daughter might've given it to you."

D'Angelo nods. "Uh-huh. And do you know what the last thing she said to me was the day she died? 'Do the right thing.' "

Carla looks like she wants to say something personal to him. But she gets control and just asks, "Why was that picture in your nightstand the night I was there?"

"The night you stole it?"

She cringes. "Yeah."

D'Angelo slumps back into his chair. He takes a long swig of his beer, wipes his mouth with his hand. "When my daughter got sick, Gordon paid to get her into the best cancer treatment facilities money can buy. Still, Jennifer hated him. Wanted me to leave Sidewinder and use anything I knew to ruin him. But it was my choice. She told me I could burn the photo or use it against Gordon and turn myself in to the feds."

This is excruciating, but he needs their help to get to the truck. He sees Carla's face soften. Crockett seems unsure. Shire's expression is glass-hard, not ready to give him an inch.

"I took the picture with me when I went out of the country to deal with some problems for Sidewinder. The night I got home from my trip, I'd been alone for two weeks. I needed company. So, I stopped at a bar." He pauses again. "I met a very attractive waitress who followed me home. I put the picture in the nightstand with my passport." He looks at Carla. "The next day the picture was gone."

"Ah, jeez," Carla groans.

Scott says, "You studied that photo for two weeks? What did you expect to find in it that you didn't already know was there?"

D'Angelo chuckles ruefully. "I looked at my young face in that picture and saw a man who believed he was protecting his country. A man my daughter would be proud of." He stops and shakes his head slowly. "And now what's my job? Trying to prevent Mexicans from coming to work in America?"

Shire amps up the hostility again, glaring at him across the table. "Face it, D'Angelo, your boss isn't doing the good work you were so proud of anymore. He's not a hero. He's a money machine.

And you want us to give you that photo so you can save his sleazy ass?"

It's time to tell them everything.

"You're half right. I need the picture to honor my daughter." He pauses and looks at them. "It's how I'm going to destroy Gordon McKint."

CHAPTER

42

DESPITE VOLKER'S WHINING objection, the EMTs take one look at him and Joey and call the police. They try to get him to ride in the ambulance with Joey, who is still drifting in and out of consciousness, but Volker insists on following them to the hospital in his own car. No way is he going to be held for goddamned observation. With Carla gone, he's short a waitress. And Shire's caught up in dealing with her ruined boat and the search for Carla's body. The Orca is not going to sit dark during happy hour. He tells the EMTs he'll meet them at the emergency room.

As he drives, his face swelling and pounding with pressure from his smashed nose, he worries about how much to tell the cops. With that scary D'Angelo prick and this amped-up freak from Anchor Point out there somewhere, the last thing on earth he needs now is the police making him look like a snitch. One or both of those maniacs will kill him for sure.

And what the hell is their connection? Cosmo D'Angelo has cop written all over him. The Anchor Pointer with the stupid beard is strictly from the receiving end of law enforcement. And what do either of them have to do with poor Carla, lying cold and dead at the bottom of the bay? How the hell did she get involved with those two?

At the hospital, one of the city cops, David Parrish, takes Volker's statement. Short, bald, and fat, Parrish is a frequent Orca customer and seems to actually like Volker. "You say he didn't steal anything?" he asks. "I mean, really, George? Guy just walks in, beats on you two, and leaves? Drives all the way down from Anchor Point to do that? They run out of innocent victims to whale on up there?"

Volker holds an ice pack on his face. "Maybe he hates longhairs."

"That wouldn't explain young Joey's concussion. Kid's as clean-cut as a Mormon."

"David, I don't know! Those hillbilly junkies might do anything. The guy could be shooting fentanyl straight into his eardrums for all we know."

"Okay." Parrish slaps his notebook shut. "If he's on some kind of druggie rampage, we'll hear about it again real soon."

On the drive from the hospital back out to the Orca, Volker passes the police station and notices Carla's truck in the impound lot, right where he parked it. Which makes him think about Carla. Which makes him think about the whole Carla-screwing-Billy-Griest peccadillo that started all this. Which makes his face hurt even more.

Funny. For a while there, he felt like killing her. Now she's dead and gone, and he misses her so much. How the hell is that possible?

His head is pounding now. All this thinking isn't good for him. He has to cut that shit out.

CHAPTER

43

D'ANGELO WATCHES CARLA closely. After hiding from him for
months, will she believe anything he says? Will any of them?

There's no doubt what Shire thinks. "You expect us to believe
you're going to bring down Gordon McKint? After he's saved your
life? After all the money he's made you? And after he paid to help
your daughter when she was sick?" Shire slits her eyes so tight she
looks like she's in pain. "You're a lying sack of shit, D'Angelo."

He debates going back into threat mode, decides to keep it neutral, but puts a little edge in the voice. "You get me that photo, I'll
testify against him."

"But Cosmo," Carla says, "Shire's right. You said your daughter
asked you to do that months ago when she gave you the picture, but
you didn't. What changed?"

"Kevin Dykstra," D'Angelo says.

"Who?" Crockett asks.

"A young guy in our Phoenix office. Techie hipster type with
one of those man buns. Skintight jeans with the cuffs turned up. A
nice guy, and one of my people. Supposedly he had information on
Sidewinder's finances. McKint had him killed."

Carla says, "The suicide in Flagstaff?"

D'Angelo raises his eyebrows, impressed she knows that much.
"When I heard about it, I made some quiet inquiries. I hit a stone
wall. Somebody clearly didn't want me to pursue the matter. That's

when I knew that Gordon and a guy named Phil Lundren waited until I was out of the country to eliminate the kid. A friend I have at the FBI told me he thinks someone inside the Bureau tipped Sidewinder off that Kevin Dykstra was about to blow the whistle."

"Yeah," Carla says, "the bloggers think McKint has spies inside the FBI too."

"You have no idea what the man is capable of."

"You're saying you changed your mind because of that young guy they murdered?" Crockett says. "I'm sorry, but you and McKint did all kinds of shit together, didn't you? All those years?"

"Look, Gordon McKint and I eliminated some very bad people who needed to die. But he knew I'd never take out a noncombatant like Kevin Dykstra, a civilian—especially one of my own people. I am not going to let Gordon McKint bring his jungle tactics to America to make another buck for himself."

He realizes he's leaning over the table, nearly shouting at them. He sits back in his chair and feels his pulse racing. Calmly he adds, "So, one of you needs to go get me the photo from Carla's truck."

Carla says, "Why can't we call the cops anonymously and tell them about the picture and where it is?"

D'Angelo shakes his head. "They'd just turn it over to the FBI."

"But that's what you want to do, isn't it?"

"Carla, if someone inside the FBI is tipping off Sidewinder, I have to be sure that picture lands in the hands of people I can trust." He looks from Scott to Shire and back. "So, who's going to town? It's got to be one of you two. Carla's supposed to be dead, and it's best if she stays that way."

"It's gotta be me," Shire says. "What possible excuse can Scott give the police for going into Carla's truck? I know half the cops in town. I can charm them."

"Yeah," Carla says to Shire. "But only if you want to. I'm worried about you and the girls getting involved."

Shire gives D'Angelo a look of sheer menace. "You better not fuck us, asshole."

He has to smile. Shire's about five foot five and as cute as a baby animal. Right now he's half convinced she would hunt him down and murder him in his sleep.

He holds his hands up in surrender.

Shire gives him one more baleful stare and turns to Carla. "So, how do we do this?"

"You have a picture in your phone of me and you and the twins in the Orca." She turns to D'Angelo. "George took it on the girls' birthday. He threw a party for them. Shirley Temples and cupcakes."

"Sure," Shire says. She pulls her phone out and scrolls through her photos.

"And?" D'Angelo says to Carla.

"Shire prints that out and hides it on herself. Then she goes to the police station, all upset over my drowning. She tells the guys there's a picture of her and me in my glove box. It's the only thing she has to remember me by."

"I've heard worse ideas."

"So, they let Shire into my truck, and she comes out with the picture of us and the twins in her hand, right?"

"And the photo of McKint in my pocket," Shire says.

"Exactly."

Crockett looks at D'Angelo. "And then you'll leave Carla alone, right?" he says, fear replaced by determination now.

That's all right. D'Angelo can see that Carla has gotten to him. Badly. He can't blame the guy. Since he saw her face the first time again this afternoon, he's been regretting that it all went this way.

He nods. "It's a deal." He stands and stretches his cramping back. "Okay, Shire, you go to town. Carla and Crockett and I'll wait here." He gives them a cold look to be sure nobody wants to argue with the idea of them acting as more or less hostages. They all nod. He looks at his watch. "Make it as fast as you can, Shire. There's a wrinkle I haven't told you about."

"A wrinkle?" Carla says. "I don't like that word."

"This morning Carla's name went out on the Coast Guard's site. That set off a flag at my office. My betters were a little surprised that someone at Sidewinder has been searching for a certain Carla Merino—without his superiors knowing about it. Let's just say they're less than delighted with yours truly."

Carla's first to see where this is heading. "They're sending somebody to Homer to replace you. And get me!"

"You bet," D'Angelo says. "Right now, if they track my phone, it will indicate that I'm still out on the spit, near the marina.

That's where they'll look first. And these goons will come heavy. Understand?"

Carla nods, grim faced. "And you didn't bring a gun?"

D'Angelo reaches behind his back, pulls his pistol out, and shows them.

"You manipulative motherfucker," Shire says. "You said you didn't have a gun."

"No." D'Angelo shakes his head. "I indicated I didn't have one in my pockets." He replaces the pistol, pulls his jacket down over it again.

Shire looks like she's going to leap up from the table and choke him.

"These guys can't be in Homer already, can they?" Crockett says. "It'll take them a while to send somebody here. I mean, all the way from Phoenix or something?"

"Unfortunately, Alaska is crawling with ex-military and ex-Agency personnel. Sidewinder could easily have somebody on one of the bases in Anchorage or Fairbanks itching to sign up for a little freelance work muscling a good-looking cocktail waitress."

Carla holds her head in her hands.

Shire mutters something D'Angelo doesn't quite hear.

He checks his watch again. "We have to get moving. I talked to Phil Lundren around eleven this morning. He's the guy running the hunt for you now. Even if he's already found someone in Anchorage, they won't arrive in Homer until this evening. And there's nothing to bring him up here to Anchor Point. But by now Lundren has Carla's vehicle registration from my search data. And he'll know about Shire's boat, and the two of you working at the Orca too. The only thing he *doesn't* know is where the truck is. Shire needs to grab that picture before Lundren's guy pays a visit to Volker and finds out about the impound yard."

Shire is already out of her chair, holding her phone up to Scott. "Can you print this photo for me?"

"Sure." Scott stands. "In my office. I've got photo paper for my portfolio of jobs."

Shire follows him out of the kitchen.

D'Angelo sits across the table from Carla, definitely wishing it hadn't gone like this. "That night I picked you up, I'd just got back from a terrible, messy assignment. I was worrying about Jennifer and what to do with the photo. I needed to get my mind off things, badly. You were nice to me. I'm sorry this turned out like this."

She works up a pinched half smile. "No one dragged me into your house. Or your bed. Jesus, I've slept with some problematic guys before, Cosmo, but you are the worst ever."

"I was just thinking the same thing about you."

She laughs. "What about those two?" She gestures toward the sound of Scott and Shire talking in his office. "I went with you looking for a good time. They were minding their own business before I dumped this on them. Shire has little children, for God's sake."

She's right. He's enlisting amateurs in dangerous work. That's the kind of thing that will get people killed. Man, he really is getting too old for this job.

Carla's watching him.

D'Angelo looks at her. "Tell me something. Nobody made you go through my nightstand either. Why did you look in that drawer in the first place? That's the part of all this I haven't figured out."

"It's embarrassing. I was just looking for a little something to remember you by. A memento. It's stupid."

"Because you didn't intend on seeing me again."

"Let's say I wasn't sure." She sighs. "It's me, not you, Cosmo. I've gotten used to very brief, no-strings affairs in the past few years. Like I said, it's my problem."

"Yeah. Well, it's mine too now."

Shire comes back into the kitchen with the color print of her and Carla sitting at a table in the Orca with the tiny blond twins on their laps. They're all wearing pointy party hats with rubber chin straps. The girls hold their mocktails up to the camera, little umbrellas in each glass. The women salute with bottles of Pacifico.

D'Angelo hands it back to Shire. "Listen, when you get to town, keep your eyes peeled for a guy who doesn't look like the usual fishermen or tourist types. He's going to be stiffer, not having a good time."

"Oh, you mean an asshole who looks like you?" Shire says brightly. "I'll be back in an hour. With the picture." She runs to her car and takes off down the gravel road.

D'Angelo says, "Man, there were times when I could've used a dozen like her."

CHAPTER

44

C ARLA STANDS AND watches through the window as Shire drives away. Scott is still at the sink doing dishes. She and D'Angelo sit at the kitchen table again. She says, "Why can't I have my life back if you're going to put McKint in jail or something?"

"The man is known to hold a grudge, Carla. And Lundren already thinks you were planning on blackmailing Gordon with the photo. He'll use all of Sidewinder's resources to find you."

"And so did you?" she says. "You thought I was going to try that? Blackmail?"

He shrugs. "People do crazy things."

"Come on. You know she wasn't going to do that," Scott says. "You can tell Sidewinder."

Scott is at the counter, meticulously drying a gleaming frying pan. Carla watches him hang it from a hook on the pot rack. The thing looks like it just came off a shelf in a Williams Sonoma. Jesus, he's a neat freak. She can't decide if she wants to marry or strangle him.

"I can tell them?" D'Angelo scoffs. "When this hits the fan, I'm going to be the first one they take out."

"Why?" Carla asks, the word *blackmail* still echoing in her head for some reason.

"Carla, I had the photo for two weeks without telling them about it. Not to mention keeping its existence—and yours—secret for another two months." He laughs coldly. "My only way out of all this right now is to bring the feds the photo and testify against Gordon. They'll put me in the Witness Security Program."

"Well, shit! I'm not going to get witness protection. I don't have anything to testify about!" She feels the heat in her cheeks. "I have to run for the rest of my life? This is the end of the fucking road, Alaska! It seemed like a sure thing. Look how well that worked out."

D'Angelo reaches over and pats her arm. "Take it easy. I do this for a living." He motions for Crockett to join them. "Crockett, come and sit. Listen to me."

Scott takes a seat next to her. Carla lays her hand on his knee, manages a smile.

"Here's the deal." D'Angelo pulls a cell phone out of his pocket. "This is a phone I borrowed from Volker. It can't be connected to me. I can call someone who will give you a new identity."

"A new identity? Why would you do that for me?" Carla asks.

"I don't want you to get killed because you picked me instead of any of the other cops who drink at the Sierra." He chuckles. "I'll bet I'm not the first person to say this, Carla, but you have terrible judgment about men."

"You and my mother should chat."

D'Angelo holds the cell phone up again. "Let me make that call. This guy will want you to move very fast. Probably tonight. You up for that?"

"Today?" She's just starting to like Homer, not to mention Shire and the girls. And yes, this awkward but sweet carpenter who seems intent on helping her. After years of more or less meaningless hook-ups with men, having one who clearly likes her, a decent guy who could be something more, is a great feeling. She's almost forgotten what that's like.

"You totally trust this person, right?" she asks D'Angelo.

"He's my escape pod. Even if the feds put me in WITSEC, I'll be calling this guy."

Scott says, "You don't trust the federal Witness Security Program?"

"Call it my second level of security. The feds make me disappear, and then I disappear from them. It's like being twice removed from my known life. This guy is my plan B." He makes the call.

"Sure," Carla says, still thinking about having to leave this place, running again, hiding, starting over someplace new. She stands. "I gotta get some air." She sees Scott give her a bereft look. She goes out and leans against the railing on the porch.

She's not there a minute when a crow flies in and lands on the railing a few feet away. Its ink-black feathers shine in the sunlight as it tips its head to one side, sizing her up. It squawks at her, beak open wide. She looks back over her shoulder at the kitchen window. She can see Scott watching. The crow squawks at her again in a demanding tone.

Scott comes out with something cupped in one hand.

"Hey, this crow is tame or something," she says.

"Yeah. I found him tangled up in fishing line on the dock this spring. His wing was damaged. I brought him home in a box and took care of him until he could fly. He's free to go, but he keeps hanging around." Scott sprinkles some small brown chunks on the railing. "He likes bacon bits. I keep a jar in the cupboard."

The bird hops over and pecks at them.

"Bacon bits." Carla laughs. "Those can't be good for him."

"I'm his friend, not his wife."

"What's his name?"

Scott looks bemused. "I never named him. I guess I figured he was going to take off and I'd never see him again."

"And you didn't want to get too attached?"

Scott swallows. "Something like that."

Carla watches Scott feeding the bird. It would be nice to stay, but the sun is strong again. And once more it makes her feel like it's beaming down on her for the benefit of whoever comes looking. These new guys who even D'Angelo is afraid of. She's going to have to go with his plan. She can hear him in the house talking on the phone.

Scott looks at her fondly. "You want to feed the bird?"

The crow looks up as if he knows they're talking about him.

She takes a few bacon bits from Scott and holds them out. The crow hops up to her hand and plucks one from her fingers.

"He's a smart bugger," she says.

Scott smiles. "They're members of the corvid family. Like ravens and magpies and jays. They have the brain–to–body mass ratio of whales and great apes. May be just as smart."

"Maybe he can think up a way to get me out of this mess."

"You're getting what you want, aren't you? When Shire comes back with the photo, D'Angelo will take you to Anchorage and use it to bring McKint down. And you get a new ID. That's all good, right?"

"Yeah," she says tiredly. "I guess. I don't know."

They're still very close, and she lets her head fall against Scott's chest. The idea of living in this house in the woods runs across her mind. It's too bad they can't give it a try. Then something D'Angelo said overshadows that, something about getting money from McKint for the photo. It really hadn't occurred to her. But now . . .

D'Angelo walks out onto the porch, still talking on his cell. Carla pulls away from Scott and leans against the porch rail.

"Okay, sure," D'Angelo says into the phone. He turns to Carla. "How old are you?"

She shoots Scott a quick glance. This is a once-in-a-lifetime opportunity. "Thirty-three," she tells D'Angelo.

Scott grins.

D'Angelo cuts her a dubious glance but repeats the number into the phone. "Height and eye color?" he says to Carla. She tells him. Then he says into the phone, "I'll send it to you in one minute. She'll call you when she gets to Anchorage." He fiddles with the phone and says to Carla, "Look at this."

The phone makes a clicking sound. It dawns on her what he's doing. "Did you just take a picture of me?"

D'Angelo nods, and she hears the unmistakable swoosh of an outgoing text.

"God. You could've let me comb my hair," she says. "What's left of it."

"I think you're supposed to look like a madwoman in your passport photos. It's some kind of rule."

"Great," Carla says. "What happens now?"

"When Shire gets back here with the picture, you and I are going to haul ass to Anchorage and call Mr. Plan B back. He'll tell you where to pick up your new ID and some other things you'll need. Then I take the photo to the FBI office. My contact in the Bureau in D.C. gave me the name of a guy I can trust there. They'll put me in protective custody."

Scott says, "Wait, doesn't your plan B guy have to be paid for the ID? That can't be cheap."

"That's the fun part. There's a slush fund on the dark internet Sidewinder uses for all sorts of off-the-books things." He grins. "I'm using their dark money to help Carla disappear."

Carla tries to smile. This is her way out. She'll go live someplace where nobody knows her. Change her name, her hair. Start over. Sidewinder will never find her. She should be relieved, right? Yet the weight of that lands on her like a falling building. And that word *disappear* keeps popping up.

Scott's says, "What's the matter, Carla? You look bummed."

"I can never see anyone I know again. I can never see Shire or the twins. I had friends in Phoenix." She hesitates, looks at him. "I can never see you again."

Scott's cheeks go so red he looks like he's been slapped.

The crow lands on the railing again and crams more bacon bits in his beak.

She walks back into the house, Scott trailing behind her.

D'Angelo apparently can see what's going on. "I'm going to stay out here and wait for Shire, keep an eye out for trouble, make friends with this bird."

Back at the kitchen table, Scott says, "Carla, I didn't expect anything serious. You know? But I would have liked to take you fishing some time, down to the river behind the house, maybe in the fall when the cottonwoods leaves are all yellow and the steelhead come in from the sea."

"What are those? Steelheads?"

"They're trout. Really big, really beautiful rainbow trout." He pauses, swallows. "I would've liked to take you out on the boat trolling for king salmon on a calm winter day too, when the snow is falling and there're hardly any other boats on the water. Just loons and cormorants and otters. I would've liked showing you that."

Carla feels a thickening in her throat. "That sounds nice," she chokes. "And I wouldn't mind hanging around to see you cut a swath through the women in this town." She has to keep joking now. "I could've helped you pick out some replacement undies for those tighty-whities of yours. Promise me you'll do that, at the very least."

That makes him laugh. "I think I could go as far as maybe some black ones."

"Now you're talking." She leans over and gives him a kiss before he can move out of the way. He doesn't move at all, just sits there and takes it, eyes closed. She pulls back. "Thanks for everything you've done for me."

D'Angelo comes back in from the porch, grumbling. He shows them a spot of blood on the tip of one finger. "That bird almost took my hand off." He stops in the doorway and looks at Carla and Scott. "You two all set now?" he says. "Good. Soon as Shire gets back with the photo, Carla and I are out of here."

45

SCOTT—THINKING ABOUT Carla leaving for good—sits fidgeting at the table with her and D'Angelo.

"What's taking Shire so long?" Carla asks.

D'Angelo looks at his watch and shakes his head, lips tight.

The crow shows up at the kitchen window demanding more food. It hammers the glass with its beak. "I'm thinking of naming him Nuisance," Scott says.

"He *is* relentless," D'Angelo says. "Does he ever get enough?"

Scott stands and goes to the pantry for bacon bits. "I think he'd eat constantly if he could."

"So would I, if I could," D'Angelo says.

"He's super smart. And vicious. If a songbird—a nuthatch or a chickadee—hits one of my windows, the crow will hear the thump and come flying in to peck the stunned bird to death."

"Sounds like the people I work for."

"Bunch of dicks," Carla says.

Looking at Carla, listening to her run that beautiful foul mouth of hers, Scott's heart flops around in his chest. He wishes they were still alone here at his house. Just Carla and him. He wishes that could've lasted a lot longer.

D'Angelo looks at his watch yet again. He doesn't say anything, but he looks concerned.

Scott says, "Should you try calling her on Volker's cell?"

D'Angelo shrugs. "Yeah, maybe. I doubt Lundren is monitoring Shire's calls. But I'd rather use the phone as little as possible. Let's give her another minute."

As though on cue, the sound of gravel crunching out in front of the house turns them that way.

"That must be her," D'Angelo says. He goes to the front door, followed by Carla. Scott hesitates, feels something tighten in his chest. If Shire has the photo with her, this will be the last time he sees Carla.

Carla and D'Angelo walk out onto the front porch to meet Shire. "I'll be right there," Scott calls out. He needs to get some composure before watching Carla leave. He lingers at the table a minute longer, looking at the crow peering in the window. "I'm going to get a few more bacon bits for my fine feathered friend."

He goes into the pantry, feeling like the wounded teenager he was when Lu Ann Freeman threw him over for that douche-bag Charlie Whiting. Almost staggering under the weight of it, he walks back out into the kitchen. The crow bangs on the glass. Again Scott finds himself imagining Carla living there with him, sitting on the porch, hand feeding the bird in the afternoon sun. And again, that fantasy is shattered.

"Stop right there, D'Angelo!" an unfamiliar voice blares from the front of the house. "You move a muscle and Blondie gets her head blown off!"

Scott's whole body clenches.

D'Angelo says something in reply that Scott can't make out.

He tiptoes to the window over the sink, heart fluttering.

D'Angelo and Carla are standing side by side at the top of the porch steps, facing the driveway, their backs to him. Scott can see D'Angelo's pistol protruding from the waistband of his pants. Shire's car is parked close behind Scott's truck. Her driver's side door and the door behind it are thrown open. Shire is walking up the drive-way toward the porch, her back rigid as a two-by-four, a short, bald man with a red beard tight behind her, clutching her ponytail in his left fist. He presses the muzzle of a black pistol against her head with his other hand. He's wearing camo pants and a white T-shirt with some lettering on it. Something about him looks familiar. Scott can't think why.

"I mean it," the man says. "Any move at all, it's going to rain blond hair and brains."

"Do I know you?" D'Angelo asks evenly, as though people point guns at him or his friends all the time.

The red-bearded man nudges Shire ahead until they're even with the left front fender of Scott's truck. They stop there, the man crouching against Shire's back. Scott can see that, even if D'Angelo had a chance to reach for the pistol behind his back, he has no shot from the porch. Not with Shire and the truck shielding the goon. He's keeping his hands at his sides where the goon can see them.

Heart stuttering, Scott ducks lower and creeps to the living room, opens the gun safe. He reaches for a rifle but thinks better of it. He isn't a great shot, and his marksmanship isn't going to improve with someone shooting back. He pulls out his bird gun—an old Browning pump shotgun—and loads it with bird shot, not the rifled slugs he uses for bear protection. It will be harder to miss with the scatter shot. The trick will be to avoid hitting Shire.

He hears the gun thug say, "The picture, tough guy. Where is it?"

D'Angelo stalls. "I'm still looking for it. Got any ideas you can share?"

The goon doesn't have the photo. Shire must not have found it in Carla's truck. Or she has it on her and the thug doesn't know that.

One thing is for sure. The man is going to start hurting people if he doesn't get what he wants. Shotgun in hand, Scott sneaks back through the house and out the back door onto the deck. He scrambles down the stairs and over soft tundra mosses, behind his shop to the gravel pit, and kneels behind the excavator.

Breathless, his ears roaring, stomach going sour, he thinks that this is what it must be like to be in combat. He's grateful he's never done that but now wishes he'd been trained the way D'Angelo must have been. Scott's been called a hero. But this is very different from the night the *Polar Huntress* sank, everything happening so fast it went by in a blur, being pulled out of the raging sea by rescue swimmers the next thing he knew. Here and now, time is slowing, jelling, every second stretching out as he tries to decide what to do. He edges forward behind the big, mud-clodded tracks of the machine until he can see the thug holding the gun to Shire's head a few yards away. His Crockett Construction truck is behind them from this angle.

D'Angelo is saying, "I can show you where it is."

The man twists Shire's ponytail and shouts, "Don't fuck with me, you dago cocksucker! I know you have it." Shire groans in pain or fear.

"If I had the photo, shit-for-brains, why would I still be here?" D'Angelo says. "Think about it."

That seems to flummox the man momentarily.

Scott could step out from behind the excavator and shoot. He can't miss from this distance. But Shire is too close to the guy. The bird shot pattern is unpredictable. He doesn't want to put a BB in Shire's brain. He still has a feeling he knows the man's face from somewhere. Where? He hesitates.

D'Angelo says, "Look, friend, leave the women out of this. They don't know what you're talking about. Let them go, and I'll take you to the photo."

"Okay, wise guy. Maybe I just shoot Blondie here, and you'll see I'm not dicking around." He lets go of Shire's ponytail and steps back, leveling the pistol at the back of her head. Shire squeezes her eyes tight in terror. Carla moans from the porch. There's no question, the guy is going to pull the trigger.

D'Angelo still has no shot, not with the man that tight against Scott's truck. He yells, "Wait!"

But this guy isn't waiting. He levels his aim on Shire's head and says, "Good-bye, Blondie."

Then the crow shrieks, fluttering onto the edge of excavator a yard from Scott, demanding food. The man turns his head to look toward the sound, pistol still trained on Shire. He squints at Scott and the bird. He hesitates.

Scott doesn't. He raises the shotgun and points as he would at a flushing spruce grouse. The blast explodes in his ears, the gunstock kicking against his shoulder. The man flies sideways, slams against the door of Scott's truck, and hangs there on the side-view mirror, a dark stain blooming across the left side of his T-shirt. He's still holding the pistol in his right hand, that elbow resting on the mirror bracket.

Scott pumps another shell into the chamber, puts the bead on the man again. Out of the corner of his eye, he sees D'Angelo shove Carla aside and start down the porch stairs, pistol in hand now.

The thug moans and raises his gun. When it goes off this time, the report is lost beneath the simultaneous roar from Scott's shotgun. This load catches the guy in the side of the head. He bounces off the truck again and pitches facedown into the gravel.

Scott runs out from behind the excavator to see if Shire's been shot, but it's D'Angelo who staggers and sinks down onto the top porch step, holding his right side with one hand.

Carla yells, "Scott! Cosmo's been shot!"

CHAPTER

46

Ears ringing, brain scrambling to absorb what he's just done, Scott runs through the cloud of cordite fumes to the man lying on the driveway. He half expects to remember where he knows him from. But the left side of his face and one eye is missing. A jumble of bones and meat oozes intensely red blood into the gravel around his destroyed head. Scott feels his own head swim, thinks he might faint. "Jesus, I shot him," he hears himself crying. "I thought he was going to kill Shire."

"Hey!" D'Angelo barks at Scott. "Snap out of it. He *was* going to kill Shire. You did all right." Shire and Carla are crouched over him where he sits on the top step, still clutching his side. He groans. Through locked teeth, he adds, "I wish you'd fired that second round a little sooner."

Scott looks at the bloody mess on the gravel, head spinning. He turns away and staggers to the porch. Carla lets go of D'Angelo. She scrambles down the stairs and pulls Scott into a hug.

"I never shot anybody before," he says to her, ears still ringing, but not from the shotgun blast now.

"It's okay," Carla says. "That guy needed to get shot. Are you all right?"

"I don't know. I guess." Scott wants to stay there pressed against Carla. But he finds the strength to pull away. He turns to D'Angelo. "What about you?"

D'Angelo lets out a pained yelp as he pulls open his Windbreaker. There is a deep-red stain spreading on his right side, just above his hip. Reaching around to his back, he grimaces. "It went right through. We'll get it patched up in a minute. But first, I need the guy's cell phone and wallet. Now. We gotta keep moving. These guys don't come alone."

Scott feels himself quail at the thought of rolling the man over to search his mutilated body.

Apparently D'Angelo can tell he's not up to that. "Shire," he says, "go through the man's pockets. Can you do that?"

Without hesitation, Shire kneels over the body and pulls out the man's phone and wallet. Scott wishes he had her strength. She brings them to D'Angelo. He checks the phone and holds up a photo, shows it to Shire. "This is how he recognized you in town."

"How did he get a picture of me?"

"You have a Facebook account?"

Shire rolls her eyes. "Who doesn't?"

D'Angelo says. "Lundren sent it to him. Here's one of me. And this is Carla's Arizona driver's license photo. They apparently don't believe you're dead. There's a picture of Volker in here too."

Shire looks at the photo of Volker. "It's from the help-wanted page on the Orca website. The picture's fifteen years old. George is trolling for new waitresses."

With another groan, D'Angelo pulls the dead man's driver's license out of the wallet. "Well, this explains how he got here so fast. The guy's address says Anchor Point. He's local."

"That's it," Scott says, stomach churning. "I ran into him and a couple of older rough-looking guys on the river last fall. Maybe ex-cons. One of them had one of those teardrop prison tattoos under one eye. They came roaring up on four-wheelers, trashing the riverbanks and plowing across the spawning beds. I told them that was illegal, and they bitched me out and drove away."

D'Angelo says, "You ran off three thugs with a fishing pole?"

"I had this with me too." Scott holds the shotgun up. "There'd been a brown bear on the river eating salmon carcasses." He pauses, his voice going quaky. "I thought I knew him. Jesus."

D'Angelo looks at the guy's phone again. "Well, the good news is he hasn't called Phil Lundren back since he got the incoming call when they set him up. That means he didn't tell them he'd grabbed Shire and was coming here. So when they start looking for him, they won't be coming to Anchor Point. That's very good news."

Scott's head is clearing a little. "What's the bad news?"

D'Angelo wipes sweat from his forehead and winces with pain. "He texted an Alaskan number just as he pulled up here with Shire. The name on it says *Pop*. He sent your name and address, and said, 'Come now.' "

"Oh no," Scott says.

"Yeah, we've got company coming. Let's hope whoever this 'Pop' is hasn't relayed this info to Sidewinder. And pray he's isn't coming from close by."

D'Angelo hauls himself up and leans against the railing. "This guy texted about fifteen minutes ago. We gotta move fast. We need to get me patched up and get out of here. Soon." He winces again. "Shire, did you get the photo?"

She raises her eyebrows and pulls the photo out of the front of her tracksuit. "He didn't see it."

"Good," D'Angelo says. He turns toward the house. "Come on, patch me up now."

Scott says, "What about the body?"

D'Angelo nods toward the gravel pit. "Is that your excavator?"

"Oh, man," Scott groans. "How deep you want him?"

"Use that hole right there." He points to a deep excavation close by the machine. "And throw his phone and gun in with him. You have lime?"

Scott feels like he's going to puke. "Yeah, a couple bags in the shop."

"Make it fast. When it's done, park your excavator on top of the disturbed gravel. And wash that blood off your truck. Is there any shot damage?"

"A couple BB holes in the window. But this is Alaska. It won't attract any attention."

"Okay. Keep that shotgun with you in case his partner shows up." D'Angelo turns to Shire and Carla. "Come on, help me. Nothing fancy, just a quick patch to stop this bleeding. Then we all have to get the fuck out of here." They head into the house.

Scott yells, "There's a first-aid kit under the kitchen sink." He staggers toward the excavator. He's always considered himself a good man in an emergency, and he proved it when it was needed on that crabber. This is way more than he ever thought he'd have to do.

47

D'ANGELO SITS AT the table watching Carla open Scott's first-aid kit. "Hurry, ladies."

"Let me see that wound," Shire says to him. She sets the photo on the table and crouches next to his chair. She pulls his jacket open, yanks up his shirt, pushes him forward. The pain rips through him. "You're right," she says. "There's the exit hole." She grabs a dish towel off the oven door handle, presses it against the wound.

Carla yanks out gauze patches and tape and helps Shire bandage the entrance and exit wounds with efficient skill. Shire says, "There's a lot of blood. Let's hope it didn't nick an artery."

He looks at the bandages. "Good job, Shire."

"Seaman's training," she says.

D'Angelo is woozy but pleased by their equanimity, their apparent competency. "Thanks." He pulls his bloody shirt down over the bandages. He can hear Crockett starting the excavator. He picks the photo up off the table, glances at it. "Okay, let's go. And tell me how he grabbed you, Shi—" He tries to stand but falls back into the chair.

"Cosmo," Carla says. "Rest a minute."

He'd like to argue, but he's not going to be able to stand up anyhow. "One minute," he says. "Shire, tell me what happened."

"At the cop shop, I gave the birthday-party story to the desk sergeant, Artie Veggich, and got your photo out of the headliner, but when I got back to my car, that guy stuck his gun in my ribs. He pushed me into the driver's seat and climbed in back between the girls' booster seats. He wanted to know what I took out of Carla's truck. I showed him the picture of the twins."

D'Angelo says, "He was watching the impound yard. He had the same problem we had, couldn't get to the truck in broad daylight. Then he saw you go through it and come out with something in your hand and thought he was golden."

"How did he know my truck is in impound?" Carla asks him.

"Volker. Sidewinder sent the thug to the Orca first thing. He talked to George. I hope he left the stupid hippie alive."

Shire says, "He told me to take him to you or he'd kill my girls." She looks at D'Angelo. "I'm sorry. I didn't know where else to go. I thought if I brought him here, at least *you* would know how to stop him."

D'Angelo manages a smile. "Oh, yeah, you can see how well I handled him." He holds the old photo up. "Here it is, folks. The last true fact about Gordon McKint. It can't be denied, altered, or faked." He gasps in pain. "Man, I hope this thing is worth what just happened here."

He fights the growing nausea, his head whirling, his pulse erratic. The damage is a lot worse than he's let on. Carla and Shire hover around him. They look a bit ashen themselves but seem tough enough for just about anything. He's more worried about Crockett. He can hear the heavy diesel growling of the big excavator approaching from the gravel pit. Not everybody is ready to blow a man's head off and then dig a hole to put him in. He makes a mental note to refer to Scott by his first name now.

"This is my fault," he says as evenly as he can. "I thought we had more time before they shipped a professional here. They must be in a big hurry to put a lid on this if they're using homegrown goons like that guy. Carla, we need to get you and this picture out of here. Right now."

He pushes up off the table. For a second he thinks he's going to fall back again, but he stays on his feet this time.

"Shire, you need to get out of here. Now. Go!" He gulps air again, sweating.

Carla grabs Shire's hand. "When am I going to see you again?"

They both look at D'Angelo. He shakes his head. "Carla, don't put Shire in danger by contacting her. Think about the kids. Understand?"

Carla nods, eyes tearing up.

They walk out. D'Angelo gets as far as the porch railing and has to stop again. Carla and Shire walk down to the driveway and stand near Shire's car, saying their good-byes, their backs to the body lying on the ground next to Crockett's truck.

D'Angelo takes the moment to check the bandages. The bleeding seems to have slowed, but he certainly isn't going to be able to drive all the way to Anchorage with Carla. The nausea builds. He leans on the railing, thinking he'll vomit.

He gets his stomach under control as Scott shifts the big machine's levers and deftly scoops the dead man off the driveway with a few inches of bloody gravel. Ordinary people can be tough when they have to be.

Scott swings the boom around in the direction he brought the machine from. With a belch of exhaust, the excavator jerks forward. One bloody arm flops out between the huge steel teeth of the bucket. A thin veil of gravel sifts down to the ground as the machine lurches over to the waiting hole.

Ordinary people can be very tough.

As the machine clanks off, he hears Shire say, "Listen to me, Carla, get yourself settled somewhere and find a decent guy. You can't just keep sticking a dipnet into a school of men and taking home whatever you haul in. You hear me? Find a real keeper this time. You owe it to yourself." Shire pauses. "And at your advanced age, you better do it fast."

"Fuck off!" Carla laughs, and hugs Shire. "I'm not going to miss you, you know."

"I know," Shire said. "I'm not going to miss you either, honey."

Shire breaks free and waves to D'Angelo. He summons the strength to say, "Wh—when I get stitched up, I'll come by with the engagement ring."

She laughs and gets in her car.

As he scans the end of the driveway and the forest around the house, the nausea washes over him again. It's not the first bullet he's ever taken. But the sickness in his gut and the crashing energy tell him this one is serious. The pain in his side races along his ribs to his collarbone. He has to talk to Scott and Carla and modify the plan.

Shire's car backs down the driveway and disappears up the road, leaving Carla alone. "Carla." He waves her up onto the porch. "I need to tell you some things."

He hangs on the railing. The chugging of the excavator drones on from the gravel pit. He feels his blood pressure crashing and clutches the railing to brace himself, dizziness flooding his brain. He fights it off and stays very still, closes his eyes for a moment listening to the rumbling of the excavator. Nothing hurts for the moment. He's drifting.

"Cosmo! Are you in there?"

It's Carla. She's standing on the porch next to him.

He opens his eyes. She peers into his face. He waves her off. "I'm fine."

He's not.

The excavator goes silent. In a moment, Scott pounds up onto the porch, shotgun in hand. He takes one look at D'Angelo and gasps. "You're white as a ghost."

"Yeah, yeah, I know," he says. "Listen to me."

Scott is dazed. Eyes unfocused, lips trembling. D'Angelo has seen the look before—on the faces of men who've killed someone for the first time. He's sure he once wore it too.

"I won't make it to Anchorage. Scott, walk me to your truck and drive me to my car. It's just up the road. I'm going to drive myself down to the hospital in Homer."

They object and sputter. He cuts them short with his fiercest stare, and they go quiet.

Scott holds one elbow and helps D'Angelo down the porch steps. Every step is a grinding pain in his side. He's squeezing the stair railing so hard he can feel the wood grain. "You drive Carla to Anchorage in your truck. Drop her off at the airport first so she can call my guy, and then you take the photo to the FBI office. I'll give you the name of the agent there. Have them call him at home, get him out of bed, whatever. You tell them my name. Who I work for."

He gasps, swallows hard. His throat is tight. "Carla, you have to be there before midnight. That's when Mr. Plan B will toss the

phone that goes with the number I'm going to give you. You understand? You call from a pay phone in the airport. No cell phones."

They nod. They help him into the back seat of Scott's truck. He
falls back against the seat, sweating again, shaking with chills. His
feet are on top of the power tools on the floor, his knees even with
his chest. "This person on the phone will tell you where to pick up
the new ID. Do exactly as he says, okay?"

Carla leans into the open door, face taut with concern. "Sure."

She opens her mouth to add something. He holds up his hand.
"Scott," he says, "take this." He hands him the photo that has
brought all this trouble down on them. "Put it in an envelope and
write *Agent Mel Ritchie* on it." He spells it. "My guy in DC has
assured me that Ritchie will get it to him." He pauses, once again
dizzy, nauseous. "I have to trust them. I have no other choice now.
This is for Kevin Dykstra. And for my daughter."

"You can't drive yourself to town," Scott says. "You're bleeding
to death."

D'Angelo groans. "I'll be at the hospital in twenty minutes. It's
all downhill from here. Literally. I can stay alive that long. Take me
to my car. Now." He adds, "And Scott, bring this"—he hands Scott
his pistol—"and the shotgun too." He struggles to reach into his
jacket pocket and turns to Carla. "This is for you."

"A flashlight?" she says, looking at the small black tubular metal
item in his hand.

"It's a stun pen. Look." He pushes a button, and Carla grimaces
when an obviously powerful electric arc crackles between two metal
points on the end of the device. "You press that end against anyone
who grabs you and hold it on them until they're down. Got it?"

Carla cringes as he puts the weapon in her hand. "I don't know
if—"

"Just take it. Let's go. I'm fading."

Scott hops in the truck and drives him to the stolen Subaru.
They help him out of the truck and into the small car. It's almost
more than he can stand. "This town and its goddamned Subarus."
He gasps for air. "Scott, there's a bag in the back seat with all my
things in it. I don't need the local cops going through it at the hospital. Hang on to it for me?"

Scott puts the bag in his truck.

D'Angelo starts the Subaru and rolls the window down. Carla and Scott look at him gravely. "Listen," he says, "I know you two have gotten attached. Are you going to be able to split when you get to Anchorage?"

They both insist they will. Sure.

"Because you do have to disappear, Carla. Phil Lundren is trying to put a lid on this. To put a lid on you." He grits his teeth against the pain. "You understand?"

"I get it. I need to disappear." Carla runs up to the Subaru's window and kisses him on the cheek. "Go. I'll be fine."

Crockett says, "What about you, D'Angelo? What if they come after you again?"

"I can take care of myself."

Carla scoffs. "Oh, you're doing just fucking great."

D'Angelo grimaces and puts the car in gear. "Give this to Volker." He holds out the bloody cell phone. "And Scott, I'll be back for that bag someday, with a new name and a new look. We'll cook something good. Osso buco, maybe. While you're in Anchorage, see if you can find some Italian anchovy sauce. *Colatura*." He gasps, somehow manages a smile. "It's sort of like Thai fish sauce, except it doesn't smell as much like sex."

He puts the car in gear and drives, not at all sure how far he's going to get.

48

WHERE THE GRAVEL road meets the pavement, D'Angelo turns left toward Homer and the hospital. In his rearview he sees Scott's truck turn right, heading north. It's six thirty PM. They still have time to get to Anchorage before Mr. Plan B disappears. But not a lot extra. And what about him? How much time does he have? He's fading, but he thinks he can make it.

He drives the stolen Subaru on the narrow, winding two-lane to the highway in a fog of pain and light-headedness. With two miles to go to the Homer hospital, his vision becomes so blurry the highway seems to be floating side to side. Twice he nearly veers off and into the weeds. When the big parking area overlooking the bay lunges into view on his right, he careens into it without using the turn signal. A horn blares. A howling "Dickhead!" roars from the pickup truck tailgating him. God only knows how slowly he's been driving, or for how long.

He rolls to a halt in the parking lot and noses into a spot facing the guardrail overlooking the cliff. He'll just pause a bit, get his breath back, clear his head. Then he can rejoin the procession of tourists and fishermen descending on the town, roll down the long road to the hospital. Nothing to it. He only needs a few moments to rest.

The seat is pushed back as far as it goes, and he lies back against it and peers out at the view from under his hat brim. The ocean.

That's where people go to relax, right? Who needs a little relaxation more than he does? And there it is, right in front of him. Several hundred feet down, of course, and not the open Pacific, just this long narrow bay where he's spent the past twenty-four hours or so. This peaceful place would be a lovely respite and refuge from the world of intrigue and violence he's survived in all his years—if he hadn't dragged all that along with him here.

He presses his hand against the entry wound. There's no pain now, just a thick, leathery feeling on that side of his body, and a similar one settling over his brain. A groggy, letting-go feeling of surrender that is so seductive. Is this how Jennifer felt at the end, when the cancer was running amok like a wave of fanatics overtaking every outpost of her immune system? It's the kind of feeling that could convince a man to put his weapon down and his hands up.

That thought jolts him alert. How did he come to be here soaking in his own blood, on the edge of a cliff in Alaska, so far from all the war zones he's seen in his life? Is this the ignominious end he faces? Death in a parking lot full of happy tourists instead of surrounded by his brothers in arms?

He forces himself to peer out the windows and assess his environment the way he's been trained. The tranquility of the place is frightening. The sun is high in the northwest, hours of daylight yet to go, the sky cloudless again for the moment. Beneath it the sea is silver-blue and flatter than he's seen it at any time since arriving here. Ant-like boats crawl across the silky surface, trailing strings of sunlit diamonds in their wakes. The lonely cone of an island volcano, a perfect Mt. Fuji replica, seems to quiver on the waves. On the far shore, the mountains stand watch, a white, serrated horizon.

Behind him the parking lot thrums with the sounds of unhurried people on vacation. *No hostiles, no enemies, no threat here*, he tells himself. He can hear the woosh of traffic. He looks in the rearview mirror. A pickup towing a big aluminum boat races down the hill, fishing rods bristling from their holders. Those guys waste no time gawking at the scenery. There are nonnegotiable tides to consider, fish who need to be reminded where they're perched on the food chain. The world is on fire, a conflagration of hatred and mayhem on nearly every continent, and they're going fishing. He envies them their insouciance. If he lives long enough, one day he'll take up the sport, see what all the excitement is about.

He grips the wheel, pulls himself up a little more. All he has to do is make it as far as the emergency room curb and roll out of the car and onto the pavement. Somebody will take it from there. That's what hospitals are for, right? To yank people back from the brink of death. That's what doctors do. The good ones. But not always. Not Jennifer's doctors. The best that money could buy. Not that they didn't do everything possible. They did. They said so, over and over, as horrified and surprised by the cancer's explosive final assault as he and Jennifer's mother were. *"Everything possible."*

His right side is numb to his shoulder. His head weighs a hundred pounds, his body a thousand. He falls back against the seat again. Lights sputter at the corners of his eyes. Maybe he should just throw the door open and fall out, right here in the parking lot? Even in the midst of the spectacular scenery, somebody will surely notice a six-foot-four-inch man sitting in a pool of blood. Maybe.

He'll wait a minute longer, see if he can summon the strength to drive.

Squinting, he tries to focus on the finger of land jutting into the bay. The spit. That's where he'll open his joint, Tentacolis, just down the beach from the End of the Road Hotel & Resort. He'll serve fried calamari rings drizzled with his own secret Sicilian aioli. There'll be *stimpirati*: squid cutlets sautéed with capers. Stuffed squid tubes in tomato sauce. A cold salad with tentacles and fava beans. An invertebrate feast.

He'll cook everything himself, putting the chef's personal touch on each dish. The David Chang of Homer, Alaska. He'll only be open from lunch through cocktail hour. Sleep late mornings, make good strong coffee, walk on the beach. Cook all afternoon. Have evenings off to make new friends—mostly female, of course. For a moment, he's aware that he's dreaming of food. And women. Again. A sound startles him. A squawk. He's awake. Maybe.

A grimly black raven pitches out of the sky toward him, a gang of crows behind it in pursuit. Is it the same aerial skirmish he witnessed this morning on the balcony of the hotel? He, of all people, knows that wars go on and on. But why this one? What was that word Crockett used? *Corvids.* The raven and the crows are all corvids. Why are they fighting among themselves? Sectarian differences?

The birds wheel straight at him, as if hurled against the land mass by the wind. But there is no wind. As they pass low over his car, the harassed raven rolls one glistening eyeball at D'Angelo and speaks to him in the secret language of corvids. D'Angelo understands it perfectly: *The strong will always be assailed by the envious weak.*

It's something he's heard Gordon McKint say.

Then the birds are gone.

Now he's at the stove of a sunlit kitchen, a glass of vodka in one hand, a sauté pan in the other. He can smell the garlic melting in the shimmering oil, feel the noisy popping splatters stinging his knuckles. He can taste the breaded tentacle clusters, rubbery between his teeth, salty on his tongue.

Out front, the commercial fishermen, the sport anglers, the charter captains and deckhands, the shop owners and artists, the bartenders and waitresses of Homer, are lining up for his food in the endless Alaskan summer light. Carla Merino is there. So is Jennifer, his daughter. Rebecca, his ex-wife. Every woman he's ever known. He should welcome them. He pushes open the door and feels the sun on his face, as bright and warm as a smile from God Himself.

CHAPTER

49

FOR THE FIRST half hour or so, Carla lets Scott drive in silence, sensing that he's still upset about slaughtering that man with his shotgun. She's trying to put the dead man out of her mind and is thinking about Shire and the twins, already missing them. She abandoned her girlfriends in Phoenix with barely a word, and now she's losing the only friend she has here in Alaska. Except for Scott, of course, whose place in her life she's still trying to figure out. Even if she could stay, what would he be to her? A best male friend and confidant? That would be a first. She's long known that she can't be platonic friends with men. A serious love interest? Too soon for that. Not that it matters. She's going to have to give him up too. She would've liked to find out at least.

Between those feelings and the excitement and terror of the shooting, the adrenaline rush of driving away from all that, she hasn't thought about what D'Angelo said since she got in the truck. Now the door of the glove compartment, two feet in front of her, turns her mind back to it: *The guy running the hunt for you thinks you were planning on blackmailing Gordon with it.*

The photo is right there inside the glove box. She watched Scott put it in an envelope and stick it in there.

She tries to put that out of her mind. D'Angelo's guy is going to set her up someplace safe. What does that mean? What kind of place? And how will she live for the rest of her so-called "new life," wherever that is? Yes, she still wants to stop Gordon McKint, but she has to think of herself now too. Maybe if she gives it back to Sidewinder, they'll stop hunting her. But if she gives it back, nothing will stop McKint from his plans for the border. Is she willing to give up that idea? She'd like to think of herself as the same idealist she once was. Still, the thought of a huge ransom from McKint is tempting. How exactly would someone do something like that?

The truck hits a pothole and breaks that train of thought. She glances over at Scott, wondering how long she's been staring at the glove compartment. He's watching the road ahead, deep in his own thoughts. She closes her eyes, exhausted by the day and by an inchoate idea lingering in her brain now. *How much money would that thing be worth to McKint?* After what she's been through, she owes it to herself, at least, to wonder. Somehow, she dozes. When she awakes, they're crossing a wide, glacial river.

Scott looks over at her. "Feeling better? You slept for almost an hour."

"Did I?"

"You needed it."

His concern stabs her. He's too nice for his own good. "Listen, Scott, there're things you should know about me."

He looks over at her. "Why do I need to know them? You're going away."

"Yeah, well, after I'm gone, I don't want you remembering me as some kind of angel who landed in your life. Guys do that when they get unexpectedly laid."

"I'll try to keep the angel fantasies to a minimum."

"Well, you saved us from that maniac. I guess I know something about you now. And this is something you should know about me."

"All right," Scott says.

The forest speeds by her window, densely green. She gets up the nerve to tell him what she never even told her husband. She wants Scott to hear it for some reason. And it's a way to stop thinking about that photo and McKint.

"When I was fifteen, my mother had a boyfriend living with us. He was a big catch for her. A poet, and a professor, or almost a professor. Ten years younger than my mother. His name was Ashton. Seriously, a poet named Ashton Bolt."

"A boyfriend in the house," Scott groans. "Aw, man."

"It's not what you think, exactly."

"Look, Carla. It's none of my business. I don't need the messy details."

She shakes that off. "Maybe I just need to tell it to somebody."

Scott is quiet as she tells him about Ashton Bolt, who he was, why her mother needed him.

"One night at dinner we were celebrating. Ashton had won a big award for his poetry and was on track for tenure at the college. He had too much wine and made some shady comment about us all doing a three-way. He made it sound like a joke, but there was no doubt in my mind that if my mother and I indicated any interest whatsoever, he would have jumped all over it."

"With you and your mother? Jesus," Scott says. "What did your mother say?"

"Nothing. She just smiled and ate her quinoa."

"Oh, brother."

"So when Ashton finally got me alone and got what he wanted, I told her." She stops, catches her breath, a little surprised at how painful this still is. She'd thought she'd gotten over that part. "You know, for a half a minute, I seriously believed my own mother would stand up for me, say something to protect me. Just once." A small laugh escapes her lips. "Not a chance."

Scott groans. "That's terrible, Carla. What a mess."

"It got a lot messier. I was so pissed at her, I told my guidance counselor. Ashton got charged with statutory rape, hauled off in handcuffs. He lost his job at the college. Almost went to prison."

"Well, the dumb bastard should've kept his hands off you," Scott says.

That makes Carla warm inside. "Thanks, Scott. That's what I wanted my mother to say. I wanted her to choose me over him. The whole thing was just a bothersome embarrassment to her."

"So, what's so terrible about all that? He shouldn't have done that."

"It's the part I never told anybody."

"What?"

"I seduced him."

Scott looks at her, confused.

"I initiated it. I jumped on him the next time we were alone in the house. He didn't put up much of a fight. But I started it." Carla chews her lip. "It was not my finest moment."

"Did your mother know that?"

"Of course. I told her. I wanted her to know I had ruined Ashton, her boyfriend." Carla sighs. "We had a terrible fight. She went off about how my slutty behavior was affecting her reputation. Not that my behavior was bad for me, mind you—it was making *her* look bad. That's what bothered her. I got so mad I threatened to kill her with a kitchen knife if she called me a whore one more time. We're both lucky she believed I'd do it." Carla takes a minute to watch the country roll by. "I swore I would never let anyone have enough power over me to make me that angry again. Never."

The whole McKint thing flashes before her. Her life upended. Talk about having power over her. Scott is quiet again, driving carefully.

"The next day I moved out, got emancipated. I lived with a girlfriend's family for the rest of high school. I wouldn't even talk to my mother for a year. Hung up if she called." She hears herself say that and, not for the first time, regrets setting the terms of their estrangement so intractably.

Scott is looking at her, waiting for her to continue.

"Anyway, her reputation managed to survive. She's still a player in the Phoenix art scene. I see her name in the papers sometimes. Some gallery opening or show. She got what she wanted. She got rid of me."

"I'm sorry your mother was so rotten to you."

"I believe you are. You're a sweet guy." She reaches over and squeezes his elbow. "The women of Homer are going to be all over you, mister."

Scott coughs. "I don't know about that."

"I'm serious. You're good in bed, and you actually listen to what a woman is saying to you. That's a deadly combination." She's happy to be talking lightly again.

He takes his eyes off the road and studies her for a moment, apparently trying to see if she's teasing him. "Wow," he says, quietly. "Good in bed."

Carla laughs and punches him in the arm. "Just focus on the part about listening to them talk, okay?"

They drive on and come to Soldotna—all fast food and slow traffic, car lots and auto parts stores, coffee stands on every corner, big-box stores—and then on across a flat landscape of grassy swamps and stands of stunted black trees. The road enters the Kenai River valley and snakes through heavily forested hills. When it meets a bigger highway, a sign indicates Anchorage to the left. Scott turns, and they begin to climb into the Chugach Mountains. Though it's nearly summer solstice now, the higher peaks are dotted with patches of residual snow like dollops of whipped cream. Carla drove through all this country on her frantic way to the end of the road two months ago, remembers little of it. She takes it all in now, knowing she's never going to see it again.

She looks over at Scott. He seems calmer. She's happy he's gotten his mind off the killing. And she's gotten hers off McKint and that photo. She pokes him in the ribs again. "Good in bed."

"Quit it," he says, but he doesn't look like he really wants her to stop saying that.

She looks at the glove compartment again and forces herself to look away.

CHAPTER

50

THE WEATHER IS grim again when Scott drives down out of the mountains and they're at sea level once more. Rain splatters the windshield. Under the brooding sky, marshes and sea grasses stretch from the highway to the barren mud flats of Turnagain Arm. Several dead white trees lean together in one direction as though still trying to get away from the relentless wind that bent them that way.

Scott's exhausted after more than three hours on the road. He rolls his window down and inhales the salt air as they cross a small, silty river flowing out of a valley on their right. A half mile farther along, in the otherwise wild country, a strip mall sits incongruously at the juncture of the highway and a small side road heading up the valley to the Alyeska Ski Resort along the river. There's a Quick Stop with gas pumps at one end. He glances at his gas gauge. Plenty. He doesn't slow.

"I have to stop," Carla says.

"Carla, it's only forty minutes to Anchorage. We're making good time, but it's ten thirty. You have to make that call before midnight."

She gives him a hard look. "Bathroom."

Scott groans and puts his turn signal on.

Though most of the tourist shops are closed for the night, the Quick Stop is surprisingly busy with people traveling between

Anchorage and the Kenai Peninsula. Cars at the gas pumps. Winnebagos parked in front of the store. Tourists and fishermen bustle in and out, arms loaded with junk food and drinks.

Scott pulls around to the side of the mall and parks. There are just a couple other vehicles, fewer people in sight. The sky is still showing dim but persistent daylight under the wet-looking clouds. On each side of the valley, the mountains tower into black rain clouds. At the far end, he can see the ski resort tram stretching uphill over slopes now snow-free and lushly green. "I'll wait here."

Carla nods and gets out, walks around the corner to the Quick Stop.

Scott yawns, the long drive and the nearly sleepless night on the boat conspiring to put him under. He thinks about Carla. She's been quiet most of the way. He hopes she's as disappointed about leaving him as he is about losing her. Not that it makes any difference: she has to get out of Alaska.

He's still thinking about that as his eyes close a moment, and then he's sleeping.

*　*　*

Scott is yanked awake by a man's high, almost womanish voice. "Where's Jules?"

He startles, not sure where he is or what time of the day or night it is. He spins around to find a skinny, older man in the back seat pointing a pistol at him. The guy has long white hair and a weathered, leathery face that Scott has seen once before. A single teardrop tattoo drips from the corner of his left eye. He's wearing a long army-surplus khaki coat. This time Scott remembers: he was one of the men Scott confronted on the river behind his house. He was with the red-bearded guy Scott shot today.

"Turn around and look straight ahead," the man says. "Answer me. What did you do with Jules? He's not answering his phone!"

Scott faces forward as told. *Carla is going to walk right into this.* "Who's Jules?"

"Bald guy. Red beard. My son, Jules!"

Scott shrugs, stalling, heart banging. "I don't know anybody like that."

The guy presses the muzzle of the gun against the back of Scott's neck. "Is that so? Well . . ."

The passenger door swings open. Carla slides into the front seat, a bag of chips in one hand. "I can't believe how busy that place is at this hour," she says. "There must've been . . ." She sees the man. "Fuck!" Her right hand goes for the door handle.

"Open that door and he dies, girlie," the man says.

She goes rigid, staring straight ahead.

"Put your seat belt on." He waves the gun her way and then points it back at Scott's head. "And sit nice and quiet."

Scott says, "Come on, mister. You don't need her. Why don't—"

"Shut the fuck up!" He cracks Scott on the back of the head with the gun butt, then pushes the muzzle into his neck again. "Okay, now that everybody's said all they wanted to say, we need to go someplace a little more private. Drive, carpenter."

Scott starts the truck. He feels the back of his head with his left hand, taking the moment to look over at Carla. D'Angelo's pistol is lying on the seat between them. Scott knows little about hand-guns. He's not even sure he could find the safety on the thing very quickly. He's a hunter, not a gun nut. Even if he could grab the pistol, he'd never be able to turn and shoot before the man blew his head off. This is going nowhere but downhill, fast.

He rubs the back of his head and glances down at the gun so Carla sees him do it.

She slides the bag of potato chips off her lap, covering the pistol.

Scott's fingers come away with blood. He puts the truck in gear. "Which way?"

The man points to the small road branching off the main high-way. "Turn right onto that."

Scott knows it leads to the resort farther up the valley—he was an avid downhill skier while at college in Anchorage. For several miles the road winds through unpopulated terrain as it parallels the silty glacial river that drains the mountains. The bottomland is a thicket of alders and willows. A good place to hide a body. Or two.

With the man's gun touching the back of his neck, all he can do is drive.

CHAPTER

51

THERE IS NO traffic on the small road at that hour, but Carla peers through the windshield like she's expecting something good to come their way. What exactly, she's not sure. This guy looks every bit as dangerous as the creep who almost killed Shire in the driveway. She glances at the bag of potato chips covering D'Angelo's pistol. No chance.

Jesus, every time she gets her hands on a bag of chips, she ends up facing death.

Scott hasn't driven a mile when a narrow gravel trail veers off into the scrub on the right side.

"Turn," the man says.

They drive down the rutted track, willows slapping at the fenders, until it opens out onto the riverbank.

The man says. "Park it."

When Scott turns the engine off, Carla can hear the river flowing past with a hissing sound like a long continuous whisper. It's wide and swift and a slate-gray color, heavy with silt and mud.

The man slides across the back seat and opens the passenger door behind her. "Here's how we're going to do this." He waves the gun at Scott. "You stay put. Hands at ten and two. You take them off the wheel, she dies." He taps her on the shoulder with the gun. "You, missy, are going to ease out along with me now. No fast moves."

He steps out of the back seat and opens her door, the pistol trained on her. Scott sits with his hands on the wheel. "Do what he says, Carla."

"Yes, Carla," the man says. "You're going to do exactly what I want. Then we're going to find out what happened to my boy and why you both want to die so badly tonight." He spits on the ground. "Oh yeah, and where that high-priced picture is. All the big questions. Now get out, girlie."

Carla unbuckles her seat belt and climbs out. This has got to stop.

She turns to the man and says, "If I give you the photo, will you let us go?"

"Carla!" Scott says. "Don't!"

"It's here in the glove box," she says. She nods toward it.

Scott groans.

"Open it," the man says. He points to the glove compartment with the gun. "Don't do anything stupid." He holds her door open with the gun hand, the pistol pointing into the air for the moment as she bends back into the truck toward the glove compartment. She's breathing heavily, almost panting.

"Carla," Scott says. "What are you doing?"

The man leans in close behind her. She can smell some kind of fried-food odors coming off him. "Give it to me."

She pulls the envelope out of the glove box and turns to the man. As she goes to hand it to him, she fumbles and drops it. She bends after it.

Scott must see what she's going to do. "Wait!" he says.

She comes up out of the crouch with the stun pen and jams it into the man's neck under his jaw. The thing throbs with the high-voltage discharge, crackling in the quiet night air. She feels the power vibrate in her fingers.

The man yelps. His pistol flies out of his hand and clatters on the rocky river shore. He staggers back, trying to get away from her. But Carla keeps lunging at him, pressing the stun weapon against his wrinkled neck. He trips and falls backward onto the stones. Carla stays with him, riding him down, still pushing the crackling weapon into his neck for another second until it sputters out.

She rolls off the man and hears Scott unbuckle his seat belt, his car door open. He runs around to her and helps her stand.

The man lies sprawled on his back on the stones, eyes closed. His face is hideously contorted, jaw slack, eyelids still twitching. She steps back away from him and closer to Scott. "Oh my God." She feels like she too is about to pass out. But there's something else. A sense of calm relief, almost elation. "What did I do?"

"You just saved our lives." He hugs Carla, holds her tight, cupping the back of her head with one big palm, pressing her face to his chest.

She looks down at the stun pen in her hand. For a second she doesn't know what it's doing there. "I think this thing ran out or something."

"It's a good thing, or you would've killed him."

"I think I wanted to. I'm so sick of these guys coming after me."

He nods. "Yeah, I know what you mean."

Carla pulls back from Scott and holds one hand out level in front of her. It's steady. "I'm not even shaking. I don't know why. I think I'm just too tired to be scared anymore."

"You looked scared when you reached for that stun pen."

"That was more like temporary insanity."

She's suddenly chilled. The valley is in shadow as the sun sets to the northwest, the night air off the river damp and cold. She puts the stun pen in the hoodie pocket and hugs herself. "Who is this one?"

"The bald guy's father."

"The guy you shot?"

"This is who he texted. He must have been almost to my house when he saw us pulling out onto the road, saw my name on the truck. When his son didn't answer his calls, he decided to follow us. He waited until we stopped where he could grab us."

"How long before he regains consciousness?" Carla asks. "And then what happens?"

Scott shrugs. "We can tie him up and leave him somewhere long enough to get you on a plane and the photo to the FBI. But he knows my name. My address. And I don't have a new identity to run to."

"What are we going to do with him?"

"I don't know yet."

"You don't have a plan?"

"How the hell could I plan for this? All I know is we gotta get you to the airport."

The man starts gurgling and coughing. Scott and Carla turn to look.

Scott kneels over the man. His face has gone blue, eyelids twitching madly, arms and legs thrashing. Foam bubbles at the corners of his mouth. "He's having a seizure or something."

"Scott, he's choking!" Carla crouches beside Scott. "We have to call an ambulance."

"Roll him over so he can breathe!"

It's too late. With one massive shudder, the man goes still.

Scott holds two fingers against the big artery on his neck. "He's dead. Heart attack or something."

"I really did kill him!" Carla says.

"He must've had a bad heart."

"Great. Just fucking great. Now what?"

Overhead, they hear strange laughter. They look up to see a raven flapping toward its roost in the rocky cliffs. It makes that *ha-ha-ha!* sound once more and disappears into the shadows. Headlights move along the road to the highway, tires whoosh on the pavement. Then the night goes quiet again.

Scott stands. "We have to keep moving. We can't leave his body here. Your DNA is all over him. His is all over my truck." He crouches and grabs the man's body under the arms and drags him toward the water.

"Wait," Carla says. "His gun." She picks up the pistol. "And I want to see his phone." She pulls the man's phone out of a pocket in his coat, muttering, "Jesus, I sound like D'Angelo."

Luckily, the old guy is bone-skinny. Scott drags his light body to the river and lays it on the bank. The heavily silted water is the color of wet concrete and looks almost as thick.

Carla has a thought. "What if he floats down to the highway?"

"I'll sink him. The water is so silty, he may never be found." He bends and picks up a rock the size of a football.

Carla stands over him with her arms crossed over her chest, cell phone in one hand, like an ordinary woman watching her husband perform any mundane yard work task: planting a shrub, pulling weeds. Except that in her other hand she's holding a huge pistol.

She watches Scott put three heavy rocks on the man's chest. He buttons the coat over them, grabs the body under the arms again, and wades into the river.

Jesus. They've killed another man and they're throwing him in a river like so much trash. She used to be a social worker. This is never going to end if she antagonizes McKint any further. She needs to give him that photo.

Scott is knee-deep in the current now.

"Be careful," she says. She'd like to have him helping her a little longer, but she needs to tell him what she's decided to do. It's either that or blatantly deceive him when they get to the airport.

Scott shoves the body away, and the river carries it off. It floats downstream for a moment, arms outstretched. Then it rolls, and one hand comes up out of the silty river like a wave good-bye. It sinks and is gone. Scott wades to shore.

"Give me his gun," he says. He takes it from Carla and hurls it as far as he can into the river. "The stun gun and the phone too."

She hands him the stun pen but hangs on to the phone. "Wait a second."

Remembering D'Angelo's actions, she tries to check on recent calls, but the phone is locked. "Damn. I can't tell if he called anybody and told them we're on our way to Anchorage." She throws the phone into the river. "These guys are going to keep showing up!"

"Maybe not. There's probably a bounty on this," Scott says. He picks the envelope up off the ground and waves it at her. "Maybe on you too."

"Is that supposed to be reassuring?"

"No, I just mean I'll bet these two were planning on keeping the money in the family and didn't share our info with anyone else."

"Listen, Scott." She hesitates. She needs to at least give him a hint about what she's thinking of doing. "What if I just give the photo back to McKint and go and live wherever Cosmo's guy sends me with a new ID? Sidewinder won't bother to look for me then. Not if they have the photo."

Scott's disappointment shows. "Carla, I thought you wanted to do the right thing and crush McKint. He's getting more powerful every day. You want to give the picture to him now? After all this? Two guys dead today? D'Angelo in the hospital?"

"I want to stay alive. That's what I want to do," she says flatly. "I'm just trying to think it through." But she's already done that.

He's going to be decent. Of course. "Okay," he says. "It's your decision. But either way, you're going to need that new ID. I'm going to get you to the airport so you can find a pay phone. Let's go."

She's moved by his loyalty and devotion. But she has to think of herself too.

He hustles her back into the truck, returns the envelope to the glove compartment, and turns around on the riverbank. They head back up the gravel track toward the road to the highway and Anchorage.

"Maybe a half hour," he says.

Carla barely hears him. Thinking. If she's going to keep up the nerve to do what she wants to do with the photo, she's going to have to make a clean, unsentimental break with Scott. That's going to be hard.

CHAPTER

52

IT'S ELEVEN THIRTY when Scott pulls into the Ted Stevens International Airport. D'Angelo said Carla must go into the terminal alone or his guy won't show himself. Still, Scott doesn't want to just let her out at the curb like some departing visiting relative he's getting rid of. He pulls into the short-term lot and parks. They've barely spoken since dumping the dead man in the river. She's been calm all the way into town. He's not sure if that's genuine or if she's just numb. "How are you doing?" he says. "You know, with what happened back there."

Carla turns toward him, face unreadable. "I've seen people die before. At the hospital in Phoenix. Lots of them." She's gone cold to him since the river.

"Yeah, but . . ."

"But I killed that one. Is that what you were going to say?"

Scott looks away, out the windshield at the airport. Says nothing. What can he say?

"Do you want me to cry? Would that help?" she says, a knot of anger or hostility in her he hasn't seen before.

Why's she being this hard?

"I'll walk you to the door," he says. "I won't go inside. You can make the call and meet this guy on your own." He pauses. There is still one thing that needs to be said. "Back at the river, you were talking about not giving the photo to the FBI. Giving it to McKint instead."

She just looks at him, not as coldly now. Just distant. "Yeah?"

"You okay now?" he asks.

Carla nods, her mind obviously elsewhere. "I'm fine. I was just upset. Tired."

Her face is taut, brow stitched. He hopes she's trying to think of some possible way to stay in Alaska a little longer. He hopes she hates the idea that they'll never see each other again as much as he does. He knows it's ridiculous to feel this attached after such a short time. But, after what they've been through, it seems like years.

"We just met, Scott," she says, as if reading his mind. She's pushing him away. She gets out of the truck and doesn't say anything more as they start toward the terminal. She stops abruptly. "I left the sunglasses." She turns back to the truck. "Can you unlock it?"

Scott points the key ring, pushes the button. The door locks click open. She opens the passenger door, leans in. She apparently drops the sunglasses and seems to be fumbling for them on the floor of the truck. It takes her a few seconds. Finally she closes the truck door. Although it's nearly dark with the late hour and a heavy mass of new clouds building over the mountains, she puts the sunglasses on. She looks suitably unrecognizable. She's already disappearing.

When she's at his side again, he presumes to put one arm around her shoulders. She doesn't resist. They walk to the terminal that way. But something has changed between them, and he can't read it.

On the sidewalk, in front of the Departures doors, she turns and looks at him, and he pulls her closer before she can step back. She smells of soap and shampoo from the shower they shared. It sends a pang of longing through his chest, but it's way too late for that now. "It'll be okay," he says. "You're safe now. Those two guys were the end of it. I'm sure."

"I hope you're right." She looks away from him. She's still not all there. Her mind is spinning. There's something she's not telling him.

"Again, I'm so sorry I put you through all this." She seems to be trying to put some warmth into that. He guesses that's as much as he can hope for now. Twenty-four hours ago he was sitting in his boat alone in the dark, Carla just one of the numerous women of Homer fueling his overheated fantasies. Now she's about to become a memory he's never going to forget. "Really, I'm sorry things got so screwed up, but thanks for pulling me out of the ocean. You are the Great Rescuer of Wayward Waitresses, Scott Crockett."

That has a note of finality in it that panics him. When she shifts her weight to step away, he reaches for her arm. "I'm thinking when I get home, I'll go anchor up over there behind the island again and wait for the next tide to bring me a new woman."

Her face relaxes a bit, and she cups his cheek with one hand. "I hope you do, Scott. I really do."

He bends and kisses her then. *She* may be too tough to cry, but he needs to get out of there before he's bawling on a public sidewalk. She returns the kiss and steps back.

He can see she's really going to go now. He pulls a Crockett Construction business card out of his jacket pocket. "In case you need me. For anything. Call it a memento. You forgot to steal anything from my bedroom."

"A memento," she says, and rolls her eyes. "That's a habit I think I've kicked for good."

"Go," he says. "You have to make that call in the next couple minutes."

She takes the card, gives him one last look, and bolts across the concrete. The automatic doors of the terminal open to swallow her and close again. She's gone.

She's going to be all right.

And what about him? When he gets home, the first thing he's going to do is bulldoze another six feet of gravel over the top of that body, grade the driveway to be sure there's no trace left there either. Will that be the end of it? He can hope. Still, there are some things no amount of gravel will bury.

He turns away from the terminal and heads for the parking lot. His feet are still wet from wading into the silty river, his pant legs soaked. The air is cool and pregnant with moisture. Ominous black clouds build over the Chugach Mountains to the east, no doubt bringing precipitation from Prince William Sound. It will be raining again by the time he gets out of the airport. Exhaustion crashing through him, he stands and looks at the grim sky and thinks about the long drive home, the empty house waiting for him at Anchor Point. He thinks about the days ahead, alone again.

Well, there's really no reason to drive all night in the rain. Maybe he'll pull into a Walmart lot and sleep in the truck among all the RVs. In the morning when the stores open, he'll go to Costco, stock up on bourbon and beer, steaks, a big chunk of the cheap Jarlsberg they sell. Maybe look for one of those specialty food delis and buy that Italian anchovy sauce D'Angelo mentioned. He might even drive downtown to that fancy Nordstrom store with the great-smelling saleswomen. Take a look around. Check out the menswear department.

Right now, he needs to get that photo to Agent Mel Ritchie at the FBI.

53

INSIDE THE TERMINAL, Carla finds a pay phone and dials the number D'Angelo gave her. She looks at the clock on the wall. It's a few minutes before midnight. The number rings three times. Four times. She looks at the clock again. The minute and hour hands are almost vertical now. "Fuck!"

Someone picks up on the other end. "Go to the Cinnabon shop," the voice says. Carla's heart is pounding so hard she can barely hear the person. It sounds like a woman's voice. "The table nearest the window."

The phone goes dead.

She walks to the Cinnabon place, fingering the photo stashed in her hoodie pocket, still turning questions over in her mind. Will McKint stop looking for her if he gets it back? Will D'Angelo—assuming he survives the gunshot—still get protection from the FBI if there is no photo for evidence, no trial of McKint? She wishes she had more time.

The Cinnabon shop is empty except for the table nearest the window. A woman sits alone facing the terminal, a newspaper and a coffee cup on the table before her. She is insistently plain looking, middle-aged, wearing medium-quality clothes—an acrylic cardigan that is strictly from Target or Kohl's—her dull-brown hair in an out-of-date perm. She looks like somebody's aunt from Ohio. Carla feels a jolt of anxiety. Did she get the instructions wrong?

Then the woman smiles and waves to her as if they're friends.

Carla takes a chair facing the woman with her back to the entrance of the shop. There's a black travel bag under the table. The woman slides it over with her foot. "Look inside."

Carla pulls the bag up onto her lap. It contains a neck pillow, an iPad tablet, an *Atlantic Monthly* magazine. There's a travel kit with a toothbrush and deodorant and such, and an orange prescription pill bottle of zolpidem. There's a small red handbag. Inside that, she finds an iPhone, a wallet, and a passport with the photo of her that D'Angelo snapped on Scott's porch; it's been transferred onto a blank background. She studies her face, the badly cut short hair sticking out around her head like some punk rocker's. The passport says her name is Anna Katherine Martin. Carla glances at the date of birth and can't help smiling. She's thirty-three again. Well, if they kill her now, she's going to die young.

She opens the wallet and finds an Oregon driver's license with the same name and age. There's an address in Bend. There's a Social Security card, a Visa card, J.Crew and Nordstrom cards, a handful of twenties. At the bottom of the purse, there's an Oregon State Credit Union checkbook, a house key, what looks like a safe-deposit box key, and a set of car keys.

She feels a cloud of depression drift over her. This one small bag holds her whole new life. Or, should she say, Anna Martin's life? Which is the same thing now.

"You're Mr. Plan B?" Carla asks. This isn't what she expected at all.

"Plan B?" The woman smiles at the name. "I work with the person you refer to. Open the phone and go to the Alaska Airlines app."

A boarding pass appears for Alaska Airlines flight 91 to Portland. Boarding soon. First class. She's never flown first class. There's a connecting flight to Bend.

"Now, you head to security and find out how good Anna Martin's ID is."

Carla just looks at her. "You can make somebody into another person with another life? Just like that? In the few hours since he called this afternoon?"

"Well, it wasn't exactly 'just like that.' Anna Martin was constructed over a period of time. The bank accounts, the passport, driver's license. There are records going all the way back to Anna's high school transcripts. In case you want to go back to college or something. All we did today was fill in the physical details to match you. And then I got on a plane to meet you here."

"I see." She hesitates. "You must do other things too. I mean, not just new identities."

The woman leans back in her chair, smiles crookedly, quizzically. "You have something else in mind that needs to be taken care of?"

Gut twisting, Carla debates whether to go ahead with what she's about to say. Right now, she's probably safe enough. She can still call Scott and tell him she stole the photo from the glove box, give it back to him to deliver to the FBI. She can still follow the original plan, go to Bend, get another job in another bar, dye her hair black. And then what? Wait tables for the rest of her life? Or just until she meets some man who'll take care of her? Take a few classes at the community college? Join a softball league? Is that all there is? And exactly how vengeful is McKint going to be when that photo ruins him? How far will she have to go to elude him? Bend doesn't sound nearly far enough. Even Cosmo D'Angelo wants to be what he called "twice removed."

But there's another way to go too. She wrestled with the thought of it all the way from Anchor Point to Anchorage, staring at the glove box in Scott's truck. The old man she killed at the ski resort finished that debate. How many more times can she do something like that?

She gets up the nerve and says, "If I had a ton of money, could you create a life someplace that was, uh . . . say, a little more exotic than Bend?"

"Almost anywhere is more exotic than Bend." The woman is watching Carla closely. "Why don't you tell me what's on your mind?"

This is the hard part. This is where she has to really trust this strange woman and her incredibly plain face. Carla reaches into the pocket of her hoodie, but hesitates again.

"Someplace father away. A *lot* farther away."

"I see," the woman says. Apparently she does. "Our mutual friend spent a fair amount of money on this plan. But what I think you're talking about would cost much more. More than you have."

"What if I had something that's worth a lot of money?" Carla shakes off all caution now, takes the photo out of her pocket, and slides the thing across the table. She briefly flashes on Scott and feels like shit for duping him this way. For betraying D'Angelo too. Not to mention his dead daughter, that young guy they hanged in Flagstaff, the FBI, and all the people who are working to stop McKint from becoming the monster he seems determined to become. She won't even allow herself to think about the poor people under his thumb on the border.

She pushes the photo over to the woman.

The woman looks at it. She can't hide the effect it has on her. An eyebrow goes up. "If this is genuine, you're right, it is worth a lot of money. Probably more than you realize." She leaves it on the table between them. Doesn't touch it.

Carla nods. "I got it from—"

The woman holds up one hand. "I don't want to know how you came to possess it."

She studies Carla for a moment and then looks around the empty restaurant and over Carla's shoulder at the entrance. Carla turns and looks that way too. In the terminal, travelers come and go, wheeled suitcases rhythmically clacking across the floor tiles behind them. The woman says, "What do you want to do with this?"

"I have a feeling you know what the picture is about," Carla says.

"I know it's something Gordon McKint would rather not have out there in the world right now."

"Our friend said it will bring him down."

"Again, what *exactly* do you want to do with this item?"

Carla almost can't believe she's hearing the words coming out of her own mouth. "I want to sell it to Gordon McKint—without getting myself killed trying. Any ideas?"

The woman leans over the picture again. Then she sits back in her chair. "Our fee is twenty percent."

"So, you can do it." Carla's stomach plummets.

"It would take some planning." The woman's inert face becomes almost animated for a second. "We let McKint know we have the original photo and tell him our price. We tell him to deposit that amount in an offshore account we've set up. Maybe using crypto-currency for the first leg of it."

"Okay," Carla says. It makes sense to her so far. Sort of.

"When he makes the payment, we deposit your portion in a secure banking institution. Someplace very discreet and very off-limits to U.S. authorities."

"And?"

"We give McKint the original photo, as agreed. Then Anna Martin slips into her bikini and stretches out on a beach towel in the Seychelles or the Maldives or the Cook Islands." She shrugs. "I've heard the Aitutaki Atoll is very nice."

Carla feels her throat constricting as she forms the next question. "And McKint's people won't come looking for me? Wherever I am? Sidewinder is international, isn't it?"

The woman shakes her head. "Look, apparently this original print is uniquely important. Otherwise that image would be on the front page of every newspaper and website in the country. So if and when McKint gets this actual piece of photo paper in his hands, the threat to him is over. He'll have everything he wants. His popularity is growing daily. Looking to punish you will be more trouble than it's worth."

"But won't he be pissed about the money?"

The woman scoffs. "We'll ask for an amount that is the cost of doing business of the kind he does. Once he destroys it, he's not going to put any effort into finding you." She pauses. "Now, on the other hand, if you turn it over to the authorities or the news media and you destroy his political dreams, or maybe even put him in jail . . ." She lets that hang for a moment. "Well, in that case, then I hope you keep a very low profile and live a long, quiet life in Bend, Oregon."

"The cost of doing business," Carla repeats, pushing aside the chilling threat implied in that last bit. "So, what would that be? How much should I be asking for this thing?"

The woman pulls a small pad and a pen out of her purse, writes something. She tears off the sheet and hands it to Carla.

Carla stares at the number, mind blurring. She counts the zeros. "You're joking."

"I've never learned how," the woman says, ruefully. "Trust me. That'll be like a speeding ticket for Gordon McKint."

"It's way more than I was going to ask for."

"That's why you need us. We work for a percentage. It behooves us to get the best price the other party will pay." She stands. "Okay, I need to catch my own plane out of here. And you, Anna Martin," she says pointedly, "get on your plane, have a drink, and take one of those zolpidems. Sleep. When you get where you're going, put that photo in your safe-deposit box and settle in. Try to look like you belong there. Enjoy your new apartment, your car. Shop for a bathing suit. I'll be calling you when I get the banking set up. Shouldn't take more than a few days."

Carla tries to convince herself this is happening, but one more thing worries her.

"Um . . ." She clenches her jaw, not wanting to bring it up.

"There's something more?" The woman glances at her watch. "Quickly, please."

"In all that offshore banking stuff I'll never understand . . . I'm sorry, I just . . . How do I know you won't keep all the money somehow?"

The woman smiles broadly. "Well, good for you. It's a legit question. And the answer is, you have to trust us. But let me tell you this: we work with a lot of very scary people. If there was ever so much as a rumor that we had betrayed a client . . ." She actually shudders. "I don't want to think of what would happen to us."

"God," Carla says, a chill running through her now, "what a way to make a living."

"Yeah. I should've stayed in nursing school." She leans over the table and takes the scrap of note paper from Carla's hands. Below the dollar amount, she adds a ten-digit phone number. She holds it out for Carla. "If you change your mind in the next twenty-four hours, dial this number."

Carla reaches for it.

The woman pulls it away, her face suddenly so dark Carla almost whimpers. "Listen very carefully. Call this number only if, for whatever reason, you decide to abort our new plan. Do you hear me? There will be no discussion. I won't even answer the phone. You're the only one who has the number. If I hear it ring, I cancel all arrangements, and you'll never hear from me again. You'll be on your own in Bend. What you do then with the photo is up to you. That's one more thing I don't want to know about until I read it in the papers." Her face goes even darker. "Tell me you understand. If my phone rings, we're done. Right?"

Carla says, "I understand."

"Good. Use this to call me." The woman hands Carla a cell phone and the piece of notebook paper with the two numbers on it. She pushes the Anchorage newspaper she was reading to the middle of the tabletop. "Set that photo on the paper so today's headline and date show, please. I don't want my DNA on that thing when we hand it to McKint."

Carla does as she's told.

"Thank you." The woman takes her own phone out and snaps several pictures of the photo sitting below the headlines. She straightens. "Well, Anna Martin, it's been a pleasure meeting you. Bon voyage." She sidesteps the table and strides out into the terminal, just another average-looking American traveler on her way home to someplace almost certainly as plain and ordinary as she looks.

Carla waits until she disappears in the crowd. She looks at her own face on the passport photo and says, "Anna Martin, what the fuck have you just done?"

CHAPTER

54

HALF PAST MIDNIGHT, Anna Martin smiles her way through airport security without a hitch. The young TSA agent is so smitten, he looks like he would escort her all the way onto the plane and help her buckle her seat belt if she were wearing a black mask and a vest of dynamite.

Sitting at the departure gate, she tells herself yet again that this is what she has to do. *Bend isn't safe enough. Not far enough. Sell McKint the damned thing. Take the money and really disappear.*

Why is she still not sure?

She thinks of Cosmo D'Angelo. Is he even alive? Scott, a decent, hardworking guy who risked his own life and had to kill a man because of her. Shire, risking her life too, and her daughters'. And— talk about lives—what about that old man and his son? Criminals, no doubt. Thugs. But two human lives she helped end in horrible, violent ways. A father and son gone missing now. She sees the old man writhing in agony as she pressed the stun pen deeper into his neck, hears the sound of his last gasps echoing in her brain. None of this had to happen. D'Angelo was going to decide to use it against McKint anyway. She squirms in her chair, crosses her legs and uncrosses them again.

Does it make a difference now whether she sells the thing back to McKint or gives it to the FBI as originally planned? Either way, that bullet isn't going to miss D'Angelo. Either way, she can never go back to Homer, never see Shire again, or watch Irene and Alice grow up. The only difference will be that if she sells it to McKint, Sidewinder won't send any more goons looking for her like the two they sent today. And she'll have the money to go so far away nobody will ever find her if they did try. *Take care of yourself.* Why not? She tells herself there is no reason to abort this. None. *Just get on the plane. Go to Bend. Wait for that woman to send someone to pick up the photo. Then you disappear a second time like D'Angelo advised, impossible to find, and impossibly rich for the rest of your life.*

She takes the magazine from her bag and opens it across her knees, looking for something to get her mind off this. The boarding area is crowded with tourists of all stripes. Fishermen, couples, families, all heading home from Alaska. The airline has announced that people with special needs and people with children may board the plane now.

Sudden loud voices from the terminal startle her. Carla looks up from the magazine. A group of young men walk past, speaking rapid Spanish. They're wearing knee boots and Carhartt work clothes. She's been in Alaska long enough to know that there are many Mexicans and Central Americans working in the canneries and fish-processing plants all over the state. The money is a huge income source for their families back home. One of them is just a teenager, from the looks of him. She can't help thinking about Hector Zuniga, a Mexican boy that age she knew at the hospital in Phoenix.

Hector would show up once a month to pick up a supply of a new tuberculosis drug that wasn't yet available in Mexico. From his lack of improvement, the doctors suspected he was selling the drugs south of the border instead of taking them. They asked the social work department to talk to him about staying in America long enough to get the complete treatment, but Hector had family in Mexico he was helping support. Carla was unable to convince him to take his medicine. He eventually stopped coming to the hospital.

The young cannery workers disappear down the hallway, shoving each other and laughing, happy to be on their way to the high wages and endless overtime of the slime lines, doing a job few white teenage Americans want. And what's going to happen to them when McKint slams the border shut?

She failed to help Hector Zuniga, but at least she tried.

And what is she trying to do now? Blackmail Gordon McKint? Give him the photo to destroy? Is there any way to construe that as the right thing? Any way at all?

The loudspeaker announces that first-class passengers may now board flight 91 to Portland.

She should be getting up, moving through the line with the other premium passengers. She puts the magazine back in her bag but doesn't stand. Her intestines twist. She thinks she's going to need the restroom. Something electric buzzes in the big vein under her jaw. She sits pinned in place. The boarding continues.

As the mob of general passengers boards, she tries to put her doubts about the extortion scheme out of her mind. *It's under way. You don't have to do anything more. The woman with the plain face will take care of everything now. Relax. It's done. You'll be safer, not to mention richer. Much, much richer.*

There's a cool draft slithering through the boarding area. The damp late-night air from the Jetway reminds her of the night before on Scott's boat. She shivers and pulls her hoodie tighter around her and closes her eyes, thinks of being in the sleeping bag by the galley stove, warming up after her dunking in the icy seawater. Is there a part for Scott in her insane scheme? Who would be happier living on an island than a man who loves fishing and boats and the sea?

There she is again, attaching herself to a man. She shakes her head at it. Those leopard spots are hard to shed.

By now Scott is on his way across town to the FBI office, unaware that she took the photo from the glove box. Unaware that he has nothing for the feds but the empty envelope with the agent's name on it. It'll mean that Gordon McKint will never get prosecuted. It'll mean that Sidewinder Security will become even more gigantic and powerful and take over more and more police work across the country until McKint has a private army of his own, right here in America. And it will mean that the poorest people along the border with Mexico will have even less power, less hope than ever. All of that so she can live like one of those rich women who buy her mother's artwork in Scottsdale.

She's on her feet and running through the terminal and out of the security area before she stops to pull out the phone the woman gave her. She dials the number on Scott's business card. He answers on the second ring.

"Scott, it's me."

"Carla! What the hell have you done?" His voice is frantic. "I'm at the FBI office. Where's that picture?"

"Come back. I'll be standing outside in front of the baggage claim."

She hangs up before he can say anything else. He immediately calls back, but she doesn't answer. She needs to explain this to his face. She owes him that much.

On the way to meet Scott in front of the terminal, Carla stops at the Alaska Airlines service desk and makes arrangements to take the next available flight to Portland. Even in the middle of the night, the flights are almost full. She'll have to fly coach. She's lucky to get a window seat. Once she gives the photo back to Scott and dials the abort number, she'll be sitting in the cheap seats for the rest of her life.

Outside the terminal, she stands on the curb and pulls out the scrap of paper with the two numbers the woman wrote down. The chilly night air swirls around her. She holds the phone in her left hand, the paper in her right, and starts to punch in the phone number with her thumb.

She hesitates and looks at the *other* number on the paper. The *first* number the woman wrote down. The one with a dollar sign in front of a digit with a lot of zeros trailing behind it like a train. A train to an entirely different future. She forces her gaze away from it and continues to enter the number for the woman who will not answer.

Her eyes shift from the phone in one hand to the note paper in the other, and back again.

Now the ten-digit number is showing on the screen. Her thumb hovers over the green send button. She has only to lower it onto the glass and the blackmail plan will be aborted. She will give the photo back to Scott. Scott will give it to the FBI. Carla will go to Bend, Oregon. And all those tropical places the woman named will go back to being little dots on a map of the world.

Her thumb continues to hover as her eyes move back to the dollar amount. How absolutely astonishing it is that this number scribbled on this slip of paper contains everything she could ever wish for. A new life in an exotic place. No more backbreaking night shifts hauling trays of food and drinks, fending off amorous drunks. She thinks again about Scott Crockett at the helm of a boat in the dazzling blue Indian Ocean. Anna Martin's boat. She even indulges a brief fantasy about the well-dressed thirty-three-year-old Anna strolling into the Cactus Flower art gallery in Scottsdale, Arizona, before she departs for the South Pacific. She admires one of local sensation Sara Merino's original mixed-media pieces. Then purchases something else instead.

The last time Carla saw her mother was in April, a week before she fled from Phoenix. Sara came to Carla's apartment that afternoon, unexpected, unannounced. She looked good. Clothes artistic but not ridiculous, hair freshly done, smooth skin the result of fastidious facial maintenance to offset the Arizona sun. Carla's first thought was *Thanks for showing up without warning so I'd be sure to look a mess.* She said, "Mother. What a nice surprise."

Sara nodded at the thick sarcasm. "Let's not start."

"Okay, fine, what do you want?" Carla let her in. Defenses on high alert.

Sara walked to the couch as though Carla had offered her a seat. She had to move a magazine and some junk mail to clear a cushion. Carla remained standing.

"Sit. I have something to tell you," her mother said.

"I can hear standing up." Carla leaned against the doorframe like she wanted to be near an escape route. She *did* want to be near an escape route.

Sara took a second to glance around the living room. Carla saw her scan the walls, empty but for one of Sara's own small self-portraits. No other art of any kind to critique or dismiss. No way to demonstrate her expertise. "I'm dying."

Carla was about to scoff. Dismiss this as more familiar drama from her mother. But the air between them went so cold she shivered. Confused, she pitched her voice to sound unconcerned. Still wary. "We're all dying, Mother, from the day we're born. Are you planning something artistic for your departure? A Viking burial in a flaming boat, maybe?"

She saw her mother stiffen. *Good.* "Clever," she said lightly, the anger obviously simmering beneath it.

Carla pointedly looked at her watch. "I have to get ready for work. So, what are you dying of?"

"That's better," Sara said. "Pancreatic cancer. I've got months, maybe as long as a year."

Perfect. Her mother had finally found the one situation her daughter couldn't disapprove of. Cancer couldn't be declared drama, bombast, self-indulgence. Carla waited for her heart to calm, for the anger to change to something like empathy or compassion or pity. She might have to wait all day for that to happen. Cancer! "And what? Is this our big reconciliation? Mother and daughter reunite? Shall I call the papers? Or will you post it on Facebook?"

She hated the way her mother made her behave. Hated it!

She waited, wedged against the doorframe, thinking something more would come from within. Something kinder. Nothing came. Maybe because this wasn't really a plea for sympathy anyway. Carla could see that now. It was her mother's parting shot, leaving Carla forever the ruthless bitch who could find no kindness for her own mother who was dying of cancer. Oh, it was perfect. Just fucking perfect.

Sitting amid the clutter of papers and TV remotes, a plastic laundry basket heaped with Carla's clothes at the other end of the couch, her mother waited too, maybe thinking the same thing. It was win-win for her. Either Carla set their enmities aside and embraced her, or Sara died the martyred woman with the heartless child.

Checkmate.

Neither spoke.

It could have been a painting: *Still Life With Mother.*

They stayed that way for the longest time.

* * *

When Carla hands the photo back to Scott at the curb in front of the baggage claim, she sees the wounded look on his face. He's in the idling truck, window rolled down. "You could've told me," he says. He winces. "But stealing it?"

He's right. Stealing it from the glove box that way was as small and shabby as all the other stollen mementos. But much more serious. And unneeded on her part. Scott had already told her that it was up to her if she didn't want to give it to the FBI. That if she turned it over to McKint, he wouldn't hold that against her. And she has no doubt about that. He's far and away the best man she's ever managed to drive out of her life.

"Why didn't you tell me?" he says. "I killed a man for this thing, Carla. I killed a man today."

"I know," she says gently. "So did I." She's a little surprised by how unemotional she's being about that death now, even though she can still see the agony on the older man's face. "You'll be okay." She pats Scott on the arm.

The traffic is thick in front of the Arrivals doors. The air wet with rain and noisy with the hubbub of the incoming passengers. Hundreds hauling their luggage to dozens of haphazardly parked vehicles. Shrieking reunions. Loved ones hugging. Weary travelers shouting for cabs and hotel shuttles. Horns. The diesel rumble of heavy buses shifting into gear.

But Carla isn't arriving. She needs to get to the Departures doors. Back through security.

"I have to catch a plane," she says, and turns away and walks back into the terminal. What else is left to say? Even if she can find a way to see him again, he will never trust her. Not completely. And he shouldn't.

"Carla!" he calls out from the truck.

She keeps walking.

* * *

At 1:40 AM, Anna Martin boards flight 101, Anchorage to Portland, takes her seat at the window in row twenty-two. As the plane fills, she turns her face away from the line of fidgeting travelers accumulating in the aisle, looking for their seats, stuffing the overhead compartments. She stares out the window at the rain-splattered concrete. On the far edge of the city, the still-snowy Chugach Mountains look soggy in the wet night air. But to the north, a wide band of clear pink sky shows under the darker clouds along the horizon. The great mountain, Denali, juts into it, blue and white and unimaginably huge.

Yes, there is plenty to love about Alaska. Will she ever see it again? Not likely.

She's nudged out of her melancholy by a man settling into the middle seat next to her. He's a nice-looking guy, about her age—her real age—and well dressed in a casual, comfortable-with-himself way. Nice smile. He scrutinizes her fingers to see if she's wearing a ring, the rest of her for all the usual reasons. His face shows how amazed and delighted he is to be seated next to an attractive, possibly unmarried woman. He fastens his seat belt with great purpose, as though he fears someone might try to move him for some reason.

"I was kicking myself for ending up in a middle seat." He smiles. "Now I'm not so sorry." It sounds like a cheap flirtation, but there is something warm about it. He's not going to give her any trouble. "Robert," he says, holding out a hand to shake.

She smiles back and gives him her hand, nearly says, "Carla," then almost corrects that to "Anna." Instead she nods and goes back to looking out the window at the baggage handlers smashing luggage onto the escalating conveyor belt in the drizzling rain. Back to thinking about leaving Alaska.

The plane is fully loaded now, and the safety instructions are under way. The man next to her, Robert, is determined to get a conversation going. "I hate these red-eye flights, don't you?"

She's not sure how to answer that. Who loves getting on a plane at two in the morning?

"But what are you going to do?" he continues.

Again, she just smiles at him, turns her eyes back to the window, and keeps them there for the next few moments, a little confused that she isn't sure whether or not she wants a good-looking man's attention in the middle of the night. That's a first.

He turns it on her again. "So, you headed to Portland? I mean, visiting? Or do you live there?"

He's a handsome guy, wearing simple but good clothes. He's age-appropriate for her, clean and well-groomed. Smells good. She could do a lot worse, and certainly has, too many times. Is he the "keeper" Shire was talking about? "Yes," she lies, "Portland. I live there."

"Really? Me too." His hopefulness amps up a notch. "What part of town? Maybe we could—"

She realizes her error. Luckily an announcement from the flight captain interrupts the man, and she closes her eyes as if listening to it over the general clamor in the plane. She keeps her eyes closed and pretends to be sleeping as the jet lifts off.

In the heady moments of ascent, she tells herself that every single thing she has worried about for the past two months since the night at Cosmo D'Angelo's house is now behind her on the ground and unable to ever reach her again. That Bend is far enough. Safe enough.

She wants to believe that.

When she opens her eyes, the man is waiting. "So, what do you do in Portland?" He really is handsome and even charming, in spite of his obviousness. As these kinds of chance meetings go, it's not a bad opportunity.

She thinks about it a moment longer. If she says no to him, is she finally shaking off this desire to be desired? Maybe she'll end up one of those proudly independent, aging unmarried women who don't date. Don't use makeup. Don't comb their hair some days. Because they don't want to look like vain former beauties—like her mother, for example—still clawing for the attention of men. Is that what's in store? There must be a way to just take care of yourself, for yourself.

She can't figure that out at this late hour. She's done for the day.

Hopefully the photo is in the hands of the FBI by now. Scott on his way back to Homer. Shire and the twins safe in their beds. Cosmo D'Angelo in the hospital. Even George Volker back to being . . . well, George Volker. And most hopefully, Gordon McKint about to be indicted. There is nothing more she can do about any of that, and she's too tired to think about it.

There's another thing she can't do anything about. Her mother's cancer. The thought of that makes her suck her teeth. Carla tried. She sent Sara the smoked sablefish to let her know she was thinking about her. But look at the trouble that brought. Now there can be no contact with anyone from her past anymore, ever. Including her mother. She should be grateful for the convenience that provides. It's not her fault now that she won't be there at the end of her mother's life. The way daughters are supposed to be. Good daughters. But it doesn't change the truth of how she feels about it, or about herself.

The man named Robert in the middle seat next to her is saying something about the scant food the airlines serve on these middle-of-the-night flights.

She turns to him. "I'm sorry," she says, and pulls the zolpidem bottle out of her bag and pries the lid off. She pops one of the little white pills in her mouth, swallows. Closing her eyes, she presses her head against the humming fuselage wall and feels the plane rising into the dense Alaskan clouds.

She yawns, settles deeper into the seat, and mumbles, "I'm just not myself today."

ACKNOWLEDGMENTS

Some portions of the story previously appeared in Opening Days, published by Barclay Creek Press (2010).

I'd like thank the many people too numerous to name who read (and re-read) and advised on this novel over the past ten years: friends and colleagues here in Alaska, and across the country. With special thanks to the patient folks at Folio Literary Agency and at Crooked Lane Books. And of course my wife, Lin, who never stops believing in me.